P9-DIG-004

CHILD LIT   18⁰⁰

YADULT
PT 6466.26 .R68 A75 2004
Provoost, Anne, 1964–
In the shadow of the ark

NORTHAMPTON COMMUNITY
DISCARDED
COLLEGE LIBRARY

GIFT

NORTHAMPTON COMMUNITY COLLEGE
Paul & Harriett Mack Library
3835 Green Pond Road
Bethlehem, PA 18020

In the Shadow of the Ark

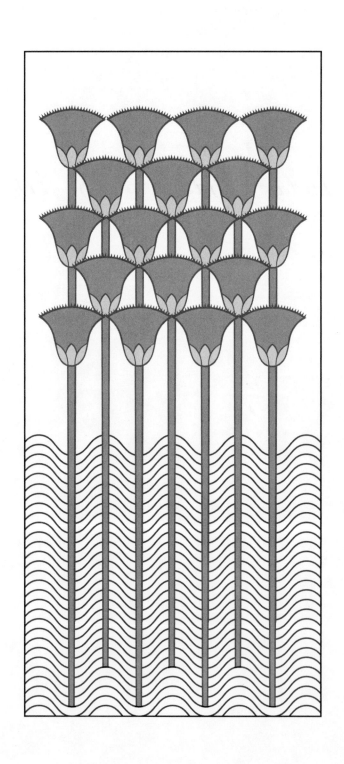

In the Shadow of the Ark

ANNE PROVOOST

TRANSLATED BY JOHN NIEUWENHUIZEN

NORTHAMPTON
LIBRARY
Bethlehem, PA 18020
COMMUNITY COLLEGE

Arthur A. Levine Books

AN IMPRINT OF SCHOLASTIC INC.

Text copyright © 2001 by Anne Provoost
Translation copyright © 2004 by John Nieuwenhuizen

All rights reserved. Published by Arthur A. Levine Books, an imprint of Scholastic
Inc., *Publishers since 1920,* by arrangement with Em. Querido's Uitgeverij BV.
SCHOLASTIC and the LANTERN LOGO are trademarks and/or registered trademarks
of Scholastic Inc.

No part of this publication may be reproduced, or stored in a retrieval system,
or transmitted in any form or by any means, electronic, mechanical,
photocopying, recording, or otherwise, without written permission of the publisher.
For information regarding permission, write to Scholastic Inc.,
Attention: Permissions Department, 557 Broadway, New York, NY 10012.

Library of Congress Cataloging-in-Publication Data

Provoost, Anne, 1964–
[Arkvaarders. English]
In the Shadow of the Ark / Anne Provoost ; translated
by John Nieuwenhuizen.
p. cm.
ISBN 0-439-44234-6
I. Nieuwenhuizen, John. II. Title.
PT6466.26.R68A75 2004
839.3'1364—dc21   2003009622

Book Design by Elizabeth Parisi

1 3 5 7 9 10 8 6 4 2   04 05 06 07 08

Printed in the U.S.A.   23
First edition, August 2004

The translation of this publication is funded by the Flemish Literature Fund
(Vlaams Fonds voor de Letteren — www.fondsvoordeletteren.be).

The story of Neelata's mother
is based on the story of
Darius I, told by Herodotus
in the third book of his Histories.

And God saw that the wickedness of man was great in the earth, and that every imagination of the thoughts of his heart was only evil continually.

And it repented the Lord that he had made man on the earth, and it grieved him at his heart.

And the Lord said, I will destroy man whom I have created from the face of the earth; both man, and beast, and the creeping thing, and the fowls of the air; for it repenteth me that I have made them.

But Noah found grace in the eyes of the Lord.

— Genesis 6:5-8

In the Shadow of the Ark

Prologue

We left our land because the marshes where we used to fish were flooding. The tide line was getting ever closer to the slopes where we dried our catches. For years we did our best to move up with it, but in the end it became impossible. The waters threatened our houses, children drowned, harvests and catches rotted. We decided to go away, a long way to the East, to the place where, according to the wandering Rrattika, there lived shipbuilders who were constructing the largest ship of all time and who were looking for workers. We bought a donkey and a tent of animal hide. With great difficulty, we learned to handle the tent. Then we traveled inland, away from the marshes and the duck ponds where we had lived for generations. My father had asked brothers and cousins to provide lights for our departure. One last time he gazed at the many boats he had built; side by side they lay at the edge of the water. As we left, he sang, but if you listened carefully, you could hear that he was uttering curses.

When we looked back from the first hill, we saw, far behind us, the torches fanning out, everyone disappearing into their own houses. I knew what they were saying to one another around their hammocks. That the rising water was not the real reason for our leaving Canaan. That my father had caved in to my mother's will. That we would be sorry and would be back before the change of season.

I had no need of the torches and the polite farewell wishes. I would much rather have left without anyone noticing. Yet I let out a shout from the top of that hill, "It is going to be good out there, much better than here! You will hear about us in songs and stories!" My voice broke, I was so hoarse from the hard work of the last few days. I was straining so hard that the jars hanging off my yoke shook and knocked into one another. I was about to shout something else, but kept my words back because I thought I saw a light appear in a doorway. Was someone coming out with a new plea, the deciding one that would keep us here? I rested one end of the yoke on the ground. One single slope we had climbed, and already I felt the need to sit down.

Nobody came out. In anticipation of daylight, small oil lamps were being lit from the fire of the torches, and the torches were being extinguished. My father said, "Don't bellow like that and look after your things, Re Jana. Don't flaunt your good fortune if you do not want to draw the attention of everything that is intent on thwarting us." I took up my yoke and walked on. There was no good fortune to flaunt, he knew that as well as I. There was only the dull, thoughtless carrying out of my mother's plan.

*   *   *

A strange caravan we made. At the head walked Alem-the-ragged, a tracker who was not related to us, but who journeyed with us to show the way. He was a Rrattika. Like all Rrattika, he was shabby, lived from hand to mouth, and did not ask how we were when he greeted us. We called him "the ragged" because of his long mustache, his drooping shoulders, and his clothes, which were gray like the mud in which they were washed. He did not smell of oil, like us, but of fat. The fact that my father had engaged him had to do with his talent. From tiny impressions in the ground and almost invisible scraps of fleece caught in thornbushes, he could tell which way the animals we were following had gone. He taught us how to "half-look." As long as you were just looking, all you saw was the little dimples the rain had made in the sand. By half-looking out of the corner of your eye, quickly turning your eyeball away, or by squinting through your eyelashes, you could see a line in the landscape, the track you had lost.

He had his son with him, a young child not half my age, named Put. The child was as dark as I am, so even the Rrattika we met thought he was one of us. He was an intent child. His father wanted him to look at the ground and at the horizon, drawing his attention to the small creases in the landscape that indicated the presence of rocks or water, but the child had no eye for these things. His attention focused on us. He was always the first to notice an ulcer growing under someone's nail or the sun scorching particular parts of our skin. Then he would call out, "Father, I'm tired as a dog," but he himself kept ceaselessly running back and forth, even long after we had sat down, sometimes even after we had fallen asleep.

3

Behind Alem came the donkey. It was young and very willing during the day, but at night it was so beset by whips and prods in its dreams that it brayed constantly and kept us awake. Its shoulders were covered with blankets to prevent chafing. It pulled the reed sled on which my mother lay. The sled was supported on the donkey's flanks with a bracket, the other end was flat and dragged along the ground. If anyone wanted to follow us, all they had to do was look for the deep furrow left on the hills by the weight of my mother's body. She was wrapped in the same dried grass–filled blankets as the donkey. Not that it was much help: After only a few days, her back was blue from the bumps and the rubbing, and the back of her head practically bald. We stopped more often to change her position than to drink.

Then there was me, Re Jana. I had nearly reached the end of my growing years. The rate at which my arms and legs were getting longer was slowing down. I was nearly as tall as my father and for my yoke I could use the ropes he had made to fit himself. I carried the jars of oils and scents. If I stumbled, they all knocked together and I sounded like a boisterous little band. Close to my body, up against my shoulders, I carried my store of water. To get used to living on land, I drank gourds-full; Alem insisted that would help. Just like dry bread stops you feeling sick on a boat, fluid in your stomach was supposed to protect you against the anxiety and oppressiveness of being on land. I accepted every word out of Alem's mouth as the truth. He was a wanderer, he had seen the world! I had never quite been able to hide my fascination with his people, with their swarms of children, with the way they shook the clothes they had slept in of a morning, like wading birds shaking their feathers, and with the way they would, from one moment to the next, string all their belongings together and throw them onto their animals' backs, hoist their children onto their hips, and disappear. They could go without food for days on end; even as children they learned to get used to the feeling of gnawing hunger. Privation was a mere inconvenience.

Last came my father. He assumed that a Rrattika could only rarely be right, and paid the price for it: He refused to drink unheated drinks, and often the only thing he would take in before nightfall would be the sun-warmed drops from blackberry flowers. And so the land made him sick. He plowed up the ground with his stick as if it were an oar rather than a support. He was not used to walking far; in all of his life he had rarely covered any distance greater than a few times the length of his fishing boat. He had great strength in his arms, but hardly any in his legs. Yet he never stumbled, his attention to the unevenness of the path never slackened. His balance was important, because he carried the silkworm cage, which had been specially designed for the journey. The small mulberry bush had its roots in water, so the silkworms were constantly threatened with death by drowning. And he carried the brazier, that glowing escape from hunger and cold. But above all, he was fulfilling my mother's dream: He was taking her away from the water. He was making good his promise to go and live in the stony desert, to find other work and another place to live, away from the marshes with their nerve-racking tides.

For weeks on end we walked. We left the landscape we knew. We crossed riverbeds, filled our water bags, and made our way into a dry region full of limestone rocks that showed through the thin

5

layer of earth. We passed pastures full of sharp grasses, crooked acacia trees, fig trees without fruit, and spent the night under tamarisk trees with ragged bark and leaves soft as down. For every day that passed, my father made a knot in his belt. In the end, the belt became so short it would no longer fit around his thin waist. His face was gray. The emptiness, the boulders, the absence of reeds and mosquitoes made him wretched. Every evening he washed my mother with the water he had saved up. He heated it to the same temperature as her skin. He only allowed himself enough to keep going. All through the journey to the shipbuilders, we begged him to drink. Only after we had passed the cliff from behind which hammer blows could be heard and he could see the gigantic ship we had been told about, did he, without saying a word, grasp the water bag by my shoulder and drink greedily like a small child, until the bag was empty and so limp that it blocked his view of the ship- yard.

The wandering Rrattika had not lied. Past the crumbly ridges, in a place where you would expect nothing, or at most a small set- tlement, a shipyard had been built, which spread like a lake. Apart from a pond, surrounded by scrub, where people came and went constantly, the place was dry as dust and strewn with rocks. The first thing that greeted you was the smell of pitch. Then the sounds. The air was full of the sounds of hammering and planing, and the rattling and grinding of drills reached you right over the top of the ridge. Then, once you had reached the top, you suddenly had a view of something like a city being built. In an area with so few forests, the sight of so many stacks of timber was overwhelm- ing. Wood shavings whirled like mere dust in the wind. In every conceivable spot stood the tents, stone houses, and barracks of the countless workers who were running around, busy as ants. Most conspicuous was the tent on the slope of the hill where all paths seemed to lead. It was red, as if drenched in ox blood. The tent's opening faced the valley; it looked straight at the heart of the shipyard, at the spot that made our mouths go dry as powder.

Over a wide excavation in the hard ground stood a gigantic scaffold with a boat-shaped structure trapped in a web of vertical and horizontal girders. This was what people in the marshes had been laughing about: the ship in the stony desert. It did not yet reach very high, still showing only its ground plan. Its future scale was visible, but the design revealed the lack of confidence of the builders. Yet the stores of timber and pitch all around revealed its makers' ambition. That was the first thing we, as people looking for work, sensed: that the project down there was being carried along by something powerful, that it had gone far beyond being just a dream. Quite possibly, that was what made my father reach so thirstily for the water bag.

1

The Descent

The sun stood at an angle behind us. We could make out the small fires more easily than the women who were doing their cooking on them. We put down our burdens: my father, the cage and the brazier; Put, the case with the ornaments and the shells; I, the yoke; and Alem, the hides that made up the tent. I sat down from sheer exhaustion. More than anything, the wind had tired me, that perpetual tugging at your hair, the dust in your face, the whistling in your ears. Keeping low down to the ground was a help. Then it seemed to forget about you and blow over the top of you in its search for somewhere to hurl itself. I led the donkey so that its large body on short legs might partially shelter my mother. When it stood in the right spot, my mother blinked her left eye rapidly, and immediately little Put came to undo the cloak she was wrapped in. I knew it was time to rub her with oil; it was already much later than usual. She had to eat, and she should sit up for a while, held in my arms. I wanted to gather some of the bits of wood I saw lying about, boil water, and set up the tent so we could sit and watch the activity in the valley from there. Everyone was tired after the long trek, and now that we had arrived, a long rest seemed a proper reward.

But my father kept striding up and down impatiently. Some marram-grass cutters were climbing up, sickles in their hands and baskets on their backs. When they had passed and the way was clear, he stood by the edge of the steep path. It was wide, much wider than the goat trails we had been following earlier, and frequent use had worn steps in it. "Pick up your things," he said. "We're not there yet."

I suppressed a sigh. Put stopped tugging at the cloak. Not that my father's words surprised us. We knew him, we understood his hurry to get to the construction and its builders. Only Alem-the-ragged seemed not to have heard the order. He followed the grass cutters into the scrub. He asked them questions I couldn't understand, and they replied breathlessly.

My father called out once more, "We're not there yet. Make haste, Alem." His voice sounded a little higher now, sharper and less hoarse thanks to that bag of water. I could guess what he was doing: He was celebrating his arrival. He was deadly tired from the journey, and the only way he had of making it clear to himself that he had reached his goal and that the deprivations were at an end was to speak resolutely and loudly, silence others and see his orders carried out.

Alem calmly turned his head toward us above the shrubs. He didn't look in order to listen, it was more as if he reacted to an unimportant sound, maybe a dog barking aimlessly.

But because my father stretched himself to his full height and pushed his chin out like a real drover, Alem slowly came toward us. Without looking away, with a flick of his fingers and a sharp sucking in of air through the corner of his mouth, the wanderer called his son to him. Put obeyed instantly. His knees flashed one after the other from under his little tunic. When the child had come near him, Alem grasped his hand and pulled him close. Put reached no higher than his elbow, yet so close together, they resembled a pair of brothers, one a smaller copy of the other. Already Alem no longer bothered to look at the shipyard. From the corners of his eyes, he was looking at the landscape we had traversed. I noticed the rapid sliding of his eyeballs, and I knew: It is over, he is getting ready for something else.

My father too had noticed that look. Throwing up much more dust than was necessary, he went over to the pair. Alem did not wait until they faced each other close up to say, "Dismiss me here, lord. Let me return to the marshes." The wind blew up his hood.

My father wore his hair short, and his body was uncovered. He was less bothered by the incessant whistling of the wind in his ears than by the flapping of the wanderer's mantle and tunic, a form of attire he disdained; like me, he couldn't understand why anyone would wear things like that. "So soon, Alem?" he asked. "You haven't seen the shipyard at close range yet."

"I have seen enough, lord. In Canaan, they are waiting for us. They will not break camp until we are back."

I heaved a small sigh, which nobody heard. Then another one, to draw Put's attention, but he stayed motionless under Alem's arm, as if he were stuck.

My father's back shone. For the first time since we had left, it was covered in a thin layer of sweat. "The day is nearing its end. It is not long till night falls!" he said. A branch snapped under my foot. All three looked at me. Their glance startled me, because I was not aware that I had moved.

Alem looked away from me as fast as he could. He seemed to need to swallow something before he could say, "Night is only the disappearance of colors. I have guided you to your goal, I will put the few hours that separate us from the dark to good use." He held his hand out to my father.

For a moment, my father stood motionless, but then he gripped the hand and shook it. He opened the case at Put's feet and paid them with shells and rings. "Take the donkey too," he said once Alem had folded his wage in his mantle. It was a generous gesture, to give a donkey to a Rrattika; I had never seen anyone in the marshes do anything like it. It seemed an extravagance, but the animal was tired and possibly ill. Alem prostrated himself before my father, but my father failed to notice. From the ledge, he was already staring out over the shipyard again.

I first embraced Put, the little boy who shuffled his feet in the dust so much it made you cough. The child did not look at me. He kept staring at the ground as though there was something on that spot that demanded all his attention. I pointed at his beads, at the string of small bones and teeth I had threaded for him. He put his hand over it as if it was a sore spot.

Then I let Alem-the-ragged embrace me. Alem had kept us away from the wild animals. When we set out, he had said, "He who wants to find the builder of the ship must follow the animals. They know the way. But he must not overtake them. They are dangerous, and they are thirsty." Because of his sharp nose and his ability to guess from a few hairs in a hollow what animal was ahead of us and how far ahead it was, he had guided us safely over the hills. I held him close, and he put his arms around me. He held me for a long while, his hands and fingers moving up and down the small of my back. He was wearing more clothes than I. I only had on a loincloth and around my neck a carefully woven collar. He wore a long mantle that left only his hands and feet uncovered. It made his embrace more like a swaddling, like the wrapping of someone shivering from a fever. He put his mouth close to my ear and said my name. I did not move, giving him time to change his mind. I shut my eyes to recover from the shock of his leaving us.

"I am not coming, Re Jana," he whispered. "This place makes me feel bad. I came this far because I did not believe the stories. Now I can see it with my own eyes: a ship without a river, without a lake, without a sea. It really is as mad as it sounded in the songs." He stood with hips and thighs and knees pressed close to me.

"You haven't been to have a look," I whispered back. "There are things you can't see from here."

"I've spoken with the grass cutters. They're pretending to go to work, but they're off. The only law that holds good here is that of madness."

I looked up at the sky, at the absence of even the smallest cloud that might have made the space around us seem a little less endless. "We haven't finished yet. There was so much you were going to teach me still," I said, putting my fingers under the neckline of his shirt and stroking his collarbone. That was something I had been almost addicted to doing ever since I first met him; I picked at the edges of his clothes because that was where his skin began.

"Go and find yourself a man. Do with him what I have taught you, and you will be happy." He pressed his lips to my eyes, first the left, then the right. He was much older than I, more than twice my age. For weeks, he had consumed the same food as we, but he still smelled of the things his people ate and of the fat mixed with ash his people rubbed into their skin. He had always drunk all the water from his water bag. Never had he saved part of it to wash himself. His scent had become precious to me, but now, at our parting, he smelled again like the Rrattika who happens to be passing by, who does what you ask of him because you pay him, but who has no idea of what drives you.

My father said, "We haven't got all day." Alem-the-ragged and little Put greeted my mother with a bow. She blinked, at the child too. We followed them with our eyes until they had reached the shrubs farther along. That was the last I saw of Alem. He had taught my father to track. He had taught him the position of the sun and the movement of the stars. And after my father had seen all the stars and was asleep, Alem-the-ragged called me to him. Me, he had taught love.

2

The People
Building the Ark

The track to the shipyard was hazardous. We went down in a zigzag. Stones flew out from under our feet. Far below we saw people stop to watch us. We drew attention because of the clatter of all the things we were hauling, the rattling of the stones that rolled away, the slow, cautious sliding of my mother's stretcher along the slope. Only once did we stop, on a terrace with a small meadow from which we could take a closer look at the shipyard. A little out of breath, my father looked at the activity below. The area looked cluttered, and it was hard to get an idea of the arrangement of the workshops. In a fold in the landscape, dozens of animals stood looking at us. Some were in enclosures surrounded by low stone walls, but most of them wandered about freely and unattended. I expected words of displeasure, but he just breathed in the scent that met us and said, "Mulberry trees, thank god!"

Once the slope was behind us, all that separated us from the settlement was a depression in the ground, which, judging by the gashes and gouges in its sides, must once have been a quarry. The ground was dusty and soft. My father found a hollow about my mother's size and removed from it anything that could hurt her. He spread her woolen cloak out over the top, brought the stretcher close, and rolled her into the hollow. He washed her more thoroughly than usual: With finger and thumb, he kneaded the soles of her feet, he turned her on her front and stroked her spine, first with the palm of his hand, then with his fingers. He put infusions on the sores on her lower back and shoulders, dried her, and rolled her back onto the stretcher. He rubbed oil into her skin and tied her loincloth around her hips. He bandaged her heels: They were in the worst state. Her torso shone, the designs on her stomach and shoulders seemed to come to life in the low light. He combed her hair and decked her with shell ornaments. All this time he spoke to her in a low voice, "They will look at you here. Someone as beautiful as you, they cannot have seen before." I listened to it as to a song.

When he had finished, and I had made good use of the time by gently rubbing spit into the sore spots on my feet, we left the quarry and moved toward the settlement. We passed dozens of dwellings in front of which teapots bubbled away in stone fireplaces. The people who were busy around there glanced at us, perhaps startled at our appearance and the things we carried, but showing no excessive curiosity. We walked directly toward the construction site. It was not a simple matter to get that far with the stretcher. There was a lot of clutter all around. Planks and stones, tools and other equipment seemed to have been left scattered around haphazardly. Children were running around barefoot amongst it all, dogs and goats walked in and out. A sort of path had been left open, but even that was covered in people's personal belongings: drinking cups, combs, blankets, spoons and cooking utensils, and I realized that this was only a path by day. At night, it was a sleeping place for many, for workers who slept like dogs under the open sky. Never had I seen so many stacks and bundles of things that did not belong together. You wondered how people here could ever find anything.

I stopped in amazement, but my father urged me on. He kicked things out of the way to make room for the stretcher. This was no different from what the local people who were lugging things around did; it was the only way to get anywhere. The closer we came to the shipyard, the fewer dwellings and the more people we found. They wore long cloaks and carelessly sewn footwear. They carried tools: planes, chisels, drills, and other woodworking gear. Some carried a stick, as if they'd prefer to beat a path rather than follow one.

At close range, the ship looked even larger than it had from the cliff. The structure was enclosed in scaffolding that gave precarious support to a number of people. Orders were shouted, buckets hoisted up. Without taking any notice of their questioning glances, my father joined the workers. He clambered under the scaffold and disappeared behind the tangle of bamboo and sunscreens. He reached out to the hull and tapped on it, listening to the sound. He reappeared and started to walk around the gigantic structure at a rapid pace. When he reached the bow, he disappeared from sight.

He was gone for a while. I swatted the flies away from my mother. Already her lips were white and dry again, and I had no water left. But my mother did not ask for anything to drink. Her eye shone. If the ducks had not taken her will away, she would have been able to say it: "Here we are then, this is it. No need to go any farther."

I held back my smile until she happened to look my way. The noise of all that activity filled my head, like in my childhood when not only my father, but also his brothers, his cousins, and his friends scraped the layer of tar from their boats and applied a fresh one. Because the noise was so overpowering, and the movements of the workers around me so purposeful and fast, the shipyard seemed to grow and grow. It covered the whole world, and I forgot that there was anything else beyond the horizon. I had no trouble seeing in their gestures the joy that drove the boys with the planks and the nails. *This is where the songs we sing are made,* I thought, *here is the beginning of the stories that will still be told many years hence.*

My father appeared at the stern and came running back to us. He had inspected the whole structure and the sheer size of it took his breath away. He had seen that it would be a sturdy ship, with a shallow draught and a flat bottom, and would ride high on the waves. He squatted next to us and carried on at my mother as if he expected her to contradict him.

"He'll lose the bow!" he said. "He's bent the top end of it the way you break a duck's neck." His face was full of color now, he no longer resembled the man who, only a few days ago, singing hoarsely, had cursed the birds passing overhead. "How does this man think he is going to keep a straight course? His ship is going to crack down the middle if he doesn't bend the ribs up more evenly." As if he expected her to have the answer, he asked my mother why the Builder was not building in oak. Oak was water resistant and indestructible! It was easy to split! Had there not been enough pine boats that had perished? "What sort of people are we dealing with here?" he asked. "Who are they? Which race do they belong to?"

My mother blinked her left eye a few times. Then he repeated the question to me, but I shook my head. These people were pale, their bodies were shrouded in long cloaks. The girls were adorned with feathers, the boys had patterns on their forehead, black designs that disappeared into their hairline. They did not resemble any of the wandering people that we had seen trekking past the marshes. Nothing made us suspect then that we had come to a people we knew.

3

Good Water

We hurriedly followed the path that led straight up to the tall, bloodred tent that we had already noticed from the cliff. It stood with its entrance facing the shipyard and was screened from its neighbors by piles of pottery shards on one side and on the other by carelessly stacked but sound timber. The tent was not made of animal hides, but of tightly woven goats' hair. It was large and seemed to tremble on its poles. Pigeons flapped above its roof. This was the dwelling of the Builder we had heard stories about in the marshes. He was said to be old but vigorous, a man of un- shakable will. He was said to have knowledge no one else had, and which he was not prepared to share for pearls or shells.

We passed the pond where a number of women stood.

"She is thirsty," I said to my father, nodding toward my mother, but he kept walking and did not wait for us.

The women made way for us. "Have your clothes been stolen?" they asked, exchanging rapid glances. They spoke in a strange accent. They used words of which we only recognized parts or which we hadn't heard in a long time. "And what is the matter with her?" they asked. They turned their heads toward the dark, beautifully made-up woman on the stretcher, her hair dressed in waves, her toenails colored, flower designs on her shoulders and stomach. They looked as if they could not imagine ever being treated with so much respect. They asked one another the question we had heard so many times on the way: "Could she be a queen?"

My mother looked up at them. I do not think she was disapproving of them. She was curious.

"She is crippled," I said.

"Who beat her too hard?"

"No one. It just happened."

"Why are you dragging her around? Is she looking for work?" The women burst out laughing. They all carried a jug. One of them poured water into a beaker. She was a stocky girl with broken teeth who stoppered her jugs with wads of grass. A piece of gauze covered the cup. Small stones, bits of twigs, and leaves were caught on the gauze. The stream of water made a gentle gurgling sound. But the water had a muddy smell. I did not have to look at my mother to know that her eyelid trembled like a butterfly's wing.

I went up to the girl and asked, "Can I have some water?" She picked up the beaker and handed it to me, but I thought she had not understood me and said, "I mean fresh water. Clean water, to drink."

She pointed at the jugs around her and said, "That is what we've got."

"But where is the source?" I insisted. "Where is the lake or the river the ship is going to sail on?"

"There is no lake and there is no river."

"Then where is the well you are going to divert here? Where is the spring that will fill this basin with water to lift the ship?"

The girl flushed. I could see she was taking offense at my nakedness, my insistence, my language. "I tell you, there isn't one," she snapped.

My mother was blowing and puffing, bubbles appeared at the corner of her mouth. I knelt by her, wiping her mouth clean and said, "You are right. Here there is no water. We won't need to move away from a tide line, for there isn't one." She blew more spit bubbles. She had no other way to express her triumph.

4

My Mother

My mother's mother was called Enah. Enah was the daughter of Manilada, who lived for another forty-six years after she had her last child. Manilada was the daughter of Elokane, who only lived till the age of twenty-six. She died and was never forgotten. She was the image of her grandmother Kan, who bore nine sons and nine daughters. She had her last child when she was forty-five and lived for another thirty years after that.

My mother was a fisherwoman, like her mother and grandmother. Her boat was named after the tern. She knew the marshes the way others know a field or a hill. All the time she went out with the fleet she was greatly respected. I can still remember the way she would walk to her boat. Her movements were fast and abrupt. She paid no attention to the way she moved until she was aware of someone looking at her. Then you could feel how she changed. When anyone at all, even a child, was watching her, she began to stride. She contained her strength. It took an effort: She was too impatient for elegance.

One day she was standing in the water next to her boat. She was using a sieve to lift small fish, no bigger than a child's hand, out of the water. Suddenly her knees gave way. She grasped the edge of the bow and pulled herself up. For a brief moment, she managed to keep herself upright on the narrow board, then she tumbled into the boat. All I could see was a couple of fingers and the sole of a foot. I heard her scream, the shriek with which I had heard her chase wild boars and snakes. Only just for a second, then almost immediately everything was quiet again. The short boat, which was not really made for sailing, only for putting the catch in, enclosed her like the shell of a nut.

I was only a little girl, my teeth had not even changed yet. Because I could not swim, I stood in the water as far out as I dared. I was expecting that the little boat would come toward me, that she would step out of it and ask me why I was wailing like that, but it did not come, it drifted away from the edge. Water creatures brushed over my skin, insects landed on my face and my ears. I lowered myself into the water up to my neck. I tried the movements I had seen my mother make. My head went under. I reached up with my little hands. I swallowed water and coughed. I scrabbled around until I could feel the wood of the keel.

I climbed into the boat along the tow rope. My mother was lying amongst the dead fish. She lived. There was no blood. She looked at me with a clear, questioning look. But she did not reach out her hand. She did not help me to get on board. She blinked her left eye, that is all she did. No one knew we were there, we had left that morning without any plan. Then the sea opened her gullet, and the water started rising.

5

Rrattika

*I*t was not easy to get my mother as far as the red tent now that my father had walked on. It was uphill and the ground was sandy. Although there were a lot of job-seekers standing about, no one offered to help. They were all too busy, speaking to each other in rapid-fire sentences, gesticulating vigorously with hands and arms and keeping their eyes on the entrance to the red tent.

As I came closer, I could understand snatches of what they were saying:

". . . many people here claim . . ."

". . . but he is a real . . ."

". . . boasted he could . . ."

I went as close to the tent as I could. I hoped to find my father amongst the waiting men, but realized he was already in the queue inside the forecourt. I left my mother underneath a guy rope, the best place to make sure she wouldn't be trampled. I went to the side of the red tent. Clambering over stacks of timber, shavings, and pot shards, I found a spot on a heap of cut-up branches where I could squat unseen. As long as those waiting in the shipyard were quiet, I could hear what was being said behind the goat's-hair cloth.

"One of them says he is a boat builder," I heard someone say.

There was the gurgling sound of tea being poured into beakers from large jugs. I imagined there were four or five men, the Builder, his sons, and presumably also a servant who laughed like a monkey and interrupted impudently while serving the tea. One by one, the candidates in the queue were examined. No doubt wearing just loincloths, they showed off the soundness of their limbs. I heard someone question them in a gentle voice about their experience, skills, age, and strength. I recognized a pattern in the assignments: Most people were needed for the scaffolding on which work was going ahead steadily and which was absolutely essential for everything. And then they needed men to handle the pitch. For that, they sought young men who would not complain, who were able to do much and prepared to do anything. The interviews were brief, but because there were many, it was a long wait for my father's turn.

My father's voice at first sounded quiet and hesitant amongst the others. Gradually the sound of pouring and slurping stopped. My father chose his words carefully. He spoke about bending ribs, caulking seams, and fitting bulkheads. Gradually his diffidence disappeared. He spoke the way I had been used to him speaking: blunt and convinced he was right. Of course, he knew what he was talking about. He had designed and built large-sized boats, and only very rarely had one of them been wrecked. Although his reputation had not spread to this region, he spoke as if it had.

It worked. Occasionally there was a brief rejoinder, a reply from the gentle voice. Was that the Builder?

When my father had completed his argument, no one spoke.

The pigeons settled down. The men waiting in the front annex too were quiet, and no longer made a clatter with the tools they were carrying.

"I want him with the woodworkers," I heard someone say behind the canvas. It was a new voice, one I had not heard before. The voice was emphatic but not peremptory. It delighted me, the way finding a smooth stone under a rough one could delight me. Every now and then, a squeak sounded through it. I stood still, holding my breath to listen to it.

To my surprise, there was no rejoinder, only a muttered objection that could not have come from my father. There was a tense silence full of coughing and shuffling. Eventually I heard my father say the words people in the marshes use to take leave, so I quickly got off my stack of branches and hurried back to the front.

My father reached the forecourt before me. He came walking backward through the entrance of the tent. Following him was a young man in a striped shirt. He was no older than me, and unlike all the others I had seen in this shipyard, he was blond. He wore a braided belt around his waist and shoddy footwear.

"You will have a very important post," I heard him say to my father. "None of us have skills like yours." I recognized the voice from inside the tent. There was something the matter with his breathing; I could hear that squeak again.

My father pretended not to notice the young man. His hair streaming, his face blotchy from the exertion, he looked around him trying to locate my mother and me.

The young man did not seem to notice and said, "My father is ill, and we need people who are highly skilled. My brother Shem is doing the scaffold, my brother Japheth the pitch. They both have experts by their side, foremen who help them in their work. I want to have you beside me for the timberwork."

My father spotted me and came toward me. The young man followed him, nearly brushing past me. Close up, I saw that he was not blond, but that his hair and eyebrows were covered with sawdust. On his forehead he wore the same black design as all young men here. He was bony and had the lightest skin of them all. "Can we come to an agreement? Shall we see each other in the carpentry shop at sunrise?" he continued imperturbably.

My father handed me his stick, shrugged, and muttered a dour "Yes." "Pick up the stretcher," he said to me curtly. He took the other end and without giving the young man another look went ahead of me down the path.

I could not understand what was going on. My mother's eyelid was trembling. She panted and snorted. My father must have heard her, but did not look back; he kicked the litter on the path out of his way and kept walking. I looked back over one shoulder, then the other, but on a path like this it was hard enough not to stumble, so I made no further effort to see what was going on behind me. I walked on quickly, the way my father wanted.

Only when we had got behind the stacks of timber did he lower the stretcher. He looked at me and then at my snorting mother. He bent over her. He clenched his fists and held them before his stomach, as if he had been hit below the belt. Very slowly he sank down. He pressed his mouth against the eye that he had stitched closed long ago to protect it from drying out. He said, "I cannot work for them. They are not sound people. They are not trained. They are Rrattika!"

That was what they were. Rrattika, people who wandered, who turned up occasionally to beg or to plunder the dwellings of people who had settled. They hardly looked like the Rrattika we knew; with their light skin they looked deceptively different, but they had the same manners. They understood nothing about water or about boats. They had no love of home, no matter how hard they tried to stay in one place for a long time. They kept cattle in their own way: They stole herds and drove them along mercilessly for days on end.

From behind the stack of timber I could see the red tent. There were even more people about now; men had come out of the tent and stood looking around in agitation. It was not clear where the light-skinned young man was. They all wore those outsize cloaks, which kept flapping against their calves. Their clothes were the color of sand, of timber, of the gray water they were washed in. These were the teeming people we knew, who had been our rivals for years and whom my father would not allow us to look at. Now they were looking at us and we stood here, amidst their dwellings, their paths, their households. I found it a lovely sight, but my father was horrified. To be rid of their smell, he breathed through his mouth.

My Father's Departure

I had only observed the poor water, but my father worked it out from many things: the shelters with their canvas and pegs, the cooking fires that reappeared in different places, the absence of ovens and wells, the latrines that were no more than shallow pits, the worn-down hooves of the goats, the grain kept in woven bags, not in baskets. Everything showed it: These were wanderers. They carried knives in their belts because they assumed they would always have to fight for a place at the spring. Eaters of roots and nuts they were, they knew nothing about cultivating the land.

Now we understood how Alem could have found the way so unerringly. He had brought us to his brothers. Had it not been amazing how much he knew about this enterprise? That a man had conceived a grand plan, that his three sons were involved in it, that he was building a ship out of the wood of trees rich in resin, that the ship was to have compartments and should be covered in pitch inside as well as out, that it would be tall, three stories at least, and long, longer than any construction ever designed, and that, as a result, very many workers would be needed, men who knew how to deal with scaffolding, and tar makers, and men who knew about bending and planing ribs. That the plan had not come from the Builder, but had been inspired by a higher power. That compensation would follow the building, a reward if the work fulfilled all the conditions. How had Alem discovered all this? From the stories he had been told during his wanderings?

We called Alem and his kin "Rrattika," after the shiny, worm-like insects that you cannot squash because they are already so flat they wriggle out from under your foot. Of course, they also had a proper name: Leave-fire-behind, a name from the time our people did not yet have fire-pots and would wait, fearful of wind and rain, for the wanderers to leave so they could get the glowing coals out of their campfires. They had those remarkable folding tents that, when there was a storm, they would pull down and sit on top of. That in particular made us laugh: In bad weather the tents did not protect the Rrattika, but the Rrattika the tents!

"Is that what we came all this way for?" said my father. "Did we give up everything to work for vermin?" He said he could not bear to look at it, that indifference to quality, that disorder, that total lack of anything made to last, to stand up to wind and weather. "If it was not for that ship, they would finish off their remaining provisions tomorrow, fold up their tents, and chase their children ahead of them," he said. We returned to the foot of the cliff from which we had earlier carried my mother with so much trouble. There we saw a group of grass cutters.

My father asked them to look out for a man with a donkey and a child. Could they ask him to return immediately? Could they inform him that the boat builder and his wife were waiting for him to guide them back to the marshes of Canaan? My mother groaned. With a visible effort, my father turned toward my mother again and took her face between his hands. "I was looking for tradesmanship, but all I find here is ignorance," he said. "What do these people know about the building of a ship? They tempt us into coming here with their promising stories. From afar, it sounds as if it would be a privilege to work for them. The man who engaged me is still almost a child. Should I work for a child?"

"You promised the light-skinned young man that you would be there," I said.

"That was a feigned promise, Re Jana. His two brothers were in the tent, two big men with wide shoulders. What would you have wanted me to do? Give them the chance to chain me up and force my knowledge from me?"

"But their construction is beautiful."

"It is too big. Its size raises suspicions of insanity, Alem was right about that. If it will float at all, what purpose will it serve? Anyone who has that much to carry would build a fleet."

We were standing in the quarry that separated us from the cliff. In the half dark, the expression in his eyes was not easy to see, but the dismay on his face was. He looked around as if he was waking from a terrifying dream. I knew what he did when he decided to stay in a place: He arranged the stones that were lying around in such a way that they offered protection and weren't a nuisance if one turned over in one's sleep; he broke up the ground so he could let it run through his fingers, pulling up thistles and sharp-edged grasses by their roots. Now I could see him inspecting the surroundings, working out how he would arrange things. He would spend the night here, and that was my wish. I wanted to be near these people, these brethren of Alem-the-ragged. I loved the hammering and the humming, I recognized Put's songs; they were the melodies that lulled me to sleep on the way there. Being so close, I imagined I was one of them, that early in the morning I would roll all my belongings in a mat, throw it onto my back, and start the journey, fulfilling the longing of my childhood.

But all my father felt was revulsion. He felt cheated, by the tellers of tales, by Alem who got away so fast, by the workers on the scaffold, who from afar created the impression they were working from a detailed plan. He pointed out the tongue-shaped hollow where the traces left by people with picks were clearly visible. "Let us wait for the wanderer here," he said. "Let us put up the tent and spend the night here. That climb we can tackle tomorrow morning."

I put down all my gear. "Tomorrow morning" brought nothing before my mind. Our future had been wiped out, a new morning was not conceivable.

If he had not taken things in hand, I would hardly have moved that evening. He set up the tent. He built a screen out of sticks for my fire. I prepared his tea with water we had bought for many shells from women by their cooking fires. I shelled our last nuts. I did not think about what I was doing. I was acting in bewilderment. I could not believe that we would have to scale again every hill we had climbed, that we would again have to stand and wait for water by the wells like outlaws, that we would again be threatened by adders and scorpions. I could already hear the voices of our kin in the marshes: "They're back, and the season hasn't even changed yet." I did not want to go back. I knew how to find good water; that task would take me less than half a day. And my mother did not want to go back. It was not till after she had eaten that her breathing calmed down.

She was asleep when the sounds behind us changed: The hammering and planing turned into grinding and stirring. The workers were going home from the bathing place. We watched the coming and going of people with torches, and the workers under their shelters of canvas, sticks, and pieces of string, so exhausted they dozed off during their evening meal, their heads leaning against a post or a stick.

"Did you notice their little fields before?" my father asked. "They've planted the seedlings without preparing the beds. In autumn they will have to chew the stones they left in the soil."

I had noticed the fields. They were small and arid, of the kind that need frequent watering.

"But that is not the worst. They do what Alem does: They let women and children search for water and then claim it for themselves. If they ever wash, it is with the cattle. Their drinking water they keep hidden inside as if it were precious stones. A woman's quality is judged by the taste of the water she brings. Is that how you want to live, Re Jana? As the slave of a thirsty man?"

His argument left me cold, I could hardly bear listening to it. I let him talk without interrupting him, I was too exhausted to speak. When I was filling his beaker, I spilt tea on his hand.

My father slept sitting up that night. The sight of the many workers who had no tents, not even a ground sheet, and just lay amongst the rocks with their tools and water bags beside them, their heads resting on stones, had made him fearful. The drone of so many people breathing, interrupted by the screaming of small children, made him think of flight and famine. How could he be one of them?

My sleep, by contrast, was full of excitement. I dreamed of the belly of the ship and the steady slap of water. All night I felt close to the lagoon and the sea, even though I was several weeks' walk away from home. Its very absence made the promise of water seem much more lovely than it would have been beside a well or on the shore of a lake. Toward morning, I was full of feelings of both admiration and mockery. The sounds from the awakening shipyard struck me as unreal. They seemed mainly intended to attract the gullible. But the very madness of the enterprise restored my confidence. Only someone who knew what he was doing could devise a plan on this scale.

My father got up even before daylight. He did not take the time to wash and drank no tea. "I'm going after Alem," he said. "I will find him and bring him back here."

How could he find Alem? The wanderer had been gone for quite a time, and as was the habit of his people, he always carefully brushed away all traces of his camps with branches. My mother puffed and panted. She blinked her eye and made her breath whistle. But my father girded his loins. To me he said, "You look after her." And he set off up the steep slope to the cliff.

7

The Divining Rod

*I*t was early, the sun still far away with the gods. I dragged my mother over to the pond. It took me ages to maneuver the stretcher amongst the sleeping bodies. I was panting and sweating, even though the air was still cool. Some women were stirring, but far away, solitary, stealing about, shadowy, without making any sound. If I got to the pool before everybody else, I might find water that had not yet been muddied. I scooped up a handful, but noticed that even without sediment it kept its smell: My mother let it dribble from her mouth when I offered it to her to drink.

I knew what I had to do. I took her to the gallery where fires were being lit under beams. The beams, planed smooth, lay in their scaffolding like the rib cage of some gigantic animal, each one in its jig heated where it had to bend, some weighted at their ends. Shortly, their curves would be adjusted with struts. The fires and the slow bending of the timber would not be left unattended for a moment.

Where a fire is kept going, there are people, and people can keep an eye on things. I took the divining rod from my mother's hip-belt and covered her body with her cloak. I arranged her hair; if I put her head down the right way, you could not see the bald patches. I put her pendant in the hollow of her neck, and when she was ready I left her in the spot where the truss-benders were working. As I left, I could feel her eye following me.

I held the divining rod in front of me. It felt familiar, like a finger that had always been there. It pointed toward the rising sun. From Put, I knew how the Rrattika search for water. They knock crusts of sand from rocks, they dig holes in the ground and twist cactuses from their roots. Any little drop satisfies them. Put had demonstrated it to us in detail. When the donkey brayed its thirst, the child would stop and start walking around in circles like an animal that smells trouble. He would hold a cup in one hand, a gourd in the other. He would stop in a particular spot and kneel down. The donkey would stand next to him; it too had smelled water and knew Put would get it out for him. Put would dig with his hands, and when he had gone down an arm's length, his hands would be wet. He looked so pleased with himself when he did that. The first time my father saw him doing it, he could not have enough of it and called him Put, Digger-of-hollows, a name he would keep for the rest of his life.

But that sort of water will not do for us. For people like us, the little hand-dug well is only the beginning from which we start looking for a spring. What I wanted to find was the source that filled these little hollows. We daughters of Kan have a talent for water. The marshes where we live are fed by rivers. They run into the lagoon, the lagoon into the sea. The sea is supposed to swallow, but a few times each season her gullet tightens up and she sends us her salty belch that makes fish gasp for air and plants discolor. "The sea is having her time," people say, and that is when we young women have to move inland.

We start at a pool. From there, we follow the deep, invisible vein we can feel beating and sometimes foaming. The vein guides us to a cavern, a crack in the earth. There we make camp and lure strong-armed men who dig the wells for us and draw the sweet water.

That is how I knew life, that was the order I was used to. To see that there were different rules in this shipyard confused me. Here women lugged water jars like thin-legged donkeys. But was that not exactly why it was the right place for me? With my mother's divining rod, handed down from generation to generation, and my ability to find the veins that flow under the earth, I would be a very attractive catch for a people with no understanding of water. Alem had kissed me in exchange for water; he had, night after night, shared his knowledge, told his secrets, not hiding any aspect of love from me. My skill could be my hallmark; their lack of it, coinage in my hand. Understanding what I could mean to the Rrattika gave my feet wings, even though my soles were still aching from our long trek.

All through the morning I walked. The divining rod led me amongst the sickle-shaped hills, and from there into rocky terrain only inhabited by the wind. In the rocks there were many caves, all looking the same. With their inviting air of mystery, they all seemed intent on making visitors lose their way. Nothing grew in the hollows that led to their entrance. The undulations in the sand made me think of the ripples on the water back home when the wind rose. Because the wind could not get amongst the rocks, there were unexpectedly many flies. They instantly covered my mouth. The sun climbed higher and became hot.

My common sense told me to turn back. The surroundings were confusing and threatening, the sort of place one does not return from, but I knew I was approaching my goal: The divining rod writhed against the tips of my fingers and pointed forcefully at a particular opening in the rock face. This cave, like the others, must have been closed at one time by a gate, but that had collapsed and decayed. The cavern seemed to have a regular shape, like a hand, with recesses and passages. I smelled the scent of earth mixed with moisture. The farther I penetrated, the more uneven the ground became. I stumbled. All around me lay strange objects that rolled away with a hollow sound. It was some time before I recognized them as skulls and bones. I tried to convince myself that they were the bones of dead animals, but my eyes were rapidly adjusting to the darkness, and around me became visible the remains of wanderers, left behind for centuries. The skulls were stacked in rows in this burial place, amongst them small ones, from children and newborn babies. In holes to the left and the right of the path I was walking on were thigh bones and ribs, stacked separately. The deeper into the cave, the more orderly the stacks, resembling huge, regular structures.

I wanted to go back, away from this spot that felt offensive to me, almost barbaric — we put our dead on papyrus boats that we burned on the lagoon. But the divining rod in my hand trembled uncontrollably. I thought it was fear making my hands tremble like leaves in the wind and causing the tip of the divining rod to move, but the trembling turned into thrashing, the end of the rod even hitting my face.

I went so far in, the darkness almost made walking impossible. The cave tapered into a deep passage, a narrow opening too dark to venture into. It was open at the top, but the light was so faint that it was like penetrating the night. There were galleries, connected by narrow passages. I came to a spot that seemed to go down into the very underworld. I made slow progress. There were a number of deep holes, each of which could mean death, but I kept going along the narrow ledge, because it was the only way to keep away from the terrifying stacks of bones, which seemed to be ever taller and built according to an ever stricter plan.

I do not know how I found the passage to the spring. It seemed no more than a fold in the rock. Because of the divining rod, I forced my way through. The ground was wet, my feet slipped, any moment I expected to hit my head on a protruding rock, but the water was so close, I forced myself forward. *Just let my father try to get me away from here,* I thought. *Just let him try to convince me now that his idea is the right one.* I went in the direction of a familiar sound, stretched out my hands, and after some searching, felt water so cold that it was as if it bit my fingers. It was a trickle, no stronger than a baby goat's pee. But if I was patient, my jug would fill.

8

Meeting Ham

*T*he sun had only just passed its highest point when I returned to the truss-bending workshop, the jug heavy in my arm. My mother had disappeared. The spot where I had left her had been churned up, and her woolen cloak lay crumpled up amongst the rubbish.

My father is back, was my first thought, but I could not imagine him having taken her without leaving a sign for me. The furrow left in the grit was a zigzag, not the firm, straight line left by someone who knew where he was going.

My thoughts raced like wildfire: *Who had gone off with her? Who would abduct a cripple? How would he ever survive the shame of such cowardice?* My mother was beautiful, she was flawless and gorgeously adorned, but so useless because of her inability to move that no one had ever even thought of taking her.

The trail led past the fires to a long shed that, judging by the objects that were being carried out of it, was a carpentry workshop. I followed the trail at a run, indifferent to the good water sloshing out of my jar.

I found her to one side of the shed. She was in the company of a young man whom I recognized, before I even saw his face, by his striped cloak and the sawdust in his hair. In my hurry to get to her

I ran even faster. At least, I thought I was running fast; whoever looked at me probably only saw me stumbling. I had the jug on my hip. Already I had carried it in front of me, on my head, and on my other hip. Now I was exhausted. I dumped the jug next to the stretcher, a movement that made the young man jump up. The clumsy way I sat down was, of course, partly out of relief: She was here, she was safe, we had not been mocked by someone who wanted to play with her as with a doll. But my relief vanished when I saw that she was not well. Her eyes were dull with deprivation. Her carnelian beads burned on a skin that looked desiccated, she was beyond sweating; I could smell her sores.

"She is thirsty," I said without looking at the young man I blamed for everything. My voice sounded strange, no doubt because of the cold water, of which I had drunk quite a lot.

The young man moved out of my way and bowed his head. "I have shown her the shipyard," he said. "I have offered her drink. . . . She did not answer. . . ." He seemed to understand it was his fault, for he blushed down to his neck. With him was a slim dog, sniffing the wind. The beast had licked her face, I could see it by the smudges on her cheek. And one of the handles of the stretcher had been damaged.

When I put the jug down by the end of the stretcher, her eye opened wide, she shivered, I could not moisten her lips fast enough. "Quiet," I said. "Calm down, everything will come good." I was calm and restrained only to her. To the young man I said, "Why did you take her away from her spot? She was in a well-chosen place."

He straightened his shoulders. "She is the boat-builder's wife, and I am looking for him. I was hoping she would help me. What is wrong with her?"

"She became crippled while she was fishing."

He reached out to the dog, stroking its head.

I let a scoop of water trickle into my mother's mouth. She swallowed and looked at me. It was good water, I knew. But it was also the water of the dead, so I gave her no more than necessary. The look in her eye asked for more, her skin was burning, she had been unprotected in sun and wind for a long time, but I had already decided on my way back that, for the time being, washing her with the water was safer than giving it to her to drink, so I got up to take her over to the pond.

"Help me move her," I said.

The young man was surprised by the request, but seeming to decide it was fair, he got up and took hold of the heavy end of the stretcher where the water jug was. I walked in front, my back to him. I heard the wheeze in his breath. The greyhound followed us at a short distance, occasionally coming up to the young man, but never to me.

I was quite aware that this was not right, that in this shipyard a man did not carry stretchers or water jars. Passersby looked at us and quickly turned their eyes away, clearest proof that what they saw disturbed them. His willingness to walk with me despite those looks made me feel generous. In a way, it was astonishing that my mother and I had come here from the marshes to be helped by the Builder's son.

We got to the pond, where a small herd of goats was busy drinking. But the animals quickly drank their fill, and I could get to work. I filled a hollow of the right size with the finest sand I could find, spread the cloak over it, and rolled my mother off the stretcher. I found a bowl with a small crack that someone had left behind, filled it with water from the jug, and settled myself astride her hips.

The dog stood close by. It could smell my oil, of course, which was mixed with myrtle, cinnamon, sweet Klamath, and cassia, according to an ancient recipe, handed down to me through Manilada and Kan. The dog was emaciated, his haunches almost transparent, and he rocked on his tall legs like a mosquito in a draught. He seemed as underfed as his master, nervous and thin as a grasshopper.

The animal's breath on her face bothered my mother, but she did not let it show. As always, she looked straight up, her eye searching the sky for passing birds.

The Builder's son observed my actions with the concentration of a child, watching the way I poured water over my mother, cup after cup. The water ran off her and soaked into the cloak. I shifted different parts of my cloth around the tip of my finger to rub her body. This was when patience and meticulous care were needed, because poor circulation had made her skin extremely sensitive. Fortunately it was cooler here, close to the pond. But there were hornets and flies. They seemed maddened by the scent of my water.

"Why does your father keep her alive?" he asked when I had finished the slow and gentle washing. "Why drag along a woman who does not move when you order her?" He had knelt down next to me.

"She is dear to us," I replied and started on the oil. The skin absorbed the fluid and slowly came to life.

The young man watched it intently, his mouth half open, with a look that would have made my mother blush, stimulating the blood flow, had she had less pride. His amazement was not surprising: My mother was beautiful. She gleamed like a freshly shelled nut. Her skin was dark but smooth, and only flawed by the sores on her back. He looked at her neck and her breasts, this boy who was not used to nakedness. Now and then he raised his hand as if to touch her.

I did not know then what sort of person I was dealing with. I knew he was the son of the Builder of the ship, and that he had taken charge of the woodwork. But I knew nothing yet of his fondness for almonds, of his ability to go on working in an enclosed space on even the hottest days, or of the softness of his fingertips, barely calloused by the work. I soon discovered that his name was Ham and that he was the youngest of the three, but I had no inkling of the rest. That is why I did not tell him that my bedridden mother had grown out of my walking mother, that there no longer was any difference between the two. The memory of her moving was her moving, the memory of her goodness was her goodness, it made it impossible not to take care of her. I did not really expect him to understand, we had not found understanding anywhere, so why expect it here?

"My father will not turn up," was all I said. "He wants to go back to the marshes of Canaan."

"Why does he want to leave?" His breath wheezed even when he was not exerting himself. Little sounds came from deep inside his body. They were like a separate, smothered conversation he was carrying on with his dog.

"He cannot take this project seriously," I replied.

He pressed his hands into the grit under him. His cloak was torn at the neck. I could see his collarbones, his skin, and his chest that was hairless and smooth. His skin had been washed, not rubbed with oil. It was mainly his cloak that made his appearance grimy: There were stains on it, and near the hem, the stripes were invisible because of the dirt.

"He will work with the finest timbers. I will give him tools made by the best blacksmiths. And a great degree of independence."

"I'll tell him," I said.

The passersby were still staring. I was not sure what bothered them most: me or him or the fact that he was with me. He lowered his voice, almost to a whisper now. He raised his hand to his shoulder. His sleeve fell back to his elbow. He had pale, hairless underarms with deep-lying veins and fingertips splayed at the nails.

"We have lost our direction. My old father is ill. As long as he was in control, everything went well. But now we have to carry on without him. We have grown up here in the desert — what do we know about boats? My foreman is no help. He stood on a jetty once, so he calls himself an expert. I am looking for someone who really knows how it should be done. I will wait for your father. I have been waiting for him for a long time." Unthinkingly, he touched his jaw and the curve down to his neck. I was not looking, but I saw it anyway.

Because he was my own age, and because he had been careless with my mother, I allowed myself to say, "A man begins building a gigantic ship. Then he falls ill. Nobody knows how to carry on. Yet the work goes on. Why not wait till the old man gets better? Or dies?"

"Don't joke," he said. "Do not underestimate us. We know exactly what we are doing. We cannot suspend building. There is no time. Completion is extremely urgent."

I laughed, the way you laugh at a child making up a story. He could have turned his back on me. I was a stranger on his territory, and he was the son of a man of consequence. But he did not turn away. He watched as I rubbed my mother with oil. Because of his watching, it was not as usual: There was more feeling in my fingertips than normal. Because he was also looking at me, at my face, and at all of my body, which was glowing from exertion.

"Where is your tent?" he asked.

"In the quarry, at the base of the cliff." I pointed out the direction. The spot I meant was not visible from there. A carpentry shop, a ship under construction, and a whole settlement lay between. It was still quiet everywhere, people had found shady spots, which they shared with the animals.

"How will I know that your father has returned? How do I know you won't suddenly disappear without trace?"

"You will know because the stars will move," I said. "Because the moon will fall and the horizon will tremble."

He did not laugh; he did not seem to be the sort of boy who laughs much. "You're not taking me seriously."

"Do you want me to make a promise?" I asked.

"What are your people's promises worth? Your father has broken the first one he made."

"You will not know," I said, ignoring his taunt. "We'll disappear like fire under the lid of a brazier." I shook out the cloak and arranged it over my mother. She too was pleased at the way I had stood up to the young man, I could see it in her eye.

He got up, as if about to help me. Without a word, he let his cloak slide off his back, leaving no more than a sleeveless undershirt. His movements made the hornets buzz away. He shook off his shoes and walked to the water. At the edge of the pond, he took off his undershirt. I kept looking in surprise. His skin was paler than any I had ever seen in the marshes. He was as skinny as I had imagined, with long arms and legs covered only in thin, unblemished skin. He waded out to a spot deep enough to cover all of his body as he lay down. All I could see were his pale, smooth shoulders, with his matted hair falling over them.

He stayed in the water a long time. As I came to the pond to rinse the cloth I had used for washing, and then walked back, he watched me, first from the corner of his eye, then with his whole face turned toward me. I walked the way Alem had taught me, my back stretched, my chin pointing down. After a while I realized that it only seemed like he was watching me. He was looking at something else, at a thought, at a perception as transparent as a god. Although I did not know why, I felt that by looking at me, he understood something. I held an idea out to him, gave his thoughts form and wings. But something was in the way; I could see it from the way he was chewing the inside of his cheek, like a famished man, without causing as much as a ripple on the water.

9

Ham's Grooming

I was not surprised when Ham came to the quarry that evening after sunset. My mother was already asleep, and so nearly was I, but I could feel him approaching. The greyhound was with him, his nails tapping on the stones. I got up, took a cloth and my oil, and lifted the water jug onto my hip. I knew how to move without waking my mother; that too I had learned from Alem. I crept outside and started following the moonlight reflected off Ham's cloak, not moving too quickly so the water would not slosh. He walked to the shipyard, and for a moment I thought he might lead me into the ship. But he stopped at the foot of the scaffold. He disappeared behind the stacks of timber waiting, ready for the next morning. There I found him, squatting by the fire that smoldered under the vats of pitch. The greyhound had disappeared as soon as the smell reached its nostrils.

I spread out the cloth by his feet. I found a bowl waiting there that had been carefully wiped clean, so I poured the contents of my jar into it. He undid his belt, pulled his cloak over his head, and lay down on his stomach. It was dark, and I could not see his skin very well, but at times it shone like silver in the glow of the fire. His body seemed out of proportion from rapid growth, but even so I could feel a controlled strength in those bundles of muscles and ligaments, the staying power of a pack animal. His frame made me think of bushes, of flexible twigs, of reeds in the marshes.

I bathed him the way I bathed my mother. He shivered when he felt the water. It was so clear under the moonlight that my hands were reflected in it every time I wrapped the cloth around my fingers. His head was turned away from me, and I could not see if his eyes were open or shut. A strange odor came from the bone ornament around his neck. I carefully removed it, putting it aside so as not to wet it unnecessarily. Around us there were only the sounds of countless night animals and the crying of owls.

He was sensitive, I could feel that from the way his skin opened itself up to the water. I knew what I had to do. I would press seeds for him. I would rub the furrows in his neck with oil until I could peel off the dirt. I would comb his tangle of dark hair until it was smooth again and shiny. I would teach him how marsh people kept themselves clean and scented. I would clean his fingernails till they shone like a duck's bill. I would give him aniseed for his breath. Oil and generous acts I would lavish on him, because if there was one thing I had learned, it was that sensitives must be well treated.

I applied the oil and rubbed it into his arms and legs, until his skin would accept no more and became smooth as chamois leather. I pressed my thumbs deep into the skin along his spine and rubbed his lower back firmly as if I were polishing it. With my thumb I pushed on his tailbone, I found the hollow on the inside of his heel. His body grew warm under my fingers.

I said, "I will show you my spring if you will carry the water for me."

His muscles tightened. He raised his upper body on his arms and looked at me for a few moments. Now I could clearly see those short but thick eyelashes, the beard, still downy, and the slight movement of his nostrils. His eyes were full of dismay.

"Give me a donkey then. The pens are full of them," I insisted.

He shook his head. The tips of his hair dragged over his shoulders. "If I give you a donkey, you will all go away. You still have no idea what we are doing here."

"The Builder builds a ship in a place where there is hardly any water?" The fire was warm, I turned my other side toward it. And sitting that way, I could have a better look at him. "Everybody here is working hard, so something wonderful must have been promised."

He bent toward me and, in a single movement, took the cloth from under him to cover his body. With his free hand, he grasped my shoulder, pointed at the red tent farther down, and whispered, "My father is in conversation. He is speaking with his god the way I am speaking with you." His sudden movement was bad, it threw up the dust and made him dirty again.

"Which god?" I asked.

"He who is well-disposed toward us, the Nameless One, the Unnameable; forget all others. This god looks after us, the others do not do that. The Unnameable is so angry, so disappointed. My father tries to calm Him, but it is in vain. His mercy is nearing exhaustion. He says He is losing faith in mankind. He wants to destroy all evildoers. Only the noble-minded and the just will escape, with them He will continue."

I knew of the fear Rrattika lived with: the fear that their name would be extinguished, the way it happened to the godless and to criminals. Their lives consisted of a constant series of efforts to escape the curse of oblivion.

Although I had dried him off, his forehead was already covered in droplets again. "I see how you care for your mother, and it touches my heart," he said. "You do it out of love, as I build the ship out of love. You do not offend the Unnameable. He is astonished at so much goodness, as I am. I know what you people think, you consider us scum, you have named us after vermin. But give us a chance. Bring your father to me and help us placate the Unnameable." He put on his cloak without letting go of the cloth he was covering himself with.

I helped him a little, not too much, because I was looking at him more than helping him, looking at his movements and the play of the shadows they caused. When he was dressed, I moved away from him a little, so I suddenly found myself too close to the fire, and it felt as if my head were burning. Anxiously I asked, "You are building the ship to make your name immortal?"

"The ship must ensure that we will not be wiped out," he said.

"An appeal for mercy?" I asked. Again, I could hear the wheeze in his voice.

He touched my arm with his fingertips. "For mercy, it is too late. The Unnameable has made His decision. We must help each other. It is now a matter of belonging to the elect."

The dog started barking, and Ham jumped up. He grabbed me and dragged me away from the glow of the fire. He pushed me between the stacks of timber, where I made myself as small as I could and kept still. Someone came and stood by him, a man with a quick step and a short shadow, an apparition from nowhere, without a lamp in his hand, without a stick, as if the laws of the night did not apply to him.

"What are you doing?" I heard the man ask.

Ham remained silent. He began walking away from the pitch vats.

"This is not the girl you are waiting for," the stranger said, his face turned toward the shipyard.

"But look at the water she brings," I heard Ham plead.

"There are other women with good water. She is not the one. I will give you a sign when she arrives."

"She is good, she is beautiful," Ham continued.

They disappeared amongst the stacks of timber. I could just see that the man who walked beside the son of the Builder was of very small stature. He was not wearing clothes like the Rrattika, but was naked. His arms and legs were thin, his hips narrow like a boy's. He had to take large steps to keep up with Ham. It may have been the poor light, but his skin seemed even darker than mine.

"We have to get away from here," I said to my mother, whom I only washed near our tent now, after that one time by the pond. "These people are expecting a great calamity. Their god is preparing an overwhelming punishment. He is going to destroy all who are not chosen." We quickly agreed: This cleansing we did not want to experience. We did not want to witness the suffering that would come with it. The gods of the Rrattika were not familiar to us, and this one did not seem the most benign. The

Rrattika had chosen a god of whom they lived in fear. That was remarkable: We were in the habit of choosing gods who would leave us in peace instead of provoking us.

And so I stored up water in order to be ready when my father returned. Going to the spring, I followed a different path every time to confuse anyone who wanted to follow me. It would seem there were different levels of water quality. I saw women who had access to reasonably good water: They sold it at high prices, and if they were unmarried, well-to-do young men hung around them. I did not make a show of how good my water was. I could have acquired clothes, jugs, and blankets for it, but what use would that sort of baggage be if we had to flee the disaster? I led a donkey from one of the enclosures and hid it in the bushes. Stealing a pack animal seemed harmless: There were so many of them inside the little stone walls, at least a pair of every form and kind, and as many as seven of certain kinds. Having to be out for hours cutting grass counted for nothing compared to the security of knowing the animal was there ready. At that time, we no longer believed my father would bring Alem and the donkey back with him.

Three nights in a row, the young son of the Builder came to get me. Each time he took me to the warmth of the pitch vats. I was restrained when I washed him. As Alem had taught me, I did not touch his face or his stomach. Yet afterward I walked back to our tent with my hands tingling as if they had been exposed to the sun for too long, and into my deepest sleep I could hear him repeat to the small, naked man in the dark, "She is beautiful. She is good. Look at the water she brings."

10

Alem's End

O n the eighth day after his departure, my father returned carrying little Put on his back. He also carried the carefully woven bit of our donkey and Alem-the-ragged's gray cloak. Put had an empty look in his eyes. It was ages before they were in a fit state to tell their story.

Alem was a hero, said my father. He had found him from directions given by reed carriers on the way. Alem had not gotten very far, because the donkey had been ill. My father had asked him to come back to the quarry to get my mother and me, and Alem had happily agreed. Of course he wanted to be of service again, he understood without explanation that the boat builder would not prosper in this shipyard. But because of the donkey, the return journey was slow. The animal became bloated. They had spent quite some effort trying to save it, but it was hopeless. First the carrion eaters had come, small dogs who were after the intestines, but the scent of blood had attracted larger animals. Alem had warned of the danger, he had said they should go on that very evening, but my father had laughed off his fear and said he was glad to have found him, that there was no rush now and they should save their strength.

The monster had appeared from nowhere, none of them had

sensed its approach. They had only heard the silence and wondered why the lizards disappeared into chinks and cracks. Then
the shadow fell on them. It was a striped animal, its eyes glistening, slaver dripping from its jaws. It wrapped its paws around
Alem like an embrace. They heard the cracking of bone. They
saw how Alem was knocked to the ground and immediately
thrown up in the air again. The incisors closed around the back
of his head right through his hood. Probably the animal had observed Alem from behind the bushes and seen how he moved; it
knew exactly where, under all the clothes he had on, his vertebrae were.

The tiger dragged Alem into the bushes. Alem grabbed at the
grass. Again the incisors closed over his skull. Something tore.
For a moment, the animal let go. Alem tried to scramble up, but
the tiger clawed at his legs the way it does with fleeing prey.

Alem had pushed himself off with all his strength. He had
thrown himself on top of the tiger, as if after due consideration,
he responded to the embrace. Very deliberately, he put his hand
into the beast's mouth, first the fingers, then the wrist. "Get
away, get away!" he shouted. "I'll hold it here." He pushed his fist
into the wide throat. The tiger slammed its jaws shut. The hand
cracked.

My father grabbed hold of Put and fled. He did not hear
screams. All through the night they waited. Only the next morning did they dare go back. When they got there, all they found
was the cloak and some splintered bones.

My father grieved deeply for the man for whom he had
shown nothing but disdain during our journey. My grief was

even deeper. Alem had taught me about love and shown me the world. Ham had predicted a disaster, he had read the signs, but why did it have to strike Alem? I tried to explain to my father that a donkey was ready waiting, that I had water and food, that, even without a pathfinder, we had to get out of this place as fast as we could.

But he was not to be swayed. "Return that donkey this instant," he said. "It will attract the wild animals. We cannot go back, the hills are full of untamed beasts lusting after our flesh." He sat down with his silkworms and fed them the mulberry leaves I had picked on the slopes earlier in the day. My mother rolled and rolled her eye, she was full of horror at Alem's death. And Put, the little man, rolled around in the gravel until he bled.

Because I did not have a place where I could hide with my horror, I went to the carpentry workshop. I had to go past the fire below the trusses. I had the feeling that it was about to leave its pit and come at me, leaping from one tinder-dry little patch of grass to another, to pour its heat all over me. The donkey, which I was leading by its halter, felt it too. It shied at every crackle in the wood. My stoical character, my willingness to take things as they come, had always reconciled me to my mother's ailment and the restrictions it imposed. I did not feel condemned to live with her, rather the opposite: I was sorry for her because she had to put up with my crude help, with my lack of reliability and skill, and my inability to protect her from the sores that develop from having to lie down. But now everything became less self-evident. With her endless, nerve-racking blinking, she had taken us away from our home, our boats, our waterways. It had cost Alem his life. We were stuck in a place where soon people were to be punished, and the only one of them I knew was a young man with a skin so fair it made me lose the feeling in my fingertips.

Ham saw me from his workbench. He hurried across. Because he looked at me without speaking, my grief burst forth. I had felt it growing in me, but when it reached my head it still took me by surprise, like a belch: It rose up in me and I overflowed. Water streamed from my eyes, my nose, my mouth, thick tears that fell from my cheeks onto my breasts.

"Does the Unnameable look like a great cat with stripes?" I stammered. "Is he a murderous, slavering monster?" I kept seeing Alem before me, his body, with its unusual scent, and which I had rubbed with oil, his cautious way of walking, intent on clues in the landscape. He taught me the gentlest possible hand contact, the touch that leaves no trace on the skin or in the sand. He taught me to move like a fish in a shoal, swerving fast without touching any other. He trained my skin, my fingertips, and the tip of my tongue.

"A man I loved has perished."

"Your father?" he asked quickly.

"Not my father. Another man I loved."

"Is your father back? Is he unharmed?"

"He has a wound in his heart, like me." I could not stop sobbing. Was this the stone coming loose, the beginning of a landslide that would overwhelm us? "Help us get away from here," I said. "See that we can leave this place safely, we have nothing to do with the punishment that will be imposed on you and your people."

He raised his hand, his sleeve fell back onto his elbow, making his white forearm visible. He wheezed as he said, "Don't be afraid. I will take care of you. But bring that donkey back. I can do nothing, absolutely nothing for you if you touch the animals."

The timber around us creaked. I wanted to grab the hand he held out, if only for balance, but he withdrew it. He looked around quickly at the workmen who came and went, their eyes downcast. Because he did not offer me the hem of his cloak, I wiped my face dry with my hand.

"What can you do?" I asked with a sob. "You do not even control your own fate! There is a dwarf who makes the decisions for you."

He hunched his back and put his hand over his mouth. The dust he worked in made him cough. Wood shavings from his hair fluttered down onto my arm. He stood away from me; his lack of breath made his face bulge and his eyes go red. He had barely any voice when he said, "The dwarf is an idiot, he's scum. He is a seer who does not know what to do with his gift. Leave him be. Leave him be with what he imagines to be his knowledge. Go away now. But come back to me tonight. You will belong to me like my shadow. If our god does not choose you, I will."

11

Washergirl
Becomes a Boy

I waited till it was completely dark. Finally, after much tossing and turning, Put had fallen asleep, and I walked to the pitch vats. Ham was waiting for me, a knife, needles, and some small bags in his hand. He carefully put them down on a piece of timber that lay across the stones like a shelf. He pulled me down and asked me to move as close to the glow of the fires as I could. He bent over me to do to me what was done to Rrattika boys when they became adults. First he thinned out my hair, cutting some of my curls close to the skull and pulling the longer hair across to cover it. Then he spread beside him the needles and the little bags, from which he shook black dyes. He asked me to close my eyes. With the needles, he made small cuts in my forehead, forming the emblem of the male.

I did not slap his hand away when drops of blood trickled to my temples. I did not kick his needles into the fire, nor did I blow his dyes into a heap. I did not open my eyes, but I could hear him sigh with the effort. He no longer smelled of cattle, but of cassia and sweet Klamath. His breath brushed over my face. The glow of the charcoal made my limbs feel weak. He applied the dyes to the cuts, dabbing the blood with the edge of his shirt.

When he had finished, he said, "Bathe your mother by the

pond tomorrow. Cover your body with a cloak. Wipe out your memories of Canaan. Become one of us. Earn planks and nails and build your mother a shelter that is more durable than a tent. You will be highly esteemed because you have the best water."

I nodded in confusion. The shallow cuts on my forehead burned as if salt had been mixed into the dyes.

"Don't let anyone know where you obtain your water," he continued. "Not me, not my brothers, not my father the day he is going to ask."

I still did not reply, I was still unable to talk after this morning's news. I had to get used to the way events closed in on me, as if I were lost in a cave that, like a snail shell, became narrower and narrower.

The next day, a boy bathed his crippled mother by the water. He did not scoop water from the pond, he had brought his own water, which was clearer and didn't smell. The boy did not wear a cloak — that would have been too impractical when using that oil and that water — but a sleeveless tunic, irregular in shape so you could not see that a pair of small breasts hid under it. All attention was focused on the garment that was decorated with shells. No one here wore anything like that, not just because sleeveless garments gave poor protection against the dust and the sun, but because, so far inland, shells were too precious to be sewn onto clothes. The meticulous way the boy worked was astonishing. His fingers moved so carefully and incessantly they seemed like ants, like steadily moving workers who would go over an obstacle rather than walk around it. Amazement could be seen on all faces, first of all the servants'. They looked furtively at the water in my bowl, nudged one another and whispered. They stood at the edge of the pond and gaped at every one of my movements. I was using my old sponge, even though it was falling apart from frequent use. And, of course, they paid attention to my mother, her face, and the adornment, which emphasized her beauty. They only withdrew when there were calls from a distance.

Shem, Japheth, and Ham approached, the sons of the Builder, and the bystanders made room for them, whispering. I did not have time to get up and watch them coming. Before I realized, they had walked past me and my mother. All three wore cloaks that nearly touched the ground. Dust fell out of them when they took them off. It was obvious they were brothers, they resembled one another, though the differences between them were not small. Shem had more of a paunch than his brothers, but had a narrower face. Japheth's appearance was coarser, his lower jaw protruding as if it had been pushed out by a brutal blow. He had large hands and black furrows in his neck. Ham was much smaller and thinner than his brothers, still almost a child compared to them.

Shem and Japheth got undressed first. They sat in the water and made scratching movements over the surface to keep the insects away. The servants were next. They made their toilet in their own way: They scraped the dirt off the backs of their hands with their teeth and poured pond water over their shoulders. They all suffered from itching: You could tell from the way their faces relaxed when they sat down in the water, as if they put out a fire deep inside their bodies. Ham was fiddling with his belt, which was hopelessly tangled and seemed to need all his attention. Even after he stood with his feet in the water, his gaze kept avoiding me. He was only knee deep when he threw himself into the water, as if he had felt a snake brush against his calf, and a moment later he plunged his head underwater.

As Shem and Japheth came out of the water to put their cloaks back on, they smelled my oils. They stood next to me, their legs spread, examining my jug, the bowl with the water, and the sponge that floated in it like a hunk of bread. "What do you do to her that makes her weak as wax?" they asked.

I stood up and bowed my head. My shell-covered tunic made soft clicking sounds and hid the rapid rise and fall of my breast under it. "We are marsh people," I said, fearful that my voice would betray me. "We have a talent for water. With this, I can wash you the way I wash my mother."

Shem had a hairy chest, Japheth was hairy just about all over. They looked at each other and smiled. They took the belts their servants held out to them and tied them low and tight around their waists. They walked to the red tent, looking back now and then, and went each into his own part of the tent. Ham went after them, but he did not look back.

I packed up my gear. I stood in front of the tent, made a greeting, and offered the Builder's sons a wash and oil treatment. They wanted to stand up, but I told them that was not necessary. I put down my bowl and knelt. I ignored the fact that they had just bathed in the pond, washing them the way it should be done. Because they were not used to me yet, I began with their hands, their arms, their feet, Shem first as he was the eldest. He was a bit giggly and friendly, talking with his brothers, but not with me.

Next I washed Japheth. His skin was gray. I was generous with the water, letting it drip from the sponge onto the pebbles and grit, something he watched with amazement. He asked me to braid his beard. His reactions were more sensitive than Shem's, almost irritable. He seemed to find my touch pleasant, but had no patience to enjoy it. He squinted, so I had no idea what he was looking at. I could not relax his tension.

Last I washed Ham, the same way as the others, no longer or more slowly. As I rubbed his arms, I could feel his pulse beat. He had not dried himself properly after his bath in the pond. Water was dripping from his hair down his neck, and as I wiped the drops with my sponge, I could see him repressing an urge to close his eyes. His breath was not wheezy, he was breathing more freely and lightly than before.

There was another part to the tent, made from much heavier canvas. Its curtain was down, the gaps plugged up with straw. Sounds came from behind it at times, the knock of stone against stone, low male voices. There the Builder lived; there also lived the dwarf I had seen near the pitch pots. But the Builder could not leave his sickbed, and nobody asked for a boy to bathe him. I could feel Ham grow tense under my hands when the dwarf came and looked at us through the curtain and said, "How curious, a boy who is as particular as a girl. Didn't you have a sister who is terribly like you?"

"His sister gets the water. She is away at the spring," Ham replied quickly, and the dwarf went back.

From that day on, I was assured of work. They did not ask me to come again, they simply assumed I would. They asked bystanders where he was, this washerboy who dragged his crippled mother along with him. After their daily labors, they waited with sluggish impatience. When they returned, they pushed back the canvas and did not request anything, but their eyes were burning.

12

A Righteous Man

After work I would sit down with my father. One day I noticed small pieces of charcoal lying under his feet: jet-black traces of someone who has been drawing.

"What were you doing?" I asked.

Nervously he looked away into the shrubs, and I knew that somewhere in there, there were boards with sketches of a vessel. I said, "Father, are you a righteous man?"

Surprised, he straightened his back. His eyes became clear at my question, he forgot the chaos in the quarry and out there. "I do not know if I am," he said slowly. "But I strive to be."

"Then go to Ham and offer your services. You have promised."

13

A Mark in Time

My father worked for Ham during the day and, in the evenings, built a house for four with the timber we earned. He placed the house at the end of the quarry, not far from the ash dump where he obtained the charcoal for his sketches for the ship, and far enough away from the tents and barracks not to be bothered by the constant sound of grinding hand mills. He worked fast. It was the desire to sleep in a hammock again, and no longer on the ground like cattle, that made him drive nails into timber long into the night. But every morning, long before I left for the spring, he was already at the scaffolds. Sometimes he would walk up to the red tent even before sunrise, carrying a lantern, avoiding the sleeping bodies of the workers.

What did he do there? He spoke with Ham. Parts of the ship were demolished, ribs pulled down and set up anew. He was building a genuine ship, not just some structure that looked like one. He knew of the need of ancient peoples to leave behind markers in the landscape, a stone table or a lime-filled furrow in the shape of a snake, and he felt indulgent at the thought that he was contributing to an effort to leave a mark in time. My father made the ship seaworthy without believing it would ever sail. In this region, water was not part of one's thoughts; if you thought of calamity, it was drought you imagined. He was realizing a dream. What he was building was a ship of ships, so perfect it would be a shame to launch it into the water. It was enough for him to know that in the future famous characters would be linked with the structure, and that in its ruins people would search for the remains of kings and children of the gods.

The woodworkers worked hard. They secured tree trunks on a frame; one man sat on top of the trunk, another below it, between them a saw that they pulled toward themselves in turn. So they cut plank after plank, day after day. They constructed slipways, lugged slabs of timber onto scaffolds, and at the end of the day whetted their saws. They barely complained at having to start all over after my father arrived; they were well fed, and that seemed to satisfy them. Perhaps they too felt they were working on something that transcended them, a timber masterpiece they would refer to forever. My father measured and made jigs. He drilled mortises and cut dovetail joints; he bent over the drawings and explained them, the pockets on his belt full of nails, and a small purse with animal claws around his neck, a talisman to prevent him being attacked by a wild beast again.

"What does Ham do inside that ship?" I asked.

"He's dividing it."

"Is he hot in there?"

"There isn't a breath of wind. He's hot in there."

I have often wondered how it was that my father became confident much sooner than I did. The winds rushing through the shipyard did not affect him. Unlike me. The wind came up and dropped. It made tumbleweeds roll about and bent grasses. It whispered of things Ham would not tell us.

14

The Animals Come, in Ever-Growing Numbers

For weeks, I washed and groomed Ham and his brothers. In the cave around the well, I had built a basin, a small dam of rocks, sealed with pitch I scrounged from Japheth. I stood watching how, after a long wait, a shallow layer of water formed at the bottom. I was quite taken with the little stream, it was so small and harmless; I tried to imagine how long it would take for it to flood the shipyard and raise the ship. But when I came the next day, all I had to do to fill my jug was to lower it into the water.

They undressed for me. I stroked their backs, rolled their skin over the second skin, the layer below the outer one, which I never got to see but needed care just as much. The fear I should have felt stood no chance because I was so close to the inventors of the calamity. I became less interested in their secret. What intrigued me was where their muscles were and how their joints turned. I found satisfaction in the certainty that I would be staying with these people for a time. And I listened to their conversations.

Japheth was talking about the pitch. He had dozens of men helping him. In the evening, they scraped the vats empty and kneaded the leftovers into little dolls they gave to the children. The smell of pitch hung in the valley and made the shipyard into a place you could find blindfolded. Washing him was a lot of work. The creases in his neck were black. His skin was rubbed red by the time I was finished. The pitch was a scourge for his skin. My oil disappeared into it as into sand.

Shem's skin, on the contrary, glowed before I even started rubbing it. This man liked my touch, he did not get tense for a moment. He just kept talking, and thought it was pointless to lower the curtain of his part of the tent while he was bathing. He showed no sign of his brother's crudeness. All through my ministrations he hummed and talked. The scaffolding was his work. His task seemed trivial, but the structure must not move, not even in a storm. Hence he chose safety and good margins. He used twice as many posts as necessary to hold up his scaffold. If I did not stop him, he would pour all my water out over himself.

Ham took me the longest. He was so hot, the water must have been a shock to his lovely skin.

"We're building a labyrinth," he said to Put when the child asked him.

"Why a labyrinth?"

"No one on board must be allowed to escape. It is better they cannot see one another. We are making a unique structure."

I tried to involve Put in everything I did. He missed his father. I did not want him to be distressed. I wanted to embrace him, he was still so small and so charming, a relief after all the other children I had known in the marshes, who always had a nasty look about them; they snatched food from your hands and were sickly because of their strange habit of eating earth and baked clay. While I worked, he looked after my mother, who lay in a corner of the red tent. He had often assisted me, and now I could see how much attention he had paid: He carefully moved her arms and legs, gave her water, chewed the bread for her, and talked to her like a shepherd to his sheep. She improved rapidly. On the spots that had grown bald during our trek, downy hair started to grow.

Shem, Ham, and Japheth did not object to Put's presence. "He is a boy with more than one heart," they said, and fed him cakes dipped in syrup.

Months passed, and we got used to the Rrattika. The trouble was, they did not seem to get used to us. By now they had regularly seen my mother by the pond, had long since studied every detail of her finery, but even so they hurriedly looked away whenever they saw her alert eye directed at them. Not a day passed without remarks about our dark skin, our habits, our language. And there was always the feeling that one day we could just be sent away. There was a lot of talk in the shipyard, but most of it I could not understand. It was mostly exclamations and sounds that went with gestures, and never became the proper conversations I so longed for. They looked at us and we at them, and the distrust in those looks continued being stronger than the curiosity.

Every day I went to my spring. Thanks to Put's talent for wandering through unknown landscapes, we could throw any pursuers off the scent by following winding and unpredictable paths. The little boy stayed close to me because I had the spear. He was afraid of the animals that threw up golden clouds of dust every time they moved. Their numbers increased by the day. They came from the four corners of the earth: from the north, white, thick-fleeced beasts with drooping heads and loud breath; from the west, birds that had flown across the seas and landed only to take to the air again immediately, as if they were uncertain of their destination; from the south, slow-moving, shy animals that mainly moved by night, ill at ease because they had never before left the hills where they were born; from the east, the long-distance runners, that stood stamping and pawing on the slope because it was not in their nature to sink down and rest. There were strange creatures amongst them, animals that looked like nothing at all, or rather looked like everything: like a bird as much as a turtle, like a giraffe as much as a gazelle. They were all shapes and sizes, but they all stopped in the hills around the ship-yard. They stood grazing unperturbed or lay in the sun. Some were too shy to go inside the enclosure and hid in the bramble. And there were beasts of prey amongst them, slavering or hiding their fearsome fangs behind a friendly-looking muzzle. One day Put recognized the tiger that had devoured his father. He grabbed me, tugging at my shell-studded tunic till it nearly tore, but the tiger seemed to be lastingly sated. It was lying under a tamarind tree, watching the passing calves and deer without the slightest trace of voracity.

"Why are they here?" I asked a Rrattika who was hauling planks.

"They want to dwell in the shadow of our tents. They know we are chosen and they are no more stupid than you and your ilk coming here. Like all of us, they long for the paradise that was. No mountain or river will stop them."

The more animals gathered in his kraal, the more expensively dressed were the visitors who came to see the Builder. They looked longingly at the dozens, the hundreds of cattle of kinds and sizes they had never seen before. "Do they all give milk?" they asked. "And the birds, are their eggs edible?" The guests brought gifts, they all wanted to contribute to this enterprise they admired.

No one, not even the highest-ranking visitor in embroidered garments, was allowed inside the building site. I too tried to get in there, but the greyhound growled at me and snapped its jaws.

15

A Woman's Well

Shem and Japheth each had a wife. They had been chosen not for their youth, not for their beauty, not for their wealth, but for their presumed fertility. Taneses was Japheth's wife. I saw her from time to time by the pond. She swayed and made a rustling sound as she walked, because she was as heavy as a loaded pregnant donkey. Her dress made the flesh around her armpits bulge. Her breasts were covered in purple veins, and her arms lay against her sides like two separate bodies embracing her. Her smooth calves always bore the imprints of the straps she needed to keep her sandals in place. She groaned under her own weight when she sat down.

Shem's wife was Zedebab. She had been chosen because, while being taciturn, she managed to make a promising impression. She looked at children as if they were her own. Her ears were pierced from top to bottom, and she wore earrings with little bells that jingled as she walked, so she would never have to look back when someone called her because all she could hear was her own tinkling.

You don't ask a woman about her spring, but because I looked like a boy, Zedebab and Taneses approached me. They stood in the entrance to the servants' part of the tent and wouldn't let me leave until I had heard them out. "It is strange that a boy who has come from so far away could win the favor of our men so quickly. They will no longer accept any other water. And how strange that they are suddenly so concerned about their skin. Where does your sister obtain this water?"

When they wouldn't leave me alone and kept trying to trap me with their questions, I stayed away from the red tent for awhile. Then Ham came to the quarry to fetch me. "My skin is itchy," he said. "I've been scratching it raw. Come to the tent with your water and your oil." But he understood my caution. I must not be exposed, for if I were, how would I ever be able to come to him?

Once the dwarf had come after him. He followed Ham like a troublesome dog, confusing him with his questions and gestures. "You are looking for that sister of his," I heard him say. "I know it. You think she is lovely, and you want to be near her." He led Ham back out of the quarry like a small child. I had not even been able to greet him.

16

The Ban on the Eating of Meat

One day a flock of mallards flew over the shipyard. My mother was the first to notice them. Through her breathing, she urged me to go after them. I walked into the hills, to the spot where they had landed. I carried my spear, the one my father had once shaped for my mother. When I approached, the ducks took off again, but they did not get very far. They were exhausted. I decided on the fat drake that reminded me of one of our decoy ducks.

Put had followed me. He stood watching a bit farther on, his slingshot hanging from his hand. If he had been able to creep up on it, he would have been able to hit the duck. With his slingshot, he could knock a nut out of a tree, and he had killed scorpions in cracks in the rocks. But he would not use it against warm-blooded animals, not even against the tiger that had killed his father.

I killed the duck quickly and painlessly, to show that it is not the killing itself that is reprehensible, but doing it carelessly and painfully. We baked it and cut it into small pieces, which we then ground up. We added salt and spices and first served my mother. Put was somewhere at a distance, amongst the shrubs; he did not understand why eating the duck made us feel in a festive mood.

But we enjoyed ourselves. We liked having meat on our menu, and duck was our favorite.

We had lain down contentedly when a large group of men came into the quarry. They wore long cloaks and carried a sedan chair. Right at the end came the dwarf with his wide nostrils and bulging lips. In the sedan chair, sitting very straight, supported by embroidered cushions, was an old man. In front of our house, he gestured for the group to stop. We watched, genuinely interested in what was going on, unaware of having done anything wrong. The old man surveyed our house, substantial and solidly constructed, like a boat. His irises were so green, I stared at him for seconds before lowering my gaze as I should. The rims of his eyes were red as raw meat, his face was lined and his eyebrows remarkably dark under his white hair. There were spots all over his skin, small creamy-looking lumps, which showed anyone who had an eye for it that he suffered from a serious illness.

There was no doubt, this was the Builder, the man who spoke with his god as with people, and who had stayed hidden in the innermost part of the tent for months. His cloak, which must have hung on a hook all the weeks he had lain on his bed, sat crookedly on his body. But his glance was bright and his words clear when he said to my father, "I am told you are the person who has been helping my sons during my illness. You have produced good work. You are an expert."

My father stood up and bowed. He too had understood who the gentleman was, and said, "My lord, I thank you for coming in spite of your health. . . ."

"Certain matters take precedence over one's health," the old man replied. His speech was not slow, as you might expect from one so ill, but emphatic and compelling, as if he was steeling himself for something that was inevitably going to happen.

My father bowed and thanked him again.

The flat-faced dwarf said nothing, he just stared suspiciously at me and at my mother on her stretcher. I hardly dared move. I was terrified he would see I was not a boy. I kept my eyes averted, but my mother looked back at him frankly. Both of them had a look of horror in their eyes, like two demons who recognized each other. He looked inside our pots and jugs and walked to the waste pit where the carcass of the duck lay. "Look!" he said in a thin voice, picking up the bones that had been carefully chewed clean. He took them over to the sedan chair, stretched up, and gave them to the Builder.

The Builder did not flinch when the bones dropped in his lap. He simply said, "You are not one of us. Your customs and traditions are strange, even repulsive." Not many of his teeth had survived the ravages of time, which caused spittle to escape his mouth. But the absence of teeth did not make him hard to understand — on the contrary, we would clearly remember every single word he spoke.

The Unnameable had not granted permission to eat animals, he said, and consequently, whoever did so would be punished. As he spoke, more water birds flew over the shipyard. They disappeared behind the cliff and landed somewhere past the clay pits, deep in the hills. The Builder was not distracted by the sound of their wings. He had a string of pearls in his hand that he passed through his fingers with a clicking sound. "The living creatures were created on the fifth day," he said. "We on the sixth. We were given dominion over them, but not permission to kill them, except as a sacrifice."

My father understood the import of his words much sooner than I did. The old man had not come to thank my father. He hadn't even come to reprimand us. A much more drastic sentence awaited us, the carrying out of a threat that had been hanging over us all this time. My father could feel it coming. Quickly he went to stand close to the Builder, moving so abruptly that the pieces of wood on his belt rattled, and said, "Do not send us away, lord! We are already being punished! Our being here is our penance!" His voice was hoarse. The cough behind his hand was not to gain time, but a spasm of fear. "We did not kill the duck in order to eat it. This duck deserved to die. He took everything from us. He crippled my wife, and after that we had to move away from the edge of the marshes because she was going mad with fear."

The old Builder had not expected a reply from my father. He had come to make an announcement, not to listen. But what my father said seemed to capture his attention. The servants stopped shuffling their feet. There was not a breath of wind, not a cry from an animal or a child to break the silence that followed.

My father hesitated. Never before had he told my mother's story, because she did not want him to. She would hold her breath till she went blue in the face, she managed to make her lungs whistle, and with her glance forbade him to say another word. But this time, she was as quiet as a mouse. She listened as to someone else's story.

"Before she was paralyzed, she bred mallard ducks," my father said. "She clipped their wings almost as soon as they had come out of the egg. She would heat up stones that she replaced constantly. She picked up the chicks one by one and pinched off the tips of their wings with a small pair of pincers. She fed them until they were grown." I remembered how my mother would wake me up when the eggs were ripe and the squeaking coming from them became so intense that we knocked cracks into the shells with our fingernails. "The chicks thought she was their mother. Once they were grown up, she did not kill them. She used them as decoys. She used to laugh at them because they could not fly. She said they stuck to the water like foam. One day, they escaped. Their strong will made them fly. Shortly after, she fell into her boat, and all she could do after that was blink her eye."

The Builder sniffed. He poked at the bones as if he hoped life would return to them. My mother lay on her stretcher, breathing deeply. She turned her eye toward my father and blinked, showing her approval of what he had done and permission to go on.

"We do know that eating them does not help. But killing them is satisfying. They taste good and give strength. And there are so many. . . ."

The Builder shifted on his cushions. When he planted his fists by his sides to hold up his body, I could see his elbows trembling. The duck bones rolled off his knee onto the floor of the sedan chair and onto the ground. For a sick man who had just left his tent for the first time, his voice was strong when he said, "The animals have been counted, the numbers are very exact. You

must not mock them. Whatever you do, whether you take revenge on an animal species or not, do not laugh at them, do not
compare them to foam on the water. There will be no mockery
on the ark."

We were not chased away that day. Possibly, it was my
mother's story that saved us. But I was struck, as if by a lightning flash, by the understanding of the secret Ham was hiding.
The Builder was building an altar. There was an epilogue to the
prophecy of doom: The disaster could be averted. To that end, a
sacrifice was needed, a sacrifice of a magnitude never witnessed
before. That was why we saw the enclosures next to the shipyard
filling day after day, week after week. These were the sacrificial
animals, the carriers of an ardent wish or great remorse. They
would be chased onto the ship as a tribute to the Unnameable.
They were the grim guests at this feast. The elect were those
who made the correct offering, the most perfect animal or the
most valuable kind. That was why there were so many different
kinds: The Builder's offering would be accepted above all others.
I had seen it before years ago, when after yet another sudden
flood, our people decided something had to be done. We pulled
down the walls of our most beautiful huts and rolled up our reed
mats. We filled our boats with them. We slaughtered our buffalo,
the best looking, the fattest first, and put the meat on the mats.
My mother offered her ducks. One by one, she chopped off their
heads and carried them onto our boat in broad baskets. Our yard
that had always been white with duck shit now glittered like a
red lake. We carried our winter stocks on board, many jars of

rice. We dismantled the huts where the supplies were stored and brought them on board too. Then we untied the boat from the jetty and pushed it into the wetland, toward the lagoon, behind which the sea was waiting. So this was the purpose of the Builder's ship. It was a purification, a trial by the Rrattikas' god to test their loyalty.

The servants lifted the Builder's sedan chair. All that time, I had stayed unobtrusively near the fence because of the dwarf, but now that I understood why the animals were here, I sprang forward. I moved so suddenly that the sedan carriers stood aside for me. The dwarf snorted loudly through his wide nostrils.

"Are you going to make a sacrifice?" I asked. "Is this ship the carrier of your intense prayer?"

The Builder raised himself from the cushions. For the first time I could see all of his head, its proportion to his neck and body. The Rrattika liked to make us believe he was more than five hundred years old, but you can't expect people who forget their birthplace as easily as their last campsite to be careful at keeping track of the years. He was old, but not as old as they said. He raised his finger at me.

"Who are you, boy, that you ask me a question like this? Are you not the one who grooms my sons?" He did not wait for my answer. He looked away from me, raised his other hand, and immediately the servants started moving. They straightened their shoulder cushions and hoisted the sedan chair onto their shoulders. This took them a little while, and the silence became oppressive. The old Builder stared straight ahead. The dwarf rattled the bones at the end of his staff. The secret they hid was greater and darker than their ship.

My father chewed nuts for my mother. If it seemed to us unreasonable to build a ship in the middle of the desert, it was just as unthinkable not to take animals that were so tame you could practically catch them with your bare hands and break their necks and pluck them. And those stores that grew and grew? People came from far and near carrying sacks and jars. The workers received part of the grain, part went to the animals, and the rest was stored; there was enough food to keep an army going. In the carpentry workshop and the pottery, work was continuous; there were more wood shavings, shards, and splinters heaped up than anywhere in the world. But why the order to make those amphoras, larger than anyone had ever seen, and so heavy they could barely be lifted? They stood in rows at the edge of the shipyard; walking past them was almost like walking through a tunnel, but if you asked what they were for, you only received an empty look in reply.

"This Builder is not building a ship," my father said to us. "He is building a box, an ark, a coffin." He made drawings on leaves, on tent flaps, on planks. How to spread the weight? This Builder's god seemed to want a living sacrifice, why else all this concern about sufficient air and light in the hold? But we had transported cattle on boats, we knew how long it took for an animal to get used to the rocking and how dangerous it would be if panic broke out in the herd. And how do you embark the animals? You don't put grazing animals near meat eaters, because the herd would try to get away from them and the load would shift. Wouldn't it be simpler to slaughter the animals first?

When I got to the red tent to groom the men that evening, I was stopped at the entrance. Two servants blocked my way. "The Builder has ordered his sons to take care of themselves," they sneered, pointing at the pond where the goats drank.

Ham's Ruse

The days passed. I was out of work. I hoped Ham would try to do something to meet me, but he did not. Perhaps his skin was becoming scaly, perhaps the itch was getting worse and worse, but he did not make time to let me look after him. Now that the Builder was better, the building of the ship was being hastened more and more. Japheth and his men were working on the pitch harder than ever, coating the ship on the inside as well as the outside, and the scaffolding that carried the pitch workers was larger than ever, stretching all the way up to the bowsprit. A number of workers had to be dismissed because the height made them sick. They were replaced by slaves.

Ham was working with my father on the layout and the partitions. They bent over and made drawings in the sand. They had no need to look for shadow: They stayed in the shade of their construction. Ham complained. There was not enough space on the ship, the divisions had to be tighter. The spaces had to be taller, with more light. My father's sketches became more and more elaborate. Ham constantly had to ask for more explanations because the wind wiped out the drawings in the sand. He threw his adze and drill to the ground.

Two decks with a space of nine cubits between them is what

my father designed, with wooden stairs and walkways, and with walls held together with crossbeams. A third deck had to be added. Every attempt to make the interior of the ship more convenient, with more doors and partitions, was accepted by the workers without complaint. Even more, it enthused them; they seemed to assume that a perfect ship would do greater honor to their god, and therefore they would inevitably do well because of it. But they made no connection between their work and the animals that were gathering near the shipyard, and when I talked to them about the disaster that was supposed to be coming, they said, "But isn't the ship well made, exactly as ordered? So why would there be a disaster? Our obedience will bring us prosperity, not punishment."

I had given up all hope of ever being with Ham again when unexpectedly I was summoned by two boys. They were both chewing constantly as they stood in front of our house and said, "You must come with us. This is a matter of life and death. Leave your mother here; this is urgent." They walked out of the quarry. Taking my things, my bottle of oil on my belt and my water jug on my hip, I followed them.

They took me to Ham's part of the tent, and the moment I was inside, they pulled the front flap down. Ham lay on the stretcher in the corner, coughing uncontrollably. I was not surprised. I had known from the start that he was the sort of boy who breathes through his skin instead of through his mouth. I knelt next to him. I tapped him on the chest, gently pounding with balled fists, loosening the phlegm. It was hot and oppressive in his part of the tent. There was good air movement in the tent if all the partitions were up and the outside air could enter freely, but when they were down, it soon became stuffy. Ham liked having them down.

It took him an intense effort to say, "The dwarf has told me your mother's story. Now I understand why you are so solicitous. She has already suffered her calamity, she should not have to undergo this a second time; punishment for a punishment is undeserved."

He spoke rapidly because he could feel the next coughing fit coming, and when it came it seemed as if he was going to suffocate on his phlegm. "Water, give me some of your good water," he panted. He drank from my jug and poured the rest over himself. He ordered me to get more and to come back as soon as possible.

Never before had I walked into the hills so fast, never before did I take so direct a path without worrying about possible pursuers. I hurled myself into the darkness of the cave, kicked skulls and bones aside as if they were mere rubbish, and dunked my jug in the basin. I did not have a spear in case I came across a wild animal. The only thing I thought of was Ham.

When I came back into the red tent, I no longer heard his coughing behind the partition. The servants admitted me and quickly lowered the flap. It took some time for my eyes to adapt to the half-light, but it was soon obvious that Ham was not moving. I lowered the jug, bent over him, and saw him winking with his left eye.

My blood turned to sand, my breath to water. Astonishment and fear gripped my heart, as it used to years ago by the marsh.

It was a suddenly sinking boat, a springing tiger, it was a blinding insight that should have set me screaming but left me voiceless. In a flash it was clear to me: The water of the dead from the cave had struck, the catastrophe was overtaking me.

When he noticed how much he had scared me, he lifted his head and laughed. He put his hand on my shoulder. He was not paralyzed, he said, he just wanted to be treated as if he were.

It took me ages to recover from the shock. My hands washed him as before, but I did not feel him.

He was sorry about his trick, he kept laughing at me affectionately. The coughing fit was genuine, he said, but he knew it would pass, as always. "Wasn't it a good thing to do to make the dwarf think I was about to die? How else would you have gotten in here?" He asked me to straddle him, the way he had seen me do with my mother.

I did. I rubbed him like my mother. I massaged him till his stomach was taut and his skin glowed. I no longer avoided his face. I moved slowly, to give myself time to recover.

He grasped my hands. He entwined our fingers till the bones cracked. My touch made his cheeks flush. He smelled of the milk he'd had with his breakfast. I bent over him and released his body's juices the way Alem-the-ragged had taught me.

When I wanted to leave the tent through the servants' section, the dwarf blocked my way. He said, "From now on, you'll come and wash Ham again every day with that water of yours. No matter that you're a meat-eating stranger. Ham will soon have to take a wife, and who would want a scabby, coughing boy whose breath rattles with phlegm?"

I nodded. It had already happened. I already was his wife. "I'll take care of it," I said and left, walking with a man's angular movements.

In the evenings, after work on the ship, my father built a bathtub. "A woman who knows a man must be able to immerse herself," he said. "And in something better than a cattle pond."

I sat down in it. The cold took my breath away. It had been so long since I had been completely underwater. The tub was beautiful, well made, with a polished edge and a base so smooth it felt like skin against mine.

"I did not know you could do this," I said.

"What is a bath but a boat turned inside out?" was his reply.

I knew the true reason for this gift. Both my mother and he thought I let myself be sullied by the Rrattika. They could not get used to the idea that I lay down with someone who had no home. But they did not stop me. Ham inspired compassion in them, he was precious to them, they already thought of him as a son.

18

The Arrival of Neelata

A short time later Neelata arrived, the slim city girl. Put was the first to see her coming, he let his millet porridge get cold to watch the commotion on the cliff. She came accompanied by ten beautifully dressed men on magnificent horses and six lady's maids on mules. They had come a long way; that was obvious from the dust on their legs and on the horses' flanks. They came toward us along the same path we had taken when we arrived. None of the riders dismounted for the descent. I had never seen a horse before. I knew such animals existed and that they looked like donkeys, that they were stronger but less able to bear the heat, but this was the first time I witnessed their nerve. They took the slope like reckless children. Some of them occasionally became so frisky their riders had to rein them in. Like Put, I was used to the deliberate movements of donkeys, and we found this bravery so exciting we forgot about our meal and walked to the bottom of the slope.

Once the descent had been accomplished, the cavalcade started moving more quietly. There were animals amongst them without riders, their bits attached to the animal in front of them, carrying sloshing jars on their flanks. The best-equipped man was a merchant, a gentleman with snow-white hair wearing a shiny robe, but we only had eyes for the young Neelata, whose appearance moved me, and who caused Put to burst into a heart-warming poem of welcome. She rode at the end of the file; her horse laid back its ears as it passed us. The caravan made its way amongst the tents, and we followed, past the scaffold and the ship under construction, straight up to the red tent.

The first one to come out was the dwarf. I had never before seen him so excited, he jumped up and down uttering cries like the monkeys in the hills.

The merchant was Neelata's uncle. He was visiting the Builder in order to leave his niece there. Why he did this, I only found out much later, when from a deep hole in the cave, she told me to leave her to perish; but it was obvious that the request he made was very considerable.

One after the other, the men dismounted. They entered the tent. Neelata was asked to wait. She let her horse wander toward the pond. She wore a dress in a blue that is no longer made, and her eyelashes were coated in mineral. It had been months since I had seen anyone with made-up eyes. She seemed like a giantess, she was slender as a memorial pillar and wore clinking beads around her ankles. She walked up and down for a while and finally sat down, her legs pulled up, her feet uncovered. After slaking their thirst, the horses stood still with drooping heads.

We saw everything, Put and I, hidden amongst the stacks of finished planks. Put was shuffling his feet so much he threw up the dust.

"Go ask her why she is here," I whispered.

"I don't dare," he said. "You're not a real boy, you go and ask."

He poked his little fingers into my side, and I left the spot where we stood.

I wasn't any braver or less shy than him. I had almost forgotten how to start a conversation. Since being here, I had made several efforts to talk to people in the shipyard, but had found their minds very limited; when they were not working, they usually just sat staring into space, and the number of words they used was very restricted because, in the little world they lived in, they could manage with very few. But this woman was different, I'd realized that the moment I saw her: She looked at me, followed my movements, and questioned me with her eyes. I made sure to look back. I couldn't get enough of looking at her eyes. They were almond-shaped, the outer corners pointing up slightly. Looking at her, at those lashes and those lips that shone in the early sunlight, filled me with regret. Here was I, who loved finery and beautiful colors, wearing the male emblem on my forehead.

I kept hesitating, and Put was getting impatient. He left his hiding place and went up close to the horse she had been riding. He put his arm around its leg so he could feel its belly. He took a deep breath and said, "If I had a horse, I'd run away from this place as fast as I could." He spoke to me, but loud enough for her to be able to hear him. I knew what he was thinking. The horse was large. Whoever sat on it was safe. The animal moved smartly and fast, he could imagine escaping from a tiger on it.

Neelata shielded her eyes from the sun with her hand so she could see Put. When she saw that he met her glance, she smiled and gestured behind her, in the direction of the animal enclosures.

I thought she meant that there were plenty of cattle there, so many it no longer mattered who owned them, there was plenty of milk for every thirsty person in the camp, so there was no need to run away, and there was no reason why you shouldn't take a mount if you had to go somewhere. But that's not what she meant. In her hand, she held a small pumice stone, such as I had always wanted to have. With it, she indicated the whole world. "It would be lovely to be able to believe that you can save yourself on horseback." Her speech was different from the local people's. Her tongue seemed to explore the language she used, word for word, as if the sounds were brand new, unfamiliar to the mouth that had to shape them. "But a horse will not save you, little boy. Nothing will save you from the catastrophe these people are expecting."

Put followed the movement of her hand attentively. He stayed right next to the horse as if it were his.

Neelata clacked her tongue to reassure the animal and continued. "Although it is perhaps better this way. Perhaps it is not a bad thing to be able to believe you can escape this place if you decide to." I needed to hear no more to realize that what she said was more about herself than about us. Her uncle left her in the shipyard. The jars that had been brought on the horses' backs stayed here and were guarded day and night. She moved into a tent with decorated borders that her uncle had put up for her, and which also housed the six lady's maids. Like us, she was not accustomed to tents; the impermanence of the structure made her nervous and uncertain. But she was not going to leave before the catastrophe struck. She was going to become Ham's wife.

I was asked to resume the daily grooming of Shem and Japheth. With someone like Neelata around, there was a greater need for cleanliness and body care. She would come into Ham's part of the tent while I was working on him and ignore my presence. She was not suspicious, she had no reason to suspect that, like her, I was a marriageable woman who was ready for a man. Sometimes she hugged him, and I heard her say, "Take me as your wife."

Ham glanced at me and shook his head.

"Aren't you pleased with what I have brought?" she asked.

She was older than Ham. And she was tall. In her arms, he looked like a child. What was she doing here? A young lady from a merchant's family belonged in markets, in stone bathhouses, or at the wells where the travelers gathered.

I tried to worm out of Ham under what conditions she had come. But he avoided my question by rolling two enormous round nuts, hairy as rats, from a basket. Their bumpy movement, coming straight at him, made Put jump back in fright.

"Look at what she has brought," said Ham. He picked up one of the nuts and tossed it from one hand into the other. A sloshing sound came from it. He took a sharp stone and cracked the shell with it. Juice spurted from it. The inside was of a color I had never seen. Inside the tent, it just seemed white, but the next morning, when we were on our way to the shipyard and Ham, after much asking, opened another one for Put and me, I realized that the white was of a purity I would never see again. It was whiter than milk, whiter than the first teeth of a baby, whiter than the shells in my mother's nets so long ago.

Ham held the cup-shaped nut to our mouths and asked us to take a sip, Put first. The little boy tasted it and uttered a sigh.

"What is it?" we asked.

"Food and drink," said Ham. "Nuts that stay good forever. We keep them against difficult times." About the contents of the jars he said not a word.

Neelata's proposal of marriage did not make me feel concerned. Whenever I rubbed Ham's chest with oil, the beating of his heart told me of his affection. He asked me to lower the tent flap. I knew Zedebab, Shem's wife, was keeping an eye on me, and Taneses, Japheth's wife, even more so. Their total insensitivity to the scents of a body made me reckless: Even when I was bleeding, I'd walk into the red tent. In her moon face, Taneses had tiny little eyes, which she sometimes turned away so you'd think she was blind; but she wasn't, she saw more than most of the others. She looked at me suspiciously when I carried my clear water into the men's tent. I'd make my movements more angular, but no reassurance showed on her face. Did it show? Did she suspect I was leading them up the garden path with my tunic covered in gently clinking shells? Did she notice that there were grooming sessions for which Ham carefully prepared? He let down the tent flap and stretched out on the ground.

When I'd finished my work, I regularly walked past the decorated tent. I wanted to look at Neelata's powdered lashes and the ornaments she wore. But very soon, I no longer got to see her face. She was enveloped in an ocher dress with a hood. Occasionally her hands or ankles showed, otherwise all I could see was her outline. Too late, I saw that Neelata and the wives of

Shem and Japheth made a threesome, and that a marriage be-tween Ham and Neelata was the logical outcome of their soli-darity. And too late, I noticed that Ham was attracted to her. He sat watching her from the bushes, the way he had watched me months ago. I washed him daily. He blinked his left eye and asked to be treated like one paralyzed. He let me rub him until his skin was taut over his bones. Then he entwined his fingers with mine and pulled me down over him. But with Neelata, he did the same. And I did not see it.

19

The Song of the Dwarf

As the ship grew taller, the atmosphere in the red tent became more excited. The dwarf composed a long, involved song that he performed with a great show of tricky dance steps for the Builder's sons one evening during the grooming session. It was a song in which he offered his services, and I listened carefully.

"You should organize a little hammock for me," he sang, "from which I can survey your hold. If any animals, against your father's orders, are having a roll in the hay, I'll abuse them so thoroughly they'll die of embarrassment. I'll do this in a manner that so entertains the elect that they'll actually hope the animals will start all over again! And I cost you nothing, just the weight I carry, and believe me, that is slight, and will only become less."

The brothers slapped their thighs laughing. The dwarf was in the habit of pretending to live on air and water. Every time the sons had a meal, he would scream loudly as if in disgust at whatever the women had prepared. This amused the sons no end, if only because it infuriated the women so much that the less tolerant amongst them would pick up a sandal to beat the dwarf with as soon as he appeared. We all knew that as soon as the brothers had had enough, he scraped out the pots in the servants' area, but everybody kept insisting that the dwarf was surviving without food.

While the dwarf was holding forth, I was doing Japheth's hair, plaiting it in a checkerboard pattern. I gently tugged at tufts of hair to stimulate the circulation. But I was listening so intently that at times I forgot to go on working.

"The time will be long, an endless tedium of half sleep. I will have to remind the elect of their manhood to prevent their members shriveling before the goal is reached."

"We'll think about it!" the brothers shouted when his song was finished. The dwarf completed his dance and left the tent. As always, he left behind a smell of fermenting fruit. I tried to carry on plaiting quietly, but had trouble controlling my movements and not tugging too hard and hurting Japheth. Here was talk about a lifetime on the ship. The dwarf's song was about people! He was saying things about members shriveling! Was this a form of self-sacrifice, like the gestures of atonement we had seen the Rrattika make on our journey here, in places where the sun had driven the river underground? They left men without any disability, injury, or insanity — in other words perfectly healthy men, capable of work — behind in a dry well, on occasion even on a cross. These men died slowly. They attempted by their own deaths to avert the deaths of many, and they did this because they had been chosen for it. Was this what they were planning, these uncultured wanderers, who with this structure were so intent on raising themselves above those around them? Was this ship in the wilderness an exercise in endurance, a test of fortitude, a slow starving of a group of people and animals who would, little by little, lose their strength and sink into the half sleep that precedes death, and in doing so save all those who stayed behind? More than once, Ham had said to me, "I will save you." Was he going onto the ark himself? Did I want to be saved at the cost of his life? Would they one day pull up the gangplank and go and die in that gigantic cocoon, while we, the workers, the ones who had wrought this insanity, would stand around it, and hear, day after day, the sounds from inside the belly of the ship becoming weaker? Had I worked to make their skin spotless and supple, their hair clean and their fingernails shiny, only to have to watch them willfully letting it all shrivel and dry and wither in the belly of a gigantic coffin?

I must have misunderstood, it could not be possible, this must have been an old song that was about someone or something else.

But I could see in Put's face that I had not misunderstood. He sat next to my mother, his mouth open, motionless with amazement.

I think I must have dropped the comb. Getting up, I knocked over the bowl of water. It made the dust, sand, and grit of the floor bubble up, turning it dark like skin. I left the tent, following the dwarf. He was in the adjoining servants' area, where the leftovers of the meal had been taken. He sat bent over the pots like a vulture, unable to speak. His hands shook so hard that the contents of his spoon dribbled down his chin and breast.

20

Entering the Ark

I did not return to the Builder's sons but walked to the ark. The base of the scaffold that led to the upper deck had been closed up for the night with reed matting and many ropes. In front of it, the greyhound lay in the dust. When I approached, it stood up and sniffed the air around me. I walked away, went to the back of the structure where the still-steaming pitch vats stood, and joined the children who were pestering the workers, exhausted after the day's work, for pitch dolls.

There was a little boy with a big head who stood smack in front of one of the workers, watching intently how the ears of his doll were modeled. "Finished?" he nagged constantly, until the man with the sticky, pitch-blackened hands lost his patience, pulled the ears off the doll, and squashed its head down into its body. The boy muttered that it was all right, he would wait. When finally, clutching the doll in his little fists, he went off with a satisfied sigh, I followed him stealthily. Uttering gentle sounds, the child made his toy walk through the air. It was a while before his interest in his prize slackened and he stopped holding it with both hands. To my relief, his attention was drawn to a stick in the sand. As soon as he was only holding his doll loosely in one hand so he could reach for the stick with the other, I snatched it from him and ran off through the tents and screens. The child howled, but I did not look back. I went back to the entrance of the ship, kneading the pitch until it once again became warm, releasing its smell.

As if offering it a treat, I held out the black lump to the greyhound. The animal sniffed, but stiffened at the smell and reared back. I approached it once more, pushing the pitch against its nose. It pulled back even farther.

Squatting, I hooked my fingers behind the ropes, pulling them loose. I forced myself through the gap as fast as I could. The dog stormed at me, barking. I shoved the reed mat against the opening. The animal pushed its nose against the gap with a high-pitched squeal. I kept following its snout with the soft ball, distracting it until I had finally pushed all of the matting back in place. After securing it with a few quick knots, I started running up the sloping planks of the scaffold. My footsteps made a shocking amount of noise. The planks bounced in their mortises, but the more racket I caused, the faster I ran, and the more the boards rattled. I could not believe how high the upper deck was, and I was convinced that down in the yard everybody was already watching me. Any moment I expected the grim blare of bugles.

The upper deck was not yet finished. A wide edge running from the prow to the stern still needed to be covered. It would have made a quick way in if it had not looked so deep and dark that I did not dare to poke my legs through. The real gateway, the entrance for all those who would embark, and for everything that would be brought on board over the next few weeks, was closed off with a hatch set in a sloping wall rising from the deck like a lean-to. I managed to open it through a small hole just large enough for my hand. I entered the ship and pulled the hatch down behind me.

My eyes had to adjust. It was not only dark, but the air was full of dust and grit. Under my feet, I felt a layer of shavings and splinters; obviously nobody had bothered to sweep up the rubbish and wheel it outside. I imagined it would never be removed, and in time it would be trodden into a carpet on the bottom of the ship. It would muffle the sounds of feet and hooves, making all that would happen here soundless.

Through the gap in the unfinished roof and the ventilation holes, some light entered. Though I knew better, I had imagined an empty space, a huge hall of timber and pitch, with just a few booths deep down in the hold. But I found myself in a narrow gallery that led down in a spiral. Dozens of spaces opened onto it. I entered some of those at random and found that they were divided into pens and cages. They had bamboo bars across the front and small doors that stood open but could be secured with wedges. Inside the cages stood food bowls. Some had perches, some did not. Each cage was a different shape and set up differently. They were arranged one behind the other at a slight angle, so that the occupants of different cages could not see one another.

I do not know how many side passages I entered. It was eerily quiet around me; all I could hear was the occasional squawking of the birds who had found a perch for the night on top of the ship, and the dull, low sound of their droppings on the deck. I walked on endlessly, past hundreds of cages, one after the other, and it was as if some insane designer was leading me in circles. Descending deeper and deeper, I came to a level where the compartments became more impressive, with better hatches and doors: This was where larger animals, those with broad flanks and tall shoulders, would be housed. From this point on, the floors were level, and differences in height were spanned by ladders and stairs.

A few side passages were different; there were no bars, but proper doors with latches. The doors were made from good timber and fitted well. There were no holes or cracks; whoever stayed here would not be disturbed by whatever went on in the gallery. The floor in this section had been planed smooth, and torch holders had been fitted to the walls. There were cupboards and wardrobes, rings in the walls and stands for amphoras. I opened a door almost jammed by wood shavings and creaking on its hinges. It gave access to a comfortable hut hung with mats and with straw mattresses stacked against the wall. This hut had been hastily swept, the dust brushed out and left lying by the threshold. I could see my own footprints on the wooden floor. There would be people staying here: Only people lie on straw mattresses and cover themselves with blankets.

There were holes in various places in the floors and ceilings. Through them dangled rope ladders that looked as if they were meant for light, quick creatures. I went down one level on one of them, the ropes creaking under my weight, and I came to new cages, larger than the ones higher up, with capacious fodder troughs and mangers. I was now at one side of the ship, probably right next to the outer wall; if I tapped on the wood now, they would quite likely hear me out there. I kept still. I wanted to go back to the center section, to the gallery that seemed to curve toward a particular spot deep in the belly of the ship.

By shuffling along carefully and giving my eyes enough time to adjust to the light that was growing ever fainter, I finally reached the open space at the end of the gallery, the only area that was not divided up into small cages and pens. This could be closed by a set of low double doors with wedges along the jambs in case the timber shrank or swelled, but for now they stood open invitingly. The space was walled with thick planks; outside sounds did not penetrate here. It felt like a cave from which you could not see the setting of the sun, let alone the sunrise. Once the door was shut, no light would ever penetrate this space. This had to be the place where what I feared would take place.

The space was rather like a reception hall, with low seats along the walls, similar to the ones I had seen in large reed buildings constructed near the wetlands by important men to conduct discussions and drink tea. There were sacks of grain, fat jars of oil, pots and pans, spoons and stirring sticks. On the floor was a layer of sand to make a fire on, there was a hollow in the ground for playing shovelboard, a harp stood in one corner, and a lyre hung on a nail.

This was not a place for dying. This was a living space, full of promise, where people would be talking and laughing, with the dwarf perhaps, if his song had made enough of an impression. It was the center where the builders, after much feinting, made their intentions clear. If this was a coffin, then where were the indications of a slow death? The stands for the amphoras were gigantic. How much drinking water could a jug that size hold?

The ship sent a double message. It was a senseless structure in the middle of the desert, obviously intended to stay here and be scoured by the sand that would eventually smooth out the grooves and remove the layer of pitch. I had expected gloom and darkness, but what I had discovered was a city turned in upon itself, a hillside thickly built over, looking out on itself. This structure was intended to hum with life. Here there was room for stores of food and drinking water; here there were going to be people prepared for many things.

I left the central space and hurried back up the gallery, but standing there again, looking at the maze of passages and ladders, made me feel even more overwhelmed. What was the builders' grand plan, what bizarre dream had brought them to this? Who was the god who imposed this on them? And what was I doing here, in this cave full of pits and hollows for which there was no map and over which night was now rapidly falling, in this succession of snail shells, in this monstrous inner ear? Me, used to open plains, to wide waters, and boats with honest bellies full of fish and mats and jars, but never a roof. A roof is only for very long journeys, for leaving the wetlands, going up the river and then farther, up to the lagoon, and beyond that out to sea, being quite certain that the starting point will disappear and will never be found again. . . .

I heard a sound from a little higher up. Footsteps, very soft, because they were muffled by the wood shavings on the floor, but becoming clearer as they came closer. Put had followed me, the little villain who accused *me* of being curious! I darted into an open cage and waited for him to get closer. I would give him a fright.

When he got to my level, I jumped out with a yell.

But it was not Put. Someone shouted back: a woman's voice. In the half dark, it did not take me long to see it was Neelata. I recognized her figure. She dropped her basket in fright, and its contents spilled out. She did not try to stop her things falling out, she just looked at me, aghast. I bent forward, grabbing for her things; round objects amongst them started rolling down the gallery; they would go on rolling as far as the ship's well. They were small, painted boxes and smooth, colored stones for playing games, but also combs and beads and her little pumice stone.

"Don't shout like that, please," she said. She did not scold me, but rather sounded surprised, as if this were a sanctuary.

"The dog let me past," I said.

"I know. I saw you."

I felt around me for her things and put them back in the basket.

"They'll beat you if they find you here," she said.

With every movement of my hand, I became more aware that these were her personal belongings, that she was apparently bringing those on board, that obviously a place on the ark had been provided for her. "I was curious. I wanted to know . . . Is this a ship for people?"

She gave no reply. She was counting the small stones, painted in glossy colors. They were part of a game that I knew. She had to have all of them or the game would not work. She rubbed them on her sleeve before putting them in the basket.

"This is where we are going to wait till the water rises." She looked at her stones. I was amazed at how well she could see in the gloom, because she kept polishing them and looking at them. "You are good with water," she said when her basket was full. "Can you feel it coming? Will you warn us when it comes?" Hearing her talk about rising water made me think of the lakes where I had grown up, of floating reeds, of jumping from one flat boat to another, holding a taller person's hand, spluttering and screaming with laughter if one of them capsized. But for her, the words had a very different effect. Nervously, she looked at the walls of the ship and at the layer of pitch, as if she suspected there were holes in it.

"Water is a blessing," I said. "Water brings wind and life. It makes the crops grow and gives the world color. It should not make you feel bad."

"The amount of it scares me," she said. "The featureless, disorienting bulk of it."

That is how I came to know the real purpose of the ark. It was built because of the water. I must have made a sound of relief somewhere deep in my throat. How could I explain to her that water made me feel secure? The ship was a shelter. Not an altar, as I had supposed.

"I thought it was a shrine for a holy sacrifice," I said.

"Which animals are coming here?"

"All animals."

"So there! If it were a sacrifice, only the clean animals would be coming. Imagine making a sacrifice of a swan! A piglet! A camel!"

"What is a clean animal for people who do not eat meat?"

"An animal that can be sacrificed, naturally," she said. I tried to see her as well as I could. She stood quite close, but because of what she was saying, the darkness around us seemed to get denser.

"Why is nobody saying this?"

"Don't you ask Ham questions?"

"He doesn't tell me anything."

"Ham is silent for his god. The water we expect is savage. It will be of a terrifying beauty, but it will be all-consuming. It will not be like the water you sprinkle on our men. What do you think would happen if everybody knew what was coming? The Builder exhorts us to behave righteously. We need know no more than that, for how would you distinguish righteousness from fear of punishment?"

She left the space, and I followed. I felt excited thinking of the kinds of water I knew from stories. I had heard of raging rivers and waterfalls. How beautiful, I used to say, what a treat for the skin, water that scours the dirt away and that rubs your muscles loose. Of course, I was mainly used to water that came up under you, brought by a sea behind a lagoon, I barely had any concept of streaming rain.

"Does he feel regret, then, this god of the Rrattika?"

"If He felt regret, He would create a new kind of human being. It is not human nature that is evil, it is just that humans have allowed themselves to become surrounded by evil. They will get another chance after the depraved have been killed. The Unnameable will populate His new world with the same humans as before. Is that not a tribute to humankind?" She was silent for a moment. I could feel her watching me.

I stood in front of her with my mouth open. We were deep inside the ship, in the middle of the gallery, in a spot where nobody could hear us.

She said, "I have followed you because of your water. I want to know where you obtain it."

"My sister draws it from a spring," I replied calmly. "It is a long way from here, a really long way."

"And you don't know where it is?" she asked. "Then why is it that whenever I follow you into the hills, I never meet your sister?" She turned her head on that long neck of hers. She was, of course, thinking about how wicked what I did was. Unless I was a woman, I could not keep secret a place where there was water. Refusing to tell her the location of the spring was enough to split the planks we were standing on. But I was thinking mainly of the many who would die. Ham had told me about the god who was going to kill all those without principles, but now, in this place, the prediction sounded much more disturbing.

"My mother is lame," I said quickly. "We have an orphan with us. We try to stay alive."

She did not seem to want to insist. She wanted to let me believe that she did not need my water, that she could find water herself that was just as good. All this time she was looking at me intently. She put her hand on my hair and said, "You are not who you pretend to be. You're disguised." She grabbed me and kissed me. I could not quite work out what caused her sudden sparkling laugh, her excitement. I could only frown and listen as she said, "You wash Ham and you are a girl! It is his ruse! Me he will save, he has said. Does he promise you the same?"

I could not manage a reply. My tongue felt thick and dry.

"Has he taken you as his wife?" she asked seriously.

"Yes."

"Me also. How many sleeping places are there, have you counted them?"

"I haven't counted them."

"The ship is large. There is room for you as well as me. But is there room for my mother, even though she does not deserve it? For Zedebab's twin sister? For your mother, who has suffered so much already?"

"No," I said.

She moved her hand along my arm. "That's why Ham tells you nothing. He cannot believe that he will have to choose. His god bewilders him. He cannot accept that the ship he has built is too small for his dreams."

21
A Conversation in the Tent

*I*t was worst for my mother. Just when she had become convinced that rising waters no longer threatened her, this is what I discovered. I did not tell her. I would not have known what to say; the things I understood I could not tell, and what I could tell — that water was coming, that it would be terrible — I did not understand. Children drowned, I knew that, and the water in some pools could make you sick. But what water took account of your righteousness? And who were the depraved that had to be killed? Were they the men and women who sang at night near the big tents, the foremen with their dancing wives, the warriors carrying swords who wandered about chewing herbs and saying they could see themselves walk? Were they the women of the family farther along who threw their food scraps onto our path? The man who staggered drunkenly across our little fields at night? The child who had eaten a piece of my sponge?

But, of course, my mother felt that we were concealing things. As soon as I came near her, she made it clear with her one eye that she wanted explanations. Before I realized, I shouted at her, "Stop nagging at me. I'm telling you, I don't know what they are planning!" That is how short-tempered I had become since I had understood I did not have Ham's love to myself. Put and I felt slighted and gulled, we racked our brains to find a way of discovering from which direction danger threatened. Would there be water that selected by poisoning? By drowning? Was it a question of seeking refuge on the right hill or in the right tent? Was the ship the right place, and if so, why all those animal cages? I assumed that everyone I knew in the yard would be saved. They were all people of good will, and if indeed they had sinned in their lives, the sins had only been lapses, not something that was part of their nature. And they were not evil. Even my father, with his natural aversion for the Rrattika, did not find these people depraved. What disturbed him about them was the absence of good qualities. He found them uninspiring, unable to arouse feelings. They were dim, characterless people, suffering a lack of enterprise, desire, or curiosity. At least, most of them were. As he got to know the Rrattika better, he saw the exceptions. The Builder he found outstanding: He was passionate, he had a plan, it was not surprising he had won a special place in the heart of his god. And similar to the Builder were his sons, with Shem the most sympathetic, and Ham and his timber workers the most challenging. Their attitudes were quite similar to those of the marsh people; they were totally different from the dull-witted, stinking pitch pourers, or the potters who, if a pot broke, pulverized it to prevent anyone from getting some gain out of the shards.

My father was not shocked by the news that people would go on the ark: He had built the living spaces. "Should this horrify me?" he asked. "How many predictions of disaster like this do you think I have heard in my life? I can't keep count of the prophecies of doomsayers, that's how it goes in good times. These people have had some fat years, that's when the fear of losing everything arises. People who have to scratch out a living don't waste time on this sort of fantasy." But his voice was not steady. His beaker trembled as he lifted it to his mouth. Porridge was left in bowls, and at night we listened to each other's breathing.

I became more attentive. Painstakingly, like one gathering shells, I searched for signs and prognostications, even if they were not meant for me, and I noticed Put doing the same. The way Ham behaved with me had not changed. I reluctantly resigned myself to the thought that I had to share his love with Neelata. What had I expected? My parents had warned me, we knew Rrattika formed unions with woman after woman and arranged rosters for the night. And Neelata was so attractive — that was why I felt flattered in a strange sort of way when she conceived a passion for him. The main problem now seemed to be that Ham's part of the tent was suddenly busy with visitors. As if we were being guarded, the curtain that closed it off moved constantly on its rod, and grass plugs kept falling from the gaps in the canvas.

I no longer went home when meals were served. Even if the grooming was long finished, there would always be someone with dirty hands or sore muscles, and I would be asked to stay. The cleanliness of their limbs made them dependent. Before, they had not known the desire for oil, but now that they were accustomed to their skin being clean, a dirty fingernail or a crust in the navel suddenly appeared much worse. They could no longer bear knots in their hair. Their clothes were washed four times as often as before. And I did not refuse any service: I thought that from inside the tent I would have a better grip on whatever was going to happen, and that I would count for something.

If, after the bathing, Shem, Japheth, and Ham went to watch the dancing women, I did not go with them. I found a spot in the servants' quarters near where the Builder and the dwarf were, and there mixed my oil according to my grandmother's formula. I took good care not to make a sound. For a long time, I sat there and listened to the conversations behind the partition. It required patience. Question and reply were widely separated because each weighed his words. But on days when the Builder was in reasonable health and, thanks to the drink poured by the dwarf, his voice forceful, I could understand every word. Sometimes it was about the payment of the workers, sometimes about the layout of the ship. One time it was about the provisioning.

"There will be shortages. Perhaps we will go hungry."

"You must procure all edible foodstuffs," I heard the dwarf say, "and take them all with you to provide nourishment for you and yours."

"How will I know if it is sufficient?" asked the Builder.

"You can take everything you can think of. The ship is large. Stow it full."

"There is still no good water. There would be good water, you said, the Unnameable would provide it."

"Do not humiliate me, lord, by making me search for water," said the dwarf. "That will have to come from the women."

"And when food becomes scarce? What shall we eat? The ashes from our fireplaces?"

"There are always fish," said the dwarf.

"Who will want to eat them? I know there are people who enjoy eating them, but my boys have not been brought up that way. They will refuse it."

"The insects then?"

"Insects? Am I taking insects? Nothing was said to me about that. Insects survive on driftwood, as far as I know. They do not need our ship."

"You could eat the warm-blooded animals! The clean ones seem to have a good flavor."

"Revolting!" exclaimed the Builder. "How can we eat something that is as warm as ourselves?"

"Have you never noticed, when making a sacrifice, that flesh becomes entirely different over fire? Doesn't its stench turn into an agreeable smell? Why do you think it is that the Unnameable liked the smell of Abel's sacrifice so well? Because he likes meat!" The dwarf was getting more and more worked up, I recognized the way he was speaking. He spat and sucked trying to swallow the spit he had lost.

The Builder tapped his staff on the ground. "Keep that barbaric talk to yourself. I don't know how they did it where you come from, but I am not an animal. I do not eat of my own kind. The Unnameable wants to save his animal kingdom, we are not meant to cut into that cake, are we?"

"It was just an idea," said the dwarf.

"But after the flood? Will there be food in that paradise?" The old man's voice began to have a singsong sound, hinting at fatigue.

"You will have to grow the crops yourselves," the dwarf replied.

"What shall we eat when we arrive? Will there be grain in the fields?" The Builder was breathing unevenly. There was a soft moan, I could not work out who from. A chair was moved, I thought the old man must be going to lie down, I heard soothing sounds.

The Builder's questions were left in the air. The silence seemed unnatural, as if they were trying to stop each other speaking. I leaned forward and pulled a plug of grass from the partition to look in. Then I saw that the dwarf was bent over the Builder. He had loosened the old man's belt and pulled his cloak up. In one hand, he held a jar of ointment, and with the other, he slowly spread it over the bluish belly and groin. The Builder's eyes were closed. There were oozing blisters on his belly and groin. It was the blisters the dwarf was carefully rubbing the ointment into.

The Builder's breathing became calm again, but his eyelashes were trembling, and his eyes moved back and forth behind their lids. The dwarf continued rubbing. He put on compresses and covered the Builder's private parts with his cloak. Soon after, the eyes and face relaxed too.

When I was certain the Builder had dozed off, his lips parted and he said, "It should never get to that. We have an exact number. We know how many people are coming. If we know how much porridge, bread, and fruit they need per day . . . Thanks to the women there will be good water, both on the ship and after we arrive. We shall have to grow the crops ourselves. There will be abundance. Water will flow from the hills. Our children will get used to the taste of fish. And if that is not sufficient . . ." He started to mumble. He was searching for words, or trying to remember something. "After the flood, we are allowed to eat the animals," he said eventually. "That has been promised."

"Exactly," whispered the dwarf. "That has been promised."

"Between here and paradise, it is simply a matter of careful calculation."

"Exactly," the dwarf whispered again.

"For me and my sons," said the Builder. "And for my sons' wives."

The dwarf held his hands still. His gaze was intent. Bending forward, he put his mouth to the Builder's ear. "You forget that the Unnameable has said 'Noach and his family, and part of his family is his dwarf!' That is what He has said."

The Builder opened his eyes. He slapped at his ear as if at a mosquito. "Don't play the devil," he said listlessly. "Don't confuse me."

Meanwhile, the animals kept coming, they occupied the hills like a mutinous army. Gazelle, wild asses, and bison left their plains; bears came from their caves; panthers and ibex came down from their mountains; and sloths and chameleons left their woods behind. The old names of the hills were replaced with new ones: The Bare Shoulder became the "Rock of the Cloven Hoofs" and the Empty Bowl the "Pit of the Crawlers." Rodents came, one kind bringing along the other, and they got into the stores. People came from the cities to be entertained by the spectacle of the steady stream of never-before-seen creatures. The Rrattika saw their coming as a blessing, a gift, a confirmation of their god's favor. Just here and there in the shipyard there were a few who were less artless. We heard them say to each other, "There must be a big fire burning on the other side of the mountains."

The Fall of the Pitch Workers

*I*t took a disaster to discover the whole truth. It was a cloudy, oppresive day that had made everyone shiver between the sheets on waking, and that had not cleared up, not even when it was already nearly noon, dough sticking to the stones and the porridge full of vermin. There was an unusual amount of shouting in the shipyard. Builders of small cages and reed weavers got under the feet of men moving wide, carefully measured plates, causing the plates to be bent, parts to shift, and precision work to be spoiled. The air was the cause of it all. Not a soul went out to do the weeding or gather eggs; everyone had to be in the yard, even those who had never been there before, almost as if the clouds spooked them and made them forget their usual behavior. It did not bother Put and me; those low clouds and damp air actually made us feel good.

Ham had slipped because of the damp and could hardly walk. So we had him to ourselves for once. Put stirred the oil and poured it into my hands, and I applied it generously to the sore foot. So I could tackle the pain from higher up, from his hips and the small of his back, I asked Ham to lie down on a cloth spread on the sand.

"How you loved the water I brought when you first got to

know me," I said, once I could feel him relaxing. "But Neelata brought a fluid you love even more." I pinched his skin between thumb and index finger, moving it around, letting go and pinching the next bit of skin, all the way down his leg and his foot, down to the little bump at the end of his toes, which I pressed gently and insistently.

My mother was asleep. There was no servant around. Ham stood up and ordered Put to go away. Put walked outside, carefully closing the tent flap.

"Neelata would be really amused if she heard you call this a fluid," Ham said once the boy had gone. "Hold still, I'll show you."

I put the lid on my bowl. In the corner under the mats stood the jars that Neelata had brought. Ham limped over, opened one, and dipped a beaker. The scent of fruit and yeast met us. I filled my mouth, swallowed, and filled my mouth again. It was as if I was drinking the fresh, sourish smell of flowers. In one draught, I could taste almost everything I loved: figs, cherries, blackberries, and muscat. Never before had I been so precisely aware of the path a liquid followed through my body. This must be the drink pressed from fruit that I had heard my father describe more than once. "Only settled people prepare this. People who wander cannot do it. They are unable to wait for a harvest. Fermentation and ripening are foreign to them. A Rrattika will consume everything immediately; only hunger will induce him to start looking for something edible. So better to give him honey water than wine."

Ham filled a second beaker. "Give this to our little sentinel outside," he said. I pulled the tent flap open a little way. Put was there, his chin on his knees. The child accepted the beaker, and I closed the tent again.

When I sat down, I saw that Ham had already refilled my beaker. I breathed in the scent of the liquid that slaked my thirst yet left my mouth dry. Ham intently watched every expression on my face. "What makes this drink so precious," he said, "is that water will go bad after a time, but this improves as the months pass." He lay on his back and beckoned me. He put the beaker on his stomach as if on a tray. I sat astride him, and we drank by turns.

I understood the purpose of the liquid better and better. The animals to be sacrificed needed to be treated with kindness. They must not come to the gangplank in a state of anxiety or in fear of being beaten. They needed to be in a pleasurable mood and to stay that way for quite a time to maintain quiet in the ship. I was being overcome by giddiness and a carefree feeling. I tried to hold this at bay by asking, "What happens to those for whom there is no room in the ark and who are not depraved? Will they be given huts on stilts? Are you building a settlement for them in the hills? You are sailing to a paradise with green meadows for the animals. Are you going to collect the harvest there to bring it here?"

Ham laughed loudly. That was how I wanted to see him: generous, laughing, prepared to tell me what he knew. I laughed too, although where that laugh came from or how it could have started I did not know.

"Don't be so anxious, my girl. Don't worry about those

stay-behinds. Your father is my foreman, you are my lover, Put is my friend, your mother my talisman. I won't leave you behind."

The servants placed the bread on the plates. It was a different color than usual and had not risen properly because of the thundery weather. Ham covered the jars and rinsed the beakers. By the time Shem and Japheth arrived, Ham was sitting behind his plate, his foot bandaged. He did not look at me. We kept our lips shut to prevent the smell of our breath escaping.

It was during that meal, not long after the boys who served the cooked food had carefully wrapped the vegetables in bread, placing it in the hands of those who were there, that a limping man came to the tent demanding attention. He was admitted. Part of the scaffolding had collapsed, he said. He was looking energetically around him with his little eyes, from us to the food and from the food to the top of the tent. You would have thought he was reporting on a successful enterprise if the traces of a sudden loss of bowel control had not been visible on his legs. The tear in his shirt was probably weeks old, but it made his appearance so discomfiting for us that no one could take another bite without turning our faces away. He did not need to look for words, he had already been shouting them at passersby on his way here: Dozens of pitch workers had crashed down. Young men as well as old. Blood flowed from their ears.

Ham pushed his food away and tried to stand up. I hurried to him. I know how badly a sprained foot suffers under sudden weight. I gripped his arm and supported his elbow with my body.

"Which side?" he asked curtly.

"West, in Gentan's section."

"The hollow ground?"

"No, the rocks haven't shifted. It was the tie-grass." This was the bluish grass Shem had been using recently to lash the scaffolding. He had persuaded his foreman to stop using the old grass, because the grass cutters could not find a reliable supply of it, and because it was so sharp it caused nasty cuts and inflammations.

"Gentan has fallen, lord," said the messenger. "Gentan and four of his brothers. And then some ten bearers and binders." Then he gave a list of foremen and their workers who worked at the tar vats. Now he turned to Japheth, who blinked in horror at every name.

Ham threw one arm around me and the other around Put. Without waiting for him, Shem and Japheth left the tent. As they went ahead, Ham groaned more with every step he managed with our help. The path leading to the shipyard had become smooth from use, but even so we progressed painfully, more because of Put than because of Ham's sprained foot: Put's shoulder was too low for Ham, his steps were unsteady because of the wine, and the child was too anxious about what he was going to see to give proper support.

And it was not a pretty sight, that toppled scaffold moving in the wind, the partitions knocked down and the sun shades smashed up. Scores of people stood about, and from the ground came the groaning of the wounded. The bystanders made way when we arrived. Ham limped from one wounded man to another. He tugged at us, he seemed to want to go backward and forward at the same time. He comforted men with broken backs who waited, motionless, for the pain to become bearable and their legs to lose all feeling. He wiped blood from skulls that had changed shape. He bent over to close eyes.

"The tie-grass is wrong," he said again and again. "Shem used the wrong grass."

Suddenly I saw my father. He was standing between the wall of the ship and a tower of brand-new crates, on the slight rise where I had seen him, earlier this week, deliberating with a group of men and asking one of the boys for a tray of tea. Now he stood there again talking, this time with Shem. Shem rolled up his wide sleeves, an unconscious gesture he kept repeating, his three servants behind him like bodyguards. I let go of Ham and went over to them to hear what they were saying.

As I rounded the stack of crates I saw, lying not two feet from the scaffold, Gentan, Japheth's beloved foreman, the man who, with tar, could seal joints for a lifetime. Lying amongst the tar brushes, he was hardly recognizable: His face was crushed and his arm twisted at an impossible angle under his body.

"Help him," Shem told my father. My father's hands rested on Gentan's shoulder. There was no need for him to kneel, because Gentan was lying on a raised, sloping shelf of rock at eye level, as if ready to start a whispered conversation with anyone passing by. He breathed bubbles of saliva and blood, and when he did that once more, I clearly heard him say, "Kill me!"

"Help him!" Shem said, more emphatically than before. His chin trembled. He knew he would soon find his scaffolders and have to face the loss. "You killed the duck, you know how it is done."

As Gentan's pain appeared unbearable, my father bent down. He raked some tie-grass together and twisted it into a rope which he laid around Gentan's neck. His hands became covered in blood.

"Don't do that!" shouted Ham, who had limped after me.

"Do it!" Shem hissed. "Give him a good, fast death. This is better than the pain and the death by drowning that awaits him."

People were moving behind the crates. There was wailing and weeping. My father looked at Ham in doubt. It was Ham he wanted to obey rather than Shem. Ham rolled his shoulders and held his hand out to me. Limp and clammy like a rag, that hand was, there was not the faintest ray of sun to remove his cold sweat. He kept shaking his head: "This man is Japheth's right hand, his best friend. He does not have to die now nor drown later. Japheth will admit him to the ark."

Shem turned abruptly toward Ham and laid his hands, almost lovingly, over his face. He took care not to cover his ears. Shem articulated every word carefully as he said, "There is something you still do not seem to understand. Even for a best friend, there is no place. He will drown with the rest." Ham's head seemed small under those large hands. There were flies everywhere, already attracted by the scent of blood. Shem shook his head vigorously to chase them. Then he let go of Ham and nudged my father with his knee.

My father arranged the grass rope again, as if that had not been done before. At the level of Gentan's Adam's apple, he twisted the ends together. He knew exactly how to do this, he had done it many times to injured animals to prevent them from bleeding. He held the knot tightly until the heaving of Gentan's body stopped and the bubbles in the corners of his mouth disappeared. Shem and Ham were waiting, looking at the crates, at me, at the side of the ship next to them, not seeing. Then my father released the noose.

At that moment, Gentan's wife came running, her dress billowing. Everyone knew her: Although she had a string of children hanging on her skirts, she would stand by him regularly, always ready with some snack and advice. She seemed to be saying something. It was hardly speech, at best a kind of barking of hoarse sounds that, when she saw what had happened, changed to moans.

I went to stand by Ham. His foot was now very swollen. He groaned with every step, and the blue bruising on his instep showed above the bandage. I grabbed him by the arm and led him away. I wanted to talk to him. It is possible that he was too bewildered to speak to me, but I had no time for his bewilderment.

"What is this?" I asked when we stood apart from the others. "What are you planning? Will whoever stays behind die? Is that what it means not to be of the elect? Is being righteous the same as staying alive?"

He stared ahead and said not a word.

"If you were righteous, you would now be giving up your places. You would be giving them up to the children, the lame, and the feebleminded! What do they have to atone for? For the injustice you have created? You choose yourselves a woman and make her righteous. You reject another woman and make her an outcast. There is not going to be a raised village, no hilltop for those who stay behind. Whoever is not on the ark is doomed to death by drowning!"

He did not immediately reply. He seemed only capable of shaking his head.

"But there is room!" he said finally. "The ark is huge!" His dismay was no different from mine, nor less intense. Just like me, there were things he had not heard, not understood, not noticed. He sank down on a rock to relieve his foot but could not stay sitting. He stood up, sat down again because of the pain, stood up again. His dog approached, but he shooed it away.

For the rest of the afternoon, no more work was done. Everyone walked about, talking together whether they knew one another or not. It was as if they had all fallen off their scaffolding and were wondering where they were. The workers were usually pretty thoughtless, accepting almost anything without surprise, but now their tongues came loose. The masks and mourning cloaks were brought out, the keening came from all around, brothers and cousins of the dead beat their drums.

I asked, "Why this secrecy, Ham? Why does no one know the purpose of the ship?"

"Because otherwise the Nefilim will find out, that is what I've always been told."

The Nefilim were the giants, the men who had sprung from the love of the old gods for earthly women. They towered over everyone but otherwise looked like ordinary mortals, except when they turned around, for then you could see how their backs were split into two parts held together by their vertebrae as if with meat hooks. The vertebrae were bare and brown, and as there was no skin around them, you would expect there would be pus in the hollows or that you could see raw flesh. But it was not so; all you could see were the cavities that sometimes, after a strong wind, were filled with sand that slowly ran out with every movement. They made holes in their lips through which, when they went to war, they pushed wild pigs' tusks. Nobody understood why they were still here, they were the supermen of the olden times. They were the instigators of everything that went wrong, they stole each other's water and dragged others' belongings from the trees. Because they kept on mating with the most beautiful women to be found, they kept having children, and those children had children, and all of them behaved badly. Their viciousness spread and became the norm. If they received a scratch, they would thrash a child; if they were wounded, they would kill a man.

"What if the water rises and the blond men come here, how will we stop them if they beat on the sides of the ship till the wood cracks?"

I did not say anything. I was certain they did not exist, but whenever people talked about them, their descriptions were so precise that I wondered. In the marshes, I had indeed seen tall, blond men coming past, but they always wore cloaks and I had never had a chance to examine their vertebrae.

"Now I understand why my father and my brothers always warned me about the Nefilim," Ham went on. "It was an excuse for keeping everyone in the dark, including the workers in the shipyard." He looked over his shoulder at the red tent. There was contempt in his look, and distaste.

From where we sat, I saw Put wandering about. He was still drunk. I knew he was looking for me, but I did not call him; his confusion would be more than I could bear. We also saw Japheth running past, and Shem, looking dejected. Ham leaned his full weight on me. Our arms around each other, we walked to the red tent. Every now and then he rested his head against mine in exhaustion and pain. No one paid us any attention.

23

The Builder Speaks

hem and Japheth stood in front of their father's part of the tent. Their silence had all the appearance of a conspiracy; it was clear no discussions were necessary because they had already been held, in a secluded place, at a time no one knew of. Glances and nods were sufficient. Ham looked at them inquiringly, but they seemed not to notice him, not even when, with difficulty, he went to stand with them near his father's quarters.

"He must tell them the purpose of the ship," Ham said. "It is high time!"

Shem and Japheth clacked their tongues at him, almost simultaneously, the sort of sound with which you calm down an overexcited child. Side by side they entered their father's apartment. Ham wanted to go with them, but because of his foot, he was too slow. The flap was pulled shut in his face, and when he went to push it open again, a hand repulsed him. Exhausted, he sat down and leaned back.

We could not understand what was said. All we could hear was mumbling. What bothered us most were the flies that had come inside with the thundery weather and were impossible to shoo away from the food. I shuffled back and forth to try to keep them off me. Put sat in his corner, his legs pulled up and his arms spread out. He was sitting not far from the servant with the bread; all he had to do was stretch out his hand. Because nobody had turned up, the servants had finished eating all the food, because according to them it would have soured and attracted vermin. But a few women had baked a second time, and that bread was better than the first lot. It was a long wait. Ham folded his hand around his foot as if to warm it. The light softened and rounded his features. The way he sat there, he seemed not much older than Put.

The tent flap moved before we had realized that silence had returned. Shem emerged from his father's apartment, his hand raised, Japheth immediately behind him. They gave Ham a brief look, but even after he had stood up did not address him. Shem kept holding his hand up. One of the servants understood his need for something sweet and offered him a small dish of honey with a piece of bread in it.

"He will speak," Shem said after he had dunked the bread. "But not now. The statement is not one for those who are hungry."

Ham looked around him despairingly and sat down again. He did not resemble the boy I knew; his silence turned him into a stranger. I went to my mother's stretcher and tied down her cover. I exaggerated my normal gestures, but Put did not seem to understand that I was getting ready to leave. Like me, he was dizzy and confused. The ball of bread in his mouth grew bigger and bigger. He kept pushing chunks between his jaws, but could not make himself swallow.

*　　*　　*

Put and I did not dare keep the soup on the boil or rake up the fire, talk to each other or whisper, for fear of not hearing the ram's horn. All the usual things, stacking the mats, rolling out the dough, or drawing water, we did in the most soundless way possible. We avoided the house. It seemed suddenly so small, so suffocating. It had no window through which you could see if the quarry was still the way it had been. We looked at each other, of course, that was unavoidable, but our faces were as if turned to stone and betrayed nothing. I saw Put staring, looking up occasionally at the birds and the clouds.

When the ram's horn sounded, we stopped what we were doing to persuade ourselves that it was indeed a ram's horn, that distant sound that was drowned out by our agitated breathing. We dragged the pots off the fire, put the lids on, and covered them with hay. We went to my mother's stretcher to lift her up, but my father raised his hand. "She is not coming," he said. "This is not good for her. There are too many people." I saw her blinking urgently. My father, however, took no notice. He nudged me and literally pushed me out of our yard.

We went and stood near the base of the ship. There was not much room. People streamed in and crowded together till their cloaks touched; the spots where the workmen had fallen were the only spaces that remained empty.

A silence fell when the Builder appeared. At every step he took, the crowd separated, creating the space he needed to reach the small dais that had been set up for the occasion. It was a solid structure, raised at short notice by the scaffolders. Shem and

Japheth walked on each side of their father. I knew from Ham that the old man always had some sand in his pockets, as if he wanted to make himself heavier and keep his feet on the ground. In reality, he wanted to know its moisture content; every new handful was a harbinger of change, and he may have felt the need to have a handful of earth on him, that very thing he believed he would soon be losing. His sons lifted him up and put him on the dais. He carefully held on to its railing, and it took some time for his sons to let go of him. The care with which they treated him spoke of their desire to continue with this enterprise. For what if this man were to die before his plan had been realized? In what kind of world would they wake up then?

The Builder, finding his balance, stood with his legs apart and looked at the people surrounding him. His skin was spotty, and from a distance, this created the impression that his effort was making him sweat blood and water. His voice was calm and did not shake, even when he exerted himself to reach his more distant listeners.

"The Unnameable has addressed me at moments when I was not prepared for it," he began. "I did not need to listen to Him in order to hear Him. He spoke to me despite my inattention. He instructed me to build a ship for the righteous. The ship is His hope for the future. It makes it possible to start anew, in a new place. You have worked with us on this structure. So have Gentan and his men. That they will not be able to see the result of their exertions saddens us. But they will also be spared much. They will not experience the calamity that awaits us. They will not have to see how the Unnameable destroys the world."

"What is it?" cried the multitude. "What is the calamity that awaits us?"

"A flood," said the Builder. He was standing under a sky that was as colorless as his hair. "God will allow the world to be flooded."

First there was a whispering. The whispering grew louder, swelled out to mutterings and shouts. It ended in cheering. "Long live the Builder! Long live the savior of life on Earth! Long live the bringer of a grand plan! Long live the fighter for righteousness!"

The Builder looked down on the cheering crowd in amazement. Put and I stared at each other in disbelief. My father threw up his arms. "Have you all gone mad? Do you really think they have thought of you?" But his voice was lost in the clamor. He put his hands to his mouth like a horn, but had second thoughts. He looked around worriedly. The applause was too loud, it reached too far. He turned and made his way through the crowd. He disappeared as he went to the quarry to my mother with a smile, to do what I blamed Ham and his brothers for doing: to tell a meaningless story, to keep silent about a great part of the truth in order to allay fear.

24

I Change Back into a Girl

Amongst the cheering and the resulting commotion, I became aware of a presence by my side that felt familiar. It was Neelata, her hood pulled down over her eyes. She grasped my arm and dragged me after her, weaving through the crowd. I stepped on people's feet and kicked their legs, shouting apologies nobody heard.

"These people are wrong. They think the ship belongs to them. Because they've built it, they think it's theirs," she said, hurrying along. I am not sure that I understood everything she said. I was trying to arrange my shell-encrusted tunic, which had stretched tight over my chest from all the pulling and twisting, and I had lost my necklace. She walked fast. At first I thought it was the mob that inspired her fear. But she kept up the pace even when we came to quieter spots. She went in the direction of the sheds where sacks and baskets were stored.

It was quiet amongst the provisions; even the guards were out in the shipyard to hear the Builder's words. Two of her lady's maids were waiting for us. They were holding up a magnificent blue dress that I recognized right away; I had seen Neelata wearing it the day her uncle had brought her here. It had those long, wide sleeves that fall over your hands.

"Ham is making me his wife," she said. "I tell you in all honesty that my heart is not his. But can I send him away and give up my life? Many will be left behind. The Builder only takes his own."

"What's the matter with this god of yours that he always has to be so thorough?" I snapped. My anger was not just caused by what she said, but also by having been dragged along in that hysterical and unexpected way. I was breathless from running.

"The Unnameable has created a form of life that is not perfect," she replied. She was tugging at the ties of my tunic. What next?! I pushed her away, but she persisted. She seemed so determined that I gave in.

I automatically tugged at my tunic too and asked, "Wouldn't it have been better if he hadn't?"

"Human beings are close to perfect, but only close. The Unnameable created us in His image and likeness. We are no more than an imitation of perfection. To make us perfect, He would have had to rob us of our free spirit. Only then would we be obedient. But a human being without a free spirit is insignificant. And so He took the risk of giving us free will. It is that will that is going to destroy many of us."

The words had barely left her mouth when Ham entered the shed. He too had been rushing and his forehead was covered with sweat. Leaning on a stick, he walked straight up to me. The bandage around his foot had become undone and was dragging along the ground.

"The man on that dais, the Builder, my father," he said hoarsely, "he cannot bring himself to tell people the whole truth." He handed his stick to a maid and pushed the shoulder straps of my tunic down. He knew better than Neelata how the breast cover worked, he had undone it often enough. The maids did not seem surprised when my breasts appeared. Curiously, they picked the clinking garment up and put it aside deferentially.

"God has a plan, but so have I," said Ham. "I'll abduct you from your father's house. I'll make you my servant. My father can have no objections to that."

It was Neelata who put the blue dress on me and fixed a headband over the black design on my forehead. She produced a brush and tried to fluff up my thinned-out hair with twisting movements.

I must have looked like a woman ignorant of how to be elegant. It was awful being brought amongst people that way, with my hair shapeless and without makeup. In my confusion, I wished they would at least put some kohl on my eyes. Nor could I easily abandon my masculine walk. The dress was, of course, far too long. I had to hold it up so as not to trip on the hem.

They took me to the red tent, where many were also heading. It was exceptionally busy around it, and people stumbling into the guy ropes made the whole tent shake. Put was there, I noticed him right away. As always, he stood close to the adults, taking in every word. I took hold of him with a gesture I had forgotten: I scooped him up by his bottom and put him on my hip. I needed both my arms to keep him in place, he had grown a lot lately. At first he was frightened, but when he recognized me, he threw his arms around my neck.

"Go inside," said Ham when I stood in front of the Builder's private quarters.

I felt Put go rigid in my arms. Never before had we entered this place, and now too it did not seem proper. But Ham's fingers poked into my back.

"Give me the child," I heard Neelata whisper when I tried to open the curtain. She put her hand on Put's shoulder. I had seen Put with her before. When she was not carrying the water jugs, she was looking after the animals. She was so friendly with them, we often heard her in the morning asking the goats, "Who is coming to the pond with me today?" Put let her put her arms around him, tolerating her face so close to his own. She took him from me, and he threw his arms around her the way he had done with me.

I pulled at the curtain. The thing would not open immediately; I tugged at it, but before we could move inside, the dwarf appeared in front of us. Fortunately, he was small, and his child's body could not stop us. Neelata followed us with Put, and that did not leave room for anyone else; we nearly filled the whole space.

The apartment was faintly lit and the objects in it were probably as old as the man who used them. I saw it immediately: The Builder still lived in the same tent he had lived in during all those years when he had wandered in the hills; the red tent had been built around it specially. The reed mats, the low stools, the small chests seemed to be about to disintegrate into dust. That was why so little light was allowed in: Light would destroy the space, the walls that made up the tent would fall apart into threads. In the center, next to a low stool, stood the Builder. He had only just gotten back, a servant was helping him out of his mantle. Under it, he wore a thin robe that had been repaired with fine stitches in several places.

"You have informed the people, but you have not told everything," said Ham.

"I was not given time," the Builder said. He whispered. He was afraid his words would be overheard outside, where the warriors were, and perhaps the Nefilim.

Ham made no allowance for his father's fears. He spoke stridently, rapidly — anyone who stood near the tent could listen in. "We are not numerous enough, Father. More people need to come. I have figured it, it will take us generations to repopulate the earth."

I did not dare look around, but there were a few things I could not help seeing. To one side stood a reed cage with a messy dove. Little bells hung from the top of the cage, and in its food bowl lay grain mixed with droppings. The creature must have had a fight with a rat or a hawk; feathers lay underneath it, and its flesh was visible on its back and rear. I had seen the Builder's quarters before, through chinks in the tent wall, but had never suspected the presence of a dove here.

Ham pushed Neelata, carrying Put, in front of his father. "You know I am taking her for my wife."

"I know it," said the Builder.

Then Ham grasped me by the shoulder. I was frightened, because I had not expected his movement. "I want to take a second wife, a servant who will aid us. This is the girl of my choice. This way, the earth will become more quickly populated."

The Builder sat down, leaning so far back that he touched the cage. The dove flapped its wings, shuffled into a corner, and lifted its feathers. I did not move; no muscle in my body seemed capable of it. The Builder said: "In the Unnameable's mind, everything has its hour. On the ark, we shall abstain. Impregnating our women we will do in the new world. You know what I have said: We have the promise of a land, a fertile land, no longer the dust and the barren territory we know. What has been promised to us is not a rocky hill, not even a chain of hills, but something re-sembling the paradise we have lost. No longer will we wander. We will stay in one spot and plant seeds. Only then will we pop-ulate the earth. Now is not the time for us to be concerned about that. What man will build a house if he does not have the motive of the bed? And if he does not have the motive of the bed, then how will there be children?"

Ham coughed. At every breath, his chest wheezed. "What if one of our women falls ill? Or dies? A camel's gestation time is one year. A camel drops a foal once in three years. It can have five or eight in its lifetime. So how long does it take before you have a herd? We know how much can go wrong with cattle. The ani-mals get foot rot, the cramps, bloat, bleeding. Who will advise us about the rodents, the beasts of prey, the reptiles? What do we know about their nature, their bad habits? I have seen a guinea pig eat its young. How will the guinea pig spread over the new world if we do not understand why it does this? One species will die out, what if another species then overwhelms us and occupies the paradise? What if every fruit we grow is picked by them, every stalk of wheat chewed up by them before it is dry?'. . . Of every clean beast by sevens,' that is clever, but how many men will be needed to tend them and to prevent them from grazing the fields bare? And if the men tend them, who will plow the earth, who will put up fences, and who will explore new places? We must take women and children. How can our god say that the existence of our kind is safe if there is not a child on board, and we do not even have permission to procreate?"

The Builder shook his head. "I cannot allow any exceptions. The Unnameable has said that I may take mine: my wife, my sons, each with his wife. Nothing has been said to me about a concubine."

I could barely breathe. My hands clasped the collar of the blue dress as if that would protect me from falling. I now had proof that Ham wanted to save me. For the first time I understood his obsession with the procreation of the animals and peoples. He saw the gaps in the plan of the Unnameable, he saw that He could count but not calculate. He knew how things happened with sheep. If the herd was too small and the ram mated with his mother, monsters would result.

25

The Farewell

I went with Ham into his quarters and carefully closed the curtain. I asked him to sit down in his usual spot and close his eyes. He was shaking with dismay. I rubbed with the middle fingers of both hands from the base of his nose to his hairline. I moved my fingers along the ridge of his nose, along his eyebrows to his temples. I made quick movements on his upper lip up to his nose. I laid my hands on his face, I laid them on his chin for a few moments, then equally briefly against his cheeks and over his ears. I made these movements several times in sequence, faster each time, until he became calm. I cut his fingernails so they were serrated. When I had finished, I took his hands and scraped the skin of my neck with them. Each finger left many traces.

He said, "Every net has its holes, as the child of fishermen you know that," but I did not listen. Now I understood that he could not do anything for me. He did not know it, but I was taking leave of him. All I could do was wonder if there was enough time to flee.

"How many sleeping places did you build?" I asked. Speaking was difficult, my teeth were clamped together like a trap.

"I don't know," he said dazedly. "The ship is large."

"You know exactly. Eight of them you've built, and not one more."

He coughed, dry and hoarse. I knew where in his lungs the phlegm sat, I could have brought it up with gentle tapping, but I did not.

I said, "You know I have good water. Wine seems more precious to you people. But wine won't take the place of water. Don't forget: The source is well hidden."

It was not only his face that was flushed with agitation. His neck and chest too were red. He said, "None of our women has the talent needed to find it. We are counting on you, on your uprightness."

With a sharp knife I had loosened the fibers of the top end of a small stick. I pushed it into his mouth and started scouring his teeth to make him stop speaking. "Uprightness has done nothing for me," I said, turning to the light. "I know where to find the herbs I need. The spring will be poisoned long before your women have reached it."

My words demanded vengeance. Naturally, a man makes much noise in such a moment. And because he is cursing, others will come running.

It was Japheth who ripped the curtain aside to see what was going on. He recognized me, of course. He said, "Is the masquerade finished?" I looked at him as if he were not speaking my language. He was dirty, he needed grooming. He went on, "Or is it just starting?"

"I disguised myself," I answered wearily. "I have a well, but I am going to make it unusable."

Shem joined Japheth. Japheth leered, Shem looked at me as if he were full of pity. Perhaps they were simply amazed at the fact that I would slip from one skin into another, change sex like clothes.

"If you are not a man, we'll beat you because you have deceived us. If you are, we'll beat you because you keep your water from us." Sweat beaded on Japheth's upper lip. He was forceful and solidly built, but not fluent in language, often stumbling in his reasoning.

I turned to the wheezing man in the chair, the only one who was clever enough, so clever that even I had not seen through his intention. "You've made me into a boy," I spat at him. "That has weakened me. Only as a woman did I have the right to keep my well secret. By making me a man you took away my power over the water."

Ham was now sitting completely bent forward, his head deep between his shoulders. "It is true," he said. "We had you followed. But none of your pursuers has returned. Did they see something they wanted to run away from forever? Or was the way so dangerous they perished? We can only guess." With a swift movement he pressed his fingers into the corners of his eyes to block his welling tears. "It was not my idea, but my brothers'."

Shem and Japheth dragged me out of the tent. They beat me in a detached, polite manner, as if to prove they had learned to punish instead of taking vengeance. Shem pulled the blue dress from my back; Japheth held up the scourge, a bundle of thin, flexible straps meant to hurt without causing injuries. Of course, it was Japheth who hit me; he was always the one who was least troubled afterward by what he had brought about. He asked me to squat and put my arms around my knees so the skin of my back would be stretched good and tight. He struck sixteen times. He struck me because I had disguised myself, and because, no matter how hard I denied it, I had lured my pursuers into an ambush.

It went on for an eternity. I tried not to think of him and his whip. I thought of home, of water and marshes, of the turf huts, of the cutting table where my mother scrubbed the fish and discussed with other women exactly how much salt was needed to pickle a fish the size of a hand without making it inedible; we children organized a mosquito hunt, there were prizes to be won, we kept the insects in empty snail shells we held closed tightly with our thumbs. I thought of swimming, of going so deep that all you can hear is the rising of air bubbles. But it was no help. The straps hurt. With every stroke, I became more convinced that my father was right. The Rrattika were scum. I despised them and their customs, I did not wish to be amongst them for another moment. I vaguely heard Ham coughing behind the goat's-hair curtain. He called out something, but I did not understand what he said.

When Japheth indicated that I could go, I hurried, without saying another word, away from the red tent. The blue dress on my body was ripped at the seam, my back was burning, but I did not scream. Put came after me. He did not stop shouting, "They mustn't hit you. Let them try again and I'll hit back. I'll smash Japheth's eyes with my slingshot. Shem I'll beat till he bleeds."

"Shush now," I said. "Keep quiet. Everybody can hear you, everyone can see us going, and I don't want them to."

But my admonition helped not one bit. He only cried all the harder, "I can scream if I want to. When the water comes, the

Builder will slam his ship's hatch shut and sail away. I can't swim, you can. How long will the trees we'll climb hold us? How long will it be before the water goes down?"

My father was in the house. I could not believe he was sitting there so quietly. After the Builder's speech I was expecting my father to start doing something, go to see the Builder or pack our belongings, not to meekly accept this humiliation. They called themselves the pure, the righteous, and let us kill a badly hurt man like Gentan so they could keep their own hands undefiled.

"These people have been hit with madness," he said, deadly calm. "They have never seen more water than the contents of the buckets they lug about."

"I want to get away from here, Father."

He inspected the welts on my back. "Our gods have not given orders," he said, gently putting his fingers on the sore spots.

"Perhaps our gods are unaware of their god's plan."

"My task in the ark is nearly completed, but not quite. . . ."

"I want to get away from here. I want to take the secret of the spring with me and make them tear their mantles in remorse."

My father removed a small flask from his belt and let a few drops drip onto his fingers. The oil cooled my skin, which was glowing as if it had been touched by fire. "Why did they beat you?"

"I threatened them. I said I would poison the water."

"Re Jana, you dumb child," he scolded. "Did you want to kill innocent people? Did you want to do what you blame their god for and play the Unnameable yourself?"

I turned my back away from him. I held on to the door jamb. His hand stayed suspended in the air.

"Is that what the elders did, generation after generation?" I asked, pretending calm. "Know that war is coming, know that drought is coming or disaster, decipher all the writing on the wall, talk about it, spell out the images of doom, but not act accordingly? Rather stay petrified with fear and talk about ordinary things — Is there enough water to cook the millet? Can we undo the bolt on the door? — than face the situation? If what we know means we should harness a horse, hire a tracker, and journey far away, then that is what we do, isn't it?"

My father interrupted me with an expressive cough. He put a shiny finger to his lips and pointed at the spot where my mother lay. "Spare her our doubts," he said, bending toward me. "If you must talk, do it away from her ears." Silently, he waited till she was asleep. Then he stood up to go outside, where darkness was falling. He went to the back of the house; I followed. Bending, he lifted a stack of planks from the ground. I recognized the planks, they came from the house. In the back of the shed where we kept our stores, a hole gaped. The boards had been carefully removed. He put them in my arms.

"I have my own solution," he said and walked ahead of me. He led me out of the quarry, past the shrubs where we normally urinated. "If the Builder is right, the flood will be violent," he said. "It is intended to kill, to wash away the wickedness of the world. Can you blame their god? He is sick of looking at the Rrattika. He is fed up with this roaming people, who are not evil, but hardly show any progress. There is so much that is new in the world, there is so much knowledge of justice, trade, and cultivation.

They do nothing with all that, they wander and keep wandering as if time stands still and as if these new insights mean nothing. Their behavior makes one wish for a catastrophe. It makes one hope for a purification. Only it is a pity that people who have nothing to do with it will be hit just as hard. Moving away makes no sense if everything is flooded. In which direction were you planning to go? We don't know from which quarter the disaster will strike. If we flee, we may be going toward it. And is this something we want to face on our own? No, we must stay with the others."

He walked ahead of me into the dark. He did not move fast; it was almost as if he carried another load apart from the planks. He went past the ash field, where for a long time waste was burned, but that now lay abandoned. Beyond the ash field, nobody lived, there were only the shrubs and the cliff. "Only those who are righteous will be spared, the Builder said. I have been wondering what that means for us. Have we not cared for your mother all that time? Have we not taken in an orphan child, the child of nomads, with no manners? Are we not hardworking people who are content with what we get for our work? And all those other men, the tradesmen who use their utmost skill, the artists who put their very soul into every vault, into every arch they polish and every image they carve? I have wondered what we would have to do to be well regarded by the god who is going to send the water, but Shem and Japheth give me no hope. It is a god just for them. He has chosen them, and they him. As outsiders, we don't stand a chance."

He started the climb up the cliff. I was panting. I could not believe that he wanted to take these planks up there, along this steep path, on this moonlit evening full of insects and vermin.

But he did not go all the way to the top. Along the winding path, halfway up the cliff, there was a smooth, uncultivated terrace where the scent of mulberry trees was in the air. He crossed the terrace and put the planks down in the farthest corner. The field where we stood was flat and open. It was naturally screened by shrubs. In the center, there lay a carefully cut wooden platform. Now that I stood next to it, I could see that battens and tie-beams had been nailed onto it. The joins had been sealed with hemp and tar. Planks lay around it at right angles, like fish bones.

Without taking any notice of my amazement at this isolated construction site, my father said, "What we need is a boat for everyone, a fleet for those who have thought, who are provident and can figure things. Isn't a new world with people of insight and intelligence to be preferred to a world with only those who are righteous? We'll build our own boat, a truss-boat that can take a bit of a storm. That is what I am doing, my girl, that is my defense."

I put down my planks. As I bent, I must have brushed against his back. He flinched and groaned. I could not see his skin very well in the dark, but I could guess what was wrong.

"Has Japheth been to see you too?" I asked. I whispered my question, not because I thought someone would overhear us, but to avoid recalling the memory of the pain.

"Gentan's wife told him I put the rope around her man's neck."

I closed my eyes for a few moments. "We don't have to go back, Father," I said when I opened them again. I heard him release a deep breath. He walked away from me. He went back to the terrace from where you could see the whole shipyard. There he stopped. He looked at the lights shining here and there from the hundreds of tents and dwellings below us, with the dozens of paths linking everything with everything. He stood there for a long time.

"We'll demolish the house in the quarry for the timber," he said at last. "We'll build a new one here. We'll no longer work for them. We'll hide in this place here, halfway up the cliff, where they won't look for us, close to our boat. And when the calamity comes, we'll be able to see from here what the ark builders do. And if we do as they do, we too will survive."

We built a modest house, not half as big as our first one, on the terrace that looked out over the shipyard but kept us hidden from view with bushes. Quite a way from there, so far that my mother could not hear the knocking of the hammer, my father continued building the boat. Day and night he worked; he did not return to Ham. Two whole seasons my father had worked for Ham and his brothers. Now, with the end of construction in sight, he hid from them. Deep in the night, we stole clothes from clotheslines. We did what we could to look like Rrattika. Put thought it was exciting, he had not expected us to ever get dressed up like him.

My mother did not understand what was going on, she expressed her surprise but we made up excuses and stories. She begged me for explanations, but what could I say? I had lots of questions myself: If that god wanted to destroy people, why did he not opt for a quick death, a death by fire or the thrust of a spear? Why that gruesome water, which inspires so much fear in those who cannot swim, and pointlessly extends the death agony of those who can?

"This . . ." said my father after he had watched me being grimly silent with my mother, "is what will happen to her if you tell her what you know." He held up a rabbit by the skin of its neck. Put watched with trembling lips. He had found the creature. He had wrapped it in his mantle and brought it to us. Life had almost deserted it, although it showed no signs of injury. It offered no resistance when my father moved it in our faces. Its legs hung limp. It neither scratched nor bit, it was resigned to dying. Put hoped my father would shorten its pain, but he did not. He waved it around and said, "Her mother did it, and her mother's mother. They decided it was enough. They died because they wanted to die. That was their rebellion, their reproach to us men, whom they blamed for the things that happened. If you talk too much, she will follow in her mother's footsteps." He threw the rabbit into the scrub without once looking back to it.

He stretched out the measuring rope, made drawings with red ocher, and twirled his compasses; he made this boat stronger than any of the boats he had built before, and the timber we had earned was beginning to run out. With my hood pulled down over my eyes I went to the woodworkers' yard to search among the wood shavings for boards that could be put to use. Sometimes Put came with me. He was more bony than ever — he

would only eat if we could persuade him that he was hungry —
and he spoke little. My father's decision to build a truss-boat
spurred him to work like one possessed. He wanted to be part of
every single moment of its building. He never took breaks. If we
rested or drank tea, he went away. He wandered about amongst
the tents, took boards from Ham's workshop, and brought them
to us. I stole the nails, my father the tools. If anyone caught us
and tried to stop us, we threatened them. Thieves and liars we
were; in a very short time we quite belonged to the depraved
people for whom the Unnameable's doom was intended.

26

Living Apart

I rapidly became accustomed to my life as a Rrattika girl, though it took me a while to learn to manage those wide sleeves and skirts, which were actually quite handy for spiriting away tools. Our life in isolation was simpler and less tiring than it had been when we lived in the quarry. Our crops flourished fairly well, milk and eggs we could obtain for a small payment, there were antlers and horns aplenty to be found in the hills to make ornaments and coins; anyone dexterous did not have to go short of anything. It seemed unlikely that we would suffer hardship by no longer working for the Builder and his sons. And there was time. Every nail my father bent, he could afford to carefully straighten. No one urged us to hurry. The sky was as bright blue as it had always been; it was hard to imagine that there would ever be rain.

Our view was panoramic. From our shelter I saw how a system of ropes and beams was used to hoist the amphoras on board the ark. The big urns looked like well-rounded women's torsos, one handle on each hip. I counted six men for each amphora, plus a seventh to direct the operation, and in a shady spot I discerned the figure of the Builder, flanked by the dwarf. A little later, a few women came from the hills with ordinary jugs on their hips or their heads, they came from ponds half a day's walk away and carried the best water they had been able to find. They went to where, with tubes and containers, a filter had been built to remove twigs, leaves, grit, and especially larvae, and then other women carried the purified water onto the ship and poured it into the amphoras that were waiting in their frames. The distant rasping and squeaking of the tools could be heard all the way to where we were.

Occasionally, my father went to observe the works from the shrubwood. The boat he was building in our little field was steadily taking shape, but what was a little truss-boat like that compared to the construction down below? And in the field, he was alone. My father longed for the cheerful company of the woodworkers and their music. Wherever they went they took their boxes containing not only their carefully maintained tools, but also their musical instruments, their lutes and flutes, which were invariably brought out after work. I got worried whenever he stayed out longer than expected. He was always so loud, and I did not know if he would be able to restrain himself when he heard them talking about the work. I was terrified that they would unmask him and claim him again, or banish him because of Gentan. Then who would build our boat?

But I could not reproach him, I was behaving like him. I sat amongst the shrubs to watch how the Builder's sons made their toilet the way they used to, by pouring water over their shoulders. I saw how Ham waded thoughtfully through the pond. I kept my gaze on the skin of his back, on his hair that hung sleek from the water, down to his shoulders in strands. I could never get enough of watching the way he would sit down on a rock after bathing, pull up his leg, and bend up his foot so he could examine the sole.

On occasion, Neelata dried him. And I knew that her heart did not go out to him. The thought that he was not loved was unbearable. I wanted to jump up and go and snatch the towel from her hands, but how could I? All I could do was return to our hiding place. For the rest of a day like that I kept feeling his skin everywhere: in the smooth stones that were to be found all over the cliff, when cutting the bulging flesh of white fruits, and in the evening when I rubbed my mother's back with oil. I saw his hair in the grass and his nails amongst the pips of melons. None of it was mine, I knew, but my longing could not be soothed.

Zaza

One day a woman climbed up the cliff. She wore a brightly colored dress and a head scarf to protect herself against the sun. She
walked unsteadily, her legs insecure on the ridges and loose
stones, and very soon I saw that it was because of her age. She
was old, too old to be climbing up a cliff. Grass cutters regularly
came up the track to the top, but practically never left it to come
onto the terrace. They were in a hurry and on their way down
carried heavy loads on their backs. The side of the cliff was not a
place to stay around; it was an unavoidable obstacle you scaled
and descended rapidly. But this woman was not heading for the
ridge. It was the track itself that held her attention. She was
looking around, bending over from time to time.

I could not resist going to meet her. When I approached her,
she did not seem to hear me. Her body, which had lost its shape
so that it was no longer clear where her bosom ended and her
belly began, was completely concentrated on something hardly
visible amongst the stones. She picked something, smelled it, and
that gesture made me realize what she was up to.

"There is thyme here, and mulberry farther along," I said.

She looked up. I saw her face, her neck with the ornaments

resembling scars, and felt a shock of recognition. It was Zaza, the Builder's wife, Ham's mother. I had seen her regularly in the red tent. She would enter the Builder's quarters and invariably send the dwarf outside.

Fear made my heart miss a beat. For weeks, we had managed to keep ourselves hidden from the ark builders. Now a moment's carelessness on my part could bring all that effort to naught. Now she would recognize me. She would send her sons here, and yet again our lives would be in chaos.

She carried a small knife and a piece of muslin to put the plants in. The muslin was light as a breath of air, but it was the knife that drew my attention, it glittered in the sun. It looked practical and sharp, and in short bright flashes, reminded me of how unsafe I had been feeling for some time. The constant threat of discovery and impending doom hung over my life and made me feel exhausted. Now I stood before Zaza. I had walked up to her of my own accord. I think I must have smiled at her, invitingly and friendly, hoping that would make her try to remember. I was hoping she would nod at me, say my name, or ask, "Wasn't it you who used to groom my sons?" But already she was bending over again. "I'm looking for thistles," she said curtly. "I want every kind there is."

"What do you want to do with the thistles?"

"To take with us on the ship. The command is for a complete collection."

"But thistles are a pest."

"I know it sounds unwise to take them, but once we have

taken a task on ourselves, once we've agreed, we must do it and do it well."

"But not just you alone?" I exclaimed ingenuously. I felt extraordinarily fearful and could not think straight about what I was saying. I knew I should run away, that this conversation posed a real danger to my family and the little truss-boat. But she paid proper attention to my questions. She did not give me the chance to disappear, and I was grateful to her for that.

"I have my three sons; they are too busy to bother with small details. I had more sons, but two of them have gone away. They were restless, they refused to spend years building and staying in one place. It made the commitment of the remaining three even greater. Except for my youngest. For him, it made no difference, for what does a child know? He saw his brothers leaving and did not understand what was happening."

I felt the hairs on my arms stand up when she said "my youngest." "Is that the one who is unwed?" I asked. I did not look at her, but kept my eyes fixed on the hard, pale edges of her feet.

"He is about to be married, but grieves over a girl who has gone away," she said. She kept working as she talked, pushing grasses aside with her feet, constantly comparing stems and leaf forms. "One morning he went to the quarry where she lived and everything was gone. He calls her name every day. When he lifts his head, the ashes he has strewn over his head from sorrow fall from his hair."

I stood still and nodded. She placed a plant in her muslin cloth, so small I wondered if she would find it when she got back home. Then she walked past me, and I could smell the coloring mixed with saffron and bone ash she had put on. Grateful for the things she had said, I picked a plant she could not reach and hoisted myself onto an overhanging rock. It seemed wrong, but I was glad that Ham was distressed. And that gladness confused me. It caused me to pick thistles with large prickles, without even thinking about my hands.

28

The Message of Doom Is Forgotten

My mother suffered most from our flight to the field on the slope. In the red tent, she had felt herself to be at the heart of the shipyard. She had stayed near the place she had been accustomed to: the center, the easily found place that people came to for advice and assistance. Now she suffered from the loss of status and from deadly boredom. She had a need of admiring glances. Her adornment had kept her busy every day. Her demands had become even more exacting when more and more warriors visited the red tent. They were the Builder's nephews, famed for their horsemanship, who decked themselves out with belts and skirts consisting of skeins of wool hanging down in rows. The warriors were needed to prevent an attack by the Nefilim. They had at their disposal the horses that were now arriving in the hills in ever greater numbers. Some of them rode a pony or a mule. They were belligerent, constantly practicing their skills at handling knives and swords. They spoke scathingly about the enemy, but that was not what had made my mother stare at them. They had hands like shovels and voices that would pulverize stone, but mostly they were beautifully built, with broad shoulders and firm thighs that darted out between the skeins of their skirts as they walked. Where we lived now it was rare for a warrior to pass by, and on the odd occasion when someone approached, Put would frequently throw a well-aimed stone.

Of course, my mother could have no idea how much the Builder's announcement from the dais had changed things. She lay on a high rock near the edge of the cliff and in the house on windy days. She did not hear how the taciturn, thoughtless Rrattika were beginning to talk. Young and old, they discussed the water and the flood. The children started having anxious dreams. They did not know what drowning was, but their fathers had said, "If you don't watch out, the water will close over your head!" and they woke gasping for breath. Their fear grew, like that of the very old who knew their lives depended on their family's fixed abode: Wandering about the land, they stood no chance and would be left behind in a shady spot with a couple of jugs of water and some bread. And as their fear grew, the inhabitants of the shipyard became convinced that, for the sake of the children, the elderly, the sick, and the weak, it would be better not to talk about it. In an almost magical way, all sorts of explanations arose of what the Builder had said, and no one any longer would draw the only correct conclusion: that many would die. And with the silence came forgetting. Because there was no new information to confirm the old, the usual happened: Messages of doom were forgotten despite their ominous content. Gaps were found in the predictions, unclear statements that confirmed the suspicion that they were lies. Eventually, the calamity also came to seem so very remote, as if it were not for this time but for another era altogether, not even that of their children or their children's children. The Builder had already lived such a long time,

perhaps he would live to twice his age, and when at last the water came, new-fashioned solutions they could not even think of
now would long since have appeared, or new gods, sons of this
god, with different opinions and different ways. And what else
was there to do but carry out the daily tasks, what else could they
have attempted? Plot a rebellion? Stop sleeping and eating?

At first, I made an attempt at reminding them of the message
of doom. I told people there was very little room on the ship,
that only those who made their own vessel would have a chance
against the flood, but all I got were bored, almost pitying looks.
They peered under my hood and saw that I was not one of them.
Only a minority took my advice seriously. They started collecting timber and improvising something. But although they had
been working on a ship for years, not one of them knew how to
put together a boat. Soon the timber was abandoned and put to
other uses. And because time passed without anything happening, the mood became easier. Stacks of fuel from the dung of the
cattle and large quantities of wool were available, and eggs ga-
lore. Bees willingly gave their honey. The ruminants were tame
and let themselves be milked. People laid banquets outside their
dwellings. They invited strangers; the women who saw me passing by beckoned to me, and it happened more than once that I
had eaten before I got home. I met all sorts of folks, they came
from faraway cities and wanted to settle here. Small businesses,
starting with few resources, flourished; wanderers arrived and
never left.

29

"Come Back to Us"

Amongst all this abundance, there was one shortage that became worse: There was not enough timber. The stacks we had been able to get to so easily were now guarded by the warriors in their woolen skirts. People who still had timber did fantastic deals. If we wanted to continue working on our boat, I had to resort to going to the waste pile. That was a precarious enterprise, because the pile stood not far from Neelata's embroidered tent, so I could only approach it disguised in a veil. I knew how close to disaster my meeting with Zaza had been; something like that must under no circumstances happen again. Put helped me look. He fossicked through the wood shavings, feeling blindly for something solid amongst the sawdust.

Before long, a guard appeared. The man pointed at the small pieces of timber I was holding under my dress. "Put it back," he said, and at the same moment Put screamed. An abrupt movement had forced splinters into the skin between his thumb and forefinger. I dropped my booty, took Put's hand, and saw at least five slivers of wood, their tips black, deep under his skin. He would not let me touch them. Before I could do anything about it, he ran from the waste pile toward the tent with the embroidered panels.

As if he had called her, Neelata appeared in the entrance to the tent. Fast as lightning, I dived for cover. I hid behind a piece of fence that was protecting corncobs from the sun. I had not been so close to her since we fled to our terrace, not even when I hid in the shrubs to spy on Ham. I wanted to see what was going to happen, but I also quickly looked for escape routes, figuring what the chances were of being seen. Neelata immediately came toward Put. He threw himself amongst the folds of her robe, digging under her gown with one hand until he found her hips and pressed himself against her, holding his other hand away from his body as if it did not belong to him. His blood stained their clothes. She laid her hand on his arm and bent over him.

She had important things to do: in and around her tent lay scales, mortars, pestles, sets of weights, all of which had to be carefully packed and taken into the ark. But she squatted and removed the splinters one by one. I did not know then that she kept his milk teeth in a pouch around her neck.

For many weeks, Put had been living with us on the cliff, supposedly isolated from the life in the shipyard, but it was obvious from their behavior that they saw each other regularly. She bandaged his hand and kissed his hair. He stood leaning against her. After a while, he no longer cried from pain — the splinters lay in one of the mortars like trophies — but I think because of what she said. She obviously had said nothing that could comfort him. It could not be otherwise: She was not given to lying, and comfort there was none. She said, "Timber you can no longer obtain. That time is gone. The Builder needs it, every spline is going to count."

I am not sure what happened next. Put said something, and Neelata looked in my direction. She saw me, let go of Put, and came toward me, her robes rustling. I jumped up and started running. But her legs were much longer than mine. She was used to walking in those clothes, I still kept stumbling over the skirts. She grabbed me, pulled me down to the ground, and gasped, "I knew you were nearby. If Put was here, you couldn't be far away." She was lying on top of me. Her breath brushed my face. I could not help seeing that her body showed the imprint of serrated fingernails, she had scratches on her neck and on her face. I turned my face away from her.

"You must not bear us ill will," she said. "We've done our best to save you."

I groaned and put my elbow against her shoulder. Grit in my mouth made speaking difficult as I said, "You have taken my place in Ham's heart. And hence my place on the ship."

Pushing my elbow away, she bent toward me. She pressed her mouth against my ear and whispered, "He has chosen me to be his wife because he cannot resist my uncle's terms. Your reproaches concern him, not me."

She loosened her grip. She must have thought I would not run away, but I did, and fast, and because she had to get up on those long legs of hers, I got away.

"Come back," she said. "We need you."

I jumped from stone to stone. "Come to the wedding! Come back to us!"

I ran up the hill like a hare. I did not wait for Put. I hurled myself into the brushwood far from any trodden path, so that when I arrived at the top, my legs were red from the lashing grass, the thorns, and the poisonous plants.

30

Neelata and Ham's Wedding

We hid our house with big bundles of branches and swept our fireplace. We were on our guard for any approaching footsteps. Neelata was searching for us. We saw her walking up and down the slope. It was unavoidable that she would find us. Put, sick from the tension, led her into our field on the day of her wedding. My father was busy some way farther amongst the mulberry trees. I saw them coming, Neelata in a wide dress, Put chewing on a cake, both out of breath from the steep climb. I rolled into the brushwood. He took Neelata across the field to our truss-boat. She was made up for the day's festivities, her hair invisible beneath a sheaf of feathers, her breast richly covered in clinking beads. Here everything was on display for her: The timber we'd stolen, the pitch we'd stolen, the nails we'd extorted, and the tools. Here she found the things Ham had missed. Put turned and quickly walked down the slope again. He came right past my hiding place, sobbing fit to break one's heart.

Neelata walked around and around the boat. She looked for the most trodden path and found it. It led to our house. She cautiously crossed the field and approached the stack of branches. She walked calmly, like a cow swaying to its drinking place, looking around watchfully as if she could feel me looking at her. The sun lit up her feather headdress. Like Put, she walked right past me. I stayed motionless, rigid like the stones pressing into my arms and legs.

She reached the pile of branches that covered our house. She walked around it until she found the door, threw the bundles that covered it aside, and entered.

That was the moment I had waited for to get up and approach. Soundlessly, I walked to the back of the house. There I could hear everything. Not very clearly, but I could hear how she spoke to my mother, who was lying on her stretcher. She talked about the small yard at the other end of the field and the truss-boat that was being built there. I could imagine what my mother was thinking: that the sky was falling down on her a second time, that paralysis was being added to paralysis, that unfairness would triumph. I stumbled around in the brushwood, climbing over the branches as fast as I could, the dry leaves rustling, you would have had to be deaf not to hear me coming. Headlong I walked through the doorway, feeling like a dog that responds to a whistle because that is what it has been trained to do, not because it wants to.

"Greetings," Neelata said sweetly when she saw me. She was sitting on the floor next to the lamp that was burning for my mother. My mother lay in her arms, her head hanging. Immediately after I entered, her eye turned to me. Neelata was not holding her properly, supporting her too low in the back.

"Why don't you tell this poor woman anything? Why do you treat her like a child?" she asked calmly.

"We tell her . . . we know . . . what is there to know?" My

tongue faltered, my mouth was dry as cork. I knew it: Every word from my mouth was a slap in the face of my poor, lame mother. Anything I said produced another lie, and so did anything I did not say. Our eyes turned to each other and away again in a rapid series of movements.

Neelata pretended not to notice what was happening between us. "You are building a boat, and this woman knows nothing." She threw my mother's head upward to change the pressure on her arm. My stomach moved in the same manner, and my mouth was filled with a taste I did not recognize.

"You don't understand," I replied, my lips feeling like leather. "This is not a boat. How could my father have advised you about size and proportions if he had not first designed the ship to scale?"

"What I saw is not a scale model. It is a truss-boat, with a roof. It is built from beautiful, sound planks. Enough timber, maybe, to complete the Builder's ship."

My eyes had not yet adapted to the darkness sufficiently to distinguish her expression. I mainly saw the feathers moving around her head.

"I have talked to her," she continued. "I have asked her where your good water comes from."

My mother no longer bothered trying to look at me, her eye was like a pearl sewn onto her face.

"Did she tell you?" I asked.

"I think so," Neelata answered. "But I can't yet understand her properly. It takes a little getting used to a woman who talks with her eyelid. But I suspect we have come to an agreement." She put my mother carefully but clumsily into my arms. "Here, you do it. Show her your boat and tell her what is going to happen. You are her daughter, not me." She walked out of the door, feathers flying from her hair.

With my arms far too low on my mother's back, I sat motionless. Her head hung so far back that the ends of her hair touched the ground. Her breathing was speeding up, she swallowed fitfully, and in her agitation she managed to make her vocal cords pop. But I looked straight ahead and thought: *Just say it. Just ask what you want to know and do not get all worked up.*

Of course, she became heavy after a while. This was not a good position, for me or for her, my back and shoulders were aching. I held her until my father returned with bags full of mulberry leaves, and spitting with indignation, he shouted, "Why are you holding her like that?" and took her from me.

I went to watch the wedding. I wanted to see slender Neelata standing beside gentle, sensitive, torn Ham. I made a headdress of feathers, not because I liked that, but so as not to be conspicuous. I put color on my face and drew lines around my eyes to make myself unrecognizable. I took nuts to lay on the table. I was not alone. Hundreds of people were gathering in the yard. The rich came with gifts for the Builder, contributions to an enterprise so grand it made them dream. Never have I seen so much food, so many plates and beakers at a feast. Things were broken, but nobody uttered an upset cry, everything was instantly replaced by something new.

Neelata was wearing her ordinary dress, the same one she

had worn when she came to our hiding place. She relied on her beauty and knew that a robe of expensive material would contribute nothing to it. Ham wore a cloak almost as white as the flesh of that nut with the hard, hairy shell. He had more of a beard than when I had last rubbed him with oil, and his Adam's apple stood out more sharply under his skin. I could see someone had made an attempt at washing him for the occasion; he had a rash in spots where they had been too vigorous. The warriors, carrying their daggers, helped him stack rocks into a column. It became a grand, impressive structure, in line with the columns Japheth and Shem had erected when they married. It was said that he had widened his quarters in the tent and lengthened the ropes. He had spread out the carpets from his largest sanctuary to receive his wife. That is how he looked when I saw him in the place where the ceremony was to take place, standing next to his stack of rocks, devoted but covered in spots, his hair combed flat against his head and wearing brand-new, tight-fitting clothes, the seams obviously chafing his skin. I looked at him from a distance, and could only think about how, in the darkness of his tent, he would undo his girdle and instruct me to sit astride him.

Neelata's uncle was there, his wrists heavy with bracelets. He took no part in the masquerade and did not wear festive clothes, but he did dance. He had brought the wine that was poured. To the side, there were many, many vats, whose contents the servants transferred, quickly and without spilling any, into jugs.

I drank as much as I could get hold of. I was planning to sneak into the women's quarters very late and spend the night there, close to the revelers, but before I had a chance to do so, I bumped into people I knew, Put first of all. He had been dressed up by Neelata and his face was sticky with figs. He carried a bowl that was far too full for him. I grabbed him by the collar and dragged him behind the shrubs with me.

He started sobbing when he recognized me under the feathers. "I'm sorry," he kept repeating. "She is so nice. She is so lovely. She gives me bread and honey, no one else does."

"What more did she give you? What has she promised you to betray us?"

"Nothing, nothing at all," he continued crying, but his glance kept darting about so he did not have to look at me. A false light shimmered around him; it came from the torches standing here and there on sticks pushed into the ground, which threw moving shadows. He took a deep breath before saying, "The dwarf came to see her. If she does not seal this marriage with good water, he will raise suspicions about her. He will tell the Builder that her heart does not go out to Ham, and she will have to return home with her uncle." His forehead was no longer smooth, the way I had known it. There was a frown there that I had never observed before and that softened my feelings.

"But you betrayed us, Put."

"I wanted you to help Neelata. And she you, for you were unhappy there on the cliff, I could see it."

Revelers stumbled around us, some standing up, some rolling on the ground. Their noise scared Put even more. I moved so I was between him and the rowdies, which calmed him down a bit. I did not have to talk to him for long to see how sincerely sorry he was. He sat smearing his millet porridge around his bowl without eating any. He resembled Alem, the way he looked up, the same lack of understanding of what was happening showed on his face. I wanted to take him with me, far away from those others who confused him with their own interests. But before I could say anything, a large hand grabbed me by the neck. I did not need much light to see that it was my father, even though he too was covered in feathers. He dragged me along, which gave Put the chance to slip away.

"I've been looking for you half the night. I can't leave your mother alone any more, she actually screams if I leave. What's happened to upset her like that?"

Amongst the bushes stood the stretcher with my mother. She was lying in such a tensed-up position you could almost believe the strength in her muscles had returned.

"That wasn't my doing, but Neelata's, with tales about a truss-boat," I said. "I told her the boat is a scale model, but she won't believe me!"

My father sighed. He looked over his shoulder at the merry-makers farther along, his eyes half closed as if what he saw blinded him. Then he let the air out of his lungs again in a series of long, despairing sighs. He understood, of course, what had happened: The truss-boat, our secret, had been betrayed to my mother by Neelata. Now the talking would begin, the nagging and the soothing. He said, "Take up the stretcher and come home. You don't belong here. You wanted to get away from these people, so don't go and drink their wine now."

I went with him, out of fear for his voice, the noise he was making and the chance that someone would recognize him with that stretcher by his feet. The trip back gave him the opportunity to walk ahead of my mother, with his back to her, and think about what he would say to her, later, in the quiet of the house on the cliff.

As we escaped from the festivities we witnessed something that was not meant for our eyes. From one of the sheds, servants were carrying bowls and bamboo stands. In the open plain behind the hills, the bowls were put into the stands. Dozens of them were there already, and hundreds more lay on the path, waiting to be put up. Servants walked back and forth with torches, carrying out their task quickly and silently. We thought of a sacrifice, but then saw that, except for some dust and grit, the bowls were empty. "What is this for?" we asked the servants, who, with their flapping clothes, looked like bats.

"Orders from the dwarf. Now that Ham has a wife, the rain will come," they replied. "The first rain will be for drinking, the rest for drowning."

At this rather nasty reply, my mother opened her eye wide. Her eyeball glittered, and not just because the light of the servants' torches was reflected in it.

My father tugged roughly at the stretcher. Without him having to utter a word, I understood how fast we had to get away from there.

31

The Betrayal of the Spring

We told my mother that what the Builder was waiting for was not just ordinary rain, but a different kind, coming from much farther away, and not sent by the gods we were familiar with. Ordinary rain came to make the soil fertile, to keep the boats afloat and allow fish to spawn, but the purpose of this rain was to cleanse. It would wash the dust off our bodies, refresh the grasses, and return all things to their original colors! We had been told of green fields, of forests even. A new world would arise from it, containing only righteous people.

After our explanations, she half closed her eye but did not go to sleep. I slept because of the wine I had been drinking. My father slept out of sheer exhaustion after listening for hours to my mother's agitation. And so we did not notice that, in the middle of the night, she was lifted from her stretcher and silently carried outside. I was just vaguely aware of hoofbeats. The feeling that someone came into our house, with clothes rustling, and took my mother became a seamless part of a dream. I had to stretch my hand toward her sleeping place to believe that she was gone.

Instinctively, I went to the field where the truss-boat was. That is where I found her. She was lying on the ground, and Neelata, the newlywed, was bending over her. Neelata was still wearing her festive beads but was barefoot, having left her husband's quarters just like that. Not far from her, with a jug hanging on each flank, stood her black horse, its eyes glittering, its tail up, its mane raised like a banner. In the windblown landscape she and her mount moved so effortlessly it was as if they had come specially to show up their difference from us, from my mother in particular, from that limp body with its uselessly blinking eyelid. I heard her talking to my mother, softly asking her things. In the early morning light I could see that what she had in her hand was a divining rod.

"Her language is very simple," Neelata said when I approached. "We understand each other like mother and daughter. Why don't you sit down?"

I did not sit down, I remained standing in the one spot where, as it turned out, all the ants wanted to be too.

Neelata held the divining rod and pointed it ahead. Taken aback, I realized it was my mother's.

"What are you doing?" I asked.

She lowered her arms. "This thing doesn't do anything," she said. "I wish I knew how to handle it. You know where to find water, but what use is it to you, it hasn't earned you a place on the ark. Such a pity, because you really love Ham."

"The divining rod is my mother's. Tie it back onto her girdle. Don't abuse her helplessness."

As if she had not heard, she said, "Ham doesn't know you're still here. I'll tell him. I want you to receive him every evening. Sit across him the way he likes. Make his hair shine again. Make his eyes brighten and don't hide yourself from him."

"What are you up to, Neelata? You could have taken my mother's divining rod from her inside the house. Why did you bring her outside, to this spot, and so furtively?"

It cannot have been very hard for my mother to see that what we were building was much more than a scale model. The sides had been nailed onto the stem and the stern with braces, and they had already been cut to the right width.

Neelata looked at the rod in her hand, not at me, as she said, "I told you we've come to an agreement. I have told her the world will be flooded. As thanks for my sincerity, she wants to tell me where the spring is."

I could not answer. I was trying to keep the ants off my legs.

She smiled amiably, almost like a friend, as she continued imperturbably, "Otherwise, how can I keep this lovely structure a secret, this little ship that will actually hold people? Where will I get the strength? And if it doesn't stay a secret, you and your family will drown with the rest."

I knew she was right. In fear-filled nights, I had imagined strong men claiming our boat in the hour of truth. What would we be able to do against people in fear of death, with nothing to lose?

I wanted to sleep. I wanted to go back to our little house and shut my eyes and forget what my mother had found out. In the marshes we had understood her fear, the nightmares she woke up from and her constant gasping. Now she knew we had kept the truth from her. From tonight on, that eye would again close not from sleepiness, but only from exhaustion. And we would have to reckon with her fury. Not that this fury was easy to see, it was seated in a remote spot, deep in her eye, just where her pupil dilated and contracted. I was already aware of her rage at that moment, from the way in which she dominated everything that would happen that early morning. It was she who led the conversation we were having in the field. In a sense, that was reassuring. It showed that the ducks had not taken away all of her will; she had enough left to make me speak for her. She looked at me, and when she shut her eye, it was as if she bolted it against me. Her eye did not tremble for even a moment, and she forced her will to its limit to make me say, "I'll show you where the water is."

Neelata smiled at me in a motherly way and said, "Very good!" She stood up and brought her horse closer. She wanted to lift up my mother to take her back to her stretcher in the house, but I said, "Leave her here. My father will find her when he wakes up. He must not think I have taken you to the spring of my own free will."

Small nocturnal animals scurried past, they had skinny little heads and short legs. If any eyes lit up at all in the gloaming, they were close to the ground, belonging to creatures intending no harm. We covered my mother's body with leaves.

I sighed as I mounted the horse. My despair became worse when Neelata sat up behind me, put her arms around my waist, and said, "It was hard for you to keep the origin of your good water a secret, I could see that, it tormented you every day. The thought that you were keeping something to yourself that belonged to all of us pained you, it made you stumble and spill the water. It brought tears to my eyes."

*   *   *

In the cave, bats from all over the world had nestled. Some had a wingspan many cubits wide, they were wider than vultures. Our arrival drove them, screeching, from their shelters. Neelata held on to me by my girdle when she followed me into the chill space with the high walls. I do not know if she realized they were skeletons, those hollow, angular objects she tripped over. We went through the funnel-like passageway that led to the next cave. We crossed all the spaces.

Neelata constantly trod on my heels. She was too scared to let go of my girdle, and I did nothing to reassure her. Finally we reached the fold in the rock and the narrow passage. We squeezed through to get to the last cave. There we heard the dripping of water.

The coolness of what awaited us came streaming toward us. Because I had drawn water only infrequently during the last few weeks, the basin had filled and overflowed. The whole cave was wet, the water trickled everywhere in rivulets.

"Here is what you are looking for," I said to Neelata, who was still holding on to my girdle. I turned to hand her the jug.

Did she step aside to give me more room? Did she overbalance when she took the jug from me? Possibly she simply hurried; she saw the sparkle of water and wanted to get to it. First I felt a tug on my girdle, then the groping of her arms. Then there was the sound of a scream and a dull thud. It came from deep down, from the well next to the stack of bones I had always warned Put about.

See what happens, I thought, *see what happens when you force me.* I had never been in the cave so early in the morning, and I had never experienced it so cold. I should have warned her. If I really had wanted to help her, I would have told her to bring a torch. Now she had fallen, into a well whose depth I did not know. For the first time since I had left my bed I became calm, and I called her name. "Neelata?" And again, "Neelata?"

What state was she in now, that beautiful, slender woman? It remained silent in the cave, so silent that the bats returned to their perches one by one. I kept trying to hear something, a groan or a breath, but there was nothing. With Gentan and his men, I had seen what a bad fall could do. Yet I kept calling her name. I could not believe she was no longer there, that her beauty had become useless, like a drowned dog's thick pelt.

It took a while before I began to see the possibilities her death might open up for me. I could become Ham's wife without arousing Neelata's uncle's anger.

I sat down. The skulls supported my back and my shoulders; it felt like sitting on a throne. As I slowly grew cold and hungry, I wondered what I should do. My head was full of plans, but also of feelings of guilt and fear for myself. Had I caused this, or did it just happen? I did not know how to answer that.

"I fell," I suddenly heard. The voice was coming from deep down and far away, as if it reached me from the realm of shadows. It was like the echo of words spoken in the past, or of a voice coming from me rather than from her. It would have been easy to pretend not to hear it, it could have been my imagination, the delusion of someone who is tired and disappointed. I heard her stumbling around. Her dress got her into difficulties. She tried to stand up, but there was water around her, or mud, and stones kept rolling about, probably because of her own movements. I heard her fall again and again.

I knew that the water she was standing in was cold, colder than any marsh I have ever been in. Thinking of it, I started shivering. I had been taken unawares by her arrival in the night and all I was wearing was a loincloth. It would have been better the other way around. Better if I had been wearing Neelata's dress, it would have kept me warm. And better if she had been wearing no clothes, it would have made it easier for her to drag herself out of the mud. But I did nothing to help her. I picked up something that lay close by my hand, a piece of rock, a pebble, a bone, I do not know which, dropped it into the well, and listened.

"You're hurting me," she shouted.

"I don't mean to," I shouted back. "There is nothing I can do for you. I'm sitting on a stack of bones. If I move, you'll get buried by them." My voice was so much lighter than hers. The air was so damp that my thirst had vanished without my drinking anything.

"I can't stand up," she said. "It hurts terribly. Don't throw anything. Don't throw anything, please." As if for an echo that does not come, she waited for me to suggest something. I threw no more skulls or stones, but neither did I help; to my own dismay I was not prepared to.

"Good," she said after a while, sounding bleak and shivery. "Leave me here. Take my place. Ham loves you, you love him, you two deserve each other." Her voice shook with fury, pain, or cold. I could no longer hear her stumbling about. Probably she found a way to keep her balance. And she didn't pant anymore, although she spoke rapidly and insistently; it seemed like her way of keeping up her courage.

This was the second time, she said, that she had stood among the elect but was not chosen. Not long ago, her mother had done the same thing to her.

Her story began incoherently. I thought a knock to the head might have confused her mind, but soon I understood what she was doing: She was pleading her case, she was explaining why she was being allowed onto the ark, she was making it clear why she had to become Ham's wife even though her heart did not go out to him.

32

Neelata's Story

*I*n the city where she lived, her family had incited the people against the ruler. The ruler burned with anger and imprisoned her father, her brothers, her uncle and nephews, her whole rebellious family, in order to kill them. The only exception was Neelata's mother, who was allowed to remain free so she could provide for the condemned. Every evening, when she brought the bowls of millet, she stood at the ruler's door to beg for mercy. She banged her head against the wood, pulled out her hair, tore her clothes, and loudly begged for her husband, her children, her brother, her brother's children.

One day the ruler felt compassion. He admired the endurance of the woman at his door, and her love too. Because of that, he stood up and went to meet her. He said, "One loved one you may choose, one prisoner I will release, the others will die."

After brief reflection, Neelata's mother said, "Let my brother go."

The ruler was amazed and said, "But I have your sons too, and your daughter. I have your husband. Why do you choose your brother?"

"I am still young and can find a new husband. If I have a new husband, I can have new sons and a new daughter with him. But

I cannot have a new brother, because both my parents have died." Thus Neelata's uncle was set free, a wealthy man with snow-white hair and chests full of gold. And because the woman amused the ruler, he set her daughter free too.

Neelata's mother was not pleased at her daughter's release. She feared her vengeance. She asked her wealthy brother to take her away, to marry her off to a man who would take her on a long journey. That was why Neelata's uncle had brought her to the Builder, to the man who would undertake the longest journey ever made. That is why he had brought the most beautiful and valuable presents; Neelata's mother and uncle came from a rich and powerful family.

Her story did not overwhelm me, I was not speechless. This was a story about people of ill will, those the Unnameable wished to destroy with his water. Yet I was silent. She said, "I know you are there. You are waiting for me to climb up so you can throw those horrible bones at me and bury me forever." I still said nothing. The cold air had affected my voice.

Her strength lasted a good long time; we were all well fed because of the abundance that prevailed despite everything. She said, "This is yet another way for you to prove your love to Ham. He will worship you even more. Do you know what he admires most in your people? That you are capable of killing. Your father killed Gentan. Ham could not do that. Nor can any Rrattika. Not because they are cowardly, but because they are obedient. Their obedience is completely straightforward, there are no exceptions for them." She was silent again for a long while. Her silence was full of pained anger, but it was drowned out by the question that echoed inside my head: *Did I not have a heart? Did I not know compassion?* After a time, she said, "Perhaps that is what disappoints the Unnameable most of all. Not people's wickedness, but their lack of understanding of what is wicked and what is good. People like you are needed to cut through knots."

Still I did nothing to help her. She repeated that she was in pain, but I paid no heed. Colder than the dampness around me I felt, but also strong and determined.

Her voice seemed to change. It lost its echo. It sounded so flat that the rocks no longer reflected it. She sounded hoarse when she said, "See that Put gets a place on the ark, do that much for me. I have sewn a camel-hair sack he fits into exactly. It is at the bottom of one of my chests, the large one with the olive pattern. The child will need help to get into it. The dromedary will have to be trained, the beast will have to get used to the weight and shape of his burden. It will take patience." Her words made me get up abruptly from my throne. I scrabbled upright and stood at the edge of the well.

"Why are you saving Put?" I asked, but the only reply I got was a weak "What?" that sounded far away. I repeated my question, but she did not reply. I knelt at the edge. I lay down, my body stretched out on the cold, wet ground. A few bones started rolling, some of them must have hit her, but she no longer screamed. I had resisted helping her for so long that her own body had provided deliverance.

The well was deep. I took all the skulls I could find and let them slip down the side. All the human parts within reach I threw down carefully. They hit the bottom with a splash. Stones I left alone, they were too sharp and heavy. When I could not find any more near the well, I looked for bones and skulls farther away. For a long time, I went back and forth. I kept fetching pieces until the bottom of the well had been raised enough for me to reach it with my legs. I stood on top of the skulls, some of which broke under my weight. I knelt and groped around amongst the bones until I found her warmth. First I found her hair, then her hand. I got her away from the bones I had buried her under with my own hands. It took all my strength to haul her body, she hung slack in my arms and did not react. And she was wet and slippery. I was damaging that beautiful, long body, but I could not avoid it: I could not possibly lift her, so I had to drag her. On my shoulder I pushed her up along the wall. A few times her head flopped down, but eventually I managed to push her over the edge. By her shoulders and arms I dragged her through the darkness, along the rough floor of the cave. I screamed with the exertion.

The daylight was merciless; it showed up contusions and abrasions as if they were adornments. Her ribs were bruised all around. I had nothing but sand and dust to dry her with. But my delight when she opened her eyes, her amazement at the clear light and dry air, dispelled the discomfort.

She said, "It was a burial place. You shouldn't go into a burial place." She wanted to get away from the opening in the rock wall, farther than we were, farther than where the horse waited.

"I can't go on walking," she said.

"I can't either," I replied. Numb with cold, we lay there, back to back, without moving, for every movement hurt.

When I felt a little better, I went to fetch water. The skulls I could reach I stacked up again; caring for the dead had been drummed into me.

I gave her water and we drank. I took the horse to a raised rock from where it could be mounted with the least discomfort. Then we let the animal carry us at a walking pace to my mother. She was no longer alone. Next to her sat Put who had found her even before my father woke up; he had fed her and changed her position.

After Neelata, her eye-glitter smeared over her cheeks, had fallen asleep next to my mother, and the three of us sat watching her, I said, "Her bones would not have been conspicuous amongst all those other ones. Did I do wrong not leaving her behind?" My mother looked at me quietly. And Put, the little darling, threw his arms around my legs and kissed my shins until I pushed him away.

Ham barely left a footprint in the dust when he came to get my father. We watched him climbing up the steep cliff to our field. He carried some milk cakes, baked black on the edges, the way he knew we liked them. He gave them to me without looking me in the eyes. He said, "You have saved my wife. I will thank you," and took my hand in his. His touch stung like a nettle. He had changed. His voice had become deeper and his movements firmer. He addressed my father, who was self-conscious with embarrassment at what he had done to himself: He had moved into a ramshackle house unworthy of a woodworker and still felt like a scarecrow in his Rrattika clothes. "I have a job for you," said Ham. "A task that can save your life."

I knew how much my father longed for the real work, for the big ship. So he did not resist. He threw off the stolen cloak, fitted his girdle with the loincloth around his hips, and went back to the shipyard. He greeted neither me nor my mother, he was still stunned by the fact that we had betrayed our spring without him having a say. He worked hard that day, he did not stop.

I walked to the vessel to see what kept him. All the workers were already having their meals in front of their tents, and there was no movement near the entrance. The greyhound dragged itself along the ground trying to get rid of an itch, and the matting across the gangplank was tied up. But inside the ark, the lonely sound of a hammer tapping could be heard.

33

The Niche

*A*t night, I would go to the silkworms' cage, where the wind rarely penetrated. Their cage stood on tall posts and was surrounded by a fence. If you sat down there, no one could see you apart from the caterpillars, but they were very much turned in on themselves. Ham waited there for me. I started by washing him and rubbing oil onto his skin. In the hollow amongst the bamboo, the caterpillars slowly chewing mulberry leaves above us, he asked me to sit astride him. His muscles had changed and his chest was covered in short hairs. We kissed, each in our own way: I with only a little hope, knowing the Builder had counted his passengers carefully and that, by exerting all my strength to rescue a woman twice my weight from a well, I had given my only chance back to the person it belonged to. But he kissed like a man who intends to kiss again tomorrow, and the day after tomorrow too. We lay looking up and gave names to the caterpillars above us. Some were spinning a cocoon and we encouraged them in their unceasing labor.

It got to the point where we became concerned about the silkworms' fate. We knew my father planned to boil the cocoons before they had a chance to leave them; under no circumstances could they be allowed to bite through the thread they had enveloped themselves in. A few would be chosen to stay alive, but only to lay their eggs and then die. We considered ways of escape for the moths. We contemplated removing the netting and setting them in the wind to speed up the drying of their wings. But of course we suspected that our interference would kill them anyway. They were vulnerable. My father handled the cocoons with a soft-bristled brush. Not long now, and he would start heating the water. Thus it was with most of us too; we would be destroyed to prevent us destroying ourselves. Our fate seemed linked with theirs: That was why we lived in fear that something would go wrong with them, and that one day they would all lie on the ground, shriveled up, because that would have to be an omen.

One day Ham and I would have to separate, I kept on reminding him of this. He insisted he was looking for a solution, but I could see his mind was on other things. I knew of his great longing for that new land, where everything would grow so fast you would be punished if you did not weed around your home in time. At the same time, he was concerned that knowledge would be lost: He wanted to relearn all the tunes he had learned as a child, he went to observe how people made clothes, how they constructed instruments. Whenever possible, he took examples to his tent to study them by the light of an oil lamp to make sure he understood everything and would remember in the new world. He wanted to learn which herbs were beneficial and which not; he knew about dried leaves you could smoke, but could he distinguish the real ones from the ones that would only stink? There were people who baked ceramics in colors, who made objects in copper, silver, and gold — where could he find those metals and which particular blends were most malleable? And the positions of the stars, reading the time, understanding the omens, predicting the weather, counting the days and years, there was so much he had to master before he could leave. Although his god had made no mention of insects, he wanted to obtain seven silkworms from my father, and the knowledge needed to keep them alive.

One morning, when we got up, the tents were shiny. Everything seemed to have changed color. The sand looked darker than usual and the dust was not flying about. No one had seen rain, yet it was clear to all that during the night a haze of moisture had come down on the shipyard. Put went outside and looked at all the pots and jugs he could find. None contained water, but everything felt wet.

Neelata proudly left her tent. She was still covered in bruises and walked stiffly because, under her clothes, she was in splints, but she no longer hid behind the embroidered panels. She ran her hand over the canvas of the tents and gauged the depth of the pond. Since her fall, she had sent me a basket full of eggs every day. As soon as the moistness was in the air, she came herself. She said, "I've been looking for the water too far afield. It is close by." She kissed me and gave me bread. "We are working at a solution. You saved my life. I shall save yours." Supported by her maids, she returned to the shipyard.

My father no longer worked on the truss-boat. He radiated a quiet that confused me. He told my mother in detail about his little boat, saying he would stop building it if that was what she wanted, but she showed little interest in this. What she did want to know was why he worked in the ark at the end of the day when all the workers returned home. He said, "For as long as we have been together, I have kept things from you. It was never out of malice. Now do not bear malice yourself and do not ask me questions." She kept blinking her eye, and he sat with his back turned to her until she stopped. All this time he continued weeding his seedlings. He watered them from the pond as if he had no idea what was about to happen. And he still dug the stones out of the ground.

My father's calm had an unexpected effect on Put. He begged him to continue work on the truss-boat in the field, but could not sway the man who stayed away all night and spent the day in his hammock, dead tired. Put tried to do it by himself, hammering nails into the wrong spots and hurting himself. He hurled stones around, he ripped just about every leaf from the tree that was supposed to give us shade. He behaved like a cornered animal, he barely slept anymore, he kept walking around us as if he could avert disaster by staying close to us. Our presence would stop the rolling rocks that were going to squash him, our weight would keep him on the ground when the whirlwind came.

Once, toward midday, he vomited up his food, small, thoroughly chewed pieces of fruit he had consumed that morning, frugally because they were the first of the season, from a remote bush. I terrified him by dragging him into the shrubs and saying, "Shall I tell my father how you gave away our secret?"

He pulled hair out of his head and used it to build nests like a bird. He slept underneath our hammocks, in the spot where, at home in the marshes, the dogs would lie. In his sleep, he scratched shreds of wood from the boards.

Because he was a child, his despair was unbearable. His small talent for wordlessly asking questions, his ability to make an undeserved sorrow visible on his face, drove my father to say, "Child, stop screaming like that. Do not make it hard for me. Do not force me to tell what I must keep secret."

Put sat up on his mat, I moved closer. "What is it?" we asked. "What is it you can't tell us?" My mother was in the corner of the room, she could hear his every word.

"Ham has made me carry out a job on the ship. I have made something I have never made before. Something I have never before thought about. He made me build a niche in the wall of the ship, a space with an invisible entry, a hiding place. It is a big secret, he does not inform his brothers. He is sinning against his father's will."

"What is the purpose of this hiding place?"

"The space is large enough to hide a person. Possibly enough for a couple of people."

"For us?" I asked softly.

"Who knows?" my father said and fell silent.

The color drained from Put's face at this revelation. He left his sleeping place, the spot pervaded by the scent of his body, the sweat from his overwhelming impotence, and ran from the house, screaming that he was not my parents' child, that we would leave him behind and forget him, and that he could not swim. I went after him. He ran along the field, farther up the cliffside. He ran so fast and so heedlessly that stones he dislodged hit my head, forcing me to shout to make him stop and wait for me. He was still panting when I reached him. I pushed him onto the ground, he sat down with the slope at his back. The child who was always the first to notice if I needed something no longer wanted to be with me; it made me very sad, it was as if he was hurling stones at me.

"I don't want to go in Neelata's camel sack, I want to stay with all of you," he sobbed. As I could not see any other solution, I told him the story of my little brother. I told him that, when my mother fell over into her boat never to get up again, I had not been the only one by the side of the water. Next to me lay my brother, a baby in a basket. After I heard her fall and saw her disappear into the boat, I had gone to her, even though I could not swim. I had struggled through the water, head under, no bottom under my feet, till I felt the edge of the boat. I had climbed into the boat where she lay motionless amongst the fish, whose thrashing about had got themselves hopelessly tangled in her hair. My mother had not offered me her breast. She did not sit up straight to make it easier for me. I had done it all by myself. When I had drunk my fill of her milk, we listened together to the steadily weakening crying of my little brother. I told her she should go and get him, that the sun was climbing and the water rising, but she only blinked her eye.

"It is not going to happen to us a second time," I told Put. "Now it's you who is our little boy; we will not leave you behind by the water's edge."

*　　*　　*

I asked Ham, "Whom is the niche for that you've made my father build?"

He replied, "For you."

"I will not come if that is the way it is."

"There is room for your father too."

"And my mother?"

He looked away. We were sitting under the caterpillar cage. He had a strange expression around his mouth, he seemed to be full of pride because he was disregarding his father's will. I knew what he was going to say next.

"Your mother is lame. My sin against the will of the Unnameable is already twofold. If I take her, it would be threefold. I'm doing my best, Re Jana. I'm trying everything I can think of."

"And Put?" I asked. Not that I had any voice. Something in my throat had shifted, and it sounded as if I were whispering.

"There is a separate solution for him. He will be taken care of."

I stood up and turned my back to him. I went inside our house. Put was there. He sat between my father and my mother, his legs pulled up, his hand touching my mother and his back leaning against my father. I did not tell any of them what I had learned.

Put's Blunder

*E*very morning the tents were wetter than before. Every jug, every bowl that had been left outside had water in it. The story of how I had saved Neelata spread. I was allowed to return to work in the red tent. I no longer wore a cloak, but neither did I wear the shell tunic in which I had disguised myself. Put was with me to carry the jugs. Shem, Japheth, and Ham admitted us without a word, were startled by my nakedness, and hurriedly closed the tent curtain. I took care of them the way I used to. Put helped me. He was in high spirits. He was enthusiastically rubbing oil into Japheth's buttocks and thighs, spilling an unnecessary amount. I pointed it out to him, but that did not help, he was nervous and excited, unable to control the flow.

When the dwarf came out of the Builder's quarters, Put and I tried to carry on as unobtrusively as possible. A smell of fermenting fruit hung about him, and for a moment it looked as if the wine had clouded his vision so much he would walk past us. But he recognized me. As he went by, he whispered with a sweaty smirk, "Hey, you! What's happened to your disguise? Have you had your beating yet?"

Put stood between us and could not restrain himself. The first secret, the spring in the cave, he had been able to keep.

The second, our hiding place on the side of the cliff, he had given away out of friendship for Neelata. This secret was altogether too big. He was confused, not able to order his thoughts and see the larger picture. He turned to the dwarf and said in the same whispery tone, "We are not going to drown. There is a hidey-hole, that's where we're going to be!"

At his words, I felt the same relief he must have felt: At last a response the hairy dwarf could not counter, at last he was reduced to silence. That triumphant feeling did not last long; everything around us had suddenly become immobilized. Not a canvas, not a tent pole moved.

"What did you say?" asked Japheth.

"A hidey-hole," Put answered weakly. He had twisted the cloth in his hand so tightly around his finger that its tip turned white.

"And who has built that hidey-hole?" Put could not utter a word. Japheth had to repeat his question, and then once more, his teeth clenched.

"The man who knows how to build boats," said Put. The dwarf fled outside, leaving a smell of wine behind him, his head down between his shoulders. Ham sat there, rigid as stone. Japheth got up. "Is that so?" he asked me. I bent my head. He started dressing, laughing, he seemed strangely excited. It took a long time to get his clothes right.

Shem too got up and dressed. His clothes were more elaborate than his brother's. His girdle consisted of a number of thin strands linked together with pearls. As if he wanted to demonstrate how it is done, he was ready in a flash. He went out without waiting for his brother. Japheth went after him, his skirts undone.

Ham stayed behind in the tent, a gray, gleaming shadow. The curtain had barely stopped moving when he burst into a coughing fit. Spit flew about in flakes. Put and I sat near him, thinking of my father and his sketches. We knew exactly what would happen. They would find him in his hammock. Seeing the sawdust in his eyelashes, they would blow insolently in his face and order him to get up. He would inform them, this man who had exhausted himself, who had done exactly what was expected of him and who knew that now he would pay the price for it.

"He will not betray you," I said to Ham. I put my hands flat on his skin to rub his shoulders. That seemed to be all I was capable of doing: to let his skin slide under my hands to make sure he stayed there.

"I know," he whispered. He moved with me. If I pressed, he yielded, but I was not sure that he knew it was me touching him.

Shem and Japheth did not stay away long. They were talking loudly and excitedly when they came back. "Cleverly done, what an economical way to use a double wall," they said. "But what did you have in mind, brother?" My father was not with them. Possibly, he was already lying bent double at the foot of my mother's stretcher. Possibly, he had destroyed his sketches and broken his measuring stick.

"I don't know what you're talking about."

"Exactly, yes, that's what that boat builder said too. He insists you know nothing about this, that he acted on his own. He claims he sneaked into the ship at night. Do we believe that? Can we believe that, brother?" Japheth laughed with a snort at Shem and then looked fixedly at Ham again. "And all that against Father's will. Against the Unnameable's command." Shem's manner was full of false indignation. A thin smile played around his mouth. He did not speak loudly when he said, "You are game, true enough."

Japheth hooked his fingers in the braids of his beard. His manner too was agitated. Keeping an eye on the curtain of the Builder's quarters, he leaned toward Ham and asked, "Tell us, Ham. That man is covering for you, you can be pleased with him. But we just want to know the truth. Who was that hiding place for? Who were you going to take?"

Ham saw that his brothers were not at all angry. They were curious. The idea of the niche appealed to them. He sat on the edge of his chair and looked them in the face. He fiddled with the cloth I had used to dry him, running the seam carefully between his thumb and forefinger. He was not aware of doing it, his thoughts were concentrated on his words. "What will we have for diversion? What will our entertainment be? We will not be allowed to go where our wives sleep. We will be bored to death."

"That is so," said Shem. "The days will be long."

"It would be good to have someone with us who can make us forget the time."

"What are you getting at, brother?"

"An ox would be able to guess who I had in mind," said Ham.

I am sure they all looked at me. I lowered my eyes. That did not prevent me seeing how Japheth involuntarily stroked his hair. He dug around in his thatch with his fingers. Shem took a long, loud breath. I bent over Ham's feet as if they were the only thing I was concerned about.

"The dwarf," said Ham.

I went through my knees. The ground felt like mud or water. It was the way it used to be when we were crossing the marshes. If a heavily loaded boat struck rough water, we jumped overboard. We swam until the wind dropped. It was a cold, scary action we learned at an early age. That was how it seemed when Ham named the dwarf: as if a wind had sprung up that could sink our cargo.

"The dwarf," Shem repeated thoughtfully. His gaze still rested on me and moved away when I looked back. I rubbed oil into Ham's legs.

Ham let me go on and continued, "Father can't do without him, even though he claims the opposite. Once we have properly taken off, we produce him. If it then turns out this does not please the Unnameable and He commands us to throw the dwarf overboard, we can still do that. The presence of a stowaway on board won't be Father's fault, but ours, and that will calm the Unnameable. We are only young, we make mistakes."

Shem and Japheth nodded. I hung on to Ham's leg. His skin and muscles were taut.

"Let's go and get him," said Ham. He looked at his brothers.

Japheth slipped his cloak off his shoulder, as if the heat in the tent had become too much for him. He laboriously wiped his neck. "But the child said . . ." he said, indicating Put.

"The child said what I'd made him believe," Ham said dryly.

I saw Put look at me as if for him too the ground was shifting under his feet.

"Shall we?" Ham asked when he got no reply. He waited, giving his brothers a last chance to object. But Japheth seemed unable to move. Shem blinked like someone who sees things around him go up in flames. He did come out with a brief "Yes, yes, yes," not expressing agreement, only a request for more time to think. Then he raised his hand. "Can't someone else . . . ?" he muttered almost inaudibly. "The dwarf is difficult company, why not someone nice and quiet rather than that show-off? Someone who is of use to the three of us, who takes care of us for instance, who bathes and grooms us?"

But Ham was striding through the tent. "Do you mean Re Jana, the girl who bathes us? That is impossible. The dwarf knows about the niche, the child has given its existence away. Now we have no choice." He pulled the curtain aside and called the dwarf who was sitting on the ground a short distance away. When he heard Ham calling him, he wrenched himself around as if he had been hit in the back by a stone. He jumped up and entered the tent with a theatrical bow. "You can come," said Ham. "The niche is for you, of course you can come."

The short, dark man straightened. His flamboyance left him, and he looked unsure of himself. His arms were long in proportion to his legs. He was bony and unattractive. He looked from one to the other. "Has not the god of the Builder said 'Only his'?" he asked carefully.

"That is correct," Ham continued. "But you know the other conditions. The animals can come. One pair of each kind, seven of the clean ones. We're not quite sure yet how this works with the different kinds of apes, there are so many of them, but we think your kind is admitted."

The dwarf seemed to shrink, his shoulders dropped, his pelvis tilted, making him look even shorter. His face too seemed to wither, his skin to shrivel up. Was he sighing with relief, or did something else make him gasp? He went out and disappeared into the sunlight.

No one in the red tent really laughed, the laughter died in their throats before it could reach their faces. All three sat down, crestfallen. Shem rested his elbows on his knees, Japheth leaned back as if thoroughly exhausted by what had happened. "Why are you doing this?" he asked.

Ham sat on the edge of his seat with a grimace the like of which I had never witnessed before. It was a smile frozen on his face, but his eyes trembled in their sockets.

"I don't know, I couldn't think of anything better. All I could think was: How can I stop him going into Father's quarters and telling what the child has said? I thought this was a way. . . . But this is not good. This will end badly. Let's go to the crevice."

I was wringing my sponge so hard it tore. I could not believe that because of a couple of thoughtless words from the wanderers' child, our death warrants had been signed. I could not believe that a joke on Ham's part had made Put's indiscretion irreparable. I should have run to the field on the slope to urge my father to work very hard and very fast to complete our truss-boat. But I did not. I continued the grooming until the brothers felt clean enough to go to the oracle in the crevice and, unsteady with nervousness, preceded us outside.

35

The Builder's Curse

We were requested to accompany them to the crevice where the oracle lived. Behind the request was an order, of course, they did not need to spell that out for us. The men were clean, their hair was shiny, and they brought the wholesome scent of Klamath into the crevice, but the path was dusty and so steep you needed to use your hands to manage it. Put and I carried flagons and poured water for them whenever necessary. My thoughts were with my father, I peered around hoping I might see his shape. I splashed water on their clothes and on my legs. They dried their hands on the cloak they had thrown over my shoulders for the trip. I carried a comb and a set of brushes.

Put stumbled. "We've lost our niche. We're going to die," he whispered. "But will we reach the realm of the dead? If that unnameable god wipes us out, will he not do it totally? Does he not wipe out even our spirit and our thoughts?"

"He will not wipe you out. He will let your spirit wander about for all eternity as punishment for your careless talk."

"Do you think so? Will I wander about forever?" His thin face looked scared.

"Of course not," I said quickly. "You're not bad. You're just dumb, that will save you."

"If I must wander about, I want to be with you. How will I find you in the realm? Will you look the same as you do now?"

I turned my back on him. His ignorance made me see red. Small as he was, his despair was no less than mine.

The Builder's sons had brought gifts. They were offerings to the gods their father neglected. For the priestess, they had a basket of fruit, picked, as usual, far too early. It was not their first visit to her, that was obvious from the practiced way they sat on the floor in the right posture. The priestess spread a handful of stones on the ground and said, "The water has not changed its course. It still comes this way. As ever, your father will prove to have been right." From the bowl that stood by her side, she took some bones, the vertebrae and ribs of a small animal, and threw them down in front of her. "I see the proof of his wisdom and understanding: I see a blessing and a curse," she said, bending forward. In her sanctum, she sat out of the wind, but our clothes flapped in a draft. "Your father will not treat you equally," she continued. She raised her eyes. She looked at each of the brothers in turn. "He will pronounce a curse."

I saw Ham's face turning ashen. Drops of sweat appeared on his neck and his temples.

With a slow gesture, the oracle gathered up the bones. She dropped them one by one into the bowl. She erased the traces in the sand and rearranged her sleeves. "That is all. I can tell you no more," she said.

Shem was shivering in his clothes. "I have let a woman wash me," he said haltingly. "He will surely curse me."

"No," said Japheth, his mouth twisted. "It will be me. I had thought of hiding Re Jana in Ham's niche. He will surely curse me."

Ham knew, of course, that he was the one who had committed the real sin. He had given my father the tools, the timber, and the order. His shoulders drooped. The sky was full of seagulls, we did not know where they had come from. They screamed like children and skimmed over our heads as if they expected the bones in the bowl to change into bread crusts.

My father was nowhere to be seen. We scanned the horizon and searched for him behind the bushes and around the small ponds. I asked Put to go south and went north myself. I had barely got as far as the almond trees when loud screams resounded from the hills. It sounded like the wailing of a shepherd who sees his whole herd disappear into a ravine. I was not the only one to hear it. In the distance, I saw dozens of people going up the slope toward the sound. I saw Shem, Ham, and Japheth not far from the sheds with the sacks and baskets. They ran like boys, the skirts of their cloaks flapping around their legs.

I hurried up the slope. It took some time before I could see what they were looking at so curiously, or what they were uttering their horror about. But as I got closer, it became clear that they were looking at a tree, a low olive tree in which hung a body.

My feet caught on the stones. I was stumbling rather than making headway. Inside me raged the ugliest premonition since the mallard ducks had risen above my mother's limp body. But I kept walking, and as I came closer, I was reassured. The body in the tree was small and dark. It was the dwarf. He had hanged himself, that grubby old joker who pretended he knew no distress.

Shem was shouting at Ham, "Did you have to humiliate him like that? Was that necessary?"

They took down the body and lifted it onto their shoulders after removing the rope. It was not heavy. Shem insisted on carrying it by himself. He made the descent carefully as if he were afraid of hurting it.

They took the dead dwarf to their father. The Builder was in the front part of the tent, bent over the spots my oil had left on one of the carpets. When his sons came in he looked up, rubbed the oil spot some more with his fingernail, and said, "He has freed himself of his earthly body. It does not surprise me at all. He was a messenger." Then he withdrew into his private quarters.

I made a mixture that would remove the oil stains from the carpet, but when I was about to enter his quarters, I was touched by what I saw: His wife, Zaza, was with him, and the Builder lay limp across her legs, breathing heavily. Zaza had her white hand on his back, tapping it with a gentle rhythm. His whole fragile body shook. I feared for the porous ribs and the thin skin around them. "Shem," he sobbed. "Japheth. Ham." Then it became clear to me. The dwarf had not gone without taking revenge. He had told the Builder about his sons' blasphemous plan. I left, because I could not bear seeing an old man lying with his head almost touching the ground.

*　　*　　*

When I passed Neelata's embroidered tent, one of her maids beckoned me. I bent under the curtain and went in. The tent was so low you could not stand up in it. Neelata was sitting on a cushion on the floor and the maids sat with their backs against the side of the tent. Put sat in a corner, looking like a prince in a beautiful woolen mantle, made to his size.

Neelata gestured for me to sit down. A few lamps burned, but none of them shone on her face. The whites of her eyes showed how fast her glance was moving over my face.

"Put has told them about the niche," I said.

"I know," she said. There was no reproach in her voice, any more than there had been in mine. We were both filled with understanding for the child, who was playing with the seams in the canvas of the tent, running his finger along them as if they were long paths that should be traversed. He fiddled with the edges of the tent's opening and with the cords that held back the curtain. He was attentive, but had no understanding of the situation he was in.

"And Ham piles mistake on mistake."

"That is true," she said.

I knew Ham was there, because I could smell him. He sat behind the cane partition at the back of the tent, trying for all he was worth to stop wheezing.

"Everything is lost," I said. "My hope is dead, my courage gone." I was not exaggerating. My father's silk moths seemed to have nestled in my head, there was such a nervous beating of wings behind my eardrums.

Neelata shook her head. "You still have the truss-boat. I have not given its existence away." She nodded at one of her maids. She always managed to place her lamps so that her tent seemed like a palace. From a far corner, the heavily made-up servant handed me a small pouch of herbs on a saucer.

"The Builder is full of sorrow," said Neelata. Her eyes glittered. "Go to him. Take care of him. Tell him about the cave."

"But the water is surrounded by the dead."

"Tell him anyway. And do it quickly. The rain is approaching. Once it comes, the Builder will have no more need of your spring, and then it will be too late."

36

The Builder's Heart

I walked home and chewed the herbs. I lay down and felt how, as time passed, the hammock sagged less and less under my weight. First I felt my courage returning. It came in a blast of wind. It made the planks in the wall shake. I spat out the remains of the herbs and rolled a fresh ball. The second mouthful fed my fighting spirit. I saw scenes of women struggling. They pulled one another's hair and bit each other till they bled. Amongst them were women with bleeding backs, pregnant women, lame women. Neelata's mother was there, she stood wailing at her ruler's door. I chewed more of the herb, and although I became more and more ecstatic, I fell asleep.

My father returned. The dark was already lifting, a soft light glowed through it, the sun was waiting behind the hills. The first thing he did when he got home was to put my mother outside so he would not have to react to her sighing and whistling. He fetched the bag where he kept his tools: everything he needed for his silkworms, his repair kit, and his woodworking gear. *He is leaving,* I thought, but I was wrong. He emptied the bag. He passed each object through his hands and considered if he still needed it. He found, for instance, some rabbit-fur boots that in the marshes were used to warm people who have been in the water too long.

Here he did not have much use for them. He packed up his spools of silk. Those he could not throw out, they were the result of years of boiling and twining. As soon as he had enough of them, he would have it woven into a wrap such as he had seen around the bodies of women from the east, a wrap so soft it would once and for all be a remedy for my mother's sores and pain. It would put an end to her constant suffering. He put the spools aside with care and took up the pieces of beeswax, kept to remove hair from a body but never used. He broke them up between his hands, they crumbled to the ground. Then he crushed the shells, the beads, the carefully carved bones we had carried with us all that time. The knife he used to keep his hair cropped close to his skull, the chisels for carving designs in wood, the file for his nails and his teeth, all of that he smashed between stones. Meanwhile he whispered the questions that filled his head to the point of exhaustion: What was this ship, an exercise in endurance? A proof of faith? A test of ability? What was the matter with the family who was building it, who set others to work to furnish that proof and so were able to produce a grandiose work of art, who then spat out the makers of that work of art as if they were bits of ash in bread? I could read the pain in his body, could see the blisters on his feet and the spots where his girdle had rubbed all day.

"What is it you are doing?" I asked.

"I destroy what I have," he replied. "Belongings are misleading, they give you the feeling that you have a future and prospects."

"The dwarf is dead," I said. "He hanged himself after Ham promised him a spot in your niche."

He looked up, a little surprised, he obviously had not heard this news yet. "Is that so?" he asked. And then again, more emphatically, "Is that really so?" He lowered the stone in his hand until it fell to the floor with a dry thump. He stood up and looked around.

"What is it? What's making you so excited?"

"The dwarf is dead," he said as if it were he who was bringing me the news.

"What about it? Do you mean there is room in the niche again?" I asked. "The Builder knows about it, so you can forget about that niche."

"I mean that there is room in the Builder's heart again."

He hung the rabbit-fur boots on his girdle and ordered me to put on my shell tunic. I did it up faster and tighter than usual; it did not hurt because I was still under the influence of the herbs. We left the house and went to the corral, for once without being irritated by the junk that always lay all over the paths. We led a sturdy donkey out of the corral. We harnessed it to a small cart on which we loaded my bathtub. We filled it with water that we warmed on the fires of the pitch vats. While my father was busy heating the water, I went with the donkey to the cave to get more water, ignoring the trail I was leaving in the hills.

When it was light again outside, we stood before the Builder's quarters and asked permission to enter. Never before had it been so easy to enter these quarters: There was no dwarf to stop us, and the herb-chewing boys who usually hung around outside the tent were at breakfast. My father entered first, I followed.

The old man lay on his mat, flat on his back. His wife, Zaza, lay next to him. His undershirt was whiter than his sons', but just like theirs, the part he used to clean his ears after washing was stained yellow. His hair lay flat against his head from the lying down and from sweating. It was only now that I noticed how small his head was, as if time had shrunk it, and how thin his hair.

We greeted him and said we had come to bathe him.

He stared at us so long that I began to feel we should leave. But then Zaza nodded. She put the tips of her fingers in the small of his back and pushed until he moved. He stood up and held his arm out to my father. I supported him on the other side.

My father carefully removed the old man's clothes. I backed away when his undershirt came down. Again I saw, low on his abdomen, the blisters I had seen through the chink from the servants' quarters. The wounds had dried, they were apparently healing. But only now did I notice that his foreskin had been removed. I tried not to look, but my father stared at it with distaste.

"The dwarf did that," said Zaza when she noticed his look. "He said it would prevent the ulcers coming back."

The Builder sat down meekly on the ground next to the tub. Zaza watched, nodding. "Wash him," she said softly.

His skin was as dry as a birch leaf but did not break or tear when I rubbed the sponge over it. The pores opened up. In this, the Builder resembled his son, Ham: His skin was as thirsty.

When we had washed him, we helped him into the tub. He sat down, amazed. He laughed an unaccustomed, childlike laugh. My father moved the sponge in the water, from the thin shoulders along the bony vertebrae. I rinsed his feet, his ankles, his lower legs, and his knees.

"We have water for you," said my father.

"That is good," the Builder replied, a little smile of pleasure around his mouth. "That is what was still lacking. Good, drinkable water for the journey. What a gift."

"My daughter, Re Jana, has found the spring you have lived next to all these years. If she goes elsewhere tomorrow, she will find clear water again."

"In the land where the Unnameable will lead us, water will flow abundantly," the Builder replied. "We will have no need of diviners."

"You will need people who can steer a ship," my father continued. "People who know about water. What you need is a boatswain of experience and understanding. How will you know where you are?"

The Builder closed his eyes when my father let the water run over his face. He opened them again and said, "The migrating birds will help us. Doves always find their way back exactly."

"You know nothing of winds and currents. You do not know the difference between onshore and offshore winds."

"Winds are sent, they are much more than blind elements."

"There must be a rudder blade. You must not be helpless. You must help your god. What if you sight land but drift away?"

"The Unnameable will steer us where we need to go," the Builder said. "I understand what you are driving at. But I cannot make concessions. Many feel they are called, but few are chosen."

I did not rub as I washed, I patted. My father became more heavy-handed. He rubbed the sponge up and down roughly as he said, "Her spring is deep in the caves, in a place that would fill any of you with horror. If she is going to drown anyway, why should she give it away?"

The Builder's shoulder blades tightened. Where it was less worn, his skin became taut as a child's. "She will because I will entrust myself to her," he said hoarsely. "Because I will follow her to the deepest, most terrifying place, as I would my Unnameable God if He asked me to." The old man's voice was suddenly so forceful it startled me. He gripped the edge of the tub and pulled up his leg. He raised himself up precariously.

My father took hold of him and prevented him slipping and falling. "Are you sure?" he asked as he draped a wide towel over his shoulders. "Even if it is a place from which many do not return?"

The Builder looked at him sharply and said nothing. My father nodded thoughtfully. He untied the rabbit-fur boots from his girdle and slipped them onto the narrow, calloused feet.

For the rest of the time, both men were silent. In my father's head the plea he had prepared had given way to something else, and the Builder seemed to be mainly amazed at his skin and its sudden cleanliness. When I applied the salve that Zaza handed me to the swellings in his groin, he did not object.

37

Incident in the Cave

Seven carefully chosen warriors accompanied us when we took the Builder to the spring. His sons stayed behind in the shipyard to make sure the people would not gain access to the ark at that unguarded moment. Neelata followed without having been asked to. She had her splendid horse with her. Although she had not yet quite recovered from her fall, she let Put ride it, and he sat tall and proud on its back until his tailbone hurt. Her maids came too, six women with combed hair and beautifully made-up eyes, who saw to it that nobody lacked for anything.

The Builder and his wife were put into sedan chairs. Each was carried by two young warriors. When we got to the cave, it became clear that only five of us would enter: The warriors and the maids refused to move a step out of the sunlight once they realized that the spring lay behind a burial place.

Neelata carefully arranged the blankets on the Builder's and Zaza's shoulders. To my father and me she gave more of the herbal mixture she had given me earlier. "Chew this," she said. "It will give you the courage you'll need." Her hands trembled like leaves in the wind.

"The dead do not inspire fear in me," I said.

"Chew it anyway," she said huskily. "I want you braver than

ever." When she came close to me I could smell that she had a wad of the mixture in her mouth herself.

My father tied the rabbit-fur boots firmly onto the Builder's feet. I supported Zaza. As I knew the way, we went first. Slowly we inched our way in. Neelata came last, her face gray with fear. My father and I each had a torch. That made going into the cave a new sensation; for the first time I could see the recesses and chambers clearly. Despite the light, walking was not easy: With a torch in one hand, an old woman by the other, and a jug hanging from my shoulder by a rope, my balance was precarious. Zaza did not shrink from the human remains. She stepped over them as if they were crumbling stones. But Neelata was terrified. I heard her chewing with lots of saliva that she swallowed hurriedly.

We left the first cave and went on through the others. Here the skeletons were in better order, thigh bones with thigh bones, skulls with skulls, the wild animals had not ravaged those. We passed narrow passages. We clambered through the opening that was barely wide enough for a body to pass. Zaza got through it easily, she was so gaunt she barely filled the cleft. The Builder's body was much stiffer, it obviously hurt in many spots. But he did not give up. He let us haul him through the passage. His mouth was wide open from the exertion, his body was rigid as a plank, but he did not ask to be taken back. We passed the well Neelata had fallen into and the stack of bones I had pulled down to rescue her.

Thanks to the torch, the spring did not seem as far as usual. Because we let the men go ahead, they got there first. The Builder dipped his hands in the water and laughed loudly. My father sat him down on the ledge of the basin. Zaza immediately hastened her steps. She sat down next to him on the ledge. She too plunged her hand into the water. For a while, they sat there, smiling delightedly, like two lovers in the sun. My father and I watched from a distance. Neelata waited in the darkness.

"You see? He has solved the problem," we heard the Builder say. "Even after his death, the dwarf looks after us." The fur of his boots had become matted because of the dampness. They pulled the blanket around their shoulders solicitously, but kept one hand free so they could hold each other.

We took our time. My father was breathing quite calmly. He played the sputtering torch over the walls of the cave as he said, "Here is your water, in this cave of the dead."

"The ways of the Unnameable are inscrutable," the Builder replied.

"Now that you have water, the calamity can proceed."

"This generous gesture of two strangers hastens what must happen."

"Our hope is that our generous gesture will delay what must happen. If all those people must be punished, is it not fair that they be warned?"

The Builder put both hands on the ledge and gripped it tightly. He bent forward a little, cleared his throat, and spoke emphatically, as if addressing children. "The calamity itself is the warning," he said.

"Then your god is acting rashly."

"What He does is well considered; He has given it long, deep thought."

"How should I imagine this Unnameable god of yours? Like an eternally raging hurricane? But who can possibly stay angry for the length of time this plan is taking?"

"He is disappointed rather than angry."

"If disappointment drives him, he must make clear what he expects. His directives should be unambiguous, there should be no doubt about what his wishes are. Only then can he justify punishment."

"Many things are so obvious they do not need rules."

"Those with that sort of understanding are rare. Many live in ignorance. And what is learned now will soon be forgotten again. What makes you confident your god will not do the same thing all over again in five hundred years, to your children and your children's children? That he will not destroy your cities again and will not butcher your descendants?"

"The Unnameable does not bear malice. He has only become tired of humankind. I have long discussions with Him, and I assure you, He does not act rashly. His spirit will not quarrel with us for eternity. Believe me, after this, there will be clear rules, commandments, and prohibitions that are so plain they will not need explanations."

My father shook his head. "I do not ask for rules. I ask for judgment, the understanding that makes it possible to deviate from the rules if the need arises."

"That understanding too will come. With the passing of time. And with mankind's maturing."

"Is this then the time of beginning, the time of mistakes and trials? To me it sounds more like the endtime. It seems to me that soon everything will be finished."

"Let us say that a new time is coming."

"A new time for whom? For a handful of candidates? That is reprehensible."

"It is the crime that is reprehensible, not the punishment."

"How can there be a question of crime for a people that does not have a system of justice yet? You prohibit the taking of a life, and so you've come to this state of disarray. If you do not kill when it is necessary, do not raise the ax against the criminal or the sword against the murderer, you replace revenge with fighting, with perpetual feuding, with the slaying and murdering under cover of darkness because the light of day will not tolerate it. That is what your Unnameable is now railing against: against that furtive killing of men in their sleep. Give this people a system of justice, give them a few executioners, and they would not become depraved. No god would find it necessary to destroy them. Whoever does not apply justice in punishment causes blood feuds. Whoever does not permit punishment forces it underground. Talk your god around, appeal to his reason." My father's voice sounded hollow in the cave. He stood looking and talking straight ahead, as if he was not talking to anyone in particular. But then his stance changed. He turned to the Builder. The Builder wanted to reply, but my father said, as if he had only just remembered, "Or is the Unnameable destroying us for your benefit? So that you will be able to live in a better world?"

The Builder's words stuck in his throat. He looked at the rock walls glittering with water and at the mosses in spots where there was a little light. Suddenly he started sobbing. His body sagged against Zaza's. Zaza gently patted his hand.

I was ashamed of my father. He should not have carried on like that at a defenseless old man. I wanted to get closer to give them more light, but Neelata came forward from the dark. She snatched at my torch. She pushed it away from the spring so that the couple sat in darkness. While there was little light, she tugged at my father's girdle.

"Do it. Do it quickly in this moment of weakness!" she whispered. But my father pushed her hand away and spat his wad of herbs into one of the wells.

"The places on the ark are fixed," the Builder said weakly. "I do not choose, we are chosen."

Neelata lost her calm. She stamped her feet and pushed me. I moved away from her. I wanted to see the Builder's face, and I knew that, despite the blanket, he was cold. The torch would warm him. Above all, I did not want to accidentally touch off the fury that was pent up in her. But she grabbed me before I could get away. She knocked the torch from my hand and threw it in the well. We were all frightened by the fire going out with a hiss.

"Gentan he killed to end the suffering of one single man," she whispered with a voice like a knife. "So why not defeat the Unnameable's plan? Why not kill these two people to prevent the suffering of many?"

Her outburst startled me. I had seen the Builder walk past the deep wells, and the thought that he might fall in had occurred to me. But not for a moment had I thought about the possibility that he might be pushed. How simple: We would come out and say there had been an accident. The warriors lacked the courage to enter the cave. The couple was old, their death would seem the natural outcome of a reckless walk in a slippery cave. You put off the calamity by disposing of those who had thought of it. What use would the disaster be if the elect could no longer be spared?

My father held his torch, now our only source of light, high above his head and said, "Get away from here, Neelata. Do not become involved in this. This is a matter for the rejected, you cannot do anything."

Neelata backed away. The herbs did not seem to have much effect on her. I could clearly hear her terrified breathing. She was afraid of what would happen, and afraid of going back without a torch. The Builder sat so still it looked as if he had fallen asleep. Even the gentle trembling of his hands had ceased. He stared sadly in front of him.

Because Neelata did not react, my father said, "Go back to the warriors and say we are waiting for our water jugs to fill." She shuffled away. When her footsteps had receded, my father threw his torch into the well.

It was dark in the cave, much darker suddenly than when I had been here before. The realization of what my father intended made me stagger. In the marshes, it happened occasionally that a drowned child floated by. Children fell into the water so easily, they ventured too far into the reeds or missed the edge of their raft. They drowned and floated past our house. My father refused to fish them out of the water. He could not spare a papyrus boat to burn the corpse on; the child came from some village upstream, and we could not expect any return favor from the fishermen there, our children floated in the other direction. My father weighed the bodies down with mud to make them sink. The first time I saw it happen, I gained strength from the horror that overcame me. The thought of the floating hair, the bulging eyes, and the outstretched arms made me careful and gave my father something to remind me of if I became careless on the water. The first drowned child came with a message, an urgent appeal that made me dry my tears. And so I did not notice how efficient my father's movements were, and how relaxed his voice. But the second and third time such a body floating past made no impression: I had already been warned, I already felt afraid of the marsh. When my father filled a bowl with mud and poled across to the child, I sat in the bow. I watched as he tied the child to his boat with a rope around its foot to haul it some distance farther along so that the putrefying flesh would not contaminate his waters. He went deep into the marsh, and there he quickly and skilfully disposed of the child. It seemed to me then that he threw his heart with it under the mud.

Now I heard him walk toward the Builder. His movements in the dark were just as efficient, and his voice just as relaxed, as when he made the children's bodies sink. Not far from him there was a soft sniffling. It was the Builder. Was he still weeping? Perhaps he was leaning on Zaza, her arms around him to support him.

"What if there was no ship?" my father said softly when he had felt his way to the Builder and his wife. "Or a bad ship that sank? Or half a ship, not finished in time? Or a rudderless ship without a patriarch? Would the calamity still come?"

The answer that came from the dark was Zaza's. She spoke for her husband who only managed a cough. "Then all would be lost. Then the insects will take over this world. They will consume everything until all that is left is a steppe and the wind that rages across it. Then no song will ever be heard again, no skin will ever again rub against skin. Then all dreams will perish."

We took the Builder and his wife back to the entrance of the cave in the same cumbersome way we had brought them in. Torches we no longer had, so we progressed even more slowly. We walked past deep, cold wells with this man, who had worked for years and years and now saw the end of his task approach, and whose total devotion to his vision we could not break. We brought him back into the sunlight. We carried water that was so cold it was as if it bit you with icy teeth. To keep that chill, we had wrapped the jugs in cloths.

Neelata waited for us, bewildered. She immediately stumbled toward us, her veil between her teeth, her steps uneven from the tension of waiting for us. "We counted on you to save our people," she sneered in a whisper. "If only you had killed them, these bringers of disaster, these lunatics who alarm us."

But my father shook his head. Like the Builder, he had searched all his life for grand enterprises, for dreams that reach beyond one's home. What dream could be more beautiful than building a holy ship, a gigantic object of beauty that took its makers beyond the shadow of the everyday? A project such as this is ended by performing an heroic deed, not by pushing an old man standing by a well. And what heroic deed could check what had been begun here? No matter what we tried, we would not be able to break the determination of the elect.

The Builder pronounced a blessing over the cave as he left it. From now on, all could drink the water from the spring. No one needed to be afraid of the dead who reposed there. Loudly, he thanked the dwarf. We drank and sat down to rest for a while. Neelata did not wait for us. She refused to take in even a mouthful of the spring water and returned to the shipyard with a dry mouth. I asked the Builder, "What will happen to her? Will she be punished?"

The Builder sat hand in hand with Zaza on the mat the maids had spread out for them. We stood beside it, like servants, like young people who still have everything to learn. "Neelata is not evil," he said. "She is mad with despair. But she will not be punished: She is Ham's wife."

38

All Timber Is Confiscated

After the visit to the cave, the rain came the following night, very gentle rain, the first in a long time, because remote mountaintops usually prevented it coming. The spring had only just been handed over when it already seemed just an extra supply in case the rainfall stopped again. And stop it did, after just a few hours. The bowls in the hills were carefully lifted from their stands and their contents poured into jugs. In no time, the wind had dried the landscape, which, after a few plants appeared briefly in cracks in the rocks, soon looked as barren and tired as before.

But the memory of it stayed. That turned everything upside down. Suddenly what had been spoken from the small dais in the shipyard was no longer the ranting of an old man but a prophecy. For the first time, there was a clear sign that he had been right. It might have been possible to forget that the Builder had spoken, but not that the rain had come. Once again, there was much speculation. Even the tone of the songs in the shipyard changed. I heard a cadence in them I had not noticed before. The strings of the lutes were plucked more vigorously than before. And the water that was collected, though sweet, haunted the dreams of all who lived in the shipyard.

Work on the ark went on as never before. No matter how dark it was, the shouting, the drilling, and the sawing could be heard through the night. In various places, the warriors stood and supervised like slave drivers. The Builder called my father to him every day. For hours they discussed the state of things, the caulking and the sealing. The question of whether there should be a rudder, a tiller, or an anchor was raised again, but the Builder dismissed it. They both agreed, though, that the rigging should be tall and elegant.

Ham no longer came to the caterpillar cage. He was working as intensively as my father. I approached him to ask where he had been, but he was too afraid of what the oracle had predicted to answer me. I sometimes saw him crossing the shipyard. He kept his hands inside his sleeves, and his eyes were feverish. He gave his workers their final instructions. The arrangement of the spaces was now definite, choices that had long been put off were now made, outstanding problems dealt with once and for all.

The rain returned. At first it fell in a fine mist, absorbing the dust and making it settle soundlessly. Then came the large drops. They whipped up the sand, making pits in it. We listened to its rustling as to the first words of one who has not spoken for a long time.

Everybody was ordered to hand over any pieces of wood they had.

"Why are you giving this up?" I asked the people who were carrying planks to the shipyard.

"The final offering," they said. "If we do not give it, we cannot be considered righteous."

"But don't you know that the places on the ark have been decided?" I asked, but I had barely spoken when I was surrounded by warriors. They stood close to me without saying a word, their spears raised, their faces fierce. More and more of them arrived, all insisting they were the Builder's nephews. They carried scourges and whips. They climbed the cliff and stood near our house until my father had removed the nails from it and pulled it down plank by plank. The boat they did not discover, it was well hidden under the bundles of branches in the field.

We returned to our old spot in the quarry. Those who did not have a tent slept without any protection. At night we felt ash blow over our faces, and in the morning we looked as if we had aged overnight: Our hair was gray, our faces like masks. My mother seemed the least bothered by it. There was plenty of water now, but she asked us not to wash her. For the first time in her life she allowed us to skip her massages. That was disturbing. Since we had left the marshes, she was more beautiful then ever: In the land air she didn't sweat as much and her sores healed more quickly. Her appearance was more youthful than before we left, her skin glowing and looking well cared for. The shape of her face, her shoulders, her arms were as lovely as ever. Everything about her was trim and clean, I could not understand why she refused to be bathed. Only later did we realize that she was already trying to give us the chance to save ourselves. She wanted us to take the time to think up a plan, a plan in which she wanted no part. She wanted my father to finish the truss-boat.

"There is time for that, woman, you'll see."

"How do you know there will be time?" I asked because my mother wanted to know.

"We earned it in the cave."

39

"Take Care of Him"

My mother wanted to say something else, but we did not bother listening to her. Everybody was saying so many things in those days, the sound of muttering hung over the shipyard like a muffling curtain. After a while, you no longer understood anyone, everyone had their say, we all spoke at once. That is why we paid no attention to what she said; it was no more than the whisper of her eyelid, at that moment in our lives of no greater significance than the beating of a butterfly's wing.

The muttering that hung over the shipyard came out of the new silence. It should have been a beautiful moment. The woodworkers had knocked the last nail into the ark, the last of the wood shavings had fallen, the fires under Japheth's pitch pots had been extinguished, the grasses that held Shem's scaffolding together had been cut, and the bamboo poles stacked up. The hammering that had resounded through the valley for years had ceased. The ark was finished.

There was still activity: People walked back and forth taking goods onto the ship, and all the time there was the slow filling of the amphoras with rainwater and water from my cave. All the tools and any remaining pieces of timber were loaded in case repairs would be needed during the journey. Large quantities of bamboo and grasses, mats and embroidered rugs went up the gangplank. The women rolled presses, nutcrackers, cleats, and files in leaves and stacked them next to their tents. In sealed containers, they carried extract of poppy and resin-rich bark over the gangplank. People carried their belongings to the entrance of the ship. They said things like "I have seven children, these are their sleeping mats. Can we take those on board now? The children are little, and I am worried about them in the crush. We'll just sleep on the ground for the time being."

"Don't just assume you're coming," the warriors at the gangplank replied. "You won't know whether you're chosen until the day comes."

Rain was never far away. It came and went, making the land greener than we had ever seen it. When his task was completed, Ham fell ill. The exhaustion of months struck and his strength left him. I no longer met him anywhere, he did not even come into the forecourt in the morning sun. I entered the Builder's quarters, but I was not invited into his son's.

Finally, Zaza called me to her. Her quarters were filled with pouches of herbs. With her gout-deformed hands she marked them with black symbols, pinned dried leaves onto them, and packed them in wooden boxes.

I had been in Zaza's quarters before. Every time I went in there, I enjoyed the business, all the paraphernalia of someone with a passion, the scent that penetrated through the walls of the tent. I was jealous of the things she had in there. I dreamed about what you could do with it all if you ground the herbs and seeds fine and mixed them with oil. Once or twice I even contemplated making a few of these pouches disappear; she surely would not miss them. But I did not steal from her. She was the sort of woman who taught you self-respect, to not act against your own nature. She asked me to come with her to Ham's quarters, where he lay on his mats struggling for breath. Sweat pearled on his forehead; he looked gray.

Zaza's fingers were so stiff they were no longer capable of stroking. She had made an attempt at tapping his chest, but had not managed to loosen the phlegm. I tapped his chest properly. When he finally calmed down and shut his eyes, Zaza said, "We called him the dark one because he was the darkest when he was born, and now look at him, so pale. He was to be my untameable one. Does not every woman wish for one untameable child? But he became his father's darling and that tamed him." She drew my hands toward her and held them. Her fingers were thin, age had made her bones brittle. She said, "He was so small when he was born. In the middle of the night I used to wake up to make sure he was alive. All his life, I have felt him, felt his body constantly to make sure he was putting on enough flesh. Take care of him, Re Jana, every time Neelata doesn't. Lay your hands on him and check on his condition."

Zaza fell silent when Neelata entered. Neelata brought water no one had asked for and knelt by the sickbed like us. She said, "The hard work has nothing to do with his fever. Sick with longing is what he is, nothing else."

I knew what was wrong. He tried to make her come to his tent more often, every evening if possible, but she enjoyed her evenings with her maids and did not allow herself to be lured by his promises. Nor would she let him approach her. She scratched like a cat. She was terrified of having to give birth to a child on the ship she had named "the coffin."

We put Ham into my father's bathtub to lower his temperature. Then we rubbed him with ashes to protect him against insects. We did it together, Zaza, Neelata, and I. He did not know it. He wailed and beat us away. In his delirium he took us for wild animals from the hills.

To achieve a cure, Ham, carried by his two brothers, went to confess to his father what everybody knew by then — that he had built a niche. "For the dwarf," he declared, but the lie made him cough until he nearly suffocated. The Builder ordered him to go back to his sickbed and stop worrying about what he had done. "The dwarf inspired us to do things we do not understand," he said. "For me too the temptation to admit him onto the ark was great. But he is dead. He was a messenger, and will remain that, although in a guise unknown to us."

It was around that time I saw Put talking to Zedebab. A second woman was with them, her twin sister, who was her spitting image. I saw that they offered Put a bag of dried manure, excellent fuel for the fire in which we were no longer permitted to burn wood. I walked toward them to see what had earned him this gift.

"We are offering him this," said Zedebab — or was it her sister? — "and we will offer you twice as much again if you will tell us where the niche is that the boat builder has constructed." They were both small and thin, they wore many rings in their ears, and they had the same way of moving.

Put and I looked at them disbelievingly. Never had we seen two people who were so alike, who seemed to say and think the same things. Yet after a brief remark on my part, they got into a furious argument, both going spotty-faced so they no longer looked at all alike, as if they had decided they no longer wanted to. The remark I made that touched off their quarrel was "What use is the niche to you? Whoever hides there will be found immediately."

40

The Feast of the Foremen and Warriors

There was to be a feast. The women made headdresses and tunics. The feathers were carefully chosen for their color and shape. They used the feathers of the toucan, the trogon, and the crane. They collected them in the evening and fixed them to the fabrics with thread. Because it was raining, the forecourt remained empty and everyone crowded into the red tent. The foremen sat in a circle on the ground beating drums. The Builder had wine brought in. And because he was now familiar with the delights of bathing and oiling, he asked me to wash everyone's arms and feet and rub them with oil.

The tent was too small for so many people. Legs were stretched out to me, which I oiled without knowing to whom they belonged. The fellows enjoyed their turns. They made all the jokes that Rrattika usually come up with when a young woman oils a man. The more they drank, the louder they sang. My father filled his beaker many times. To my surprise, he knew not only every foreman, but every warrior by name. He was proud of the construction, he allowed the others to slap his shoulders and congratulate him. He insisted that I drink too. "Relax, Re Jana," he whispered to me. "The rain is just a shower. It will take weeks for this land to flood."

It was not until long after midnight that I could pack up my equipment. I had done everything they had asked. The wine had not made me cheerful, only dizzy. Ham noticed. He took no part in the feast. He had pulled up his tent's curtain and watched feverishly from his quarters. I had offered him wine to relieve the pain, but his stomach would not let him consume anything except the water I fetched for him. When I got ready to go, he said, "What are you dragging your mother around for? Leave her here, we'll look after her. She won't suffer thirst or cold." My mother eagerly blinked her eye when she heard his proposal, and so I left her behind with Ham.

Deep in the night, I woke up with an uneasy feeling. How could I have done this, left this beautiful woman behind in a tent where there was a feast going on? My father snored noisily next to me, his sleep a stupor I had not seen him in for a long time. I got up and went to the red tent. I stood close to the tent, about where I knew she had been. Her breathing was clearly audible. She was asleep. Around her, all was quiet. I felt reassured.

When I returned the next morning to fetch her, she had been combed and washed. There were not many people left in the tent, only Shem, slumped full length in a chair; even feverish Ham had finally left his mat.

"Who has groomed her?" I asked with the same uneasy feeling I had had during the night.

"Not me," said Shem.

"So who did?" I asked the girls near the partition behind the women's tent.

"None of us," they said. In the forecourt, the warriors lay

among the puddles. I prodded them until they opened their eyes and asked them who had washed my mother.

"That gorgeous thing in the corner? That willing little woman who blows without scratching? We did not really wash her, no." They roared with laughter.

I stood over my mother. She smelled of the oil I had left with Ham. When I asked what had happened to her, she answered by turning her eye away, like a bird that spins from being hit by an arrow in the back rather than the heart.

41

My Mother's Will

My father could not comfort her. Nor could he calm her anger. She thought the dwarf had chosen the right way. We uttered our suspicion only in whispers, we did not want her to hear. We said it while around us the almond powder blew about, scooped from my mortar by the wind. We pretended we were talking about nothing in particular, just the nuisance of the wind, but we said, "She wants to prove she still has a will: the will to die."

My father and mother talked together for days. In their turn, they kept what they said a secret from me, me who had so often been their mouthpiece, who had always done my best to keep them close. When, on sultry afternoons, my father's restlessness became too great and he leaned against her in despair, I had lain on her other side, stretching my arms out to him across her. With his eyes closed, he had the illusion that my fingers and hands were hers. Then he would groan at the touch until the groans turned to sobs.

She asked my father to build a papyrus boat, a long, narrow one with high bow and stern, like a gondola, the kind on which we burn the dead. He took me with him to the stores where he made his choice from the stocks of reeds. There were bundles of flexible ones for covering pens and dividing spaces, thin stems suitable for birds' perches, but also bamboo thick as an arm, for making cages for large, dangerous species. My father built a boat from papyrus as he had done a few times already in his life: one for his mother, one for his two brothers who perished together, and one for my little brother who died at the edge of the water. He only took cover when it rained and went back to work as soon as the sun broke through.

People surrounded his structure. They did not know about the carrying power of reeds and laughed at what he was doing. Some thought it was an act of rebellion and that he was ridiculing the Builder and his warriors. But when the papyrus boat was finished, they looked at it full of admiration. None of them, seeing the gondola, thought of death.

My father asked Put and me to help him carry the boat far into the hills, near where the thick-fingered bushes grew. He had chosen the spot and prepared it. He had gathered bundles of branches and hidden a large jug of oil in the shrubs.

For the first time in his life, Put, that poor little boy who had no idea what was going on, killed a duck in flight with his slingshot. Away from people, we cooked it, keeping the lid tight on the pot so the scent would not escape. We ground the meat into a mush, adding salt and herbs.

My father held my mother close and fed her one mouthful after another. "Do you remember," he asked, "how your ducklings took to the water?" She blinked. I had experienced it. When the ducklings she had bred were ready for the water, she got into her boat and made them come after her. The ducklings followed her into the water. My father always thought it a lovely moment, and he invariably clapped his hands. But we children had our hearts in our mouths. We knew some of the ducklings could not swim at all. Sometimes one of them would tip over. Then the awkward little thing would float upside down in the water. The eldest amongst us could handle a raft, and even if it was late and cold already, we would clamor to be allowed to go to the rescue. But my mother forbade it. She needed to know the strength of the young birds. Sometimes one of them would manage to turn itself right side up. To our great relief, its head would reappear above the water, and it would swim a little faster to catch up with its siblings. But frequently, we had to watch its efforts slow down, see the movements of its wings and legs become stiff and change into useless splashing as if something inside it had broken. Then the duckling became still, and the fish came to claim it.

Put cried when my father spoke about the past, and so did I. We plucked at our girdles, pulled our legs up high, and rested our chins on our knees. My mother settled a few more matters. She made it clear to my father that I was to have her divining rod, which was the most precious thing she owned. I dug my hands into the earth. I knew that I was waiting for a pain that went deeper than I could fathom and felt my fear rising. While waiting like that, it was hard not to repeat the old arguments: We still had my father's truss-boat; we could manage to live in close proximity; the water might not even come.

But whenever we mentioned the water or the truss-boat in the field, even in a whisper so she would not hear, my mother's eye would fill with fear. The rising springs, the overflowing ponds, the stones that became more and more slippery, and the hills that were so much greener than before caused her to look around anxiously. She had come here so she would never again have to be at the waterline. She had suffered the journey so she would never again be carried onto a vessel. If the whole world flooded, how could she escape? Making her wait for the waters to rise would be too cruel, and so was carrying her onto a boat or an ark.

That was why, after a long afternoon of eating and talking and silence, my father took her to the spot in the hills where he had prepared the papyrus boat. I stayed behind with Put, who stuck close to me, speechless. It was an endless wait before we saw the column of smoke rise. Wild ducks and all sorts of water birds passed, flying around the smoke in a wide arc. And the next morning, after an exhausting sleep under a ramshackle shelter, with nothing but dreams of my mother, we saw long, glistening threads hanging all over the encampment. They linked boards to rocks and palisades to trowels. They were the threads of the silkworms that my father had thrown to the wind.

"It is perfectly built," my father said later on. "It is the most beautiful papyrus boat my hands have ever produced." Yet my mother had not wanted to be carried on it. Never again on a boat, she had made clear, not in life and not in death. He had had to lay her directly onto the pyre.

Here I did not know any places for grieving. At home in the marshes, I had places; I knew where I wanted to sit down when I learned that my grandmother was dead, and my uncles, who had died just one day apart from the injuries inflicted on them by wild boars. We each had our own spot, and we spread out knowing we would not get in each other's way. In the Builder's shipyard, I did not know where to go, it was so busy everywhere, and in the hills there were wild animals, and so I went to sit underneath the silkworms' cage.

Neelata came to me almost immediately. The shrubs were low, they did not provide cover for someone tall, and so I knew she was approaching long before she found me. She carried a cushion on which she was embroidering a design of roses. She asked me if I liked it. It would be for me, she said, later, once it was finished.

She continued embroidering while I spoke about my mother. I leaned against her stretcher, which I dragged behind me out of habit. You could still see her shape, worn into it after so many years. Neelata did not look up from her task as I spoke to her. That was good: Her not looking made talking easier. I spoke about my mother's life and what had happened to her. I said, "She blamed it all on her lack of will. She thought that, if only she had had the will, she could have stepped out of that boat to get my little brother." Neelata let the threads slide through her fingers. I bent over, gently biting the skin on the back of my hand, and talked to my mother. I cried for her to come back.

Neelata had only just disappeared behind the shrubs when I saw Ham approach. He brought me a blanket, a comforting piece of woolen cloth, which he wrapped around me. The wool chafed my cheeks, which were wet and taut.

"Do not cry," he said. "She has protected you from a much greater loss."

"What loss could be greater than this?"

"A death against her will. A death that comes slowly like rising water." The fever had left a red edge around his lips. He looked away from me as I told him about her. I knew it had been he who had washed her after that long night in the tent. He had done his best to remove the traces the warriors had left on her. He bore no guilt; the warriors had taken her away from him while he slept.

We made a memorial. Ham searched the area for a suitable stone, lifted it, and carried it to the spot I showed him. He carved a tern onto it, my mother's lucky bird.

He took me with him into the hills. He wanted to get away from the silkworm cage, he insisted, as far as possible. Far from all our familiar spots, he erected a column of stones; there were no feathered warriors to help him. He said, "I have taken Neelata as my wife because she belongs with me. She comes from a lineage that has made our people great." He stood behind me and wrapped his arms around me, his elbow on my breast and his hand on my neck. "But are you not my rightful wife? Have I not lain down with you long before Neelata?" He pointed at the column. "It is for you I am erecting this." His shoulder was touching my back, but I moved away from him.

I wandered in the hills and found nothing but shy animals who looked at me indifferently. Near the thick-fingered bushes, the papyrus boat still stood, decked out, ready for the journey to the underworld, but not burned because of my mother's will. Nowhere in the wide-reaching hills did I find a good place for grieving.

Contrition

*A*fter my mother's death, my father changed into a man I no longer recognized. He mingled with the Rrattika. Warriors came to see him, men I knew had been there that night with my mother, but my father did not reach for his dagger to take revenge; by the glow of the fire under his teapot he exchanged quiet words with them. His behavior disturbed me. I thought he had lost his mind. To my alarm, he began to like the things they ate.

He became an adviser unlike any the Rrattika had ever known. He encouraged them to hatch a plan. "It is important that most people go on thinking there will be enough room for everybody," he said. "It will need muscle power and skill to conquer a place. That is what you must prepare for."

Only much later did I comprehend what he was up to. He had not gone mad. He deliberately allowed them to cultivate him. He did what he had not done before: He penetrated these people's world, not because he sought company, but because he was working on a solution. He was trying to save our lives. And he was plotting revenge.

The water in the pond rose, more tents had to be moved, travelers arrived with news of flooding in faraway regions. The hills filled with water; they resembled huge sponges from which you could press fluid by simply putting your foot on them. Around us, people started hoarding anything that would float. They made rafts. They trekked long distances to gather branches, bind them together, and fit canvas around them. Others started to arm themselves excessively. They formed small militias and trained in the fields. They were the most dynamic amongst the Rrattika, people of enterprise with the courage to buck the established order. They knew that they had all undoubtedly done something that made it far from certain they would get a place on the ship.

But my father also mixed with those who did not bear arms or wear battle dress. To them he gave advice of a very different kind. He became a member of secret societies. They held meetings late at night. Together with men and women of varying backgrounds, he waxed indignant about the people who slept and slept and slept so they would not have to see the rain. We are so tired, they said, we have been working so hard. He was conspicuous with his dark skin; before long he could not cross the shipyard without being accosted ten, fifteen times. He encouraged people to sleep only during the hours of darkness. He called them to action. "Save yourselves. Do not blindly accept this fate. Be too smart for the Unnameable and force a second chance from him. Build a boat and lay in supplies."

Even now that the ark was completed, very few understood how to do this. They still started by building a hull out of many small pieces and adding ribs and thwarts later. My father showed them it was necessary to first build the strengthening keel and that the superstructure should be fixed onto that. For the first time in his life he enjoyed the luxury of building boats from the hardest and most expensive varieties of timber, varieties he had never handled before, brought here by caravans at the orders of prominent warriors in exchange for much money and silver. He got help, lots of help, from woodworkers who, now that the ark was finished, had nothing to do. When a boat was finished, it was carried under cover of darkness to a secret place in the hills. The buyers acted discreetly. They were afraid of what the mob would do once the water came.

And my father set the example in showing contrition. He was amongst the first to don sackcloth and get rid of his last belongings. He only kept the things he had plans for: a hook, his large fyke-net, ropes, four jugs, my mother's seamless cloak, and a funnel. But his yoke, the chest, the spears, even the pouch with the big cats' talons, he got rid of. Some of the people in the shipyard listened to his advice and followed his example. What else could they do? Their own wise men were not much use to them. The wise men of the Rrattika, those know-it-alls, who had previously accepted valuable items in exchange for their counsel, no longer ventured out. They hid like mice creeping into their hollows and did not move. The Rrattika found support from my father because he was the only one who still spoke. They shaved their heads and put their hair into a large pile, the plaits, the frizzy hair, and the lank tresses all mixed together. Onto another pile went all their clothes, onto yet another one their footwear. The way they stood there, their thin legs sticking out from under the hair blankets, all with the same shaven skulls, they looked almost appealing, and you could not imagine that they had called a calamity down upon themselves.

The Builder witnessed the display of penance and said, "What you are doing does not show genuine contrition. You are sacrificing, you are doing what you have always done for your old gods. If you were really contrite, you would not only cut off your hair, but also change your hearts. But you only cut off your hair."

There was sadness in the singing of the workers early in the morning. They caught each other's tones and complemented them. It was as if the hills themselves were singing plaintively. It was so beautiful I felt jealousy toward this people who, because of their common language and customs, their sense of unity and their adaptability, could survive anywhere in the world: They would always find themselves amongst their own sort and would always be at home. But their brotherliness had not done them much good. They gained no respite from the god they had chosen.

My father said, "I have worked with the Builder, but his god I am working against. I build boats for the warriors so they will survive, completely against his will. The boats are not big, but the important thing is they float. The calamity will not achieve its purpose, Re Jana, and that will be my doing."

Ham too did penance. He renounced his place in the red tent. He no longer went to eat or sleep there, but lived like us, without a house, with only a fence to shelter against the rain and a stone to rest his head on. "I've come to finish the truss-boat," he said to my father when he arrived with his pack. He provided us with as much timber as we needed.

43

The Discovery of the Truss-Boat

Shem and Japheth got wind of the fact that all over the hills boats were being built secretly. How could it be otherwise, it was practically impossible not to hear the banging of the hammers. The first to be suspected was, of course, my father. We were not surprised when, one morning, the two brothers were standing next to the truss-boat. They walked around it, examining every detail. Four cages had been constructed, two on each side. The face of the person sleeping inside and the top of the cage were less than an arm's length apart.

"This will have to be destroyed," said Shem. "How will the Unnameable's plan succeed if we allow this?"

"They are free people," replied Ham, his mouth still full of nails. "They can build a boat if they want to. The Unnameable has not ordered us to destroy other people's boats."

"But their work does not make sense," said Shem with the fixed stare of someone whose eyelashes have been singed. "This is a stony desert. If people build a boat here, it can only be in order to escape the wrath of the Unnameable. They ape His commands. They ridicule Him. This is a trick by that boat builder from the marshes, can't you see? First he persuades our old father that everybody has to be warned. Only if you do that do you give people time to repent, he says. And now that everyone knows what is coming, instead of being penitent, they go and build boats! You know what will happen: When the flood comes, the Nefilim will rush onto these boats. In no time at all, they'll populate the new world and the divine plan will be undermined, for the gestation time for the children they beget is not forty weeks but forty days."

Even the cliff had become sodden the last few days. You did not climb up the path for fun, it was far too slippery. So Shem's argument was dead serious, he was covered in mud, and he had no understanding whatever of a brother who was involved in this enterprise. He nodded at Japheth. Japheth looked around, went to Ham's tool basket, and took up the ax that had long since been used to cut down the last tree in the area.

Ham was the first to realize what he intended. He dived for his brother to try and stop him. He stood between him and the boat, spread out his arms, and said, "Do not touch the boat that will be my deliverance. If you make that leak, I too will drown: I am not going on our father's ark." Ham's greyhound whined. Japheth lowered the ax until its head touched the ground.

"Don't carry on like that," Shem said angrily. His shoes were not made for this sort of weather. They soaked up the water and sagged crookedly over his instep.

But Ham was not joking. Even to me this only became clear when he said, "The ark is doomed. How can I believe in my brothers' righteousness if they allow a crippled woman to be abused in their tent? Some of us will be blessed, others cursed, the oracle said. I will earn the blessing. I am going on this boat."

My father and I were speechless. The greyhound barked. Shem and Japheth left the field. Japheth had not spoken one word, but that was not unusual for him. Shem said no more either, which should have warned us. But we were so moved by Ham's decision that we missed some of what was going on.

That evening Ham had a nose ring put in, shaped like a snake swallowing its tail. "The symbol of my determination," he claimed. Going with us instead of with his father seemed a logical decision. He was convinced that, if the Unnameable wanted him to live, He would spare the truss-boat. In a touching way, he was certain that now nothing else could go wrong. "Our boat is just as good as theirs," he said. It was better, he considered a bit later, more maneuverable, better arranged, easier to steer. To which my father, with the emphasis of someone who has chewed too many herbs, replied, "If not, we will await death with all our strength."

Shem and Japheth did not order our boat to be confiscated. Of course, some accord was reached, though I had no idea what, but I could see that my father was shackled like a prisoner to an agreement. Suddenly he no longer talked to everybody, and he was not seen in the shipyard anymore.

Shem, Ham, and Japheth went and begged their mother, "Make Father bless us. Don't let him wait until we are on the ship. There will not be enough time then." They wanted the blessing for all three together, so he could not curse anyone.

"There is plenty of time for the blessing, I am not dead yet," replied the Builder, and sent Zaza back to her sons.

Neelata knew of Ham's intention to go on the truss-boat when the water came.

"That is good," she said. "It is a good plan."

"But we won't be together," I said.

"I'll keep Put, you take Ham."

"Put belongs with us, he is our child."

"Leave Put with me. I have a large store of honey and dates. He is better off with me than with you."

We were convinced that our separation would only be temporary. We had an unreasonably strong belief in our chance of survival. Yet we suffered the sort of sadness that does not leave you at night. The only thing that could make us forget it was the beauty of the ark: It was flawless, it was perfect. Its dimensions complied with divine proportions. It was not a ship, but a heavenly image of one. Looking at it was true comfort.

44

Camia

We had to move once again. My father and I were used to dealing with rising water levels. How often had we spent the night in our boats in the marshes because there had been heavy rain? We dug channels and, if necessary, cleared them every day. But after a while, despite all our precautions, it became too muddy in the quarry. It became so cold that we had to wear two hair shirts. We lived in a constant dilemma: Do we wash the mud out of our clothes, and if so, how do we get them dry? Supplies went bad, tools rusted, and wounds would not heal. Whoever still lived in the valley packed up their belongings and moved into the hills. Naturally, we went back to our field.

More people had come to live on the slope, like little Camia and her blind mother. Her eyes had been taken out, which made us suspicious, because we were aware that, for some of the peoples we knew, putting out the eyes was the punishment for treason; but she was so warm and affectionate with the child that she soon won our friendship. She seemed to have found a strange kind of reassurance in the fact that the same fate awaited everyone. She dispelled her daughter's fear by making up a story about a beautiful blue river that would carry all people with it; all you needed to do was shut your eyes and let yourself float, and not be afraid when the water closed above you, because that was the way it should be. Underwater you traveled faster. It was quiet there. You became lighter, and your hair moved in the current. The blind woman made gestures to go with her story, she threw Camia's hair up and slowly let it come down again.

For Put, the girl was a playmate. They knew each other's rhymes; the words were different, but the cadences were the same. The little girl seemed to thrive in our wet surroundings. Like her mother, she constantly sniffed the air; they were still getting used to the scent of moisture and the winds blowing from a different direction than they used to. She visited us, soaked but elegant, to shout words that made us laugh because even Put did not understand them. It was strange to experience how differently you see people when you know they are going to die soon.

45

The Rain

*P*laces you could once easily run across were now slippery and inaccessible. You couldn't rely on rocks and boulders for support, because they had been loosened. All around, people were digging ditches as fast as they could, but to my surprise nobody built any footbridges. In the marshes, we'd had footbridges linking everything to everything. Here all you'd find was the occasional platform that soon sank into the mud. Everybody took to sleeping on platforms. Out of bamboo and scarce boards, stilt villages were constructed. Because the water was now running off the hillsides in streams, people moved back toward the ark: It didn't matter much where you lived, you were going to get wet. We woke up with swollen throats. The little ones caught colds, their ears ran with pus, and they cried through the night. My father waded across the plots where his millet was rotting.

The wet did not come from the rain alone. It came from under us and from around us, it rose from everything. The earth slid away beneath us. Mosses grew in the fireplaces. Lakes and streams formed. Flowers bloomed in places where we had never seen any green before. The refuse that had been heaped up began to ferment, food scraps, excrement, everything became one big mash. The flies stung. In the hills, the swallows seemed to hit the ground in full flight. The blackbirds huddled in the trees, smoothing their feathers. The chickens scrabbled in the mud. The cattle stood at one end of the enclosure, their heads into the wind. Sometimes the rain caught us in the middle of the night. Then we lay curled up, soaked, waiting for morning. And when it dawned, it always was like a betrayal: All it meant was yet more dampness we couldn't bear.

Zaza blew the ram's horn. At first we didn't take notice. It was a familiar sound that was lost amongst all the others, but it started things moving. Animals came down from the hills. They squelched closer, but then held back. They came to a halt in front of the gangplank. They snorted and panted, their fur tangled. Then those who lived in the shipyard realized that the call of the ram's horn had been the signal. The beginning of the end was here, the moment of truth had arrived. In their tens and hundreds, they gathered around the ark, carrying their possessions on their backs in bundles, beating off the cattle and the animals pressing around them with sticks. But the trapdoor did not open until after dark. By evening, they were standing in oozing dung.

When darkness had fallen, the Builder, Shem, and Japheth appeared on the deck. They put out a gangplank, which only the animals were permitted to cross. Most of them entered the hold willingly enough. Because of the mud on their feet, they stepped along the gangplank carefully, even those animals who were used to climbing ledges. The warriors were stationed at the gangplank in order to prevent uninvited guests from getting on board. Those who were waiting were becoming tired, understanding they would be standing there for hours if the animals came first. When they realized Taneses and Zedebab were still sleeping in their tents, they too withdrew to rest. The animals, though, kept moving up the gangplank. The dark lent the embarkation a contrived air; it became an event such as you only hear about in stories. There was a solemn movement of paws on planks, careful and fearful, as if the rhythm it produced must never be forgotten. The composition of the boarding crowd was like an ancient recipe: seven clean animals, two unclean. They were distributed over the ship according to their weight. There were animals who panicked at the scent of others; they were kept apart. Some were refractory. The camel, for instance: Shem took hold of it by its halter, and the beast sprayed the contents of its stomach all over him. The snake was denied access to the ark. It had seduced one of the first ancestors of the Rrattika. Judging by its head, it had not really changed after all those years and was still up to no good, so it was chased back with sticks.

It turned out there were not enough cages. Ham was called away from us to help. He dragged up stakes and bars and in great haste divided the cages up into smaller spaces. Japheth carried animals into the hold, the legless ones, the ones so small you had to keep them in a jar, the animals who were so lazy or slow that without his help it would have taken them half the night.

Of each species they took the biggest and strongest. They didn't seem to comprehend that once they had taken the leaders on board, the whole herd was desperate to follow. They had to pull up the gangplank and wait for the animals to calm down before they could continue with the embarkation. From the little field on the slope, you could hear the shouting and, again and again, the counting.

Zaza shuffled across the shipyard. Till the very last moment, she kept shaking seeds out of flowers and putting dried fruits in straw-lined boxes. Neelata had handed her affairs over to her lady's maids. She now stayed in the ship day and night. She had spread out her carpets and wall hangings and made herself a nest. Taneses stayed in her tent while she still could, like Zedebab. Zedebab had strengthened hers with ropes and pegs and would admit no one except her twin sister, whom she was going to have to leave behind.

We slept from sheer exhaustion, but not for long. We were woken by people shouting farther down. Their mats had been lifted by the water. They were afloat. Quickly, they pulled up the flaps of their tents, hoping the water would run out. Only then did they notice that the water was coming from outside. All around them floated the remains of the shipyard, pieces of bamboo from the scaffolding, branches and jugs. The ark still stood, rock solid, at its landing stage. The water lapped gingerly at its keel. Toward morning, we tried to sleep some more. Lying close enough together, stopping any leaks in the cover we lay under, and not getting wet seemed much more important than the embarkation going on below.

There were no longer any clear periods between downpours, the rain was constant hour after hour. We became motionless, as if the raindrops had nailed us to the ground by the hems of the blankets we wore over our shoulders like mantles, and which had become heavy as lead.

More and more tents were pulled down, mostly by laborers who were leaving. They left the shipyard but were back after only a few days. "The Builder is right," they said. "The water is covering the whole world." They were terrified, those simple souls, they nursed no hopes of being among the elect. They were the poorest of the poor, the lowest in society, they knew they did not stand a chance. They tried as best they could to put up their tents again and keep their children dry. They did not complain. The women went on bathing their children every evening and did their best to see they did not catch cold in their damp clothes. They went on trying to cook millet. There is no point in suffering from hunger, not even if you know you are going to drown. You could not talk to them any longer. Their gaze had been turned inward, and they showed that waiting for death takes place in total solitude.

But even those who thought they would be admitted to the ark became suspicious, particularly when some thirty stowaways, who had hidden in different parts of the ship, were driven out with sticks and whips by the warriors. If so many animals were let in, there would be very little space left over for people. Was it possible they had been deceived all this time, and that only the sons and the nephews and those warriors in their woolen skirts were amongst the elect? The arrogance of the warriors, the impudence they showed when they chased the poor devils from the ship, made it clear there would be fighting for a place. That was what everyone was preparing for: pushing and shoving and fighting. People had another look at their possessions, throwing away anything superfluous, packing anything absolutely essential in even smaller bags. You wondered what these people thought they were going to do with bread that was soaked, with freshly washed clothes that were as wet as the ones on their backs, with small tools, with bags and packs that would make them sink to the bottom instantly.

We could hear questions being raised all around the shipyard: "Why are they letting the animals on first? Do they matter more than people?" When I passed by, some of them couldn't stop themselves from saying, "This is the revenge of the dead. Led on by strangers, we violated their burial place and stole their water. Now they are repaying us with water."

Things were still being loaded constantly. The Builder insisted, for instance, on taking our bathtub. The loading had to be done so fast that the contents of jars and baskets were no longer checked. At the most, Japheth saw to it that anyone who came on board left again. That is how it happened that someone brought some flat baskets on board. No one heard or saw it happen, but afterward the story got around: The carrier uttered curses as he entered the ark. In the baskets were the snakes that had been denied entry earlier. Apart from objects, only animals were admitted again that day. On the ground, near the entrance, their feet in the water, exhausted people stood where they could. They no longer dared leave their spots.

The next morning, the red tent had been pulled down. The pegs had been pulled up, the canvas lay on the ground like a dead bat. There were sounds, soft at first, rumbling like distant surf. The winds, coming from all four corners, carried the smells of storm and tempest. Then the rumbling swelled into a drumming full of fury, gods banging on the cages in which they were locked. The earth began to tremble. I saw it in the water in my jugs, which took on a life of its own, rippling and splashing. From the hills sounded the hoofbeats of rushing herds. Dripping tumbleweeds rolled ahead of the storm, kicked along like outcasts.

Put had been brave up to now. But in the fury of the storm he saw Neelata bring llamas and camels on board. "I want to go with her," he screamed. "It's too scary here!" We let him go, his pockets filled with nuts and dates. We saw him run down the hill like a lost dog, his legs crooked under his body, his face twisted with fear.

The Builder was nowhere to be seen. My father stretched the tarpaulin over our boat and shouted over the roaring, "Why doesn't that man offer a sacrifice? Whoever his god is, now is the time to tender his offering!" He poured milk on the ground for our gods, in particular for the god of the storm with his immense wings. But the earth did not accept the milk. It was already saturated with liquid.

46

The Windows of the Heavens Are Opened

*I*t was the seventeenth day of the second month. All the fountains of the deep broke open. To the sound of howling winds, solid curtains of water came down. There was not only rain but also hail. The wind raged over the land. Trees bent, chickens were plucked alive on their roosts, tents broke loose, planks and boards were hurled around. The dead floated from the caves where they had been buried.

Our shelter tore apart. The section that was left was just large enough to keep me dry, but my father sat in the rain. From where we were fighting the wind, we could see what was happening to the others. The large group waiting at the base of the ship were taken unawares by the tempest. The gangplank was still out, but guarded by so many warriors with long swords that anyone who set foot on it was immediately beaten back. Many were killed, pushed onto the gangplank by the mass of people and instantly impaled on the spears. Even at that stage, they might appear to be victims of an accident, and most of them still seemed to expect the hatch to be opened soon. There were some who had armed themselves and practiced an assault in the hills. Now they too arrived, forming small groups and going around the ship with ladders and ropes to attack it from its unguarded side. But already the chaos was too great. Even armed groups with careful plans were scattered. The hulk they wanted to climb was tall and the wind against them. Together with hordes of others, they fled up the cliff. They assumed the water could never rise to that height. To be able to overlook the land made them feel certain they would not be taken by surprise. But they were troubled by the wind. They had to lie down to stop themselves from being blown off the cliff.

We saw how Zedebab's twin sister was led away from the ship by warriors. And we saw Ham coming up the cliff! We had been waiting for him for a long time. The light was failing and the landscape changing. We had worried about how he would find the path in this storm, and now we thought he was coming for us. But we were wrong, it was the brushwood a long way below us that he was heading for. Groping around, he found a tree stump to which he tied the dog. The animal was sodden with rain and hung its head. I jumped up, my father following quickly to protect me, and shouted, "Come on, Ham, come on! The calamity has arrived! What's keeping you?"

But Ham did not hear me. Without once looking back at the dog tugging at its rope, he returned to the ship.

Here and there, small boats appeared in the landscape. Like ours, they had been hidden under branches. But around each of them, there was a commotion. I recognized the movements of those on board. They were bailing. "They're taking in water, Father! Look at what sort of boats you've built them!"

My father leaned against me like a wet, formless sack. He replied, "The boats you see down there, they all leak. For a bit, the people in them will manage to plug the holes. Then they'll start bailing. But in the end, as Shem instructed me, they will sink. I had to do this to save us. Only on that condition was I allowed to keep our truss-boat."

The rattling of the hail and the raging of the wind made thinking about what he said difficult. I felt numbed, as if from a blow that takes you beyond pain. I sat bent over beneath the scrap of shelter my father held up, motionless, as if all I had to do was wait for it to be all over. There was nothing to persuade me that this was really happening, that the world was being inundated, that through my father's doing, the little boats down there were leaking.

But while I waited, still, there was a new commotion in the shipyard.

"They're going on board," I said dully. My father let go of the guy ropes. The wind howled and the shelter flapped away behind us like a bird flying up. He took me by the hand. Together we ran to our boat and dragged the bundles of branches away from it. It was well-built, our boat, it had an upper deck with a hatch that could be closed against the rain and against people who, when they saw our vessel, would try to get in. In the bilge was a layer of sand for the fire, and stores of food and water stood in every available spot.

"The heads of the ark builders are filled with strange thoughts," said my father as we looked for a spot in the hold. "Their forebears have eaten a fruit that made them able to distinguish between good and evil. Good means obedience, evil means disobedience. They can think no further. But look at me! I make the boats leak and find delight in thus taking revenge for what they have done to my wife. Yet all I am doing is obeying the order of the elect Shem and Japheth!"

Once again, the sound of horns rang out from the encampment. We heard the clatter of hooves on the gangplank, sometimes followed by plunging sounds from the water below. We heard the crack of a whip. It must have been the last of the animals, the kinds that came from afar and had only just made it. The Builder must have said, "It is time." Ham had to carry the varan, wildly lashing out, on board on his shoulder, together with other reluctant or slow reptiles.

"Let me have a look," I begged my father.

"We have to close the hatch, Re Jana, don't be so reckless!"

"But there is so much noise. What if Ham comes and we don't hear him?"

Because I insisted, he left the hatch partly open. From its lee, I saw how Camia's mother lost her little daughter. She was blind, and in a way that was an advantage for her: She was used to finding her way by touch. She calmly called her child's name, but in her fear, Camia ran the wrong way. That was the last thing I saw. The sky turned black as a sackcloth of hair. The darkness made the chaos around the ark complete: People were storming the ship blindly, screams of fury and of pain went up, many were trampled.

Full of fear, we closed the hold. We huddled together and waited. So we sat for a long time, my father's heart beating against my shoulder. He muttered prayers I had never heard. We listened to the tumult outside, the screams of humans and animals, and the pounding of the storm.

Suddenly something battered against the hull. It sounded like splintering wood. Broken branches, we thought, or something else floating around. Briefly, we hoped it might be Ham, but we did not see his face appear at the hatch. We had heard so many noises, this seemed no worse or more ominous than the others.

Not long after, we finally heard Ham, his voice hoarse and distorted. We unfastened the bolt to let him in. But he did not come into the hold. He grabbled through the opening and gripped my hand, shouting again. I tried to understand him, but it was impossible with all the clamor around us. "What?" I shouted, but already he was silent. His fingers around my wrist like claws, he hauled me out of the hold. He threw my arm around his neck and lifted me up. I heard the sucking noise of his feet in the mud. I did not understand what he wanted, I wriggled loose, but he gripped me even more firmly and threw me over his shoulder.

"Look! Just look!" he yelled, pointing at the hull of the truss-boat, in which there was a wide, gaping hole. Next to it lay a tool, only its handle visible in the mud, but I could see it was an ax. "Shem did that! To stop me going separately. Now I have to go on my father's ark!"

The pelting rain, the seething winds and the deafening roar, the thundering of rocks rolling down the hills was everywhere around us. Through all this violence, he carried me to the ship. It rained stones, they scraped my shoulders and calves. The earth rumbled. But it was as nothing compared to what was going on farther away. There were moments when everything was lit up, more brightly than by lightning: The stars were falling from the sky. Under the onslaught of the heavenly bodies, Ham threw himself on the ground. Craters opened and were immediately wiped out by the impact of yet more celestial objects. Before Ham could get up again, blood poured down. Its drops burned our skin like scorpion bites. But he did not let go of me. Despite all my extra weight of mud and water, he heaved me even more firmly over his shoulder.

I saw how my father jumped from his boat into the ooze to go and inspect the hole in the hull. I shouted, but he neither saw nor heard me. Around us, groups of dromedaries, camels, donkeys, and deer raged in a frenzy. They swung their heads wildly trying to make progress in the mud. During one flash, I saw their wide nostrils and their moist eyes, gleaming dark green. The ark was the only place left now that the end of the world had come, now that the fury of the Builder's god seemed irreversible. Large chunks of earth broke off the hillsides, boulders tumbled, columns erected by human hands fell down their full length, bushes were washed away. When we arrived at the gangplank, Ham let go of me, ripped off his cloak, and threw it over my head and face. The warriors were still defending the entrance. If one of the Rrattika managed to hoist himself out of the mud and find the gangplank, he would immediately be forced back by whips and spears. The warriors administered the kinds of blows you can only deal if you feel yourself superior to everyone. But they did not stop Ham. I was so limp in his arms that I must have looked like some dead animal, or a bale of cloth.

The entrance to the ark was a gaping hole lit by neither lamps nor torches. There was a penetrating smell of excrement, the fear-scent of the skunk stronger than all the rest. Here you no longer felt the stinging rain, but the noises were fearsome and in their own way painful. I heard the stamping of hooves and shrieks like children's that must have come from cats, apes, or birds. I heard the sputtering of lizards, the snorting of pelicans, the whining of foxes and dingoes. And I heard Shem's voice in the distance: He was trying to calm down the animals but could not control his own desperation. Ham moved fast; someone called out his name but he did not turn around. Deep in the gallery he uncovered my face, but it was so dark in the ship that I still could see nothing. He climbed some stairs or a ladder: I could feel him lift his legs up high, groaning with the effort. He moved through long corridors. He could have put me down and made me walk, but he did not; he held me firmly like something precious.

As soon as it was possible to raise my voice above the sounds around me, I cried, "What about my father?"

"Wait. I'm going to get him," he shouted back. He went into a side passage, and when we came to the third or fourth pen, he put me down on my feet so he could open it. The bamboo-barred door swung away from us and I realized I had to bend over. There were animals in the pen I entered, although I could not see what they were; I made out their dark shapes against the wall. They seemed fearful and tired. I could hear them making clucking, coughlike noises in their throats, as if they were reassuring one another. Ham came into the pen after me. He forced them out of his way with a *ksss* sound. In the middle stood a hutch that seemed intended for animals to sleep in. He put his hand on the side panel. There was a click of wood on wood. He tugged at me, and I understood what he wanted. Feet first, I slid into the sleeping hutch. I fit exactly, as if in a coffin. Then I heard his footsteps receding in the gallery.

The cage had been built by an amateur. There were plenty of gaps for me to look through. The animals alongside me went back to their places. They made gobbling sounds like turkeys. Their fear of the tempest helped them forget I was there, so close to them. A cushion lay beside me; I reached for it and could feel that it was Neelata's, there were roses embroidered on it. The uproar in the ship continued. I could hear how places were allotted, how animals were chased out of one pen and into another. Outside there was shouting from the workmen who had helped with the dragging of timber, the lashing of scaffolding and the stirring of the pitch. They realized what the Builder had intended all along, what he needed his ark for, and why there had been such demands for speed toward the end. All this time, the warriors were busy repelling the people trying to storm the gangplank. They did it with skill and efficiency, determination showing on their faces. When my father handled his moths for the first time, he did not know one had to hold them by their lower wings. Instead he had pressed on their bodies and killed them, but did that mean he was bad? The warriors were just as ignorant about the workmen they beat off the railings. They knew only that they were doing what they were supposed to do.

For an improbably long time, the walking back and forth went on. I waited, full of tension. Then the time came: I heard

Ham enter a pen not far from me and talk to someone. *Another pen with a sleeping hutch*, I thought, noticing that for the first time in a long while, I was breathing steadily.

And what had to happen happened. With a few slashes at the ropes, the gangplank was cast off. It scraped along the bow, I heard it fall, and the screaming of the warriors shook me out of the stupor I had been in throughout the embarkation. With a strength I had not suspected was in me, I kicked the front panel of my cage loose. In his hurry, Ham had not shut the barred door of the pen properly, and it swung open as soon as I pushed against it. I searched for a way up. I climbed stairs and ramps. I got to the deck via one of the trapdoors, probably not the normal way, but the ship was shaking too much to look for anything else. I could barely stay upright out there, the wind tugged at my body, and I had to use both hands to hang on to the edge of barrels full of rainwater.

Under the gangplank lay warriors. Many had been killed by the fall. Of those who had stood below, some died because the storm hurled rocks against their heads or drove sharp pieces of wood through their bodies. They were the lucky ones: They perished quickly and from a cause they could, in their final moments, comprehend. Those who were still alive now were gripped by despair. The notable, the distinguished, the warriors, the tradesmen, they all rushed the ark. They hit its sides with their fists, they shouted curses that could be heard deep inside the ship, they pressed against the bow like dogs. And the children, all those boys and girls who used to hang around the ship hoping to be given a pitch doll, they screeched like animals.

When the ship was lifted off the ground, the hold resounded, even more than before, with the screams of creatures in terror of death. Never before had they felt the ground move under their legs. They were not used to their bleating, bellowing, barking, and twittering reverberating against the inner wall of the ship. And the thunderclaps now followed one another so rapidly they were like their own echoes. The wake of the ark caused small boats to break their moorings and drift. They either took in water or capsized. All around floated rafts with people hanging on.

The Builder shouted at them, "The Unnameable, who knows no regret, has been driven to regret. He regrets that it had to come to this." And the hatch closed.

Then the god of the Builder opened the floodgates of the heavens. The land that he had divided from the water when he created the world was now joined to it once more. The water came from the east and the west, from the south and the north. Whirlpools and eddies formed, there were clouds of spume, masses of silt and foam rolled toward us. The air became briny. Far away, tempestuously rising rivers broke their banks. The water smashed stones and rocks. The sea came rolling inland. The ark yawed and listed. The people were washed off the cliff. Everything that was outside the ship disappeared.

I could not see anything anymore because I was enclosed by spume. I knew that another tidal wave would wash me off the deck. I had to go back. I did not have time to go down the ladder, and plunged into the depths through the well hole. Crawling on my belly, I reached the pen. I wanted to get back inside the hutch;

it was, all things considered, the best place. But the ark was pitching and yawing so hard that I found it impossible to get through the small opening. As soon as I attempted to, I rolled against my fellow inmates, who screeched and beat their wings tumultuously and wounded me with their beaks and claws. *If only I had the cushion*, I thought, but I could not reach it. My head and shoulders hit the wall, now to starboard, now to port.

The tempest went on endlessly. Whenever the roar subsided momentarily, there was still a continuous dull rumbling. Then you could hear people shouting, "Here! Over here!" They all drowned, those people who thought they would fare differently, who did not realize that exceptions are not always possible. No matter how talented, how skilled, how determined in their thinking, they drowned. I managed to get a firm hold by hooking my hands and arms in the bars. The water smashed against the hull, shaking the planks of its outer skin. With my feet braced against a rafter, I experienced the way the water gathered its force, exhausted it, gathered it again and exhausted it again, in a rhythm of effortless patience.

The rumbling and the lightning ceased. A shaken silence remained, together with the sour smell of vomit. I heard nothing but the raging of the wind and the thundering of the waves against the bow. My first sorrow was not for my father or Put. I was convinced they were in the ark. My first sorrow was for Camia, the little dancing girl who now floated somewhere in the water. With much pain and effort, I got up and went back to the deck. It was night, but because burning particles were still falling out of the sky, I was able to see. There were animals that could swim and followed the ship for a long time: dogs, beavers, geese, hippopotamuses, crocodiles. Of people able to swim there were none, there were only those who had got a hold on the small boats that floated here and there. The rich had the best boats. They were made out of sound timber and had partitions to stop the water streaming in. They were leaking all the same, and sink they did in the end. The parents jumped overboard to save the children. But even that weight was too much for the boats. And so the last ones to float on the surface of the water were mainly children, wearing well-made woolen clothes and pearl ornaments around their wrists.

47

Fruit

I dreamed Ham was standing next to me. He had a torch in his hand, which blinded me. He looked like someone who urgently needed help. He was covered in blood and animal droppings.

"Did the varan hurt you?" I asked him. I knew it was not his own blood. It was that of the people he had beaten off with a pitchfork to get to the ropes of the gangplank. He insisted that I should wash it away as soon as possible.

"And my father?" I asked, but he had already gone, and I woke once more from a brief, restless sleep.

After long hours I noticed a faint glow. I could hardly call it light, it was no more than a slight break in the darkness, a faint suspicion that up above, outside, the night was past, that a dawning turned the sky almost imperceptibly paler. It did not come through the wall of the ship, because that was covered with pitch that had crusted over the cracks; if I was not careful, my hair stuck to it. It came from a different direction. My father had explained to me how he planned to bring light and air into the ship. He had, along the length of the ship, left gaps under the edge of the roof. When necessary, wooden panels could be slid across them. No doubt, this had been done, it had been necessary! Had someone now removed the panels? Was that not a bit premature, as nobody could be sure the storm would not come back?

Apart from what I could see through the bars, I only had my ears to discover what was going on. I listened to every sound. It was tiring; I had to work out which came from people and which from animals. There was a horse, somewhere, or some other hoofed animal, stamping on the plank flooring. It sounded like a human with a crutch. The Builder with his staff? One of the brothers who had hurt his leg in last night's tumult? Thanks to the sounds, I learned that the faint light was not dawn. The glow I had seen came from torches that were coming closer. The sloshing sounds no longer came only from the waves outside, but also from buckets that were being emptied into drinking troughs, I supposed, and presumably only humans did things like that. The sound did not give me any sense of relief. To me, who had spent so much time on boats, and who as a baby, so my father said, could only sleep with the rocking of water below me, this rescue felt like imprisonment, like a trial or a trick.

Thanks to the faint glimmer of light I could see that I was amongst the dodoes. With their great layers of fat they looked well prepared for bad times. The sounds they made had changed. They held their heads at an angle, making them look as if they were questioning one another, or deliberating about what they ought to do in this confined space with not a branch or a stone around. They did not move out of my way when I tried as quickly as possible to get back inside my small but safe sleeping hutch. We had survived the storm together, and they looked at me as if

I were one of them. Because of the wild tossing around of the past night, dozens of splinters had lodged in my arms.

The light became stronger, and I could hear voices. Someone approached, lugging tubs, putting them down, opening pens, throwing fodder inside, and latching them again. The dodoes were restless, hacking into the planks with their beaks as if they expected seeds to jump out of them. My arms trembled from the exertion it took, but I managed to see how the door of the dodoes' pen was opened. The hand threw fruit inside, which the dodoes gobbled up. Briefly, the gallery remained quiet. The door of the pen did not close again, but opened wider. Moving rapidly, someone slipped inside, without any sound of weight on wood, without a groan of exertion.

It was Ham. He carried more fruit, which he quickly threw into my hutch. He hardly bent forward, and there was not enough light to get a proper look at him: All I could see were his eyes like hollows in his face. "My brothers are nearby. I can't talk. I'll come as soon as I can," he said.

"Wait!" I whispered. "Come back!" My voice was hoarse from the cold I had suffered. I had not been able to warm myself in the mud-soaked clothes that had enveloped me for so long and that had saturated the wood underneath me. Outside an unceasing call was coming from the water. It was a high, wailing voice I did not recognize.

"Who is that calling?" I asked.

"An old man has sewn cork into his clothes. My father will not allow him to be pulled from the water." Swiftly, he vanished from the pen and shut it behind him. The light faded and disappeared.

The waiting started again. The rain kept coming, I heard it lashing the bow. In fits and starts, I realized I had escaped death. I had to stay motionless because on this ship there was no compassion. Sleeping in the ark hurts one's limbs, that was the first thing I learned.

48

My Father

hey returned much later, after I had already fallen asleep several times, and perhaps a whole day had passed. Once more I heard the sound of water in drinking troughs. Again I heard the voices and the footsteps. The feeding proceeded faster than the first time; the various actions went more smoothly and there was less shouting.

This time I did not crawl into my hutch. Quiet as a mouse I sat amongst the birds. I saw Shem and Japheth moving quickly through the pens, Shem with a small monkey on his shoulder and Japheth with his beard and hair tied back with string. The cloaks they used to wear had gone. They now wore, right against their skin, thin undershirts that could be washed in little water and did not offer much shelter for lice. Ham entered the pen and closed the grating behind him. I did not move until after he had opened the sleeping hutch.

A shock went through his body when he noticed me behind him. "Aah," he said, closing his eyes, when he recognized me. He looked tired. The skin of his face was damaged in several places. Along his hairline there were traces of clotted blood, the result of fights with refractory animals. I saw instantly what needed to be done, where the wounds could be bathed and what oils would reduce the bruising. I just wanted to look, but before I realized, we were holding each other's hands, our fingers entangled like ancient knots that could not be unraveled.

"We made it," I said. "We're alive," and I kissed the bruises on his face.

He pushed me away, pressing close to the wall where it was really dark. At every sound in the passage I could feel him stiffening and huddling closer up against the wall.

"You must stay in the hutch. It could have been someone else instead of me. Then we would be thrown overboard, you as well as me."

"The hutch is so small. Let me sit here when nobody is near."

"There are snakes on board. We've found two flat baskets from which they've escaped. They can wriggle through the gratings. You're safer in the hutch." Ham too was wearing just an undershirt, apparently designed specially for the journey. He had a hood against the dust, but because there was no sun here, they had skimped on the material. Hence it was so ill-fitting it was embarrassing.

"A snake is not enough to keep my father inside a small hutch. He is not afraid of them. You must have something a bit bigger for us, where we would all fit, including Put?"

He scrambled up and turned away from me. His brothers had moved on, darkness had returned and that should have calmed him. But it did not. His body trembled, and when I touched him I could feel the cold sweat on his skin.

"Is he far from here?" I asked. "Not too far, I guess, because I heard him being brought in."

He pushed me toward the hutch by my shoulders. I appreciated that I had to get into it again; with snakes about, it would really be safer, and he had to get back into the passage before his brothers would return to see what was keeping him. "Do not ask me such questions, Re Jana," he said with a sob in his voice. "I don't know what to say."

"What is the matter then?" I asked as I slid obediently into the hutch, which smelled mostly of me. I took up the same cramped position as before so that I could at least see some of him as he spoke to me from the opening at the end.

"Did you watch the disaster? It was a hundred times greater than the violence we expected. I could not get through it. Your father stayed behind in the flood."

The force of his words knocked my elbows from under me. "And Put?" I asked.

"Neelata tied him onto the back of the dromedary. He is on board but does not show himself. He is a fearful child, he will need time to get used to it."

"Take me to Neelata then," I said, managing to stay calm just a little longer.

"Keep Neelata out of this. Do you want my father's curse to hit her?"

I fell backward, stretched out in that hutch that was too small to hit your head hard against the wall. A sound came from my throat, something like the sound the dodoes made. He must have left me, though I do not know when. I paid no attention to him.

*   *   *

I made a din, but not with my voice, because that had broken down. I turned over and pounded the wall with my feet. It was a feeble noise, barely audible above the stamping of the hundreds of animals. My body fell into a violent kind of shivering that set the boards around me shaking. In my mouth, tastes came that I did not recognize. My teeth rattled, my chest went up and down as fast as a finch's. How had it been when my father drowned? He was a good swimmer, even though he hardly ever did. A boat builder did not swim, he went by boat. If there was no boat available, he would rather tie two planks together than have to swim. More than once it happened that the floats of such a punt would come apart. On those occasions I had seen how fast he was, how powerful the stoke of his arms trained by rowing. Never would he let go of his catch, he dragged the net after him through the silt. The thought that he would have kept swimming for a long time made the pressure on my chest worse. It made my body jerk like a fish on the shore of a lake. What was left for me on this ark? If Put was on board, was he not, more than ever, the child who had blabbed, who had caused my father's death? My fingers clawed, I scratched fibers from the planks because life itself seemed to have forgotten me. I hurt myself and let the drops of blood fall around me like petals.

Ham brought me food, but I did not eat. He said, "You must make yourself get over your grief. You must think of both of us now. Your noise will give us away. Stop it. My brothers ask me which animal is so restless in this corner of the ship. They ask me for a plan of the ship, because they think some animal is groaning with hunger."

I managed only very slowly. My arms and my legs were like tentacles that did not really belong to me. At best, I could keep them still when the dodoes were being fed. But afterward, the shaking and banging came back until it made the dodoes uneasy, and I kept still for their sake.

49

The Papyrus Boat

For days on end, I did not eat, it seemed pointless. For a while, I was concerned about the cuts in my skin. Briefly, I felt hungry, but that too passed. I lay in my own excrement for so long I stopped longing for water. Now and then I changed my position. I turned over and moved Neelata's cushion. I made the time, which I no longer valued, pass by sleeping.

After days, I was woken by a sound behind the wall. I felt someone open the panel by my head and recognized the hands that dragged me by my shoulders out of my hollow.

I was not sure I was not dreaming. I felt sick. Because feeling the warmth of his body was so immediate, so real, I knew I was not dreaming. Being upright again, once more feeling my proper relation to the ground, made the blood sing in my ears. I really wanted to stand up, stretch my back, and hold up my head, but my legs were not up to it. I fell, limp, against the man who had lifted me up.

He caught me. He picked me up and carried me out of the pen into the passage. Every sigh, every cough from a cow, the scuttling of the armadillo, the flap of a bat's wing, stopped him moving. He progressed by feel. Luminous eyes of nocturnal animals in stacked cages turned toward us. The man lifted his knees up high, he was carrying me up steps or a slope. After a while I felt, to my amazement, wind and rain on my face. We were on the deck.

The air brought me to my senses. The pale-skinned man next to me wore a nose ring. There was a scent around him I recognized, the scent of dread, but also of cassia. He put me down on my feet without letting go of me. The wind coming off the water, full of eddies and whirlpools, was cold. On the ship's roof sat birds, small ones, but also cranes, herons, and eagles. They were dead tired from flying and jostled for space on the edge of the water barrels.

I breathed shallowly so as not to cause myself pain. I shivered with fever. Ham felt it, but he did not take me to a warmer spot. Excitedly, he stayed right there, and I realized there must be something I should see. "There, just look!" he said, pointing forcefully at the dark expanse of water. There were so many things floating in the water. I looked at the glittering surface, the play of black on black, and the moonless sky that was like an inverted sea, and I could only wonder where the shipyard was and the hills. Where were the Rrattika with their tents and their children?

But then there was a shape I recognized. I saw a papyrus gondola, like the ones on which the marsh people buried their dead. I grabbed Ham's arm, I looked and looked until I was certain: It was my mother's papyrus boat. All other vessels had perished, only this one had stayed afloat, the one that was meant to be burned! Nobody had bothered to smash a leak in this little craft because no Rrattika believed it would float. I pressed my nails, grown long from lack of use, deep into Ham's skin.

"Why are you showing me this? Don't torture me like this!" I groaned. I felt feverish and cold, I could not cope with the memory of the loss of my mother, not now that I also had to constantly think of the loss of my father.

But he pointed again. "Look! Why don't you look?!" he said.

I peered. When I moved closer to the edge, Ham's grip on me stiffened. There was a movement on the little vessel. A human shape was visible. Someone, during the storm, had run to the thick-fingered bushes to take cover on the papyrus boat. Someone had piloted the vessel unscathed through the storm. On a pole hung, like a large flag, a cloth I recognized. It was my mother's seamless cloak, which my father had carried with him up to the end, even long after he had given all his other belongings away. And so I became convinced: The papyrus boat carried my father like a swan her young. So far-sighted my mother had been before she died: She had foreseen the discovery, perhaps even the destruction, of our truss-boat and taken care that a second vessel would be ready for us.

"Do you see?" Ham asked, enraptured. "It is him, he lives, he has survived." He hopped from one foot onto the other, while I could only stare. He lifted me up and took me away from the deck. We went along the shaft my father had designed to bring food to the animals on the level below. Afraid of waking anyone, Ham moved cautiously, but I could sense his excitement, his relief at the news he had brought me.

But I could not feel any joy. *What will he live on,* I wondered. *What will he eat when the three loaves I baked for him on a small fire just before the flood are finished? Will he fish all the time? Will he drink the floodwater? It will make him ill, being polluted with drowned lives.*

50

The Bath

*I*assumed that Ham was taking me back to my hiding place, but I was wrong. Along a succession of passages and ladders he carried me to the heart of the ark, the place where the game of shovel-board was set up and where, on a layer of sand, the fire was kept burning. Now I could see, I was finally in a place where there was light. We were surrounded by rows of amphoras. They contained sloshing water, some of which had splashed onto the ground. Provisions enough for a journey of many months were stacked up here. They still cooked on dried dung, I noticed, although they had brought much brushwood and could have spared all those on board the suffocating fumes. Ham handed me a beaker and watched as I drank its contents.

Once my thirst had been slaked, Ham carried me to another corner of the space. To the side stood my father's bathtub, three-quarters filled with clear water, next to it on the ground a small cloth, a sponge, and oil.

Ham dipped a corner of the cloth in the water and wrapped it around his fingers. He did what he had always seen me do. He said, "Abstinence, my father has said. We must abstain. From each other, but from water too. It is to be used only for drinking, not for washing. And that while there has never been so much water!" On his knees he approached me. He carried the flask of oil in his left hand. I raised my hand to take the cloth and the oil; I thought I knew what was expected of me.

I was mistaken. He did not remove the cloth from his fingers. He bent over me and washed my forehead. He brushed back my hair and looked at my face by the flickering light of the fire. He washed the red rain from my hands and arms, doing it the way I had done it for him many times. The water was exactly the right temperature. There was no sand in it, it did not sting my wounds. When he had finished, he threw herbs into the water in the tub. He laid me down in it. For the first time since I had been on the ark, I felt no pain.

"We will get food to your father," he said while the water lightened my body and my fever went down. "We'll get him salt and oil. Perhaps even some of Neelata's nuts, I expect they will float."

The water nourished me like bread. After a while, I had enough strength to raise myself in the bath. Ham helped me stand. I looked at myself; my hips were a complex web of carmine pink, purple, and thunder-sky blue. My legs were covered in burst veins that resembled underwater plants, and garlands hung over my shoulders. In the reflection in the water under me I saw that my hair was one tangled knot, standing up cheerily like that of a young badger that had fallen in shallow water.

"Food is not needed," I said. "We'll pick him up tonight. We'll hide together."

Ham put my damp dress back over my shoulders. My hair was heavy with moisture. He shook his head. "Then he must get closer. He will not do that except to rebuke and lecture us."

51

Desire

*E*very night changed into the next night, the sky seemed permanently dark. It rained unceasingly. When it became quiet and only the nocturnal animals were still moving, Ham came to me. He brought me straw and reeds, which I wove into a basket. I melted pitch from the side of the ship and smeared it over the basket. On top of the victuals Ham had gotten I placed an oil lamp with a flax wick, and over it all I constructed a roof. Then he launched it onto the water at the end of a long rope. We knew how well my father could steer a boat. Even in a floating box, he would be able to follow a flame.

Every day we prepared a new bundle. But as time went on, the stock of oil lamps ran out; I had to convert basins and hope the sea would stay calm. They did really float, the nuts with the sweet juice and the flesh whiter than shells. Ham threw them, one by one, into the water, where they formed a long, gently bobbing string of pearls.

When the occupants of the ark were awake, I kept quiet as a mouse. In my hutch, I listened to the muttering sound of drops against the side of the ship. It was as if you could hear it, the fermenting of the droppings in the cages and the rotting of the roof above, slowly eroded by the steady rain. I got used to the smell of garlic and olives, of the melon peels and date pips on the floor, of wet wool and animal fodder flavored with sorrel. I thought of my father, sleeping out there in his small hold, and could only wait till silence returned to the ship and Ham came to me.

Ham was not the only one to wander through the ship in the still hours. He heard Taneses and Zedebab, near the air funnel, tell about luminous fishes swimming around the ship. They mentioned a reed gondola too, which just did not seem to sink and carried a human. "The Unnameable will decide whether he lives," they said resignedly. A tension was building in their limbs, he noticed. Both of them longed for their husbands. There was no peace in their abstinence, in complete contrast to the dodoes: These built a nest where they happily deposited pea-green, unfertilized eggs, which I plundered to put in my father's basket. The flood was taking so much longer than the women had expected. None of them understood this continuing rain. Every time they woke, they expected it to have stopped. Their bleeding told them that more than a month had passed. What was the sense of this excess? A death by drowning takes a few minutes, a couple of hours for good swimmers. Was there a doubt, perhaps, that everything had been wiped out thoroughly and for good?

Ham seemed tireless. I longed for him constantly, I wanted him next to me as he used to be under the silkworms' breeding cage. I wanted to stroke his skin till his buttocks felt all silky. I wanted to see him throw back his head.

But he had a pact with his father! Now and then he came to me with water, oil, and a sponge. (It was good water, it had come from my own spring. The water in the containers on deck was disappointing. It was brown and full of grit that irritated the skin.) I had to lie still like a cripple. As soon as I stretched my arms out to him, he pushed them away. I placed my foot against his, but he moved it aside.

Because he was so implacable, because the pact with his father was apparently much more precious to him than our love, there grew, deep inside me, an ill-natured, tireless argument that was directed at my innermost being. To him I said nothing, because there was nothing I could express in comprehensible language. Being silent was hard for me. I wanted to hear myself say what I thought this journey would become, how I hoped to survive the isolation and the separation from my father. But what could I discuss with him?

My silence made him affectionate. I turned around when he asked me to, held my arms exactly where he liked them, and kept smiling. His breathing was so much clearer now, his skin barely flaked at all in this moist environment. While he caressed me, stroked my hair, and straightened my dress, my feeling of desolation increased. I shot into my hutch and nursed my resentment. When he came to me again, a beaker full of goat's milk in one hand, figs in the other, I kept what I wanted to say to myself.

52

The Encounter

*F*or fear of the snakes, I did not often venture out of my sleeping hutch. I had already been through this before in the marshes. A girl had once stepped into her boat before daybreak. In the hold lay a fat-bodied snake that instantly bit her foot. She fell and stayed down. We lifted her out of the boat. We tried to tell her to be still above all, to not move, and breathe as slowly as possible. But she screamed and flailed about. Her frenzy made her blood race through her body, and in no time the poison reached her heart. Moments later, her face turned black, and when we held her upright, blood streamed from her nose. The blood kept coming long after she died, it soaked through the rags we kept rinsing in the marsh. The water turning red around our boat had given me a deep fear of snakes. But as the weeks went by, my loneliness became too great. I climbed from my hutch and pushed my arm through the barred door of the pen. I could just reach the bolt that held it closed. It took me a while to get it open, but I managed: The builders had not reckoned with a long-armed dodo.

I went up the passage. I heard the animals snorting, sometimes I felt the warmth of their breath, but I did not see them. *Is it this long-lasting night that keeps them quiet*, I wondered, *and prepared to abstain although housed close with their own kind?* Feeling my way along the walls, I found the gallery that led upward. I had been here, my grasp of the design saved me, although I had counted on at least some light from the gaps in the decking, and backwater, mud, and wind were the only things coming through. Because of the dirt on the ground, I wished for something on my feet. And for better eyes when nocturnal animals moved suddenly, frightening me excessively.

I knew there was a chance I would be seen. But I was not afraid. My skin was dark; even if someone crossed my path, I could make myself invisible by keeping still. I would surely hear them coming; the voyagers on the ark moved through the hold like cattle. Above all, I was simply not afraid of discovery: I was leaving.

By feel I found a rope ladder that led to the deck and climbed it. A rope as thick as my arm lay on the deck. It was fixed to the railing with a firm loop. I threw it over the side where it uncoiled, dancing down the bow, and then hung a few feet above the water. I slapped my hand in one of the water barrels, waited a little while, and slapped again. When I had done that long enough, I walked up and down near the bow, the skirts of my light-colored cloak flapping like flags.

First I heard the soft sound of oars in the water. Then I saw my father's little papyrus boat. Barely protected from the rain, he sat next to the shelter on the deck that had been designed to hold my mother's body. He rowed cautiously, the way he would have stalked a wild boar in the reeds.

When he was below the rope, I lowered myself along it. The

rope was slippery from the rain, and the burning pain of the slide raced from my hands to my shoulders. Apart from a small lamp on the deck of the papyrus boat, there was no light. The rain caused a fine haze above the water. I must have looked like some unearthly being, the top of the rope indistinguishable because of the darkness, my hair and clothes wet through, floating a few feet above him like a tired bird, but my father was in no doubt that it was me. He pulled a strand of papyrus from his boat and held it in the flame of the lamp. The hold was lit up and I could see him: Bony and gaunt he looked, his eyes deep in their sockets. He was wearing a cap with flaps sticking out, made out of feathers and other debris he had found on the water. It protected him from the rain that kept coming down on him ceaselessly. On the deck lay his funnel and jug, and a few nets and hooks. The bow had discolored, but the outer skin had not turned black, which meant the reeds had not soaked up excessive amounts of water. My father held the burning strand as high up as he could and looked me over thoroughly.

"You're looking well," he said. His other hand firmly held his barge pole. He controlled every movement of his vessel. No wave would take him by surprise, the trim of his boat was at all times in his hand. "Your legs are plump, your face is chubby. You're doing well on that ship."

"Help me, Father. Get me away from here!"

"Why do you want to leave the ark? Doesn't Ham look after you properly?"

"Ham loves his father better than me. I have thought hard: I too love my father best."

He bent his head and sighed. Then looked up to me again. "There is no room here for two people."

"The rope is hurting me. Help me." There was a cramp in my foot that would not go away when I loosened the grip of my legs on the rope. It was my good luck that there was a knot in the rope that offered me some support. I felt it under my foot and stood on it, which made it easier but did not cure the cramp.

He was not about to free me from my situation. He said, "I do not want you on board with me. What are we two together but a dead end, a lineage that is slowly dying out? It is a choice between my loneliness now or your child's loneliness later. Just look at yourself. Your body is filling out despite the hardship you endure. Your life after the flood has already begun. You're carrying a child."

"But Father," I said nearly in tears. "I want to be with you. If you do not want me with you on your boat, then come with me on the ark. I am lonely. Ham will not let me near Neelata, and Put keeps himself hidden."

"If I am to survive, it will be by myself," he replied. "Not with that animal-tamer who has elevated his own family above all others. Not with Shem, who broke his agreement. Not with Ham, who left me behind out of fear. And least of all with Japheth." His voice was firm. After all the hardships he had suffered, I had expected him to be hoarse, but he sounded clear, like a singer or a poet.

I was freezing cold. I could not believe that he had pointed out my condition to me, and for the rest, only allowed the drops that slid off my body to fall onto his deck. It was not worthy of a man who had spent a part of his life looking after a cripple. It was dishonest, it was scandalous, but when I wanted to tell him this, my voice had left my throat like a startled bat.

"Don't send me your baskets of food anymore," he continued, unperturbed. "They tempt me, and I can't resist picking them up. But they make me dependent. The day your supply stops, I starve. I know the rules of scarcity. The first is that you do not help each other. We cannot survive for each other. Help weakens you. Starving happens in solitude."

He should not steer his boat so close under me, I thought. If I fell, I would crash onto his deck and overturn his boat.

"Forget your grudge against the ark builders, Father. Use their ark."

"I must stay in my papyrus boat. That floating coffin you're on is stable, but gives no certainty. I have said it from the start: To save mankind, you need a fleet, not a single vessel. What sort of god carries all his eggs in one basket?"

I began to understand why he kept steering that boat of his so carefully below me. If he moved away, I could throw myself into the water. He saw that I was desperate enough even to defy the man-eating fish.

"I really don't need much room. I belong with you. Those others are strangers to me."

"Think of your child. You are no longer alone."

"I want it to be the way it was, live with Mother and you by the marshes, build rafts and catch fish."

"I know, my daughter. This is the time you do not want to go through. Just as unbearable as the thought that after our death life just goes on, is the knowledge that our lives just go on now that everything has been destroyed. You want this to be past, but you cannot jump, not into the past nor into the future. You must suffer every hour of this punishment."

"Why are you like this, Father? What has happened to you?"

"Have you seen how powerful their god is? Have you seen a single one of our old gods? They have been swallowed up, Re Jana, now there is only the Unnameable. If I find myself on this papyrus boat, it is thanks to Him. Your being on the Ark is thanks to Him. Do nothing that displeases Him, we cannot stand up to Him. Forget what I have taught you and abide by His wishes." His voice was as cold as the water that ran down my back. My strength diminished. It became ever harder to hang on.

"But what will you eat, Father? What will you drink?"

"Worries are for the start of a journey. After a time, they are replaced by a healthy indifference." His torch hissed as he extinguished it in the water. He took up his oars, he rowed away from me. I hung there as if I had been beaten senseless.

There were people who had told me that every life is a continuation of a previous one. Then why did I have the feeling that I had to start from nothing and still had to learn everything? After weeks of longing, I had finally reached my father, and he sent me back. The only thing he had done for me was to confirm what I suspected: that I was carrying a child, and that therefore my place was on the ark. I could not recall a loneliness, a physical pain like this. What had happened to the knowledge I had gleaned in my previous life?

My feet slipped off the knot and I slid down. I wrapped my legs around the end of the rope. The lump rubbed the salt from the spray into my skin and pressed on my already sensitive parts, but it held me. I hung there, helpless as an animal in a snare.

Climbing up the rope seemed the same as going down: It offered no prospects. Letting go would be the simplest — disappearing into the depths, following those many others into the sea. But when I contemplated letting go, it was as if inside me frightened little hands grasped around, and so I dangled, rejected by my father, on the outside of that ship.

I called out. Ham would have been looking for me for ages. He would forgive me and take me back. But it was Japheth who heard me, cross-eyed Japheth of all people. He did not sleep; he too had his nocturnal occupation. Perhaps that was lucky for me: He had the strongest arms and the most accommodating character. Without as much as a sigh or a groan, he pulled me up. He took me under the armpits and carefully lifted me over the railing. He was going to put me on my feet, but a cramp knocked my legs out from under me. Helpless as a fish I fell onto the deck.

53

Japheth

I did not say a word, I think I did not even moan. Japheth helped me stand up. Beaten, numb with cold, I went where I belonged: the dodoes' pen. There I lay down in the clammy hay. Not for long, of course, for Japheth came into the pen and hiked up his skirts. He lay on top of me and opened his mouth as if he was screaming. I curled up to protect the life that was growing inside me, my hips twisting unwillingly, my ribs around me like armor. But Japheth was heavy and strong.

I did not think he meant me any harm. Rather, he was desperate and embarrassed. "I am so sorry, I can't help it," he said. "For the animals, abstinence comes naturally. The Unnameable has suspended their instinct for killing and mating. Why not for us? Why do we have to suffer a discomfort even the animals are spared? I hope I do not hurt you, and if I do, please forgive me." He released me and brushed my hair out of my face. He arranged my clothes and helped me up from my awkward position. I had forgiven him even before his footsteps died out.

Soon after, he was back. He was talking to someone I could not see. "Lie down next to her and feel how beautiful she is," he said.

"Yes," the other replied. "I'll lie next to her."

"Do it now," Japheth said, his voice high-pitched.

"Yes, yes, calm down. Keep your head, I won't betray you."

The other entered the pen. It was Shem, carrying his little monkey, much to the consternation of my fellow inmates. "Go now, will you?" he said to Japheth, who watched him sitting down next to me. Japheth disappeared up the gallery.

Shem wanted me to kneel down and bend over for him. He pressed my face into the hay, making breathing difficult. *Better this way,* I thought, *he won't hurt me with his bony beads.* But thinking of the pain I avoided did nothing to lessen the real pain. With Shem too it did not take long. He must have had things to do still; the animals were waking up and bellowing for their food.

They were back a day later. They entered the dodoes' pen by turns. They were touching in their apologies. They clearly underestimated my satisfaction. At least I was allowed to touch them; they did not, like Ham, force me to stay motionless. Being allowed to stroke did me good, even though their bodies left me cold. I knew where to touch a man, and how long it took before he threw back his head and offered his throat. Japheth exhausted me with his constant demands to use force, to treat him roughly. I thought his skin was probably too thick. But at least he looked at me, even if he did not say much. Shem, on the other hand, looked past me. There was a lot of disgust in his pleasure; perhaps he thought, like me, of the truss-boat he had destroyed. Of love, all he knew was the motions.

Ham came to get me as usual in the quiet hours. I refused to make another basket, and when he brought food for my father, I ate it myself. He asked me to put my anger aside. "Do as you used to. Tell me what you think," but I could not tell him what happened to me during the day. Even less could I tell him that my father had refused to take me on his papyrus boat. All I could do was sing. Songs from the past, rowing songs, hauling songs, songs for bringing in the nets. I sang them with gusto from the hutch:

> Where heads the little boat
> warping on the water,
> racing like a fire,
> and who is at the helm?

> How much costs a net,
> how much a sheet, a candle?
> How much a garth of thorns and stones?
> How much the eyes amongst the reeds
> through which you gaze at me?

As I sang, I painstakingly pulled every thread from Neelata's cushion. I thought it was a shame, I did not want to do it, but my fingers kept going back to it. The pieces of thread flew around me and finished up in my nose and throat. Because the ship's noises went on as normal, I sang even louder; I was hoping I could be heard as far as Put's hiding place. Every once in a while I stopped to listen to the birds who were sharpening their beaks on the bars as if they were getting ready for a massacre. What I did was dangerous. But I could not stop it, my voice hummed on, even when I clenched my jaws and held my hand clamped with all my strength over my mouth.

54

The Builder's Blessing

*I*t did not take Zaza long to work out that her sons were desperate. When she heard a female voice from the cages, she understood what was going on. She approached the Builder and said, "The days are long and there is time to bless the boys. Do not wait until something happens to them, do it now."

The Builder was amenable. The bouts of fever had not recurred for quite a time, and he was satisfied with the progress of the journey. They agreed to meet that very evening in their living space. They would not play shovelboard or make music; their full attention would be on the blessing and the dialogue with their god. I knew exactly when it happened: They fed the animals much faster than usual and there was a nervousness in their movements that had not been there since the departure of the ark. They were, of course, worried: The words of the oracle still rang in their heads.

I was convinced Ham would be cursed: He stole food for me every day, he wasted water, he wandered about the ship while everybody slept. By going down that rope, I had betrayed him. Shamelessly, I had put his life and his child's at risk and demeaned his love. He had been good to me. He had made mistakes, with my father as well as my mother, but never from ill will. To me he appeared upright, the least deserving of the curse. Shem and Japheth had committed the real crimes. For that reason, I opened the dodoes' pen that evening and left my hiding place. I stood by the door to their living space and listened. I was fairly sure I could hear everyone. They sang and prepared for the blessing. With both hands, I pushed the door handle and went in.

The shock I caused was palpable through the whole space. Zaza jumped up to try and stop me. Zedebab gave a yell, high and piercing, as if trying to chase away a bird of prey. Neelata quickly hid in a dark corner, Taneses following her. Shem and Japheth managed not to move a muscle in their faces and stand motionless, their arms folded. Immediately, when Ham saw me, he began beating his breast. Since he had been on the ark, he had taken to wearing a little cap with a white, orange, and blue design. He yanked it off his head, coughed into it, and put it back on. He rubbed his eyes with the tips of his fingers, as if he wanted to wipe away my image.

The only one to stay calm was the Builder. After studying me through his eyelashes, he said, "So it is you who has been doing all that singing lately?"

I said nothing, but nodded.

Japheth lowered his arms. He knelt before his father saying, "I hauled her on board. I am sorry, I do not deserve your blessing."

Immediately, Shem too fell to his knees. "He thought she was one of the sirens we've heard tales about," he said hurriedly. "He only recognized her when she was already on board, and had too much compassion to throw her back into the water, the best proof that he is a good man, so do not curse him." The others had sat down with their backs against the wall, as far as they could from the light.

The Builder looked at me again. He leaned toward me and said, more to his sons than to me, "Is this not the girl who showed us where the water was? She is with child!"

I replied, "The child was fathered by Ham, long before the flood. He has not failed you. He has kept his pact with you, which I cannot say of your other sons." I gave him a small bow before I walked backward to the door. I carefully negotiated the threshold, but once I got to the gallery, I ran.

Of course Ham knew which passages and ladders I usually used. He came after me. He shouted at me through the passages. I did not slow. I raced up onto the deck. There I stood at the railing, almost in the same spot where Japheth had hauled me back on board.

I heard Ham come panting up the ladder. I dragged myself onto the railing and squatted because there was nothing to hang on to.

"Re Jana," Ham begged from the darkness. He did not dare come closer for fear that I would jump. "What has happened? Tell me! Is it what I think? Did you hold Shem and Japheth in your arms the way you used to hold me?"

I looked at the foaming water below. It was black and dirty. The rain ran inside my collar down my back.

"Is it true what you said? Are you carrying my child?"

I gathered my courage to let go of the railing.

Ham did not approach to stop me. He just said, "Even if it is someone else's child, it doesn't make any difference. Stay with us. You are the true chosen one."

55

Neelata

*H*am went back the way he had come and informed the others that I had thrown myself into the sea. He did his best to make the news sound tragic, so the others would observe true sorrow, and it worked. The blessing was canceled. Nor did the Builder pronounce a curse, not even on the snakes he knew lived amongst them.

And I disappeared into the bowels of the ship once more. For the second time, I became invisible, dead to them. From the deck cabin, I snuck into Neelata's hut and sat down amongst the embroidered cushions and the chest full of her mother's clothes. Near the loom and the heaps of yarn and wool I waited for her.

She must have expected me, she was not in the least perturbed when she saw me. She put her arms around me and held me close.

"Where is Put?" was the first thing I asked.

"He is on the ship," she said. "I tied him onto the dromedary with my own hands. Every day, I put out food for him. He comes to get it, but keeps hidden in the darkness. The child needs to get used to things, give him time." She put a blanket around my shoulders.

"How clean you are!" she said when she felt my skin. She was dirty. She spread fodder and mucked out, but was not given water to wash. She pushed me down, I could sit properly once more in these soft surroundings of hers. She put her hand on my stomach to feel the bulge. "How odd," she said. "Our time stands still, but yours just goes on." She combed my hair. She put her left hand on the hair roots, stroking with her right.

She let me comb her hair. Then she even allowed me to rub her with oil. I recognized her scent which, before the flood, I had found so often on Ham. How long was it since I had groomed anyone, how long since my hands last rubbed oil into skin?

"What did you think of the flood?" she asked. "Was it not magnificent? I so enjoyed the cleansing, the thought that, far away, my mother and her brother, with all their belongings, drowned! I had never expected this, I thought I wanted to save the earth, but seeing the destruction gave me pleasure." For a few moments, I understood her exactly. How manageable everything seemed suddenly, how easy and clear it seemed to know that the only things you had to take into account were inside this ship. This understanding made me, very briefly, laugh, the first time in a very long while.

For days on end, I did not leave her hut. Hour after hour she talked to me, and gradually I managed to do what my father had told me to do: I no longer jumped, not into the past, not into the future. I sat out every day of my punishment with painless patience. We had to be so quiet that we learned to communicate with gestures. She made me put on her mother's dresses, forbidden on the ark. She had a little hidden compartment in her hut where she kept black pearls.

"Ham's father wouldn't allow it," she said. "Nothing that

might seduce the boys! But I couldn't possibly leave them behind. The world may perish, but not this." She hung the pearls around my neck and on my ears. She adorned me with the peacock feathers she had gathered on her rounds.

We talked through half the night. We persuaded each other that there are things worse than loneliness. Unsteady love, for instance, or a love that is not recognized. We listed the things we missed: shells the size of a fist, pebbles under our feet, the scent of the sun on a tent, pomegranates in the bowls next to our beds. We told each other what we were afraid of: that love would grow too big for a heart, that love would burst because the heart gives out. We talked about Put, about the smell of cakes and milk that always hung around him, about the beetles and the shiny pebbles he played with, about the small stains on his teeth.

"Do you remember how you rescued me?" she asked. She told me she dreamed about it, about how I dragged her out of the well and bruised her ribs. In her dream, she was never unconscious, she kept her eyes open to see my panic and helplessness. In between our talking, we listened to the reassuring noises around us. There was not a sound that did not reach us, from the chirping of the sparrows to the clattering of the cranes. We knew the fears of the animals, the nerves getting tense when the scent from the lions' enclosure reached the other cages. But we ourselves were not afraid.

One day, she took off her clothing. When the last garment, a tight undershirt, slipped over her head and arms, she said, "This is only my skin." She held out her arms to me. She said, "Open me up. Do what Ham can't do, release me."

To what can I compare her touch? I do not know. It was not stroking, rather a soft, unexpected collision of skin against skin. She put her hand on my hip and it was as if I had gone down into the sea: Shoals of silvery fish brushed against my body and sent up a cloud of air bubbles. She must have felt it too, because she nearly squeezed my arm to a pulp. When she lifted her leg to turn to me, she made me shudder. I was breathing very irregularly, but I was breathing. For the first time, the ark seemed to be more than a coffin.

So we kept guard, the two of us, curled together, around us spider-eating monkeys, which were allowed to roam everywhere to rid us of vermin. We fell asleep with our faces turned toward each other. Time and again, I opened my eyes to look at her, and saw how she too opened her eyes sleepily to look at me. In the half dark, I especially saw the glittering of the moisture on her lips. Her vulnerable throat was turned toward me. She wore nothing but a string of pearls around her neck, a string without pearls around her waist, and two bronze anklets. I did not go to sleep without reaching for her hand. Her thumb she held in her mouth like a child.

In the morning, I heard how her belly woke up first. The saps in her body started moving, then she began to toss and turn, and finally she opened her eyes. When I looked at her, I was overcome by the feeling that she was immortal, while I was here only briefly. I was allowed with her for a while. After that, I would disappear, a disappearance that was of no importance to her because she had no idea of time. Of all those on board, she was the most lighthearted, she was the only one who had no regrets and felt no guilt.

I asked her, "Tell me about that god of yours!"

"He is a god who does things for you, if you behave according to His rules. He holds a hand over your head."

Her words did not surprise me. This god had saved them from the flood. Our gods were capricious. They let herds become infertile and rivers break their banks. They did not order boats to be built when they let the water rise, any more than they made it clear that wells should be dug when drought was coming. A god who assisted his people and loved them, that was the sort of god I wanted, that was a god after my heart. Abide by His wishes, my father had said. By this god I wanted to abide.

She asked, "Are there others, apart from you and Put?"

"My father."

"On the ark?"

"No, out there, on the edge of the world. He has no one to look after him."

She stretched on her mat, touched the wall with her fingertips, and said, "Is the man in the little boat your father? He feeds the waterbirds, did you know? The Unnameable will help him if you ask Him. And if you accept His conditions."

56

Ham

*S*o I paid the price. I refused to go with Ham when he found us in each other's arms. I fought like a varan. I hit him in the face.

He gripped me by the shoulders and shook me. "I have brought you on board. You are mine," he said. "You slept with Japheth, you slept with Shem. Now you sleep with Neelata. It is enough. You're coming with me. I'll find a cage with a bolt, where no one will look for you."

I gripped his hand and bit it, and as I bit, a heavenly warmth streamed through me. I spoke to him, the first time in a long while. "Once I found you in your tent. I looked at you and saw that, like me, you were ready for love. I covered your nakedness. We made a pact, but since we've been on the ship, you've beaten me away from you. You look after me, but if I want to do the same for you, you won't let me. The new pact, the one with your father, is more precious to you! You draw strength from your abstinence and you think you are doing a good thing, but the reality is that you torment me. You don't seem to understand that you arouse my desire, and so cause me more pain than you can alleviate with oil and water. Do not come and get me now that I too have decided to obey your god." He again grasped my hand, but I lashed out with clawed fingers, scratching the skin I had so often cared for.

Neelata did not stir in her corner. She kept her eyes down, her face turned away. We burst out laughing when he drooped off.

He tried again the next evening. His footsteps in the passage sounded more determined, his fist on the door more resolute. It must have been audible in the surrounding spaces, he made such a racket. Taneses and Zedebab did not emerge from their hut. They must have thought it was Neelata trying to resist their brother-in-law.

The door was not locked, we had seen to that. We repeated our fight like an ever-returning enchanting dance, evening after evening, eerily lit by the flickering, almond-shaped flame of the lamp. It became the cause of our happiness. The daily beating was satisfying and addictive because it was an answer to the Un-nameable's instructions, because that way Neelata could dab at my wounds afterward, and I could ask myself in tears who was looking after him like this, who washed him, cared for him?

We kept it up for many days. Neelata did her work, she fed the animals and mucked out. I waited for her to come back, kill-ing the time spinning and weaving, even though it was much too dark and it ruined my eyes. I washed her and slept in her arms. Ham came to get me, but I did not go with him. My resoluteness seemed to please the Unnameable. The rain outside became more gentle day by day, the drops became smaller and no longer hit the surface of the water like pebbles. It changed into a smooth haze that rustled in our dreams.

First Light

*T*here was change coming, you could feel it. Forty days had passed since the ark had floated from the ground. The change did not excite the animals, to the contrary, they became unnaturally quiet. They seemed to prick up their ears. I could hear nothing. Then I realized that that was precisely what they were listening to: the silence, the absence of the rushing sounds. It had stopped raining.

There was a dawning in the sky, a new day broke, the first in a long time. For the first time since I had hidden there, I left Neelata's hut and stood on deck. I was cold, but the sun — the sun! — seemed intent on warming me. It was a watery disk, orange in color and still half in the water. The plankton below the surface of the water lit up. I began to get an impression of the extent of this sea. I would be able to look for miles around, later, once the darkness was quite gone and the orange light turned white. I waited, but did not see my father. Was he farther away than the eye could reach? Had he plunged into the abyss at the end of this massive body of water?

The animals recognized the light. After the silence, their joy erupted. The cock crowed like one possessed. The birds went crazy, they tweeted, they twittered, they warbled. Bumping sounds came from the sleeping quarters. I expected Put; surely he would soon appear now, the camel-hair sack around his body. But it was the others, the Builder and his wife, Shem, Japheth, Ham, and their wives. I heard their footsteps coming up the ladders. They wanted to get outside, onto the deck as quickly as possible to see the sun.

I raced down the ladders, and when they came past, I stood in the kangaroo cage, quite visible in all that sudden light. Luckily, they were in such a hurry to get on deck they paid no attention to me. It was my father's ingenious construction that made me so vulnerable. Thanks to his light gallery with its adjustable shutters, the light came in from many sides. It was of no great service to me. All it did was throw light on the hopelessness of my situation. How could I go on hiding if every footmark, every handprint, every shadowy movement could be noticed thanks to the open shutters?

Scared, I sat in Neelata's hut, waiting for her to return. She had a room divider, with woven designs in different kinds of reeds, which she had already used in her quarters in the shipyard to give herself privacy. I placed it between me and the door in case someone looked in through the gaps. She was as boisterous as a child when she came in, so excited she just put the screen aside without wondering why it was there. "It's over, Re Jana," she exclaimed. "Everything has been destroyed, just a short while and the new world begins!"

But the end of the rain did not mean that the voyage was finished. The water stayed high, day after day. My skin and my dress became tight around my belly. Neelata altered the dress, she put extra panels in the seams so I could breathe more easily. It did not help. The constriction was not because of the dress, but because of the space I was locked up in. I wanted to move, look around, go on deck, and, now that it was light, help search for Put.

And I wanted to see how Ham was. My rejecting him had its flip side: He no longer bothered with me. He no longer procured extra helpings, just now that my hunger seemed insatiable. Neelata went foraging, but she was not resourceful. I suspected she mainly looked about for Put and did not pay much attention to edible things. And there was less and less. Fresh fruit, dried fruit, nuts, and cheeses were finished. What milk could still be obtained from the cattle did not reach me. My stomach demanded more than Neelata found for me. My appetite became so great that I set out to search in the evening after darkness returned.

The ark stank, and it was hard to follow your sense of smell. But when I came near the dodoes I recognized an odor that did not belong to the birds. I opened the hutch I had lived in for so long and discovered that it had been taken over as a storage place. There were bags of raisins and fragrant cheeses. I hid as much as I could carry under my dress for Neelata. The raisins I dropped in front of Ham's door; he would feel them under his feet when he left his hut.

Neelata closed her eyes when she took a taste of the cheese. To give her a surprise, I went back to the store the next evening.

Like the first time, I opened the hutch by sliding away the panel Ham had made for me. It was not easy doing it quietly. Dodoes react grumpily to having their sleep disturbed. They rock their bodies and hit the ground with their broad toes. There suddenly seemed to be so many of them that night, much more than seven. Then I noticed I had been trapped. It was not just dodoes squatting against the wall. There was a woman amongst them, the substantial figure of Taneses.

With much rustling, she got up and grasped me by the wrists. I dropped the panel. "Neelata?" she asked. "Zedebab?" She dragged me along the passage toward the swans' cage some way farther along, where her lamp stood.

"You?" she asked. "But you were in the water. I've envied you all this time. I thought you had been spared this doom."

I hurriedly shook my head. I must have looked scared, showing my fear of her strong body.

Her voice became gentle when she looked at me close up, I heard compassion in it. "Shall I throw you in the water so it will all be over?"

I shook my head again.

She looked genuinely surprised. "Do you not want to? I would wish for nothing better than that someone would tie me up and push me into the water along the dung slide." Her grip slackened. She knew I would not run away; my only escape was the water, and she now knew I did not want to go that way. "But you can swim, of course. That makes a difference. That makes a death in the water too slow. And you're carrying a child." Her mouth smelled of the cheeses in the hutch. Her waist was wider than mine. She always looked pregnant, regularly had been before the voyage, but her children died, they dropped from her body like onions from her sacks. As women, we knew she kept her losses a secret from Japheth. With her voluminous belly and veined breasts, she had managed to persuade him that she was the best woman for him, and this had saved her life.

She released me. "This journey is a heavy load for us women. Look at Zedebab. Her nerves are at breaking point. Her twin sister drowned. The girl was not different from Zedebab in any way whatever. Yet Zedebab was chosen, and her sister not. Can anyone comprehend this?" She handed me the lamp and pushed me along the passage. With her forceful grip she forced me back into the dodoes' pen.

"I will spare your life," she said flatly. "So long as you do something in return. I need someone to slaughter a bird for me. You killed ducks for food, didn't you?" She pointed at the birds surrounding us. It occurred to me that her movements resembled the dodoes'. She too had a small head on a large body, and just like them, she placed her feet carefully so as not to disturb that large body's balance.

"No," I said. "Not the dodoes."

"A dodo is what I want," she said. "That one has been at my fruit." She pointed her chin at the blue female with the mournful voice. She opened the hutch and produced three alabaster statues, images of a bull and two calves. "Then you'll pluck it and cut it up in small pieces," she continued. "My gods demand sacrifices, but I am forbidden from killing animals. If you kill the birds, both the Unnameable and my gods will be content."

With both hands I was gripping the bars on the door of the pen. I calculated my chances of getting away. "Why these gods if you already have one who saved you from the flood?" I asked.

But she was alert. Her grip on my arm was strong, and she jammed the door with her leg. "These gods are very special. They promise something you get nowhere else. A life after death, not in a realm of shadows but in a paradise. Is that not lovely and attractive? Is that not much better than what the Unnameable promises: a good, long life?"

I tried to extricate myself. But she twisted my arm so high up my back that my shoulder cracked. "Catch it, or I take you to the Builder," she said.

The dodo angrily beat its head and spat and hissed like a fire when I grabbed it. I had to clamp its beak to prevent it from pecking out my eyes. I struggled with it, making a noise like a wild thing and filling the cage with feathers and quills and droppings. Taneses urged quiet, but of course that did not help. She gave me a knife so sharp it must have just been whetted. The flapping did not stop until I managed to get my arm across the wings. I quickly broke its neck to stop the noise. The beast did not close its eyes when it went still in my hands.

Taneses watched as if she wanted every movement to be imprinted on her memory.

I carefully plucked the dodo, removed the glory of its color, the hundreds of feathers, every one of which glowed differently in the soft light. In its pupil I saw my own face.

"Have you slaughtered an animal?" asked Neelata when I returned to her. "How could you? That way you will not save your father."

I laid my head in her lap so she could comfort me. "I saved myself!" I said. As she wiped the blood from my hands, sorrow rose in me.

58

An Accident

The number of marks on the wall doubled. The rain had stopped, but the water was not draining away. The hay in the stores was rotting, it started to ferment and became black as pitch. Something was going on with the seasons too. Suddenly, the larvae matured. Within days we were tormented by swarms of mosquitoes, which rained down on our faces and limbs as soon as we lay down. After a while we learned how to repel them by burning rags, but most of the time it seemed the smoke would overcome us long before the mosquitoes.

The mosquitoes set the bats moving. In the morning, I would find them tangled in the nets and tent-dividers that Neelata had stowed between the beams of her ceiling. I could not resist disentangling them, when Neelata was not there, and dashing them against the wall. And then there were the leeches. They sat on your face, your hands, and your feet. Your whole body became covered in little black holes, particularly those parts that were exposed to the air. From the mud and the dirt, the flies were born, they came from nowhere but drove the cattle in the holds mad.

As the days crawled by, our hopes of an early landfall diminished. Sailing became a habit, and it seemed we were losing sight of the purpose of the journey. The voyagers forgot the flood. Like me, they forgot their previous lives, and like me, could not imagine the life to come. Everyone seemed to be mostly concerned with the cares of the moment. Wasps building a nest in a spot no one could reach suddenly became more important than the thought of a new land. Out of boredom, the voyagers sang songs they invented. The songs were mostly about their loneliness. I must admit, they were good at singing, and at rhyming too, in that language of theirs! They sang about the monotony of sailing and of the sound of the water. Sometimes the songs were melancholy, sometimes so wild the donkeys started braying and the dogs howling.

I killed animals for Taneses. At first mainly dodoes, later spotted swans and jumping geese. She roasted them under the air funnel, because that was where the smoke dispersed fastest. "My gods are content," she said. "You're conquering a very special place in their hearts."

But I did not show myself to the others. Tempers were restless, I was afraid of what would happen if they discovered me. The Builder became ill again. This time he slipped into a state like madness. They thought he had been bitten by a bat, because he wandered about the hold with foam on his lips and his teeth clenched. Shem and Japheth were furious with the bats. They hit out at them with sticks and did not care if, from some of these species, both the male and the female perished. Of course, there were so many of them, all with differently angled jaws and claws.

I knew the illness from which the Builder suffered. I had seen men and women slowly die of it in the marsh country. I also knew of the preparation of quicksilver, which, if applied properly, could give relief. But offering my services would have meant death.

Because, of course, there were suspicions. They began to wonder why this voyage was not coming to an end. What was going wrong, who was committing errors, what so displeased the Unnameable that he let the water stay? There were more and more rumors that a child had been sighted. It always seemed to disappear in a flash, so no one could ever catch it. And the disappearance of the animals I killed did not go unnoticed.

My fear made me short of breath. During the day, the heat in the ark was unbearable. Neelata fanned me. She only left me when absolutely necessary, when she had to work or to go and eat. She did not feel the need to walk on the deck. But because I insisted, she went to look at that wet world outside. Excitedly, she told me about the reflections and how the sky kept changing over the water. But even under the clearest of skies, she could not see a papyrus boat.

One night, I was busy preparing a quail for sacrifice to Taneses's gods. I had broken the beast's neck and had plucked it. The fire was ready, but Taneses thought the offering too meager and wanted another one. It was an unusually rough night, as if somewhere in the distance a new storm was brewing. That gave me a feeling of security: The voyagers would feel ill and lie down on their beds. And so I got a fright when I saw someone going up the gallery. The figure that crossed my path and made me hide hastily was Zaza. She moved with unsteady steps, she seemed lost and had difficulty standing up. All the way up she climbed, and I could hear her footsteps on the deck.

I did not know why she went up there. Walking on deck right now was dangerous. The surface was slippery. She was not carrying a lamp.

What would she do if she spotted me? Would she scream? I followed her anyway, I could not stop myself. The strange way she moved showed she was in greater need than I.

It was a dark, sinister night. On deck were the glistening trails of snails that had come out of the wilted foliage looking for fresh food. I noticed she had prepared her coming: A crate with some steps against it stood near the railing.

She was not startled when I stood next to her but greeted me. "Hasn't it been a long time! I didn't really think you had thrown yourself into the water, not with that child. You look lovely and well! Are they giving you a decent life, those children of mine? How are you bearing up on this endless journey?" With every step I took, she moved away from me, her carriage alert, her toes tensed.

"It won't be long now," I said soothingly.

She moved close to the steps and looked out over the water. The sea was restless but not wild. There was a little wind. She was silent, like a ewe becoming mute at the sight of the shearer.

"My children's father says," she said after along silence, "there will be a new land, a new beginning. He doesn't say where I am supposed to find the strength for all this. I am too tired for his paradise." She had folded her arms across her gown, her forearms supporting her breasts. She climbed onto the steps, put her left foot on the first step, her right foot on the second.

"Why did you go along with this dream?"

"A man needs to have something," she replied. "And a dream is better than emptiness." She stepped onto the crate. I gripped her hand to stop her, but she just used it to balance herself.

"Don't throw my shoes in after me," she said. "They must not think it was an accident."

It seemed impossible, the water was not wild enough to do what it did: A wave came up, a gigantic, voracious wave that scooped her up but did not even touch me. I felt her push off against my arm and she was gone. Her gown floated on the water.

I rested my arm on the railing for balance and stood there. What was this? What did it mean? I had done my best, I had tried to do the Unnameable's will, and had been forced to disobedience by Taneses. Where was my father with his worthless little boat? Was he watching me, could he see me standing here, grubby, my belly curving with life? Throw your rules, your manners, your habits overboard, he had said. I had given up all my old rules. My lips formed questions for him. *What did you mean when you said, "Do everything that is asked of you"? What did you mean when you said, "Forget what I have taught you"?* Being obliging produced no better results than disobedience. My head was full of anger, anger that stank like smoke. The ship under me was burning. I had not put out the fire near the air funnel.

59

The Fire

The fire destroyed the stores and smothered an unknown number of animals. Shem, Ham, and Japheth grabbed the first water they could get their hands on, the sweet, scarce drinking water from my cave, and used it to put out the fire. While they plunged the jugs into the barrels to let them fill up they were calling out, "Where is Mother? Where can she possibly be?"

Zedebab stamped on the sparks with her feet. Neelata threw her wall hanging on the flames, which choked under the weight of her embroidery. Ham took off his cloak, plunged it in the water, and put it back on. Dripping wet, he hurled himself into the fire, beating at the flames with his hands as he searched for his mother. Taneses ran past, carrying alabaster statues of two calves and a bull in her arms. Her skin lit up with the fire behind her, looking as transparent as the statues she was carrying. Then she disappeared in the flames.

The animals screamed. As the corridors and galleries filled with smoke, they made the same noises as when the ark was first lifted up by the water. *Put!* I thought, running through the ship. But the smoke overcame me. There was only one safe place, of course. I felt my way toward it. I recognized the Builder's hut by the staff that stood at the door; it was the sign of his presence, as it had been when they lived in their tents. He lay on the wooden pallet by the wall, his mouth half open. To my surprise, his room too was filled with smoke. I moved into the corner farthest away from him, the ever thickening curtain of smoke between us. He said not a word, but looked at me with eyes used to hallucinations.

He has been abandoned by his god, I thought. Once a sea of water had come from the sky, and now not a drop to keep the smoke out of his bedroom. I stood ready to lift him off his bed and carry him onto the deck when I heard footsteps in the corridor. The voyagers had come to get their father, and I could not get away.

The fire under the air funnel had been put out. Shem and Japheth were wet through. Zedebab had tied her skirts together between her legs, making her look as though she was wearing baggy pants. Neelata's hair had been scorched. Ham held his badly burned hands up in front of him. They were all black with soot, making them look as if they belonged to my people.

When they noticed me, they stared at me, particularly Zedebab, who seemed not to remember how she knew me.

"Where is Mother?" they asked, as if they knew I had the answer.

"I do not know," I said.

My voice startled them, suddenly so open and loud in this ship. Everyone went on deck to get some air. Zaza and Taneses were missing. Worry about Zaza's fate and grief for Taneses' death formed a strange bond between us; nobody thought of asking me yet, "What are you doing here?"

"Taneses wanted to save her belongings," they told one

another. They mourned Taneses, but I admired her. She had finally taken the step. She had gone into the fire because nobody had been prepared to push her into the water, and so had entered her gods' paradise. But of course the display of grief for Taneses was mainly a way of not having to think about the shoes that lay on the deck, and about the fact that Zaza was taking far too long to appear.

The material damage was great. Of the women's quarters, only Zedebab's remained. The central living space had been destroyed. The voyagers no longer had a place for playing shovelboard or making music. The stores of food had been burned. In his attempts to beat out the flames, Ham had used the scrolls on which all mankind's wars, their dates, and the names of their victors were depicted.

But all that was as nothing compared to the loss of Zaza. She was the mother, the conciliator who understood what no one would express. On her sons' faces I could read their dismay. Neelata and Zedebab too were speechless. They had come to know and appreciate Zaza. Because there was no one else, she had taken the place of their own mothers. And she had taken so much with her, all knowledge of motherhood had been lost with her. In the new world, they would have to learn childbirth from me, who knew nothing about it.

"Let me do your hands," I said to Ham, but he thought he did not need my care.

"They do not hurt, it is my heart that pains me," he said. That sounded true. His hands were so badly burned they must have lost all feeling.

Shem was the first to be able to take stock of the new situation. He allocated Taneses's bedroom to me. The walls were scorched, her bed and cupboards turned to ashes, and her spoons and skimmers twisted by the heat, but I had a bundle of hay and a blanket. "In the new land," he said, pointing at the curve of my belly, "you will become Japheth's wife, the bearer of his progeny."

Japheth protested. His thoughts were with Taneses. I could not replace his wife, he said, and he had no feelings for me. He had not forgotten that I had prevented his father's blessing.

But Shem had no patience with his objections. "What would you rather, that Ham had two wives and you none, or the fair division I propose?"

60

The Builder

From that day on, I took care of the Builder. Neelata and Zedebab refused, Zaza and Taneses were dead, and Ham, the man who had learned the art of caring by practicing on me, could no longer use his hands. The news that Zaza had perished in the fire had a bad effect on the Builder. He lay on his mattress, shivering, eyes and mouth half open, seeming unable to speak. By the light of the small oil lamp it was shocking to see how the illness had attacked his skin. Barely any blood flowed through it, at most a pale sap that kept him alive.

"Stay with him and do all that is needed," said Shem. He left me behind in the hut that resembled the Builder's tent in the shipyard. Inside, the same chaos reigned, and it was permeated by the same resiny smell of ointment. Attached to the wall with bronze screws was a small, square, acacia-wood altar with four horns. In the incessant commotion during the early part of the journey, he had no doubt spoken with his god here, but now the illness exhausted him, no Unnameable could do anything about that. Beside his bed stood the cage with the messy dove and the little bells, and on a stand a few nondescript little plants with brown, serrated leaves in moist soil. On the shelf below, jugs, a press and sieves, covered with ash from the fire. I opened all the pots I could find and sniffed them. I found mugs with dregs of wine, but also the pots of ointment I was looking for. I boiled up an herb broth, which I fed him spoonful by spoonful.

I took care of him every day. He was restless in his sleep because the lumps on his belly and in his groin itched.

"What do you dream about?" I asked him when, on the third day, he looked at me. His irises trembled constantly, the whites around them were bloodshot, and stale-looking tears filled the corners of his eyes.

"About the newborn children," he said. "The animals have been saved, but not the newborn children. Someone needs to explain that to me." Crumbs of dried ear wax lay on his pillow. I brushed them onto the floor or blew them away.

"I had a conversation once, with a man," he continued. "We were deep inside a cave full of the dead."

"That man was my father."

"His words touched me deep in my heart. He was speaking about showing remorse. What happens if remorse is not genuine?"

"Then calamity follows."

"That is right. Calamity follows. But what if the calamity comes first? If it comes so fast and unexpectedly that there is no time for a request, for a question, an expression of remorse? Zaza disappeared so fast. She died too soon, and in the wrong way. On this ark, life does not turn into ashes, it turns into foam. Foam is what we must become."

I recognized his loss; I missed my mother. I wanted to say to him, "The fire has not consumed your wife. The water has claimed her because she sought it," but what man needs the truth in his grief? I said, "Your Unnameable god does not seem to know that the dead stay alive. They move into the next life."

"He has made us out of clay. He breathed life into that clay, life that can be snuffed out. When it is extinguished, everything is gone. We return to our original state."

"But it is that breath, that sigh, that wind that lives on. It leaves the throat and goes elsewhere. I should know, I saw it happen when my mother fell into her boat. The cry that escaped her contained her will, not all of her will, but a part of it, a part large enough to make her decoy ducks fly despite their clipped wings."

"He has never said anything to me about that. All I know is that this life passes. The living know they are going to die, but the dead know nothing. That is why a living dog is better than a dead lion, and in death, man is equal to the beasts."

"Then why are we here, if life is so temporary?" I asked.

"To worship and to sacrifice."

"Then the Unnameable has regard only for himself. People will turn against him and soon forget him. Is your Unnameable a good god?"

"He is a good god."

"Then he must console. Then he must spare his people meaninglessness and offer some prospect."

"Consolation there is already," he said dryly, pointing at the vats of wine.

"It will need to be more than that. He will have to offer what cannot be found anywhere else: the promise not to wipe us out, the hope for a better place, and the certainty that our suffering is not meaningless. A new life in paradise for those who deserve it. That is what some alabaster gods say. Is that not beautiful? Is that not something for the Unnameable, he who is so fond of good commandments?"

"Yes," he said, staring for a long time at the beams in the ceiling. And then again, "Yes, you are right. It would be beautiful to believe that Zaza's breath floats about. That she is going away to a place that is better for her than here. That is what I shall do, that is how I will think of it." When, quite a while later, he opened his eyes again, he said, "I know who you are. You are the dwarf in a new shape. I knew it when you showed us the water in the cave. You disappear and reappear, just like him."

I knelt next to his bed. I bent my head because I hardly dared look up, particularly not when he said, "Give me your message. Tell me the commandments of the Unnameable."

In a conversation I had with him a few days later, I made up a hereafter that seemed fair to me, with a place for the righteous inhabited by nothing but pure, snow-white beings. But I was not thinking of that now, because something else altogether was worrying me.

"The man who moved you to tears in the cave now sits in a little papyrus boat," I said. "He is floating about all alone on this sea."

"Is that so?" asked the Builder. He looked at me, his irises no longer trembling but looking fixedly at me. "Then we must help him." He asked me to take him onto the deck. He was not heavy, hardly heavier than my mother whom I had lifted so often. He hung on tightly to the railing when I put him down. On his feet, he was wearing my father's rabbit-fur boots. He looked out over the water, lifted up his free hand, and muttered a few prayers I did not understand.

"I bless the man in the papyrus boat," he said finally. "May the Unnameable assist him in all that he undertakes."

"And Ham?" I asked when he opened his eyes again. "Can you bless him too?"

"Ham will have to earn his blessing," he replied. "Just like his brothers." He put his hand on the railing again. I carried him back into the hold and stayed with him till dark.

61

Hunger

*A*fter the fire came the scarcity. My gums became swollen, my nails tore. Hunger makes you resentful. Someone has to take the blame for the emptiness in your belly that makes you think you are being eaten away from inside, that something is gnawing at you. I had to survive on the shriveled almonds and the moldy biscuits Japheth handed me. On top of that, we had to cope unexpectedly with the death's-head monkeys, who would wander about us and snatch out of our hands anything we lifted to our mouths and disappear with it like lightning. Their fur, which had been smooth and shiny when we embarked, became dirty and scruffy, and their once-shining faces looked dull.

I took over Taneses's tasks. The animals in the pens reacted with resentment to having to get used to a new voice and new movements. Every evening, I went off on my own to Taneses's room, which smelled of smoke and sooty dampness. Occasionally the ark still smelled of something edible, but such days were becoming rare.

Because Neelata's hut had been burned out, she shared Zedebab's. But although that hut was opposite mine, I rarely caught a glimpse of her. Like all of us, she became very turned in on herself. Her stocks of honey and raisins shrank rapidly. Her dates she had been sharing with me, but not the rest, because she saw that I sacrificed part of what she handed me to the Unnameable. She no longer entered my smelly hut. We met while we were feeding the animals, and she asked, "Why am I more worried about myself than about you?"

I said, "The soul knows many ways of fleeing," but her face remained unyielding as the night.

She replied, "I am not worried about you because you persist. You should have married Ham, my presence here is a mistake. I cannot honor the Unnameable. He is no more than the collected fear and sickness of all that moves in this ark. Anything the boys and their father cannot understand they've called the Unnameable. I cannot afford to waste my dates on a god like this."

I squeezed her hand to reassure her. "It's better not to worry about me," I lied. "I'm fine."

"I still share with Put. He collects anything I put out for him. But how much longer can I go on sharing if I'm starving?"

"Not much longer," I said. "Starving we do on our own."

She smiled, and with steps that dragged more than they used to, she went on with her work.

More even than with eating, we were preoccupied with sleeping. We slept more often and for longer periods. We spent hours arranging and rearranging our sheets and sewing larger, softer pillows to lie on; feathers there were aplenty, the birds were molting. We avoided the sun because it made us hungry. We loved the moon because night after night it brought us the sleep we longed for.

The animals became ill. The cold, the damp, and the smoke

had left them unscathed, but the hunger exhausted them, except for the hibernators, who seemed unconcerned because they did as we did: They shut their eyes and no longer left their nests.

And we were thirsty. The little water that was left had become tainted. You could not taste any difference between what came out of the amphoras and the dregs from the sinkhole. The cattle collapsed. We had to pour water down their nostrils to bring them around.

The shortages were harder for me to bear than for the others. They had been brought up in the Rrattikan belief that eating very little did not kill you. As children, they had been trained to put up with the feeling of gnawing hunger. Privation was never more than an inconvenience. They baked bread from thistles and pressed water out of cactuses. Because there were no thistles on the ark, they used sorrel and hay. But my stomach could not cope with their inventive bakery, and my bowels stopped functioning. If occasionally something decent was found, I was not included in the distribution, an omen of the way I would be treated later. I had to scrape together my own food, and so I stole what I could find, afraid of being caught, but not so afraid that I did not realize that dying of starvation was more terrible than anything they could do to me. I dried the flesh of animals that perished. I had to do it fast, or it would rot within a day. Because I did not have enough salt, I cut the meat in thin slices and dried it over the fire. The last piece I threaded onto my stick was the arm and fist of a small monkey. I saved it and hung it on a nail in a dark corner. Of course, it disappeared in no time, presumably snatched away by monkeys of the same breed, and I was left with nothing.

The days passed. By that time, no one was counting the weeks anymore, and as deprivation got worse, the ark became quieter. Shem and Japheth passed the days sleeping, Zedebab and Neelata tried making soup out of nut shells. Now and then I took something to the Builder. I had almost nothing left to put into the broth, no more than a couple of drops of oil, half a sprig of thyme, and a pinch of salt.

One evening after work, I returned, exhausted, to my scorched hut. Before I had even shut the door, I felt the presence of something alive in the corner. *The snake*, I thought, but whatever sat in the corner was bulky, and it made wheezing sounds. I did not have a lamp, I had no need of one to sleep, so I stood, petrified, waiting for the creature to move.

"Shut the door properly," someone whispered, and I recognized the hoarse, throaty voice of Taneses. I did as she told me.

"The fire was my fault, I know," she said without stirring in her corner. "I pretended to walk into the fire to escape the Unnameable's eye. That, I think, I succeeded in, but now it seems this whole ship is going to perish from hunger."

I moved closer to see her. I saw the three alabaster statues on the floor next to her. They gleamed in the darkness from the fat she had rubbed them with, these were probably the only things on the ship that still looked cared for. I touched them and felt they were warm, she had brought them here under her clothes. The scent they gave off reminded me of the small temples in the marsh country, where priestesses lived, like Taneses, women of substance who cherished their statues like children.

"Even the little boy is weak with hunger," she continued. "We must do something, Re Jana. If we don't start something, we'll all perish, even the animals."

I pulled back my hand. It was difficult to keep up my squatting posture. I was dizzy, and my belly was taut. "Little boy?" I asked, breathing deeply.

"I found that child that used to hang around with you."

"Put?"

"I let him do things for me. How did you think I have survived all this time?"

"Why does he listen to you?"

"I was surprised at how easy it was to make him obey. I did not have to hold him over the side of the ship, just threatening to was enough."

I half fell to one side. *The floor*, I thought, *the fire has made the planks as thin as wafers, I'm going to go clean through it.* But I fell no farther than against her.

She stretched out her arms to support me. "Are you all right? You're not feeling ill, are you?" she asked. Her head was right next to mine. She said in a whisper, "I do not want to exploit that child. I am not a bad person. But it is not always easy when your gods are demanding."

I shuddered again. I could smell that she had eaten more recently than I. "Is it your gods who prevent the waters receding?"

She helped me up without too much noise. "I think so," she said dully.

"I know what we can do," I said when I was on my feet again. I was still staggering, but thanks to her support I stayed upright.

"We'll make a special offering to your gods. We'll kill the most precious bird in this ship for them."

That evening I went as usual into the Builder's hut. I lit his lamp and applied ointment to the ulcers in his groin. The Builder was in a good mood. He smelled of wine and said he had practically no pain anymore. That was thanks to me, he said, and my soft hands. As I was leaving, I took the messy dove from its cage and clutched it under my dress.

"Has the time come already? Is it time to look for an olive branch?" the Builder asked when he saw what I was doing.

I sidled to the door as quickly as I could. "This creature is our last hope," I said and went back to Taneses's hut. There I did what I thought was the right thing to do. I killed the dove, plucked its feathers, and laid it before the alabaster statues while Taneses watched.

"And now the child," I said when I had finished. "Show me where he is."

"Not so fast," she replied with her eyes on the statues. "First we'll see if this sacrifice bears fruit."

Return to Ham

*H*am looked up when I came in. He had his hands in a basin full of fat that he was trying to spread over his skin with unfeeling fingers. "You are not supposed to come here," he said and continued rubbing.

"I know," I said. "There are so many things I'm not supposed to do."

All that time he had mourned. I could tell from the hairs that lay all over the floor, like a fur he had shed.

I shut the door behind me and walked into his hut. But I did not get far. I moved my foot and collapsed. I fell flat on the floor and all I can remember is the boards.

Ham lifted me up, his arms under my armpits, put me down on his bed and covered me.

"When I started this journey, I was strong," I said hoarsely. "But everything has been taken from me. I was not to be allowed onto this ship. There was no room for me, but see, my presence was immediately accepted by everybody. I understand why: I am here for the benefit of all of you."

Ham briefly closed his eyes but said nothing. With his stumps wrapped in rags, he boiled water for me. Day and night I stayed lying on his mat. I could no longer raise myself to drink, but he kept my lips moist. Every morning again I gave myself up for lost, but every morning again it was he who called me back to life.

He told me things I had heard his father tell: that he would bring me to a garden, a place free of cactuses, thistles, and rocks, in its center a tree that would enlarge the mind. I watched him preparing to go to sleep. He tried to clean his feet. When I saw how dirty the cloth was that he was using, I struggled up. I knelt before him and offered him my hair. He lifted me up and gently pushed me down beside him. With all the movement inside my belly, all I could do was lie against him at an angle, my leg over his to carry the weight. We pretended tenderness to forget the earlier violence between us. He lifted his arms, but his movement led to nothing. His hands were bandaged and the skin of his forearms was without sensation: He could only imitate a caress with his elbows. No longer could he scratch me with those serrated fingernails of his.

I did have my hands. Full of regret, I moved them over his neck and shoulders, and he did not push me away. Perhaps he no longer had the strength.

"See," we said to each other. "The ark that was to save us is closing over us like a coffin."

The animals no longer cried for food, some had lain down, others stood dumbly on their legs as if they had not learned how to collapse. Barely anything moved. And so we lay amongst the scrolls, the carpets, the mosaics, and the fabrics Ham had stacked in his hut. He had barely left enough room for himself because he had been certain he would go on the truss-boat. Here I thought I would meet my end, after many wanderings, back with the pale-skinned boy. In a state of paralysis and lack of will, like my mother. We held each other. Together we listened to the splashing of the waves against the bow.

63

Call over the Water

When the ship had become so still that it was as if, in an unguarded moment, everyone had abandoned it, a call sounded over the water.

"Re Jana! Re Jana!"

At first, I thought I was dreaming. I opened my eyes and closed them again. But the call sounded again.

I got to my feet. The ship was rocking more than you would expect from a vessel in quiet waters, but perhaps it only seemed like that because I was so dizzy. I climbed the ladders, went on deck, and leaned on the storm-battered railing. For a while, I stood and wondered at the restlessness of the water. All carcasses and tree trunks, everything that floated, had sunk or been washed over the edge of the world. Now there was life in the water, and not just predator fish. From glitterings in the water and rapidly disappearing little cross currents, I recognized shoals of edible fish. Eels with toothed jaws swam around the keel and, slowly behind them, a string of flat fish, which, in the marsh country, we called alpoes, an excellent type of fish, white and flaky when cooked.

Again, my name echoed. I went to the side of the ship the sound came from and bent over the railing. Below me, close up against the ark, I saw a whirling of water birds' wings, among them many terns, my mother's lucky bird. Dozens, maybe hundreds of birds circled around a floating object of which only the tip of the prow was visible. I recognized my father's papyrus boat and its white shroud.

"Re Jana," I heard again. "Throw down a rope and gather your strength to pull it up again."

Of my father I could not see much, only his hands, which appeared from under the sun shelter now and then. He made rapid movements with a rope he was pulling from the water.

Zedebab and Neelata came out of their hut. Shem, Japheth, and Ham shuffled onto the deck. They had all heard the call.

"He wants a rope," I said. "We have to pull." It was impossible to suppress the joy in my voice. He was alive, this man, he was safe and sound.

Shem and Japheth threw out a rope and laboriously hauled it back up. Its end reached the deck, and with a smack, my father's heavy fyke-net fell on board. Fish thrashed about on the boards. The voyagers looked at it with amazement.

I saw the revulsion in their eyes and said, "They are very good when you roast them. They are not warm-blooded. Your Unnameable god allows their consumption." Again I looked over the railing at the papyrus boat at the bow. My father waved. "Go on, you know what to do," he called.

I cut off the heads, removed the guts, and baked them over a low fire. Nobody wondered if the fish tasted good. Myself, I had never thought I would be eating alpo this way, without the tart fruits and the bread that should go with it. But the voyagers licked their bowls clean. It did not even occur to them to ask the Builder's permission. The broth I prepared was taken to him. Shem and Japheth threw the net and the rope overboard again. "Perhaps there's more to come," they said. They laughed for the first time in a long while.

When the fyke came up again it was even heavier than before. Zedebab and Neelata ran forward to help the men.

Soon we saw what made it so heavy. Squeezed in, his legs pulled up, his face weather-beaten, and his hair stiff with salt, crouched my father. Shem, Japheth, Zedebab, and Neelata abruptly stopped moving. So disconcerted were they, they had only enough strength left to stop him plummeting back.

My father peered through the net. When he saw me, the corners of his mouth turned up briefly. "Re Jana, my child," he said. Then he looked at the others on deck. I do not know if he was aware of how relations had changed. Swollen and dirty I was, but so were the others. In any case, he could see I was amongst them, which was probably the most important thing for him.

"It was becoming so quiet on the ark," he called after he had a good look at everybody. "I hardly heard a sound. And no more movement on deck, that could only be a bad sign." Once more he pulled up the corners of his mouth. It was not a smile, rather the grimace of someone trying to remember a smile. I was concerned about the way those four were holding onto the rope. Shem's grip seemed solid, but his hands were shaking.

"Looks like you got a little hungry!" my father continued. "I thought to myself, let me give them some of my leftovers. I've served quite a few on this journey, I've had lots of guests, all the birds who had had enough of swimming. Just after we set out, I even had three mallard ducks: I gave each one of them a name, Shem, Ham, and Japheth, ha-ha-ha. They didn't live long. My bread I couldn't spare them, and fish they didn't like. I've got an albatross too, but I chase it away from the roof, it has to swim, it takes up too much space." His voice sounded shrill over the deck. A strange odor came from him, some small fish hung around him where they had stayed behind in the mesh of the net. He was not very comfortable, with his knees pressed up against his throat, but as if this did not bother him in the slightest, he continued, "Of course, you need a bit of cleverness to survive in such circumstances. What use is rightmindedness without cleverness?"

I could see that Shem too was now shaking all over. "You've still got plenty to say for yourself, boat builder," he said calmly. "We're grateful for the fish, but we have not invited you."

My father looked through the mesh, his grin becoming wider and wider. The flies he had brought with him buzzed around him; he seemed to be so used to them he did not shoo them off even when they settled in the corners of his eyes. "We could cooperate," he said. "I'll take care of the supplies. That way we all get something: You have things to eat again, and I get some company. Because it's all taking a long time, and I'm getting pretty bored!" His language was even blunter than it used to be. His isolation had made him forget his manners. I ought to have been embarrassed, but my heart rejoiced, I had to make an effort not to burst into laughter. I had not experienced so much cheerfulness in a long time.

But Shem saw it differently. With his free hand, he gripped

my neck and pushed me down to the railing. "This," he shouted, "is what has become of us because we did not throw her overboard. She is the evil from the old world. Her life we'll spare because women will be needed. But she is not amongst the chosen. We will recognize her by the color of her skin, her and all her offspring."

"Stop it!" shouted Ham. With his bandaged hands he pushed Shem. "She has nothing to do with evil." It made Shem push me even harder against the railing. The pain meant nothing to me. I was mainly glad that Shem kept holding onto the rope.

"This man, who is her father, has saved our lives," Ham went on.

"That's exactly why," Shem replied dryly. "Did you think I would haul him on board so we could listen to his smart cracks day after day? God knows how much longer we'll be on the way. Let him circle us like a guard. Let him supply us with fresh fish from down there."

Ham gave his brother a long, cold look. "Being chosen does not give you the right to be heartless," he said.

"Well then, let's call our father!" called Shem.

The fate of a man in a fyke-net hanging off the railing of the ark did seem something only the Builder was fit to decide, so when the suggestion was made, everyone nodded, including Ham. And so it was that, a few moments later, the old man with his characteristic odor of wine and ointment appeared on deck. He looked at the remains on the deck, the fish heads in the sun, the mushy guts spread over them. His sores must have dried completely, because he walked upright and did not seem bothered by chafing from any items of clothing. A sigh of relief escaped me: If he felt well, he would be in a generous mood, and if he was in a generous mood he would allow my father a place on board. But the Builder did not walk toward my father. He took me by the elbow and led me away from the railing.

"Do not hold it against Shem," he said. "The boy is trying to earn his blessing. He has been waiting for it such a long time." There were whitish spots around his neck, and his lips too were almost white. The thin fingers around my wrist did not shake. I looked at them as if they were my real lifeline, as if everything depended more on this grip than on the one that held the rope. "You belong with us now, Re Jana, my girl," he continued. "Your child is now my child." The fingers curled around my arm like vines, then let go. I looked at his green eyes, his spotty skin, his gray hair. How well he looked, my countless hours of caring had not been in vain. But, of course, he feared a second, healthier patriarch on the ark. Over my shoulder, he nodded at Shem and Japheth. Slowly, they lowered my father. Over the edge of the railing I could see how the albatross, the terns, the gulls beat their wings to let him pass.

"He is a great man," said the Builder. "A great progeny will be his." Far below us, on the surface of the water, I heard the sound of oars. With splashing strokes my father rowed away from us. And while my father rowed away, the Builder blessed Shem. He blessed Japheth. And he blessed Ham. They bowed down to the ground before their father. Their eyes shone with relief.

64

Ararat

I put a couple of fish in a dish and returned to my hut via the ladders. There Taneses was busy with her alabaster calves and bull; she had a lamp that she nervously screened every time she heard someone approaching. I set down the bowl in front of her and said, "Our offering has made your gods favorably disposed toward us. See: fresh food. Now show me where Put is hiding."

When she smelled the fish, she got up willingly. She was not excessively hungry, I suspected she had eaten the dove. She gave me a look of understanding and stood by the door.

"Everybody is out on deck," I said when I saw her hesitate to go up the corridor. "The men are receiving their blessing, so we have nothing to worry about." To my surprise I saw, as we walked through the ark, that there were cages standing open. Animals walked into one another's spaces, pushed against each other and jumped on each other in the galleries. The air had a sour smell, which made it hard to breathe.

"What is the meaning of this?" I asked Taneses, but she was equally surprised at what was happening. We did not try to shut the gratings, there would never have been an end to it. We were on our way to the reptile cages when suddenly, with a long, plaintive sound of scraping planks, the ship stopped rocking.

Anything that had not been bolted down shifted, things fell and rolled away from us, animals braced themselves, Taneses and I fell against each other.

"My good gods, help!" wailed Taneses, because, again, it was as if the world was ending, but the shock was so brief that she too realized quickly that we had run aground.

"We're there," she said in a shaky voice. "The ordeal is over." She hugged and embraced me. I threw my arms around her too, I could not help it.

"I'll take you to the child before the others come this way," she said. We went past the lizards, the iguanas, and the tree frogs. I quickly glanced into every cage in the hope of spotting Put. But that was not where I should have looked for him. Taneses pointed to the shaft through which the air came in.

"Stand on my shoulder," she said, helping me up. It was not easy. We were both bulky, and when we finally managed all I found in the air shaft was a snakeskin and a camel-hair sack.

Against my better judgment, I kept searching, in my head the memory of Put sitting in a corner nibbling the burned crusts of bread. He had those huge eyes that always looked innocent, even if he had just tied a knot in your girdle while you were asleep. He was like an attentive, faithful dog, who was always in the right place at the right time: If you were hungry, he would have just picked fruit from the tree, if you were driven mad by insects, he would have already squashed a lot of them with his hands.

But I did not find him then, nor later, when the ark was empty. The joy I had felt when we ran aground turned to sorrow.

The Receding
of the Waters

*H*aving run aground changed everything. The voyagers' hope revived, they again dreamed of the land that would be lovely, undulating, without cliffs and without rocks, without ravines and caves that could harbor dangerous animals. For days, the ark lay in the water like a beacon. In the distance, the tops of acacias and cypresses became visible. The wind blew the moisture out of the gray crowns of the trees. We saw their branches covered in black seaweed, as if we were eagles soaring above everything. All that time, the Builder sat on a chair in the sun. I sat next to him, my hand under his. We watched the waters going down, which seemed to go on endlessly. What emerged was not beautiful to see. There was only slush and stones overgrown with algae. Slowly it became clear what our abode would be: a miserable little settlement by a string of ponds and lakes. This was no longer the old order, the rolling landscape we remembered. This landscape was repulsive and inhospitable, it was full of ugly outcrops, bulges, and sharp ridges. Ham voiced the questions that plagued us: "Are these the fields full of clover we have been promised? Was there not going to be a tree that bore fruit forever? What shall we eat?"

"Through the waters of death we have journeyed into life. Be grateful, my son," said the Builder. But Ham coughed as if he wanted to make it impossible to understand his father's words.

Once the water had gone down sufficiently, the Builder made his sons put down a gangplank, a new one, much wider than the one we had left behind. They used an extravagant number of un-damaged planks taken from the roof. The animals stood petrified in the full sun; they squeezed themselves into the dark corners of their cages. For others, however, things did not move fast enough: They smashed the bars and bolts with their horns or their hind legs. The birds stretched their wings and left the ark through the gallery in such numbers that the sky was obscured by them.

When the ship was just about empty, I went back to my hut to help Taneses. We searched for a good spot for the alabaster statues, somewhere deep inside the ship. I took her to the niche my father had built. I found it fairly easily behind the terns' cage, the obvious spot, selected by my father to save his family. The niche was unused, spacious, and easily locked, a place worthy of images of gods. Shem, Japheth, and Ham knew where it was, but I did not expect them to come looking for anything there now that the journey was over.

Then I took Taneses to the others. They stood watching the procession of the animals, every living creature, all moving ani-mals, all that crawls on the earth. Nobody had expected her appearance.

"Very early on the voyage I found a child," she said while everyone remained speechless. "A wild boy who would not speak. I knew it was not permitted, but my mother's heart spoke; I went into hiding in order to take pity on him."

Japheth went to her and threw himself at her feet. "I have given your place to someone else," he said hoarsely.

"I know," Taneses replied. "And now I take it up again."

Our Arrival in What Was Said to Be Paradise

*T*he Builder went down the gangplank. The new land was still soggy, but it carried his weight. When he came to a raised area on the rock he called a few words to his sons. They came out with blankets and shade cloths, they set up screens so as not to feel the damp wind and scanned the surroundings for landmarks. Meanwhile, the Builder chose a rock over which he poured oil. "Let us thank the Unnameable," he said.

A wide-eyed ewe had stopped on the gangplank, and Zedebab led it down. Carrying the animal on his shoulders, Shem waded through the mud. He put it down on the rock and held it down by the wool, the legs folded under the body. Japheth whetted the knife. The Builder took it from him. His thin cloak flapped in the wind. He made a slow, graceful movement. The ewe looked into the Builder's eyes, right through the gesture. The shudder that went through its body was the only thing that betrayed the pain. The blood ran into the hollow in the rock.

"Now that the flood is over, we may eat the animals. We were promised that," he said. They seized a second sheep, not for the sacrificial altar, but for themselves.

They asked me to look for something in Zaza's hut that would soften the taste of the meat. I brought them dried thyme, dill, and the last bit of salt I could find. Following my instructions, they put the cuts on the fire. Soon after, the scent of roasted meat filled the new air. Taneses was the first to cut a piece from the carcass. She ate, smacking her lips. The others ate hesitantly. As quails flew overhead, they sat with their backs to the fire, hoping to get the dampness out of their clothes. The legs and guts stayed behind on the rock. The ewe's head turned black quickly, but with its eyes closed and the tip of its tongue hanging from its mouth, it seemed lost in a dream. On the swampy horizon stood a rainbow only the Builder paid attention to.

67

The Emptiness
of the Land

*I*n the ark, that symbol of a death with dignity, I was the only one who stayed behind, together with the hundreds of flies that had settled on the animal droppings, with the parasites, the molds, and the fungi, and with the lingering stench of the badgers, beavers, muskrats, and skunks. The deck offered me views of surroundings where there was little to see. Yet there was something in the empty landscape that drew my attention, a point on the empty horizon, no more than a dot in the deserted plain. I dragged myself toward it. I was so big I could hardly move. The ground under my feet was not nearly as stable as I had hoped: It rocked like a ship.

As I moved away from the ark, I could not help looking quickly, from the corners of my eyes, the way Alem-the-ragged had taught me: This is how it should have been, this ship, this landscape, this small encampment with its fire, the colorless ground, I saw it all the way it had been meant to be without me. Me walking here observing it was not part of the divine plan. I belonged with the others in those perished cities where I had never been. The dot increased in size. I walked straight toward it. I recognized the faded, torn cloak and the blackened prow of the papyrus boat.

I waddled up to it and looked inside. There were traces of life, but life itself seemed to have disappeared. I walked around the boat as if I expected to find double walls or hiding places. I passed my hand over the sunshade and over the fishing net on the side. But there were tracks in the dried-up mud, footprints of someone who had gone away.

Panting from the effort of the walk, I stood for a while. The sun continued on its course. Around me was nothing but vastness.

I'll follow the tracks, I thought, *I'll go after my father, but first I'll rest a little while.* I had not sat down before I heard a rustling on the deck. I pulled away the smelly net in which dead fish were rotting and expected to discover some animal. But the creature that looked at me round-eyed and with disheveled hair was no animal. It could have been one, its movements were jittery, and it had its hands on the ground as if they were forelegs. It was Put.

I held out my arms to embrace him, but he reared back, uttering a low growl like an angry monkey.

"Did you escape here, little boy? Did the ark frighten you?"

He made no reply. He looked past me nervously, his face twisted.

"Shush, shush, easy," I said. "Nobody here wants you to die. Taneses just scared you. That time is gone. With me, you're safe." But he still would not say a word.

"Did you come too late? Had my father left already when you got here? Was he the only one you still trusted, and have you lost him too now?"

He watered where he sat, I saw the yellow puddle spread by his feet. Every time I tried to put my hand out to him, he cowered and hissed like a snake. I talked to him for hours. I kept repeating the same phrases. He listened as if he had never before heard the words I used. "You're my little brother. The world is gone, but you and I are still here."

I wanted to stay with him. I had already worked out how to make a bed with my mother's cloak for cover, so I might be with him, slowly regaining his confidence. But I could not. The pain in my belly made me stagger. Water trickled from my body. I had to go back.

Birth of the Child

y child was born in the ark. Neelata was there. I lay in the wet hay. I sang storm songs, rowing songs, and songs for hauling up nets, while inside my body the slow beat of a wave grew. It resembled the swell of the waves we were so familiar with, that sluggish, almost pleasurable pain in my back and thighs.

I'm becoming a spring, I thought, when my waters broke. The water came as a gift. It was like when you find a stone under which you think there is moisture; I experienced the same release, the same feeling of refreshment. You lift it up and you find sun-warmed water. The flow prevented me bursting apart.

Neelata pulled me down over her. She pressed her fingers so deeply into my arms that blue bruises appeared. It was no longer clear from whom the child was coming. She bore great pain. She called for a woman, her mother, I expect. "Eve!" she shouted. "You cursed slut! It's your fault I am here, because of you my body is tearing apart!" The child broke out of our body, it gushed out of us as from an inner river, with still more water, as if there was not enough of that in this world already.

Then my father stood next to us. I saw his movements, but they were too fast for me to remember them. I asked him, "If I can see your little boat, you must surely have seen ours? Surely you knew what was eating my heart?"

He replied, "What did you expect? That I should let myself be humiliated again by that scum? Did you think I would bow down in the mud after all that time? Have you not known me always as a man who takes the honorable way out? You need me no longer, I am what has to be forgotten. Your son is your future, make sure he is brought up amongst other boys."

Neelata wrapped the child in cloth. At first, I did not look at it. I lay next to it, panting, my eyes closed. It asked for nothing and I slept to the sounds of animals that were already miles away, but which I could not keep out of my dreams, particularly those of the howler monkeys, they sounded the most gruesome. Neelata's constant walking back and forth aroused my fear of the carnivores that I had seen leaving the ark: Were they far enough away, had they all really gone, were there none hiding in the pens and cages?

Only after a long time did I manage to open my eyes. The child was much darker than Ham and much lighter than me. I licked it the way I had seen the cattle do. My father was no longer there, but Ham was. He put amulets around the child.

I said, "Name him Canaan, I beg of you. Name him after the land of the marshes."

"Canaan will be his name," said Ham, laying his hand on the little head.

Every time Canaan pouted his lips against my nipple, my breasts started flowing. His smacking calmed my restless heart. I could not help feeling that it was not I who had given the child life, but it me. I watched the little hands that wriggled, kneading my breast. I listened to the rumbling of his belly while he drank. The thread of saliva that linked me with him, the little, black-edged nails with which he scratched his own face, the haughty look in his eyes and his air of here-I-am-look-after-me made me forget the desolation outside. His thirst woke me several times during the night. In his haste he bit at my breast through my clothes. As you put your forehead against a piece of alabaster when you have a headache, so I lay my forehead against little Canaan.

Ham felt Canaan with his nose and chin instead of with his fingers. He said, "My child will not grow up on this wreck. On my arm he will enter the temple my father will build."

A few times, I tried to explain to Neelata that Put was in the papyrus boat. It was difficult to persuade her that I was speaking the truth. Like me, she could not believe that Put had turned his back on us. But eventually she ordered Ham to not leave my side. She baked bread for him and for me. She cut his meat because he could not do it himself, and when everything was ready, set off for the papyrus boat.

69

The Curse

"*I*t would be better if we did not build permanent houses," said Ham. "If we do not roam the land, we will stop working together. We will fight over a piece of land. We will form single families instead of wider clans and rise against one another." But his brothers stacked stones into walls. They were afraid of the rumbling noises in the distance and the clouds that were piling up. The occasional appearance of a rainbow could make no difference to that. And the spot was lonely. Like mine, their gaze kept focusing on the horizon. Sooner or later we expected old acquaintances to appear there: Zedebab's twin sister, the pitch workers and the carpenters, the warriors and the foremen. Camia and her mother. My father. But no one came, not even a couple of Nefilim to break the solitude.

One afternoon, eight days after Canaan's birth, I heard someone move about on the ark. At first, I thought of an animal that had come looking for its old pen. Or was it Put, his fear overcome, returning to us? Put it was not, nor an animal. It was the Builder, who was approaching me with gently shuffling steps over the crumbling dung. "Why are you hiding?" he asked when he saw me lying in the hay. "I have looked everywhere for you. I have been in every pen in the ark. Why do you keep me searching?" His cloak was lighter in color than when we were on the water. Zedebab must have taken it to one of the ponds, it was no longer stiff with stains as it had been. He smelled differently than he had during the journey too. He walked without difficulty. Obviously, the illness was leaving him in peace for a while before striking again.

I had a sheet over me to protect me and the child from the flies. The sudden appearance of the Builder had made me dive under it. I was still not strong. I did not know what to say to the man who sat so close to me while I was still bleeding.

He examined the condition I was in and said, "Do not doubt yourself. You are the only one who can be exonerated of everything. You are unblemished, pure as the water from the cave full of bones. You are the only who has never raised yourself above the others by saying, I am chosen." He bent his head, his chin on his chest. He wept, like that time in the cave.

Not much later, Canaan must have made a sound under the sheet.

The Builder gasped. With his staff, he lifted a corner of the sheet. "Here!" he said. And again, "Here!" He did not immediately pick up the child; first he touched it as if he wanted to know what to expect. But then he did pick it up. He held it close and laid his dry lips on the soft skin. "This is no place for you and my grandson. Your place is in my house," he said.

I tried to pay attention to what he was saying. Did he mention a place? Was that not exactly what prevented me sleeping: that no place had been provided for me in this world?

But the Builder did not wait for my answer and walked onto the gallery with the child, out of the ark.

He took us to his hurriedly constructed abode. The place was untidy, the house of a man on his own. There was a smell of fire and fermenting fruit.

"Sit down and make this your home," he said.

I did as he said. I could not do otherwise. The walk had exhausted me and I had to lie down.

As if there was something urgent that he might forget to do, he picked up the child and went outside with it.

I closed my eyes, but not for long. Outside, not far from me, I heard Canaan crying. His pain resounded across the landscape like the announcement of great sorrow. I jumped up instantly. I ran outside and saw how the Builder held Canaan on the altar stone. On his little loincloth were bloodstains that had not come from me.

"Hear him," said the Builder, holding my child's foreskin in his hand. "My grandson weeps because he does not understand how great a service I do him."

I could not answer, my throat was as dry as a pot shard.

He wiped the knife clean on his gown and put the skin into the purse around his neck.

Is this the price, I thought, *of becoming one of them? Does this change my little one from a stowaway into a voyager on the ark? What sort of people is this to which we now belong, who live in isolation yet stay faithful to their god?* A world had perished, and now it was perishing again, and I had the same feeling as the first time: This was what my life would be like, permeated with just one thing, with but one quality: aloneness. This was how it would feel, being forever recognized by the color of your skin and knowing that that color is the reason why you listen, why you conform, wherever you go.

I walked to the altar stone. I lifted up my child, he felt like wood, stiff with fear and distress.

"Let us hope he will manage to make something of this land!" said the Builder, but already I was walking away from him.

No more than two marks in the landscape, Ham and Neelata returned from the papyrus boat. But they did not have Put with them. "Not with sweets, not with a whip, not with a rope can we get him here," they said when they saw me.

I was unable to walk, I was stumbling. I fell, the child under me, and that brought the others running. They had seen me walking and heard me crying. Shem was collecting stones, Japheth driftwood. They approached to see what was happening.

"Could he not have offered a lock of hair or a piece of finger-nail?" called Ham when he saw the bloodstains on Canaan's loin-cloth.

All together we returned to the Builder's house, Ham and Neelata out of anger, Japheth and Shem out of curiosity.

The Builder was asleep. The short cloak he had worn on the ship had become even shorter from being washed. So he lay on his bed, his legs spread out, his cloak rucked up to his waist, the scars in his loins red from scratching.

"Look at him naked and drunk," called Ham when he entered.

Shem and Japheth hurriedly went to the bed. With eyes

averted, they pulled the sheet out from under him and covered his nakedness. "Do not talk like that," Shem said to Ham. "You know he drinks to dull his pain."

"He drinks so he does not have to see what he has brought about," said Ham, not even trying to lower his voice. "When the drinking water ran out on the ark, he kept the vats of wine hidden from us."

"You cannot say that, Ham!" said Shem.

"I can say that, brother. He will not curse me. He has blessed me."

The women too came into the dwelling, Taneses's face sweaty, Zedebab's big, dark eyes full of surprise. I saw them come in and looked at them as if this were the first time I saw them. This was them, the chosen, the beginning of the new humanity. No one had changed. Taneses was as greedy as ever, Zedebab still vacuous, Neelata just as full of hatred for her mother, Shem still fanatical, and Japheth still persuaded of his own inferiority. They watched as the Builder opened his eyes. They all waited to hear what he would say.

The Builder looked at his youngest son with an open mouth; he may have thought he was dreaming when Shem and Japheth told him what had just occurred. "Go away then, Ham. Disappear from this place," he said.

Neelata raised her arms and said, "Do not send him away, not with those hands."

"He has feet," replied the Builder. "No more is needed to go away."

Ham regarded his father vacantly. He was standing, the

Builder sitting. I observed the space between them, the way they faced each other, the trilling of the air that separated them. From under the sheet, the Builder's body odor rose, unexpectedly strong.

"The dark girl and her child you will leave here," the old man continued. "Her child is the first of my new people, she the First Mother. With you, she is no more than a servant. Anything you cannot lift with those hands of yours, you will make her give to you."

Ham strode to the door. He did not turn when he said, "Your paradise you can keep, but not this woman. She is more precious to me than anything and anyone that was on the ship." Suddenly all eyes were directed at me. I had already sat down because I felt so exhausted. But now I stood up, holding the child close. I went to stand next to Ham in the doorway.

Tiredly, the Builder passed his eyes over everything low on the ground: the stones, the empty sacks, the shards of pots that had been broken during the unloading. He said, "Yes, just go. You will see what good it does you. Your child will be a servant of servants."

So here it was, the curse predicted by the oracle. Of all people still living, it hit the most innocent, the child who had done nothing to anyone yet, who had lived for only eight days and already had to recover from the fear of the knife. The curse was tied to the blessing. The blessing was the chance to leave, to part with the settlement that held no promise for me. It was raising your lips to bare your teeth, it was turning around and saying, "Good, I'm going." The resoluteness had a refreshing effect; for the first time I did not have the feeling that the sunlight that fell on me through the doorway was too much to bear.

Not that I did not waver. I could remember how light the Builder was when I carried him onto the deck. I could still feel the pressure of his frame when, sick as he was, he blessed my father. Soon, he would start feeling worse again, the periods of recovery would become shorter and shorter, the fevers more intense. The feelings of abandonment would afflict him just as much; he obviously had never blessed himself.

But my doubts were wiped away by other memories. "Then I will have what every mother longs for," I said. I spoke with my chin raised, and with very small, even elegant gestures, exactly how I imagined my mother must have spoken in the marsh land.

Now the Builder looked at me, squinting. Just possibly, he understood what was happening, and how people escape from under a curse through small actions.

"Huh?" was the only sound he uttered.

"An untameable child," I said, and walked into the sunshine, following Ham.

70

Canaan, the Land

The Builder requested us to leave the donkeys and horses behind. But the unclean camels we could have, they would take us farthest. I gathered the things I wanted to take: Neelata's black earrings, a bowl, a basket, and a couple of spoons, twisted in the fire. As soon as the camels had been loaded up, Ham came to the ark. He did not ask anything, he watched me on the gangplank in the sun. Awkwardly with his bandages, he helped me onto the smaller of the two camels, the female. Neelata sat on the other one, Canaan tied onto her belly. I saw that the little one did not move; he was asleep, exhausted by what he had been through.

We traveled past the new encampment. The Builder did not emerge from his tent. Shem stood in the small field he had laid out, his silver-tailed monkey on his shoulder. With one hand he pressed the scarce seeds the rats had not found in the course of the journey into the soil, filling the furrow with the other. Japheth was planting the small, limp vines I had seen in the Builder's hut. Neither had what he was doing in his fingers; never before had they cultivated plants. They very carefully did as they had been taught by experts from faraway countries before their departure: They sowed wheat, black cumin, millet, and barley, with spelt between them. They did their best to love their new land. I had heard them say to each other, "Let us build something large again, even larger than the ark. Let us build a tower reaching up to the Unnameable!"

Zedebab and Taneses stood leaning against each other, almost unrecognizable in their new cloaks that protected them from the sun. They poked the fire to keep it burning. They reminded me of what we used to do on the ark: spin endless yarn, mixing particular colors, burning incense to dispel the stench of dung. Later they would weave mats to keep the drafts out of the houses. They would crush the grain and beat the cumin with sticks. They would boil milk. They would have children. Snakes of all sorts would keep them from sleeping.

That is how I left the ark behind, that coffin, which, though hardly changed, had preserved none of its original beauty. First we went to the papyrus boat. I had hoped that Put would come and sit on the camel with me. But he shook his head. He rucked his cloak up with his girdle, seized a stick and walked ahead of us like a tracker. At the last pond, the camels drank until their bellies were swollen. Then, rocking like ships, we traveled westward, following my father's footsteps, which you could only see if you half-looked.

Postscript

The sons of Japheth were Gomer, Magog, Madai, Javan, Tubal, Meshech, and Tiras. The sons of Gomer were Ashkenaz, Riphath, and Togarmah. The sons of Javan were Elishah, Tarshish, the Kittim, and the Rodanim. From them descended all those who spread over the islands. These are the sons of Japheth, separated into their own countries, each with their own language, family by family, nation by nation.

Shem too had children. He was the ancestor of all the sons of Eber. And their land stretched from Mesha all the way to Sephar, the mountainous land in the east.

Ham's sons were Canaan, Put, Cush, and Mizraim. Put was the child of wanderers, found by chance and taken along. The other three were children of his concubine, not his wife, whose womb had been closed by the Unnameable. For his wife's heart did not go out to him; she had sworn never to bear children for him, but warmth she found, like him, in the concubine's tent. Canaan became a singer, famous far beyond the marshes, untroubled by the curse that had been laid on him at an early age. Cush fathered Nimrod. He was the first powerful ruler on earth. He was a mighty hunter. Hence the saying, "Even as Nimrod the mighty hunter before the Unnameable." The beginning of his kingdom was in Babel. He built Nineveh. From impudent Mizraim descended the Philistines, who later fought determinedly with the descendants of Shem. Put did not procreate. He died before he grew up, during a game with his brothers.

Canaan was the father of Sidon, his firstborn, and Heth. From them descended the Jebusites, the Amorites, the Girgashites, the Hivites, the Arkites, the Sinites, the Arvadites, the Zemarites, and the Hemathites. Afterward, the families of the Canaanites spread abroad. The border of the Canaanites was from Sidon through Gerar up to Gaza, and then toward Sodom, Gomorrah, Admah, and Zeboyim. They became famous for their skill with wood. Famed carpenters they produced, and immortal boat builders.

Those are the families of the Builder's sons, after their generations: From them have descended all the peoples who spread over the earth after the flood. The flood did not wipe out evil. To this day, the fight between the Semites and the descendants of Canaan continues.

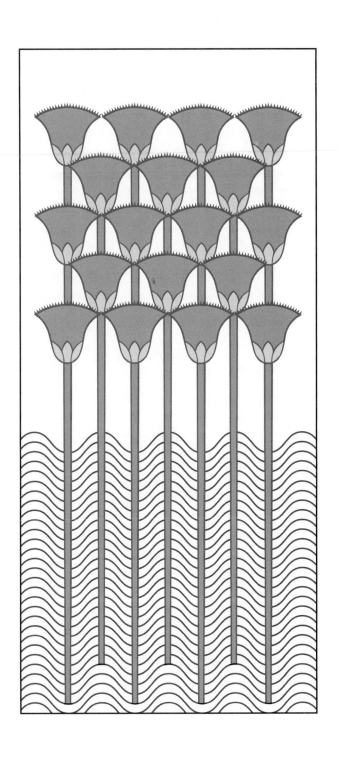

About the Author

Anne Provoost was born in Belgium in 1964 and studied literature at the University of Leuven. She is the author of four novels: *My Aunt Is a Pilot Whale (Mijn tante is een grindewal); Falling (Vallen)*, which was made into an English-language feature film; *The Rose and the Swine (De Roos en het Zwijn)*; and *In the Shadow of the Ark (De Arkvaarders)*. Together they have been translated into ten languages and have received many major Dutch literary prizes, as well as several international honors. Asked what message she hopes to convey with her writing, Provoost says simply, "If you have to talk about a message, than I would like to limit myself to one thing: stretching the reader's empathic abilities." And she adds, "I want to write books that, if they had hands, would grab you by the throat."

Provoost was elected a member of the Belgian Royal Academy of Dutch Language and Literature in 2003. She lives with her husband and three children in Antwerp, Belgium.

About the Translator

John Nieuwenhuizen's translation of *The Baboon King* by Anton Quintana won the Mildred L. Batchelder Award in 1999. He has also translated *Falling (Vallen)* by Anne Provoost and *What About Anna? (En Met Anna?)* by Jan Simoen. Born in the Netherlands, John later emigrated to Australia, where he now makes his home in Melbourne.

This book was designed by Elizabeth B. Parisi.

The text was set in Perpetua, designed by Eric Gill in 1929.

The display font was set in Opti Lord Swash.

The book was printed on 50-pound commodity offset antique paper

at R R Donnelley in Crawfordsville, Indiana.

The manufacturing was coordinated by Jaime Capifali.